Final Exam

PRESS

First edition, first printing March 2005

My thanks to Nikki Taylor for typing; to
Pamela Hollie and my agent, David Hale Smith,
for reading; to Ruth Smilan for the haunting cover photograph;
and to Jerry Kelly, who makes publishing a pleasure.
Thanks to my friends outside of Gambier for the refuge
and perspective they give me when I leave home, and
to my friends in Gambier for welcoming me back. P.F.K.

Book design by Jerry Kelly
Cover photograph by Ruth Smilan
Cover design by Jerry Kelly, Pamela Hollie, P.F. Kluge
Printed by Printing Arts Press, Mt. Vernon, OH

http://xoxoxpress.com

Box 51 Gambier, OH 43022
books@xoxoxpress.com

Final Exam

a novel by
P. F. Kluge

XOXOX

PRESS

To Doug Givens and Peter Rutkoff,
and all my morning coffee people
in Gambier...

Editor's Note

The horrifying ordeal that beset a small college in Ohio two years ago is well known, the serial murders that generated a crescendo of attention in which individual lives, institutional character, the very purpose of liberal arts education all were tested. The crimes' solution, when it came, answered only some of the questions that arose and left many of us who lived through that violent season exasperated and perplexed. The murders were eventually attributed to a person who had departed the campus abruptly and, absent other evidence, remains alive. This person's conviction has been in the court of public opinion, not of law. The murders ended but not the speculation; the "semester from hell" still resonates. No wonder some of our wisest commentators suggested we might never know what really happened.

But now we do: this book tells the story. It consists of the accounts of three people on campus at the time. Warren Niles, former president of this college, has made available a journal he kept those terrible months. Fragmentary and incomplete, this manuscript—entitled *"Night Thoughts of a College President"*—is President Niles' contribution. The second testimony comes from Billy Hoover, the College Security officer assigned to the investigation. His pages, like President Niles', are his own story, in his own voice, self-written. The third voice in this book is mine. I was a visiting professor at the time of the murders. My role in the story is smaller but, it turns out, necessary.

My editorial function has been little more than placing the testimonies in chronological order. I wish I could have done more. I advised both writers to delete substantial passages that were embarrassing, even damaging. To their credit, both men demurred, reminding me that my own account had its share of indiscretions. What results is the fullest possible account of the times we shared. Any number of reputations will be affected by this book, those of the living and the dead, the innocent and the guilty, as well as the college where our lives converged. So be it.

—MARK MAY—

Prologue: 1976
BILLY HOOVER

Everybody knew a student was missing. They'd been searching for days, searching all over—cops driving country roads, teachers and classmates walking through cornfields, combing the woods. They walked along the river, poked around abandoned sheds and trailers. Every cow pond, gravel pit, every dumpster got looked into. And, each day that passed, people got a little more scared. Scared of finding. Scared of not finding.

I heard about it from my uncle, Tom Hoover, who worked in College Security. My father had died the year before, my mother was "failing," as they say around here. She went down real fast after my father died. A lively, healthy woman—the talker in the family—turned thin and silent. I'll never know about her fall down the steps of our house, which she'd walked down thousands of times before, whether it was an accident or not. The end of her failing, that's what it was. That happened a few months before the student disappeared and Tom was there for me, getting me new clothes for eighth grade, taking me fishing, hunting, out for pizza. Some nights, he took me to work at the college—patrolling parties, keeping drinkers out of cars, escorting girl students home from the library at midnight. That was my first taste of college.

I remember wondering about that missing student, not just where he went, but why. For me, lost meant misplaced: lost keys, lost ball, lost and found. Not like lost at sea, lost in combat, lost forever. Even the posters that were all over town— at the bank, the post office, the grocery and gas station—though they were supposed to show who folks were looking for, seemed more like messages meant for the student himself, telling him that people missed him and it was time to come home now, please.

My home was—and still is—a farm just across the river from the college, which sits up on a wooded hill. My father always told me I was lucky to be born where I was, in this part of Ohio, in this particular place. Not everybody had a famous college in walking distance. That brought some quality to life, he said. Some magic. Just look at it, he used to say, pointing up at the hill. Like a castle. Or a monastery. Or a space station, shooting signals out into the stars. High and mighty talk coming from a college maintenance guy who plowed snow and scattered salt in winter, mulched leaves in autumn, cut grass in summer and spring. There were plenty locals who took potshots at the college, at spoiled kids and snobby faculty and presidents who...as my Uncle Tom put it...thought their shit didn't stink. But, low rank as he was, my father believed in that place and what he believed in was good enough for me.

It was Indian Summer that day, a kindly warm spell after a killing frost. The October heat was a surprise. Flies were buzzing, crows circled overhead and—just when the wind was right—I could hear the announcer at the home football game, the college taking yet another pounding. Our local high school team could beat them, folks said. I sat awhile on a railroad trestle, walked along the river, then set off uphill, into the woods, into a neighbor's orchard that smelled like cider, drunken bees feasting on windfall apples. I followed a deer trail back onto our place into a bumper crop of blackberry bushes, sumac, scrub oak and maple, a field that hadn't been planted for years. My father wasn't out to shake the last penny out of the ground. Leave something for the deer, he said, the wild turkeys, the raccoons and the possums.

Leave something for the crows. They were all over an empty barn at the edge of the field, up against the woods. My dad used the barn for wood, dismantling it a board at a time, when he was building benches and tables for professors who liked that weathered, broken-in-look in their garden furniture. The crows had found it now, swarming around the place, cawing like crazy, circling overhead. I walked towards them, through dry grass and brambles, floating through that last warm sunlight, late in the day, late in the season.

The smell hit me, slugged me, before I saw where it was coming from. Something hanging inside the barn, hanging at the end of a rope looped over a beam at the edge of the hay loft. A week had passed since the student vanished, a week of warm days since the crows had found him, turning him slowly as they landed and took off but never deserting him completely, one or another always in contact, never leaving the dead kid alone, never backing off to admire their work. I folded down on my knees, gagging and vomiting. The crows knew I was there but that didn't bother them. I chucked a handful of stones at them. That didn't bother them much. They lifted off the corpse, letting me see their work in progress. The eyes were gone, the ears, the tongue, cheeks, everything that made a face. All the easy pickings. When I saw that, when I looked down at where trousers had split open, where like kids pulling ribbons off a gift, the crows tugged at intestines, I screamed and ran. It was him alright, the lost student. I couldn't believe it, that I was the one to find him. I hadn't even been looking. As soon as I hit the trail that runs along the river, I saw Tom Hoover walking towards me. He always was able to find me, whenever I needed him, and now I threw myself into his arms, crying. "I know," Tom said. "I know." He told me I should stay put a minute and he headed for the barn. I could see him shudder when the smell hit him but that didn't stop him. He stepped inside, stayed a minute and came back to me. "Spoiled," he said. "Spoiled rotten." He held me and hugged me, the way he did the day they found my father in the river. "There's a reward," he said.

The reward was a hundred dollars. But it was more than money. It was death. The smell of road kill got me, ever since. The sight of anything hanging the way that dead boy had hung. A deer on the first day of hunting season, hung from a branch, gutted and bled. A pinata thing at a Mexican party. That was my reward. A gift that kept on giving. A role to play, a part in life. I was the one who found the bodies. Or they found me.

Part One:
Orientation
1999

I.
WARREN NILES
Night Thoughts of a College President

Next year, the last of my twenty years here, will doubtless be filled with tributes and farewells of all kinds. Much, I'm sure, will be made of me. That is why I have chosen this penultimate year for a long-contemplated project: my journal, my reflections on my tenure as president and what it means, or meant. I do this for my own pleasure, yet not without hope that this summing up, carefully placed and well published, might be of interest to others.

I look forward to writing this. For years I've had a notebook with *Night Thoughts of a College President* written on the cover and nothing within. What a joke it would have been if I had died and someone going through my possessions, the college archivist perhaps, had come across those unwritten pages. It would have confirmed what many have suspected: that behind those suave presidential walls, an empty lot reposed. But now, at last, I commence.

The morning after I return from Maine, I position myself in my living room window, watching the college faculty assemble at the college gates. Dressed in caps and gowns of many colors, plush maroons and somber judicial blacks, decorated with silver and blue sashes, pinks and yellows. Returning like the swallows to Capistrano, one odd bird at a time, they turn the campus into a medieval aviary. The old timers, about to retire or already emeritus, can be counted upon for a day like this. Some of them have been retired for decades but they take their place in front, death and eternity right ahead of them. Soon they are joined by junior colleagues, visitors and recent tenure-track hires, dressed in plain black robes and ordinary mortar boards on loan from the wardrobe department in the basement of the college bookstore, the sole exception being their hats—whimsical beanies, boaters, derbies—that some of them wear to show that none of this is to be taken seriously.

I walk downstairs and pause to check myself in the hall mirror by the front door. Blue robe, black piping, silver sash, black mortarboard, gold tassel. Pale skin, gray hair: dead white male walking. Student waiters scurry by, carrying trays of glasses out to the front porch. The smell of hors d'oeuvres reaches me from the kitchen, like the generic whiff of heated fodder that wafts down airplane corridors. I duck out of a waiter's way, apologize, open the door for him. Where I have lived for twenty years is not my property. It comes with the job. Other presidents have lived in it before me and others will follow. I know that that's true of other houses too; we're all just passing through. But this house reminds you of it all the time, the formal parlor, the dark dining room, the uncluttered study. It's the kind of place an undertaker buys.

I step outside and feel the heat. August has two days remaining. I understand the intricacies of college calendars but part of me nonetheless resents the way we start in August. I remember when Labor Day was the end of summer. There was time for last walks on the beaches, barbecues outside vacation cottages, resort romances ending, the first thought of school supplies and new courses, flannel and corduroy to buy, *Dr. Zhivago* not yet read and now all of it's gone the way of doubleheaders. I walk across the grass and greet the senior faculty.

When did I come back, they ask. How was Maine this summer? Is my new home almost built? When will my wife be able to tear herself away from contractors? Isn't it amazing how the weather cooperates when freshmen and their parents are here? How long has it been since rain forced us indoors? Once again, I am a president. No one more talked about, more closely observed, more deftly parodied. The average college president serves for seven years. I have been here nearly three times as long. If time itself were a monument, that would be mine. An almost unprecedented run. Can I be blamed for feeling proud?

Ninety out of 120, not bad at all: faculty arrange themselves up and down the path. The smart alecks pick the side of the path which will lead them to the shady side of the stage. It won't be long before we're all sweating. Though summer pleasures end today, the heat continues. I detect mixed emotions in the conversations I hear, exchanged condolences on the end of summer. The long vacation begins with imperative books to read, manuscripts to write. But life gets in the way and lack of talent and loss of interest and today there's a note of apology and relief, that the agony of freedom is over and more manageable pain is about to begin. Because: they're back. They're coming.

They're here. They march towards us, down the path. Call them matriculants, incoming students, underclassmen, first year students: only the word freshmen describes them. This, I confess, is a moment I love completely, this first glimpse of the young people who have chosen us. Oh yes, we're a "highly selective" college. We accept—select—seventy percent of those who apply to us. Of those applications, slightly fewer than thirty percent (our "yield") agree to come. We choose once, sort of. They choose twice, decisively.

While we sweat in caps and gowns, freshmen pass by in shorts and wrinkled khaki trousers, short-sleeved shirts, t-shirts even, running shoes, sandals, flower print summer dresses, madras shirts, a few white shirts and ties, a few earrings and nose rings. What they are wearing, I grant, is roughly what their professors-to-be are wearing underneath their robes. It's enough to make me doubly grateful: that clothing covers our bodies and that regalia covers our clothing. Amen and Amen again.

Some students smirk as they pass by. What a goof, stepping through this gamut of faculty while bells toll—for them!—in the nearby chapel. Others are plainly moved; they sense beginnings and endings in their lives. Some—prep-school graduates, I suspect, though that may not be fair—plod along familiarly, institution-wise, like juveniles moved from a youthful offender facility to adult minimum security. Been there, seen it, done it. Many students just can't decide, they're giggly, they're anxious, like newcomers at the edge of a party. Sometimes, I sense a trace of concern about being accepted, about fitting in and finding happiness and—very occasionally—I think I detect a concerned expression, the vestige of another time, when academic failure was something to worry about. These days, flunking out of college is rarer than breaking out of prison; also harder to accomplish.

Now it's our turn to parade. The junior faculty head towards the stage and then, in rough order of seniority, from mid-career to old timers, we follow. It must be like time-lapse photography, to see what professing does to the human body, turning spiky-haired theorists into fuddled curmudgeons. At first, there's only grass and trees on either side of us. Then, things thicken. I see village people, up for the parade but keeping a safe distance from our oratory. Early arriving upperclassmen, football and soccer players reconnoiter the freshmen women while lounging on the grass. I see dogs and kids and faculty spouses, cheerfully paying their respects. I walk through parents pointing cameras my way, I walk through students. I take the stage. After the priest prepares the way for me, I arise and speak.

"GOOD AFTERNOON!!! AND WELCOME to what has been and is and will continue to be the finest college of its kind!!!" An audacious claim. I repeat it. "The finest college of its kind. I know what you're thinking. What does he mean by that? Some of you in front of me may wonder. Along with some of those behind...." This is when I turn and ponder the faculty, part sullen, part sycophant. People who talk for a living resent being forced to sit and listen. They know my performances in and out. Over the years I've repeated myself. As if they hadn't!

"Look around you," I declare, in what is locally famous as my Brigham Young moment. "Consider this place, this hillside in the heartland, so central yet so remote, this hill and the river curving around below, these trees and lawns and college paths. Consider the sense of discovery you feel, when you come up the hill for the first time, when you discover this improbable, unexpected college-out-of-place. Consider that the trip you make today repeats the arrival of the college's founder, more than a century and a half ago. And he—passionate, visionary—turned a dream into a fact, a desire into an imperative. Look around at his place. It is still his place. And now it is yours as well. You are part of the river of life that flows to, and through, here. You are newcomers, each of you, the latest but not the least, and not the last. You are part of something larger and older, a college rooted in a certain time and place. Ask me to define my terms. Well, that is part of it. This is not just any college!"

I have built to a crescendo. Now I rest a bit. The founder president lasted less than two years here. He lost an argument with a faculty he couldn't control, resigned in anger and rode off into exile, wintering in a relative's cabin one county north of here. He never returned, died and was buried elsewhere.

"My definition continues," I resume. "It has to do with size. Though the college has grown, often against the odds, contending with a smallish endowment, limited resources, and a short list of graduates, however generous, our smallness—a choice enforced by circumstances—defines us." Careful now, I remind myself. Watch your cadence, those balanced clauses, those cross cutting parenthetical asides. Elegant and intelligent, that's what they say about me. Slicker than snot on a doorknob.

"We believe in small classes. We believe that what happens in class is only part—although the most important part—of what occurs between a professor and a student at a residential college. We believe in chance meetings, sidewalk seminars, casual conversation, the shared experience of life in a small place. Our faculty hold office hours, answer their own telephones and—now hear this!—grade papers the old-fashioned way, by hand, one paper at a time. If that kind of scrutiny makes you nervous, I can tell you, you are not alone. And I can add that the admissions people assure me your high school records, your test scores, your application essays and on-campus interviews suggest that you are among the most talented and diverse incoming classes in college history. So they tell me..." I pause, just a beat "...every year."

Relaxed laughter ripples across the crowd. I'm on the home stretch now, I smell the finish line and so does the audience: everyone's relieved. The shirt beneath my robe is soaked from the collar down and my belt will be sweat-swollen and sodden when I pull it out of my trousers, loop by reluctant loop, half an hour from now. The breeze feels cool on wet skin and how often, in his chosen line of work, does a college president pour sweat? I love the illusion of honest labor! I love it so much that on this, my next to last convocation, I take an out of character gamble. I depart from the text that the faculty behind me know by heart. I do this for my own sake, not for theirs, and for the sake of this very journal I am keeping.

"I travel a lot on college business," I say, dropping my voice to the level of a confession. "And I come back late to various hotel rooms, I come back from meetings with trustees, with graduates, with foundations of all kinds, potential donors and prospective students and fellow presidents. I come back exhausted. There are no words left in me. I've lost not only the ability to talk—no loss there, some of you might say—but the ability to listen and, very likely, to think. So, what does your president do at, say, the O'Hare Ramada Inn?"

A dozen faculty suggestions float into the air, obscene soap bubbles blowing across the stage, like words over the heads of cartoon characters: pornography, prostitutes, masturbation, phone sex. I sense unusual interest. I'm providing new material.

"I turn on the television. Obscure sports events, late night talk shows, colorized movie classics, cable shopping. And, recently, a certain ad. It's an ad—you've all seen them—for DeVry Technical Institute. I believe that's the correct name and I apologize if I have it wrong. The ad features a map of the U.S. that lights up, to show the institute's many locations. That's impressive: a school that moves and shifts and replicates. But what impresses me most is the parade of graduates who appear on the screen, looking up from microscopes, seated behind computers, carrying rolled up blueprints that look like diplomas. These are happy, hardworking people whose lives have all been made better by education at DeVry's. DeVry's helped them find jobs and earn money and make a mark. Their education has been a transaction from which both sides, buyer and seller, have profited. In short: a good deal.

"I wish, oh how I wish, this college could offer the same straight-forward assurances. But, truthfully, we cannot. What we attempt here is different, riskier, trickier. Success is harder to measure here. A life-time can pass and all the returns aren't in yet. We don't teach mar-ketable skills here, specific trades and vocations. Though many of our graduates prosper, we cannot guarantee the kind of immediate return on investment that some places promise. Your presence here is more than an investment. It is an act of faith. And the faith is that a deeper and human engagement with the liberal arts will serve you and enrich you in a way that goes far beyond the job that you get and the work that you do, in today's marketplace and tomorrow's. We're interested not just in what you do, but in who you are. And that, ladies and gen-tlemen, defines us."

I nod towards the crowd and linger at the podium while the applause builds. It always half-surprises me, though it's never failed. Snake oil salesman! Flack! Flim-flam man! Shill! Charlatan! Those are shouts I hear in my head. And when I look at the applauding stu-dents and their parents, I half expect to see someone raising a hand to ask me the name of that institute I mentioned, could I please spell it for them?

At the post-convocation reception, I position myself on the front lawn, mingling with parents, greeting them genially, introducing them to appropriate professors. Attendance is decent but the party doesn't last long. It's mid-afternoon and, unless they go soon, the parents will have to stay the night and that would feel wrong because the whole point of the day is about saying goodbye. I can read these parents' eyes, see them wondering if there's anything more they can do, some little thing, a conversation with me that might help down the road, the personal touch we advertise: "The president told us that early grades are low; he told us himself, his first paper in college came back with an F." And, behind it all, deep in their eyes, the sense of departure, minutes away. Act of faith.

When the guests are gone and only caterers remain, empty trays, empty glasses on empty tables, I step inside, into the living room we added a few years ago. Living room is a phrase I ordinarily resist. But in this house, the word applies. The other rooms are public spaces, designed for entertaining, where selected strangers stand and drink, sit and eat, hang their coats, relieve themselves, dry their hands on college towels, check their faces in college mirrors. Only the living room is mine. It has a television and a soft chair with a good reading lamp, a pile of magazines and books on the floor. Alumni like to send me books they think I should read. Most come from old timers who contribute volumes on the politicization and dumbing down of higher education. Just what I need at the end of the day. Titles like "Poison Ivy" and "The Tenure Trap," published by institutes with furniture store names: Republican Heritage, American Traditions.

I stretch out in my chair, settle into the afternoon itself. When late sunlight slants across the campus, every window frames a painting, a late summer/early autumn mix of green and gold. Stone walls, oaks and hemlock, grass and a few fallen leaves. The sun gets richer by the moment, even as it declines towards the hills on the other side of the river. Late afternoon. If my career were one day, it would be around this time now. Autumn of the President. A hundred yards away is the college cemetery, where three college presidents repose. It's not so many, three out of eighteen, but some stormed away and others were forced out. What's more, there's an unwritten law about college presidents: once you resign, you leave. Hilton Head and Scottsdale beckon. Sometimes I picture a retirement community that's just for former college presidents, poolside drinks at happy hour, merry old duffers swapping their favorite tenure-denial stories.

As usual at college functions, I've eaten just enough to ruin my appetite. Everything is thrown off. At dusk, it is too late to nap, too early to sleep. My wife, if she were here, would urge me to walk the dog around campus. In her absence, and the dog's, this stroll is something I cannot undertake. I head upstairs. I take off my shoes and stretch out on the bed. The day went well, I suppose. The only hiccup

was mine: that angst about DeVry's. I came out of it strongly, though.
Act of faith. DeVry's positions its graduates in the market place. At our
school, we study history, we consider eternity. So: act of faith. I roll
over. Lying on my back is like lying in state. I glance towards the bathroom. I must have left the door open, the light on, though that isn't
like me. And it wasn't me, it wasn't me at all. I see ACT OF FAITH
written on the mirror in a pinkish-red lipstick my wife favors. Her lipstick but not her handwriting. Someone else's. ACT OF FAITH and,
just below it, YOU ASSHOLE!

Trembling, stunned, I walk slowly towards the bathroom. I am an
actor in a cheap scene, not of my devising, seeing what someone has
wanted me to discover, walking forward as someone has meant for me
to do, just like this, afraid, just as it was meant I should be afraid, wondering if someone might be waiting for me in the bathroom, behind
the door or the shower curtain. I pause, I hesitate. "Don't go in there,"
I can hear an audience shouting. I nonetheless proceed. The room is
empty. ACT OF FAITH. YOU ASSHOLE! I wet a washrag and wipe the
mirror. ACT OF FAITH goes first. Then I am looking at myself in the
mirror. YOU ASSHOLE! remains, like a caption below a photograph.
A few more wipes delete it. The room is as before yet everything feels
different. Who would consider me an asshole? I wring out the washrag
under the faucet, turn to towel off my hand and see something on the
top of the toilet. A library card, a firm plastic card with the sort of bar
code that gets passed over supermarket scanners. And a name: Martha
Yeats. What an anticlimax! A history professor, outspoken and cause-
oriented, the loosest cannon on campus, the kind of tenured radical
conservative critics denounce.

I take the card into the bedroom, placing it next to the bedside
phone. Another Martha stunt. I'm expected to react, to come down
hard. That would make me a male authoritarian. Not to react would
make me soft and gutless, another "suit." A lose-lose situation. I decide
to wait. This is a company town, a residential college, I remind myself,
and Martha is tenured. She isn't the kind of problem you solve. With
Martha, you live and manage. "Hi Martha," I will say, tomorrow or the
next day. "It's Warren Niles. I found your library card."

II.
BILLY HOOVER

We found the first body near the mud wrestling pit, out behind the Psi U Lodge...

That's how I'd begin all this. But I guess I should set it up some, I should say what was going on in my mind and how I felt that night and how those feelings changed—before, during and after. That's what writers do, I hear. Tell a story and pretend like you're telling it to someone who's never heard of you or this place. Tell it to a total stranger so what happened to you, happens to them. Back years ago, they paid writers by the word or by the line. My deal is better: I get paid by the hour, and I can take all the time I want. No rush, no outside work, no heavy lifting: a desk in the back office at College Security, the same office that was crowded with cops back when we were trying to understand what was happening to us. Now it's just me filling up the lines of a spiral notebook while other guys worry about locked-out professors and false fire alarms and illegal beer kegs, all the things I used to do, knowing it was bullshit and I was bullshit, a campus cop is a Keystone Kop only not so funny, but now I miss that whole normal world and I wish I could shag a call or two, a noise complaint at night, a turd in the library stacks, an undergraduate ankle snapped in beer slides, but I've got this story to tell that I'm telling by the hour and it takes more hours than you might think to get past that first sentence. We found the first body near the mud wrestling pit, out behind the Psi U lodge. Lots of hours going into just that line. But who's complaining? I'm just a campus cop and my time comes cheap.

So okay, there's this small expensive college on an Ohio hilltop that it shares with a small village and when people see it for the first time, especially in springtime, all three days of it, and autumn, which can stretch out for months, like a long, lazy yawn, they walk around with this goofy tourist grin on their faces, like they've walked into a Universal Studios set called "College Life," where violets dot the grass in springtime, maple leaves cover the lawns in fall, dormitories look something like castles, dining halls are lined with paintings of rich and famous men. A mile-long gravel path runs through the college and the village, which is just a one-block collection of grocery, bookstore, bank, post office and restaurant. It's a college that's like a summer camp or a country club, some folks say, but to me, it's beautiful. It's hard not to drive up the hill and think that you've come to a place that's good.

Anyway, it's late August and I'm on duty, I'm cruising Kokosing Drive and there's a dog off the leash in the middle of the road—or to get it right—a dog trailing a leash, one of those fishing rod type leash-es that reels in and out, as if the owner went surf casting in a pet shop. But the owner isn't around and the dog is running around in circles, yelping. The first time I see him I drive right on by. This college town loves dogs. There's lots of professors' pets wandering freely and shitting at will, with no guff about pooper scoopers. And, when school's in ses-sion, dogs migrate here from the surrounding country, begging for scraps outside dining commons, foraging in dormitory dumpsters—rough dogs, part-time coon hunters, part-time college students. So I drive past the dog, ten miles an hour, the first of four patrols between ten p.m. and dawn. After the fraternity lodges, the street is all residen-tial, 1950s split-level stuff. Ten p.m. and not a light in any of the win-dows. That's the way it is around here: dishes dried and put away by seven. People leave their garage doors open all night long, and keys in the ignitions of their sensible shit-box cars.

Well, pain in the ass. The dog's still there at the edge of the road when I drive back and now I better get out and see who it belongs to. The yelping starts as soon as I step out, a shrill high sound, like a spoiled kid. "Hey you," I say, hunkering down a few feet away, not wanting to alarm the animal. "What's your story?" The dog quiets down some, perks up its ears, studies me. It's a small kind of a dog, a terrier, a schnauzer. Soon as I move closer the yelping starts again. I reach out, hoping to grab the leash, but the dog takes right off, dodg-ing onto the Psi U lawn where it sits, waiting for me to follow. Are we having fun yet? My next approach sends the dog back into the road. Now anything that happens, it's my fault if this little puppy never knows the taste of Cycle Four. And just then, I see some headlights passing the Delt lodge, heading my way—make that our way, moving fast. "Shit, shit, shit," I say.

I rush into my Cherokee, turn on the roof lights, the parking lights, like I'm setting the stage for an accident that hasn't happened yet. I grab a flashlight and point it down the road, into the windshield of a jeep with Connecticut plates.

"How you doing, officer?" comes the familiar upper-class voice. I spot a t-shirt, a baseball hat turned backward, a girl in the passenger seat, three others in back. Those open cans of Old Milwaukee twinkle in my flashlight beam.

"What might this be about?" I realize it's been months since I've heard that insincere politeness.

"Might be about speeding," I reply. "Might be about open containers."

"Is this a multiple choice?" someone else asks. A round of laughs from passengers in back. The customer is always right and around here, the students are the customers. $100,000 for four years and going up all the time. I'm not a cop. Cops enforce law. I mind manners. Sometimes theirs, mostly my own.

"I'll tell you what," I say. "You turn around and park in the student lot. I'll come by and check, maybe ten minutes from now. Your vehicle isn't there, I file a report. It's there, no problem."

"Oooh...he'll file a...report." That voice again. This time my flashlight finds her, a woman, caught like a deer in the headlights. Same baseball cap, same t-shirt as the boys. A minute away from saying "boy does this suck." I turn back to the driver. "Well?"

"You're on," he says. The jeep turns towards campus. He leans out the window. "Officer?"

"Yes?" Whenever they say officer, you know that something smart-ass is on the way.

"There's a dog in the road."

"I know." The dog sits calmly, on its best behavior.

"It could get hit, officer."

"I'll take care of it."

"Good. I'm sure you can handle it." Long pause. "Officer." Then they drive off, speeding up as soon as they turn the curve. I can hear them laughing, replaying the clever things they said. I stand there, wondering if there's any way a guy like me can win, talking to the likes of them. I wonder about this all the time. I keep the student directory at home by the toilet and...add it all up...I spend hours just flipping through, seeing where they come from, towns like Shaker Heights and Lake Forest, Darien and Wilmette, all those Allisons and Megans and Ryans and Joshes who live on lanes and courts and drives, which are nothing like the roads I know. I study that directory like it's a textbook in a course I'm close to flunking. I know that flunking feeling. I was a student here myself once, a scholarship student sort of. That's only because college employees get a huge discount on tuition and since my father worked here, they cut me a deal. My going to college was a dream come true; my father's dream that he never lived to see. It's just as well. I lasted a few weeks into the last semester and then it was done. I went to class pretty regularly, at least at the start, and did my work on time. I got encouraged and counseled plenty but, though the college was a mile from my farm, I never felt like I belonged. I felt slow and tongue-tied and second rate and after a while I slipped away so quietly that nobody missed me, not then, not ever. Now I'm back, another dumb goober playing cop and nobody knows I was a student here. That's okay. I take enough shit as it is.

The dog sits motionless, just like the dog on the old records, listening for his master's voice. But as soon as I move, the game is on again. The dog runs circles around me. Again, I wonder about driving away. But the students saw me. If that schnauzer winds up pavement pizza, they'd love reporting me, they'd be checking my tires for fur in no time. Alright. One on one, even up, level playing field, the dog could dodge me all night. But the leash makes a difference. I fake for the dog, step on the leash and watch the little bastard do a back flip onto the pavement. Then I reel the sucker in. The dog freezes and digs in, legs locked, so it's like pulling a statue of a dog, something with no moving parts. At my touch, it trembles. Holding the flashlight with one hand, I turn the collar with the other, until some metal comes around, but I can't read it because when I wipe at the surface my hand comes back, covered in blood. Now I see there's blood all around the dog's mouth and neck.

"Holy shit," I say. I wrap the leash around a fence post that marks the edge of the fraternity property, then step over to the jeep and radio my office. I call my uncle and ask him to get over here fast. Tom's an old hand in security. Mr. Popularity with the students. They come to him when they need a break, a case of vandalism that doesn't need writing up, if repairs are quickly made, eight kegs of beer at a party where four are permitted, well, anybody can make a mistake. Anyway, Tom is a piece of work. He got me this job, after I finished with the Army. I got married, he was my best man. I got separated, he let me live in his trailer. I cry uncle and there he is, stepping out of a college station wagon.

"Hey, Billy," he asks. "What's with this dog?"

"He was running around the road," I answered. "Barking like crazy, going around in circles."

"Looks like he's calmed down now," he says.

"Not really. You step close, you touch him. He shakes all over..."

"Jesus, he's got the shakes alright," Tom says, hunkering down.

"I told you. And..."

"What the hell..." Tom withdraws his hand, rubs his fingers together. "This is blood."

"It's blood. But he's not bleeding. There aren't any wounds."

"Tag?"

"I didn't get around to it...I just called..."

"Well, shit," Tom says. He yanks the dog forward, grabbing the collar, wiping some blood and dirt away. And coming up empty. "Just an inoculation ID. The vet's name and number. This won't do us any good tonight."

"It's not the dog I'm worried about," I say. "There was someone holding this leash when they started out together tonight."

I see Tom think it over. He glances toward the fraternity lodge, a handsome stone building that no one would mind calling home, if fraternities ever took the hint and went the way of the polo team, the flying club, compulsory chapel and the rest of it.

"You drive up and down the road?" he asks.

"Yeah. No one out walking. And from the looks of things, everybody's all tucked in. There's no parties in progress. No visiting cars or nothing..."

"Well," Tom reaches in for a ring of keys that hung from his belt, then nods towards the Psi U lodge. "Let's just check."

"You don't think..." I say. The lodge is dark, shutters down, door padlocked. It's been that way all summer.

"Listen," Tom says. "Maybe not. But it's a fraternity lodge. And fraternities are a womb of weirdness. Okay?"

"Okay," I say.

"What would they say if we didn't check?" Tom asks. "They'd say, dumb hicks. Tie up the damn dog, Billy. Could be... could be a raid from another fraternity," Tom says. "A prank, like."

It takes him a while to open the door. I point the flashlight, while Tom tests one key after another. It feels like we're wasting our time. But Tom has a point. We have to check the lodge. Now we step through the door, into a foyer. Tom feels along the wall, finds a light switch, flips it back and forth.

"Power's off," I say.

"You picked up on that, huh?" Tom reaches for his flashlight and now there are two beams of light. We step inside toward the main room. The place is eerie. It's like one of those movies, a cop investigating a crime scene where the killer might, just might, still be around. Martin Balsam walking up those steps at the Bates Motel. Only he had a gun. College Security has flashlights, which now light up the main parlor. I see wood floor, wood beams overhead. A fireplace. Benches and chairs along the wall. Must and mold and stale air.

"Ever been in here?" Tom asks.

"No. Just outside. Checking IDs and stamping hands."

"In your student days, I mean," Tom says. "Such as they were."

"They invited me..." I say.

"But you didn't go," Tom answers for me. "Withdrew incomplete. They put it on your transcript. You're not careful, they'll put it on your gravestone."

I stay quiet. Every now and then Tom turns on me. He says hard things, gets this look in his eyes, this dead look that makes me think I don't count for much. This only happens once in a while and only when it's just the two of us. It's not the real Tom, though. It's not the best of him, not the most of him. It's just another side. And it scares me.

"Christmas party is something else," Tom says. "Wassail. This big old bowl of wine and vodka and cinnamon and pine cones and I don't know what. Kind of stuff, girls drink it. 'Oh, wow, it's like Kool Aid only warmer, can I have some more?' Next thing, they're swinging from the chandeliers, they're projectile vomiting across the room. That's after the faculty leave. Some damn scene. Next day—next week—they decide they got raped."

While he talks, Tom shines the flashlight around the room, covering every surface, painting the place with light. We're both relaxing, knowing the place is empty. But the dog still sits outside. The bloody dog. Tom locks the door. The lodge is behind us and that's a relief. "I'm going to walk up and down the street," he announces.

"I've been up and down," I remind him.

"I'll walk it," Tom counters. "You see more when you walk." He means, he sees more than I do. "Just check around the lodge until I get back. Then we'll call the sheriff and leave a message for the morning shift. Over and out."

"What about the dog?"

"Take it in to the office, I guess. The morning guys can drop it off at the pound."

"Let's you and me go for a walk," I tell the dog after Tom leaves. I worry about the pound: a long-odds lottery with a death sentence at the end. My trailer's right next door almost, I see what goes in and what comes out. I can count. Leash in one hand, flashlight in the other, I head around the side of the building. Four steps along, a dark shape slumped against the wall turns into a garbage bag full of beer cans, Old Milwaukee and Old Style, cheap beer that the students call Old Mill and Old Swill. We move around the back of the building, into a parking area at the end of the driveway. And then—suddenly— the dog is straining at the leash, pulling like a husky—yelping, tugging me off the bench towards the edge of the driveway where I see some- thing that isn't going to be another garbage bag. It's someone sitting against a tree, like those college students in brochures, reading books in nice weather. Only tonight is dark and the dog is straining, yelping, and I follow along, and find a woman seated against the tree—a woman who has graying hair pulled back into a bun, who wears wrin- kled slacks and polo shirt—a woman covered with blood that comes out of a hole torn in her throat that I can't look at, that hurts me to see. It's like another mouth that vomited blood.

"Don't touch anyfuckingthing," Tom says from behind me. I had- n't even seen him come.

"I should check to see if there's a pulse," I say.

"She's dead. Trust me on this one, Billy." Tom steps around to the back and calmly points his flashlight. "Shot in the back of the head, looks like. Came out the throat. Came out big time."

"You know her?"

"Seen her. Academic processions."

"She's...faculty?" I ask. I'm ashamed of the way it sounds, hushed and reverent, as if a dead professor is more important than a dead, say, hairdresser. Then again, this is a college not a beauty salon. I can imagine a beautician getting killed: bad debts, angry boyfriend, crime of passion, all the stuff you hear about in country songs. Who'd want to kill a professor?

"Just go to the jeep and call the office. Tell them to get the sheriff here. And an ambulance. Tell them to tell the ambulance no sirens. No rush. This is over."

Tom is digging around in a blue canvas tote that's all covered with buttons and slogans like GO VEGAN and WIMMYNS POWER and there's one he laughs and holds up, so I can share the joke. The button had a picture of our college president, Dr. Warren Niles, with BIG PRICK, TINY DICK printed across it. That about takes my breath away, disrespecting the president like that.

"Wonder how she found out?" Tom says. Now he's rustling around inside the bag. He pulls out a book—one of those pocket-sized calorie-counting guides.

"I guess she was trying to lose weight," I say. It comes out dumb but it's sad, seeing someone who was trying to make herself better getting interrupted, just like that, when she's trying to get in shape. All those skipped meals wasted.

"Yeah, well," Tom says, giving me this look. "She'll be down to skin and bones in no time now." He opens a wallet that we found inside her tote bag, finds a driver's license.

"Martha Yeats," he says.

The next day, Tom drags me to a meeting in a conference room on the second floor of Stribling Hall, where President Niles and Provost Ives have their offices. I know Hartley Fuller from History, at least I recognize him, and Ave Hayes, the trustee who lives on a gentleman's farm outside of town. He's dropped in on me more than once, asking do I want to sell my land. I can understand why they're here. And Willard Thrush is no surprise: he's a shoot-from-the-hip kind of smartass who heads up the development office, which is about raising money. The question is, why did Tom wake me up and bring me along? I've got no business here. I found the body, is all.

"A bad time for Martha to get herself killed," Thrush says. "Right before college, right on campus."

"Excuse me?" It's Hartley Fuller. "You're suggesting she should have picked a better time and place?"

"Well..."

"She was murdered!" Fuller looks like he's about to jump out of his chair. Tom glances at me as if to say, see, I promised you an interesting day. In the nick of time, Sheriff Don Lingenfelter comes through the door, escorting this tall grim-faced guy who looks like a coroner. But it turns out his name is Sherwood Graves and he's a detective with the State of Ohio.

"How's life in Security, Tom?" Ave asks, calming things down. He's that kind of guy. "President Niles just invited me to look in on things," he says. Informal as hell. But the man's got deep pockets and deeper pedigree. Rutherford B. Hayes, 19th president of the United States, was a graduate of this place and Ave is his great-great-something or other. "I've been looking for a little part-time work," Ave goes on. "You get to go to all those parties."

"Forget it," Tom says. "They don't get going until after midnight. And they're a hell of a lot noisier than they used to be."

"Oh..."

"You want the same experience, just go down your cellar, turn off the lights, turn up the radio and drink beer until you're sick."

The door opens again and I'm expecting Warren Niles, our president. He knows my name. It's always, "Hi, Billy," and he's proud of it, on a first name basis with the hired hand. But it's not Warren. It's Caroline Ives, the provost. She doesn't know me from Adam.

"Maybe we should get started," she says, the way those spokesperson women do at the start of press conferences, coming on like one of the boys but not much liking the boys she's with. "The President has asked me to convey our commitment to cooperate in every way with this investigation. He wanted me to make that clear from the very start."

"Uh..." said the sheriff, pulling up his sock and rubbing his neck, all at once. "Where is he?"

"President Niles thought it would be appropriate for me to represent the college," she says and now I'm pretty sure she's not happy being here. I see Willard Thrush rub a hand over his face, like he's scratching an itch. My guess is, he's hiding a smile.

Next thing, the provost lady goes around the room and everyone introduces themselves and says where are they from. It comes my turn, I say "Security." It sounds flat. "I found the body," I add. Provost Ives gives me this funny look, like was I here to claim a reward? Then she invites the sheriff to brief us.

"I'll tell you what we know," the sheriff begins. "No surprises. Professor Martha Yeats lived alone in a bungalow a half mile from where we found her. She walked her dog a couple times a day and where she died was on one of her routes. Folks there were used to seeing her. But no one saw her last night. No mess, nothing unusual, at her place. Salad on the counter and some wheat crackers. Table set for one. No guests staying, no company expected..."

Now Lingenfelter pauses and reaches into his shirt pocket for the kind of scuffed, spiral-bound notebook people use to record gas mileage on long car trips.

"This is a summary of what the medical examiner gave me over the phone. Professor Yeats was shot at close range—a yard, say—from behind. Death was immediate. No signs of a struggle, no other wounds. We don't have a weapon—a handgun, for sure. But we have the bullet that killed her."

"What caliber?" Thrush asked.

"If you don't mind," Graves said, "We don't think you need to know that right now."

"Okay," Thrush conceded, "I guess not."

"So anyway," the sheriff resumed, "there's a chance she got killed nearby. Her shoes—it's not for sure—suggest maybe she got dragged. And there are some parallel tracks in the gravel leading to where we found her. Coming in off the road..."

He flips through a few more pages, then looks back up at us. "That'll do her."

"How..." the provost lady scans the faces across the table, our two officers, the sheriff, the state investigator. "How can we help you?"

Again, the sheriff looks at the investigator. Sherwood Graves. Like the name of a cemetery. And it fits. The man is tall, gangly, bony, ugly. If he were a U.S. president, he'd be Lincoln. Failing that, he's just plain odd. His face has been scarred by some youthful condition, acne probably. Once more, Graves nods to the sheriff, who continues.

"We get two, three murders a year in this county and they're not exactly head scratchers. Half the time the killer turns himself in, even waits for us at the scene, phones us up and gives us directions. Drug stuff, alcohol, domestic..."

Lingenfelter's voice trails off, as if he's picturing memories he decides not to share. But I can picture them. Trailer courts with torn above-ground swimming pools. Tired clapboard shacks where white-painted truck tires border dead gardens. Down at the heels garden apartments with video dishes searching heaven for excitement. Parking lots where pickup trucks outnumber cars and country western music feels like truth.

"These things are ugly," the sheriff says. "They surely are that. But they're not real hard for us. Now what happened with your Professor Yeats is different... This killer didn't stick around. He did the job and left. And maybe he moved the body. Only he didn't move the body to hide it. The purpose was to...I wouldn't know what to call it..."

"Display it," Sherwood Graves says. He leans forward from his side of the table, planting bony elbows that could put a hole in a tablecloth. "Display it," he repeats. "You might want to think about that."

"We could get lucky," Lingenfelter says. "It happens. We connect a bullet to a weapon. We find the weapon and we connect it to someone's hand. Sooner or later someone talks. The killer, the killer's boyfriend or girlfriend or ex-partner or cell mate. And it gets back to us. It's not like we solve the case. We just stick around and wait for people to be their shitty selves."

"This is Martha Yeats!" Hartley Fuller bursts out. "I hired her. I mentored her. I mourn her. This whole college is in mourning, sheriff. When something like this happens, it doesn't just destroy an individual life or a single career...a very promising one at that. It challenges our whole enterprise. What we do and what we are. And, perhaps most of all, where we are. It violates..."

"Oh, give me a break," Willard Thrush interrupts. "Martha was a loud-mouth and a flake. She got out of bed in the morning and she went to bed at night planning how to piss people off. I'm sorry she's dead but I'll bet it has nothing to do with the college. And everything to do with her sorry, kinky self. So I think the sheriff has a point. I don't see any reason we should turn ourselves inside out."

"If I may." Now it was Averill Hayes' turn. "I'd suggest you do what you can. But do it carefully."

That's when I notice the way Sherwood Graves is leaning forward, almost out of his chair, staring at Hayes. Hayes is a chummy, clubby kind of guy, a jolly good fellow. And Graves is the opposite, all angles and edges.

"Do what you can and do it carefully," says Graves. "That's our mandate?"

"We're all together on this," the provost adds. She senses an ending, I guess. Tired of the bunch of us. She'd make Warren pay for his absence, I bet. She was that kind. On the best day you ever had, moonlight and roses, she'd have this list of all the little ways you let her down. A list that only got longer.

"Fine, then," Graves says. He gets up, as if to leave, turns away, heads towards the door, where he retrieves a leather satchel he deposited at the foot of a coat rack.

"Shall we begin?" he asks the provost. He sees her surprise. "Cooperation, right? That's what you promised. You and your president."

"That's correct," she says, glancing at her watch, the way people only do in movies, signaling how busy they are. Graves doesn't go for it.

"Well then..." He gestures for her to sit down. "Let's get started." Then, as if to demonstrate his control, he sifts through the files in front of him, while everybody waits, empty-handed.

"You hired Martha Yeats for a tenure-track position in the Department of History a dozen years ago," he says without looking up. "That was before your time, am I right?"

"This is just my second year," she responds, as if she's still angling for permission to leave. No such luck.

"You weren't around then," he confirms. "And you, Professor Fuller?"

"I wasn't chair then," Hartley says. "The chair rotates among tenured members of the department." It makes a funny picture: one chair, a half dozen professors' asses. "But I was on the search committee."

"A national search?" asks Graves. "You advertised the position, people applied, you interviewed them at a professional convention, you brought two or three candidates to campus where they taught a sample class and gave a lecture, met the provost and the president and the honors majors, was it like that?"

"Yes," Hartley replies. He seems surprised by Graves' knowledge of college hiring. "All our searches are national. She replaced a professor who was about to retire. Was that your next question?"

"You guessed right, professor. Who'd she replace?"

"Hiram Wright."

"One of our great faculty names," the provost says. "Right up there with Harry Stribling. Wright lives just outside town, to this day.

He's a nationally known historian."

"Nationally known. Did Professor Wright retire willingly?"

"We've never had a mandatory retirement age," the Provost says.

"Okay. You had a national search to replace a nationally-known professor. How many applications were there?"

"Oh, at least two hundred."

"We keep applications a year or two," the Provost volunteers, "on the chance that we may go back into the same pool. After that..."

"Sure. You chuck them."

"We advertise for a dozen positions of one kind or another every year," she says. "We can't save them, we have as many or more applications from prospective faculty as from prospective students, any given year."

"Is that good news or bad news?' Graves asks her.

"Well..."

"Never mind," he says. He walks Fuller through an account of how Martha got hired. There were no local candidates, visitors or spouses that year. No suspects there. Then he goes over Martha's job reviews, which were in her second year, her fourth, her sixth, when she got "appointment without limit." Tenure. Tom Hoover calls it "lifetime employment." Short of rape or arson, you can't get shitcanned.

While they talk, I half listen. I picture Martha Yeats. They knew her while she lived. A fighter, a noisemaker, a pain in the ass. I only knew her as I found her, sitting in front of a tree, a bib-sized splash of blood coming out of her throat. Sherwood Graves wants to know about students who dropped or flunked her course or petitioned to withdraw and two or three she'd accused of plagiarism. And some professors who questioned her classes, "feminazi rally," "caterwauling 1-2," who belittled her research, the clothes she wore, the weeds in her yard, the rust on her car, the bumper stickers, the dog she allowed under seminar tables. These are things that might lead to jokes, gibes, snubs. But not murder.

When Graves starts in on Martha's scholarship, I'm back in grade school, watching the clock on the wall, waiting for the bell that doesn't ring. I even catch the provost looking at me and we trade smiles. She knows a lot—too much, maybe—and I know nothing but together we make the most bored couple on the planet. I'm picturing what she'd be like if we were stranded someplace together. And you know what? She might be wondering the same thing. That's how bad it is.

Anyway. "Women and Power," that was Martha's theme, comparing early female leaders—Imelda Marcos, Mme. Chiang Kai-shek—to honest-to-God feminists like Benazir Bhutto and Winnie Mandela. It turns out, once Martha had featured them in this article or that colloquium, they got indicted, assassinated, otherwise driven from office. It got to be a joke, Willard says: recognition from Martha Yeats was an instant jinx. The bottom line—which it takes two hours to get to—is that Martha Yeats had answered a casting call, that was all. A certain kind of part was open, a character in a long-running series called small college. She played the part: woman crusader. The lesbian thing was a throw-in. Hell, she'd arrived with a husband, a visiting professor who left after a couple of years. No one's mentioned him, I suddenly realize. So does the provost lady.

"Excuse me," the Provost says. "Hartley? What was the name of Martha's husband? I was just wondering."

"Husband?" Graves asks, his head popping up from below the table top. "She decided she was a lesbian after she got here?"

"It's not a decision," Hartley promptly corrects. "It's a discovery. And her husband's name was Robert Rickey."

"Is he around? Robert Rickey?"

Now it's my turn. I get this look from Tom, this nod that it's okay for me to speak.

"Excuse me," I say. Suddenly, everybody's looking at me. He walks, he talks. Surprise!

"Yes?" says Graves.

"Robert Rickey? He's around."

"Can you find him?"

"I suppose," I said. Maybe I should have left it at that. "He's living on my farm." I stop again. And start. In for a penny, in for a pound. "With my wife."

"Well then..." Graves says. He stops a minute and then I hear the kind of stirring you get at the end of college ceremonies, where the audience sniffs an ending. A long meeting would have gone longer, if my wife hadn't left me for Martha Yeats' ex. I even get a grateful nod from the provost as she rises, like she owes me one. "Thank you." She just mouths the words.

"Oh," says Graves. "I'll need a driver."

"Oh?"

"I could get someone up from Columbus but it would be better if it was a local. How about him?"

He was gesturing at me.

"He's plenty local, alright," Tom says.

"Don't go finding no more bodies, Billy" the sheriff says.

"You're early," Sherwood Graves said, the next morning. He came to the door of the Motel Eight with a towel wrapped around his middle, soap in his ears and dripping wet.

"I'll just wait outside here," I said. He nodded okay and closed the door. I didn't get more than a sneak peek but when you work around a college you learn how to eyeball a room in a second and that's what Graves' place reminded me of, a dorm room: papers spread over the bed, clothes on the floor, styrofoam cups and plastic plates from fast food places across the road. The room was hot, the air was sour, the curtains were drawn.

I waited in the parking lot and checked out Route 36. The first bunch of shopping centers got built along here, the ones that emptied out the downtown. They were growing old now too, losing out to newer places up the road. People said a mall was coming.

"Alright, Billy," Graves said, closing the door behind him. "First stop is Hiram Wright. He lives on...let me see...Lower Gambier Road."

"River Road, sir," I said. "That's what us locals call it." River Road is a spooky kind of place. As a kid, I was scared shitless of River Road. It had some of the roughest white people I'd ever seen and their dogs were the meanest anywhere. It was a strange place for a professor to retire, but near the end of the road, just about where you caught your first glimpse of the college hill, there was a sturdy looking red-clapboard house sitting on a narrow pie-shaped piece of land that was five feet from the road, five feet above the river. Someone was on the porch in a rocker, watching us approach. Maybe he knew we were coming. Maybe he sat there all the time.

"Good morning," Graves said, in this way cops have of staying polite without getting friendly. "Are you Professor Wright?"

"Yes." So we'd found him. The college legend, him and Harry Stribling, Butch and Sundance. They put the little jerkwater college on the map, so I'd heard. Stribling had been dead for years. He was just a name to me, a name on a grave in the college cemetery that visitors photographed, on books filled with poems that don't have rhyme—

or, Tom says—reason, on the building where old Warren Niles has his office. His name was on something else, too. Harry Stribling left the college a ton of money that went into buying land around the college, so the place would stay country-like forever. The thing was, when the Stribling Tract bought the land, the farmer stayed put, nothing changed and that was the whole point. The farmer died or moved to Florida, the Stribling Tract found a new farmer or just closed the property off and that's when you'd see "no trespassing" signs in hunting season, with Stribling's name on them. And that was only some of what they owned. No one knew how much. People were always guessing. The other thing was that the college didn't control the Stribling Tract: it was some lawyer in Columbus. Old Harry loved the college but not so much that he trusted it not to screw things up. All of this meant that old Harry Stribling gave folks something to talk about, even if they never read a line of poetry: the Stribling Tract. Where it began, where it ended, nobody was sure. Tom says it wasn't the poems made him rich. It was family money. Poems don't earn squat, Tom says.

Hiram Wright was something else again. I'd seen him around, not knowing he was special. He was the kind of guy you noticed, with a body that reminded me of Orson Welles on *The Tonight Show,* and a goatee that was like Colonel Sanders. But he dressed River Road: work boots, wrinkled chinos, old-fashioned undershirt, the kind with long sleeves and buttons in the front you see in pictures of old-time mining camps out west.

"I'm Sherwood Graves," my partner said. "I'm with the Ohio Bureau of Criminal Identification and Investigation. I'm looking into the death of..."

"Martha Yeats," Wright said, jumping in. But while he was talking to Graves he was staring at me. It was the oddest damn thing. Then, his hands came out from behind him. One of them was holding a cane, which he planted in front of him. He stood up, leaning forward on it, that much closer, staring at me.

"I know you," he said. "You're a Hoover." He came closer to me, moving slowly behind the cane. It wasn't for show. He needed it. He put his hand under my chin, ran it around my face, studying me, like I was something interesting he hadn't expected to find. It gave me the willies getting looked at that way.

"You're Earl's boy," he said.

"I'm Billy." I just barely managed to get it out. Earl Hoover had been dead for going onto twenty years but now this old guy said I'm Earl's boy, it took me back. I was a kid. I was my father's son, that's me. "How'd you know my dad?"

"Your father and I went hunting together three or four times a year, for a dozen years in a row. Out towards Newcastle, in the flood plains along the Walhonding. Up in the Killbuck Valley, on the way to Millersburg. Down to the covered bridges in Licking County. You must have seen us come and go. I saw you...it must have been you."

"My God..." Now I had it. Someone who'd drive out to our farm on a cold pink-sky November dawn, in a jeep with his dogs, joined by our dogs and my father. What I saw of him, I saw through sleepy eyes, my forehead against a chilly pane, I saw a flash of headlights, the dogs stirring. I smelled coffee, I heard the stamp of boots on the doorstep. The professor had come, my father's friend from the college, the professor.

"You're the professor."

"That's right, Billy."

"My father said you were the smartest man for miles around."

"He was one of the best men I've ever known," Wright said. He stopped and studied me some more. "Do you miss him?" he asked. I stood there, words caught somewhere between my stomach and my throat. "I know you do," Wright says. "It's written all over you." He stops but he's still looking at me. Then, as an afterthought, he glanced at Sherwood Graves. "I know you too."

"I guessed you would," Graves answered.

"Well, come in," he said. Then he couldn't resist turning back to me. "I must have walked a thousand miles with your father, over the years," he said.

I expected something low ceilinged and choppy, with lots of little rooms, which is the way all the old houses are around here. But, except for a kitchen and bathroom towards the back, Professor Wright's place was one big room where furniture—a bed, a rough wooden table, an easy chair with a reading lamp, a television—made islands in a sea of books. I spotted a murderer's row of liquor bottles in the corner and classy glasses that might be crystal. No applejack and Mason jars for Professor Wright. And there were serious copper pots and pans hanging on the wall and an oversize gas stove and strings of peppers and garlic hanging from the beams, all of it looking like a set for one of those cooking shows on cable television.

"So," Professor Wright said. "The subject is Martha Yeats." He aimed his words at Graves but he was still taking me in, maybe thinking of all those miles with my father. Maybe they were friends, just like he said they were, but it was hard to believe.

"There must have been some tension between you and Professor Yeats," Graves prompted.

"That's what they told you? Who told you that? Hartley Fuller?"

"Yes. The history chair."

"That's not a chair, son. That's a stool." He enjoyed his moment of anger, then got back to us. "Maybe it doesn't matter. History gets written by the winners, no? Bad history. And Hartley is surely a bad historian. And...in a way...a winner." He fell silent for a moment and Graves knew better than to throw in another question. "The fact is, Martha and I overlapped for a few years. So we lived across the hall from each other. A duet. My swan song and her...I wouldn't know what to call it..." His voice trailed off. "So what kind of wisdom are you looking for?" Wright finally asked. "I didn't kill her."

"But somebody did," Graves said. "It wasn't a robbery. It wasn't a rape. It was an execution. Maybe some maniac drove through town. That happens. But chances are, it was someone who knew her, who found her while she was out walking her dog, who got close enough to join her, to drop back a step and fire a bullet into the base of her skull. Don't tell me who killed her, Professor Wright. Just tell me why someone would want to kill a professor at this college. Kill her and display her body outside a fraternity lodge."

"God, what a question," Wright sat quiet. "Let the old professor ramble. That's what you want, isn't it?"

"You're the man they call the legend. You and Harry Stribling. And Stribling's rambling days are over."

Wright laughed at that and sat some more. I guess when you're talking to someone old you take your chances. It's a grab bag. You make room for memories. "Stribling's been dead fifteen years this December," Wright said. "Amazing. And he wasn't up to much for years before that. His best work was done in the thirties, most of it before he even came here. *Country Vespers, Things I Wish I'd Known.* A small shelf. Reputations are peculiar things. As you know, Mr. Graves."

Graves nodded his head. There was something they knew that I didn't. They were signaling to each other in a code I couldn't break. I wish they'd let me in on their little secret.

"Harry Stribling died in doubt. Did you know that? He thought of himself as a failure. I know they've named a building after him. He left some land behind. The Stribling Tract. They use him in brochures. He'd be amused. What he accomplished didn't measure up against what he aimed to do. I'm dying a slower death. Or living a longer life. It's the same thing, I suppose. I'll die and they will mourn me and raise funds in my name. In the meantime...so much for legends. Harry Stribling was a fine writer of the second rank. I have a name as an American historian. Harry and I were enough to give this college a reputation. And now...so what?"

He pulled himself out of his chair and went over to the long table with the bottles, poured himself a glass of something brown and sat back down. Then he reminded himself we were there, gestured an offer, got turned down.

"You'd be amazed at the number of institutions that perk along from year to year and never get closer to acclaim than a professor who appeared on 'Jeopardy.' Those colleges you see in the sports pages in columns of tiny type, places that I can't associate with anything, not with a colleague, a book, a single living idea. What are these places that make no claim on the world's attention, on the world's mind? What goes on there? Does anybody know? Is anybody checking?"

He stopped there and collected himself, staring out the window now. I was amazed at Graves' patience with this guy. It was like Martha Yeats' murder was just an excuse to get together and talk about the college.

"Martha Yeats," Graves reminded him. The gentlest possible nudge.

"You called her my replacement? Yes and no. She wasn't another me. She wasn't supposed to be. She was part of a larger change. Bear with me now..." Graves nodded. "In the thirties, this college was like the others I've mentioned, just a name on a list. Relaxed. Obscure. Upperclass. There was a flying club. They played polo. They visited brothels in Mansfield. Then there came a new president— Chambers—an imperious, driven fellow who determined to make this place..." He stopped in mid-sentence, as if he were searching for the right word, but I'd bet the money in my wallet he had it already. "...great. But he didn't have the money. He couldn't go at it top to bottom. He couldn't build new buildings, he couldn't even maintain the ones we already had. So he hired a handful of professors who might make a mark. He brought Harry Stribling up from Tennessee.

He found me at Rutgers. He got some brilliant refugees right off the boat. Philosophers, scientists out of Berlin and Warsaw. He found, he recruited, he seduced talent and he brought it here—here!—to this improbable place. It wasn't a wholesale transformation. Likeable, mediocre faculty outnumbered—and sometimes resented—the new-comers. Resented the president as well. As for the students...well...a mixed bag. Still our little college had some magic. It wasn't always wonderful, Graves. But we rarely doubted that we were where we ought to be."

"What happened?"

"What always happens. Change. The president died. The college grew. The village got pretty. Styles changed, not styles in clothing, but styles in people. Not just here, of course. Very little that happens, happens here first. Things took their time coming. But, in the end, they found us. Even here..."

"What arrived?" Graves asked.

"Mr. Graves, it would take forever."

"Just a few words."

"A loss of focus, a restlessness arrived. Ambitions that couldn't be realized here. A loss of integrity. A loss of identity, almost. An odd combination of complacency and discontent. A pandering to students. Customer is always right or, if wrong, forgiven. The devolution of an educational institution into a faculty-centric user-friendly therapeutic kibbutz. The end of almost all requirements, assembly, attendance, chapel attendance, class attendance. Dress codes, Saturday classes, you name it. An embrace of diversity which, while it enriched, also diluted and divided. What did it come to? In the head a loss of edge, in the heart, a loss of love. That's what arrived, Mr. Graves. Am I vague? I'll be more specific. Martha Yeats arrived. Martha Yeats. Are you sure I'm not a suspect?"

"Yes." Graves said.

"Would you tell me if I were?"

"No."

"Well, the fact is, I liked Martha Yeats."

"You're joking, aren't you?"

"Not at all. If you'd been a part of a college all your life, wouldn't you be curious about what followed you? Wouldn't you love to take a peek into the future? That's what I was granted. Hartley Fuller thought it was time for a change. I was out of touch with recent developments

in what he loves to call 'the profession.' My teaching style didn't appeal
to 'today's students.' Warren Niles agreed it was time for me to go and
Martha Yeats was the beginning of the end for me. My class sizes had
dwindled, I admit, and there had been complaints. I was harsh, I was
sarcastic, I wasn't sufficiently interested in students' opinions. I'd
become an acquired taste. Hard grading, heavy reading. Oh my. Well,
alright, but I got Warren to give me a couple years more. It wasn't the
money. It was pure curiosity. I wanted to be a guest at my own funeral. Now, as it happens, I'll be attending Martha's. Well, I was a speci-
men to her, she to me. There was no contest between us. The issue had
been decided, the future was all hers. Time turned me into a local
character. Also—in her eyes—an elitist, hegemonic, hierarchical patri-
arch, way past ripe, outward bound, the bell tolls for thee, old fart, fos-
sil, fogey! But published. More books than the rest of the department
combined. There was that. Well, from where I sat the view was deli-
cious. My courses were titled *American History 1600 to 1800, 1800 to
1900* and *1900 to present*. Martha's courses were calls to arms, credo,
invitations to therapy, things like *Bitches, Witches, Snitches: Women in the
Middle Ages*. I walked into a classroom in a suit, stood behind a lectern,
addressed students as mister and miss. Martha was on a first-name basis
from day one, teacher and students all in a circle, campfire style. And
her office hours! The halls lined with students waiting for an audience,
waiting to talk not just about their papers, their unwritten or half-
written papers, which she criticized, edited, rewrote, and, I suspect, finished in their presence. No, more than that. She was a mother, a sister,
a friend. Every student, I soon learned, began her class with an A. It
was theirs to lose. Grades were demeaning, she told them. So, too, it
turned out were fraternities, athletic contests, our choice of guest lecturers, the Christian symbols in the college flag, the college songs, our
policy on day care, the arrangement of tables in the dining hall, the
honorary degrees we awarded. It was around this time that, having
become aware of William Butler Yeats' 'Leda and the Swan,' a poem
which had escaped her notice until then, Martha decided to differen-
tiate herself from an author who celebrated rape, wings flapping, loins
shuddering, all that. So Yeats, rhyming with gates became Yeats,
rhyming with beets. The world was alerted to this re-naming, via an
all-student, all-employee e-mail. Oh, life was lively with Martha Yeats.
And what paradoxes! Committed to the students yet endlessly com-
bative towards the school, indifferent when not hostile to its character,

its tradition. An odd position for an historian, no, acting as if the history of the school began on the day of her arrival? As for me, I was her daily reminder of all that was wrong with the place. In my office across from hers... well, it was as if a leper had been wheeled into a maternity ward. And it was that. There were infants a-plenty and many childhood diseases. The homesick and lovesick and lonely and not sure of gender, the about to withdraw, transfer, flunk out, harm themselves, harm others, they all sought her out, all the birds with one wing. I grew accustomed to hearing people crying across the hall. And then, late in her second year, it was Martha crying.

"I was in my office after a seminar on history-as-literature, three hours in the daunting company of Francis Parkman. Seminars are exhausting. I'd venture a true full three hour seminar is beyond the abilities of half the current faculty. I sat in my office tired, mute, replaying what I'd said and forgotten to say, the inevitable highs and lows, feuds and alliances. I reached into my drawer for a bottle of brandy, poured some into a coffee cup. Across the hall, I heard someone crying. It was April, I recall, because the wet, earthy breeze came into my office—what a relief from the stuffy, caged-in seminar room. It was April because that's when students cry the most and Martha had been doing land-office business lately. Abuse and molestation are terrible things. But—forgive me—one notices how those memories tend to surface in April, close to exam time. I heard a tap on my door and Martha was standing there. Tissue in hand, red-eyed, she made no effort to disguise that she was the one who'd been crying.

"'How do you do it, Wright?' she asked. 'Or rather, how did you do it?'" She nodded towards my shelf of books. Not conference papers, not journal articles, not book reviews. Books. The very books which she'd referred to as 'out of touch, out of date, and, alas, not out of print.' This from the same woman who called Harry Stribling, our dear gentle miniaturist, a 'dingleberry from the fetid asshole of the Old South.' That was in a faculty meeting. And no one corrected her. It was amazing how quickly the old guard caved in, how the faculty who made a religion of civility swallowed their tongues when Martha spoke. And now she'd come to call. I wondered why.

"I invited her into my office and, when she sat, I gestured towards my brandy. She nodded gamely back, returned to my office with a clean cup. This time she closed the door. I poured, she drank. She'd just re-read her thesis, she said. *Cunts and Counts: Courtesans and Power in Eighteenth Century France.* Oxford University Press—'isn't that the same place that published your stuff a million years ago?'—had expressed an interest. They'd wanted some revision of course, an opening and closing which would appeal to a broader audience. And they were more than willing to wait. Then the second year rolls around and there it sits because Martha's on nine committees. She has advisees, she's writing letters of recommendation, she's liaising with student groups, the women's caucus, the gay-lesbian forum, anti-fraternity task force, eating disorders council, multi-cultural steering committee, alternative lectureships program. Out of breath, she peered up at me and asked why I wasn't laughing at her. Because it wasn't funny, I said.

"It got worse. Her original editor at Oxford had moved on and the successor, while professing enthusiasm, didn't seem as committed to the project. Then again, Martha reasoned, urgent interest would have been as disturbing as a nonchalant 'whatever.' How she looked forward to the summers! How quickly they slipped by, no longer than a three day weekend, and no more productive. Just enough time to recognize the saddest truth of all. She wasn't the same person she was when she started writing. She'd changed. 'I let this place take me over,' she said. Teaching, grading, comments on papers, committees. Students in her classroom, in her office, in her house. Students waiting for her, even now, to review what happened on the Take Back the Night March…"

Wright interrupted his story, poured himself another drink which he lifted, maybe a toast to Martha. He let us wait a little longer. He knew he was a storyteller alright. And "the smartest man for miles around." But I couldn't help wondering what all this had to do with nailing the killer. Graves wasn't rushing the old man, that was for sure. It's not like a guilty person was making a getaway and every second counted. Then the intermission was over and Wright began again.

"I realized that Martha Yeats hadn't come to me for advice. She'd come to me for punishment. Punishment was sitting in front of me, confiding failure. So it didn't matter what I said. Therefore, I said what I wanted. I told her that the most important books, more important than the books that I had written, maybe even more important than the ones that she aspired to write, had been written under far worse conditions than obtained at this college now. I told her that when people came to me and said they'd always wanted to write, I said, if that were true, they would have written. Somehow. She didn't like what she was hearing. Punishment she meted out to herself was one thing. Correction from me was quite another. She was getting out of her chair, out of my life, but I kept talking, knowing we would never talk again. I told her she was talented but that talent was promiscuous. There was always lots of talent around and...and then she was gone."

Wright sat back in his chair. "That was all. We never talked like that again. But, from what I saw, my fears came true. She had a look in her eyes. Two strikes against you before you spoke. I didn't speak. And I don't know who killed her. I couldn't begin to guess. Are you sure that it wasn't...random...an accidental crossing of paths?"

"I doubt it."

"Well, do you think we'll ever know? I'm an historian, not a detective. But I know there are questions that are never answered. Could this be one of those?"

"I hope not."

Wright followed us to the door, out onto the lawn and slowly walked us over to where we were parked. The morning was pretty much shot. I wondered what Hiram Wright did with himself, how he got through the days and nights. All the things he did, he did alone— cooking, eating, reading and writing. I was by myself but at least I had a job. I dodged loneliness. I worked nights.

"I forgot to mention something," Wright said. Graves and I were both inside the Cherokee. "I've benefitted from Martha's death. Maybe it's a benefit. We'll see. Warren Niles stopped by this morning, before you came."

"He visited here?" Graves asked.

"Don't be surprised," Wright said. "People find me here. All kinds of people. Warren comes by every few weeks. There's a bottle of cognac on my shelf that has his name on it. We talk. Anyway, I'm back in the line-up. Martha's classes. It was too late to run a search. I'm teaching Monday."

"*Bitches, Witches, Snitches?*" Graves asked.

"*American History, 1800-1900. American History 1900 to Present.* Quaint, isn't it? Like Amelia Earhart radioing the Honolulu Airport for permission to land. It should be something." He tapped my shoulder. "Stop in, Billy. Take the class if you like."

"I don't think I can," I said.

"Just do it. Do it for your father's sake. I was after him for years to take my class. I had no doubts about his intelligence. Only his confidence. Sooner or later, he'd be sitting in my classroom. Then...he died. Now, I'm retired. Now it's a second chance. Take it, Billy. For my sake too."

"That might not be such a good idea," I said. I wondered about telling him that I flunked out once already.

"He's going to be busy," Graves warned. It came as a relief.

"Well," Wright said, "drop by when you can. Alright?"

I nodded. "When I can."

"Excellent," Wright said. "It's amazing," Wright said. "I taught for thirty years. I've been retired for ten. But I'm nervous. It's in my legs, my stomach, the palms of my hands. I'm rejuvenated. I feel wonderful, knowing there's a group of lives that are going to intersect with mine. I can't tell you how it feels. I'm a professor. I profess history and literature. I'm young again. I can't wait. If I could only click my heels..." He laughed and shook his head, amazed at how good he was feeling. "I have Martha Yeats to thank. Or her killer."

"Next stop?" I ask.

"We're looking for Robert Rickey."

"Okay," I say, heading towards my property, just a mile from Wright's place. I glance at Graves to see whether he wants to talk. You know how some people, when they want to turn you off, pick up a book or newspaper to hide behind? Graves does the same thing, only without the book. He closes his eyes and folds his hands. So I drive home along the river, checking like I always do to see that the old railroad trestle is still in place. They're mostly gone now, just like the trains, and I guess I'm one of the last bunch of kids who ever heard the sound of a train at night, that whistle you can hear a hundred miles. When they stopped trains, it's like an animal we know got hunted out of the world.

Linda Thorne was a college kid, the same way there are army brats. Her father was a money-raiser, moving from place to place until he landed here and pretty much put up his feet. Linda and I went to school together, kindergarten through high school. The summer of my senior year, as a service to the community and a favor to a friend, she took my virginity. I'll never forget how it was, late that Sunday morning, grass smelling sweet, a picnic planned at the old canal locks at Black Hand Gorge. Her house was completely empty, her parents in

Columbus, and it seemed against her nature, letting a morning like that, a house like that, a Billy like that, all go to waste. She stepped away from the sink, where she'd been making a salad, she walked over, dried her wet hands on the front of the t-shirt I was wearing. "I'd like to fuck you," she said, leaning into me. "I didn't know a woman could fuck a man," I said, honestly puzzled. "Thought it was the other way around." "I'll show you," she said. So she did, a few more times before she left for college. And lots of times after I came back from the army. Now I know. A woman can fuck a man. I know that for sure.

We park by the barn and Linda comes out the porch door, smiling at me, this sad, pitying smile of hers. Robert Rickey is making arrangements for his ex-wife's memorial service, she says, but he ought to be home soon. We sit at a picnic table while Graves chats with her. I check out the place, the overgrown kitchen garden, the barn that's got my father's truck—the one he died in—parked outside. It's rusted now, sunflower stalks coming out the windshield, plants living where my dad died.

"He's coming," Graves says, watching a car bump down the driveway.

Robert Rickey is a peppery, sharp-tongued kind of guy who would last about twenty minutes in a local bar. I guess he spotted our College Security vehicle driving in and that gave him time to prepare.

"Hi, Billy," Robert says. We've worked out this no-hard-feelings thing. I started it, Robert picked up the cue. "How's it?"

"Busy," I answer. "You know that."

"Guess I do." He nods at Graves, doesn't introduce himself or offer his hand. "Alright. We were married and we were divorced. If you need the dates I can look them up. I don't celebrate them. On the night she died I was with this lady here. We drove to Columbus at four p.m., arriving at the Stone Ridge Shopping Center sixteen-plex in time for a 5 p.m. showing of *Jackie Brown,* which we saw in the company of Howard Stein, who's current writer-in-residence at the Thurber House. After the movie we kept an eight o'clock reservation at Lindey's Restaurant on Beck Street in German Village. I had a mussels appetizer, the half rack of lamb with garlic mashed potatoes and more than my share of nice merlot, followed by a double espresso with crème brulée. Honey, what did you have?" Linda doesn't reply. She just smiles. She once told me she liked men because of shoulders or butts, eyes or hair or skin. Even astrological signs; one year she screwed her way around the zodiac, sign by sign. But Robert Rickey drew her because he was so bristling smart, so quick on the draw. "I think you had portobello mushrooms on some kind of pasta. I paid by credit card and I kept the receipt which shows we left the restaurant at 10:32 p.m. Was Martha still alive then?"

He reaches in his wallet and pulls out the receipt, offering it to Graves who hesitates before taking it. Robert is messing with him and Graves doesn't like it.

"I saved the receipt because Howard and I were discussing his agent's taking over a manuscript I'm finishing up and, God willing, this qualified as a business dinner. I thought the receipt would help me with the IRS. If you take it, I'd like to make a copy."

Graves returns it to him, without a word.

"We drove back here via routes 62 and 661, arriving here just after midnight. We shared a cognac in the living room and went upstairs, will you back me up on that one darling?"

Linda smiles again. Robert is always taking chances, smart-ass chances, but he's lively, I'll give him that.

"We'll take silence for assent," Robert says. "And now let's all ask ourselves why I'm talking like an upperclass twit on *Columbo?* Could it be because I've just done funeral planning for my wife and come back to find cops waiting? Could it be I don't know how I should feel right now or what I should say? Let's say I'm looking for my voice." Now he offers Graves his hand. "Who are you, mister? What about you?"

"Sherwood Graves."

"Well, was there something more?"

"Yes, Mr. Rickey. Let's sit down." Linda goes back in the house to bring coffee for Robert and Graves starts asking about Martha Yeats. Nothing like death to flush out interest in a person, nothing like murder to make someone more than what they were. She's a hot topic: become a corpse and you're the talk of the town. Graves takes Robert through the story. They met at graduate school in Michigan. He was in English, she was in history. They hook up, live together, get married, go on the job market. Rob's transcript matches Martha's, basically straight A's, but Martha's a woman in a hot field, gender and history. Publishers are interested in her thesis. No way Rob could compete with that. Then it kind of falls apart.

"No fights, no broken dishes, no lipstick on the collar," Robert tells Graves. "Nothing even close to that. No melodrama."

He takes a deep breath and for just a minute, he's out of words, the ones he prepared ahead of time.

"I'm sorry she's dead," he says. "We were finished a long time ago but it bothers me that she won't be around doing Martha-type things..."

"Could anything she did have..." Graves didn't have a chance to finish.

"I don't know why anyone would want to kill her. Don't waste your time on the faculty. Faculty don't kill. Their main hobby is feeling badly treated. I'd put my money on a stranger."

"Until last night, I'd have agreed with you, Mr. Rickey," Graves says. He stops, enjoying the moment. Robert has been in control until now. But Graves has something. He knows it. He leans across the picnic table. "I checked Martha Yeats' hiring. The search. Nothing unusual. Nothing irregular. The circumstances at the time of her death, the scene of her death, her colleagues, her students. Nothing. I checked her love life...after you. Nothing."

"Yeah, I guess so," Robert agrees. "Just this morning, I find that kind of sad."

"In the files, though, there was a name that Provost Ives didn't mention. A candidate in a search that occurred before she became provost. Gerald Kurt Garner."

"Oh my God!" That's Linda bursting out and regretting it right away, when we all turn towards her. "The G-Man," she adds weakly, like a little girl, which it turns out she was, when she knew him.

"Please..." Graves says. He's surprised to hear from her but he recovers fast. "This isn't...a trial." Yeah sure, and he wasn't a cop investigating a murder. He was just a connoisseur of people. "If there's something..."

"Puppy love," she says after a while. Trying to sound light-hearted. "Big man on a small campus. He came from the south of the state, one of those Ohio River towns that are famous for football players. Full scholarship. He was something. He was blonde, and broad-shouldered and smart and not crazy and a smile that..." She stops. She can't help picturing him. It takes her breath away. "He wore chinos and t-shirts and sneakers, same junk they wear today but then it was a sign of innocence, not indifference. A crewcut, would you believe, and oh what a smile. The world by the balls, without half trying, and my just-barely teenage heart in his hands."

She stops and she's shaking, right on the edge of losing it and I'm standing there watching. Crying is something I've never seen her do.

"I have no idea where he is or what he's doing," she says to Graves. "Excuse me. I feel like shit."

She walks away and the walk turns into a little bit of a run up the sidewalk, through the porch, the screen door slamming behind her.

"Alright," Graves says. "Mr. Rickey? Anything from Martha Yeats about Gerald Kurt Garner?"

"No," Rob says. "But I heard that Wright's picked boy applied for a tenure-track position and Martha spiked it. Carried the whole department with her by sheer force of will."

"Do you think it's possible?"

"She fucked Wright's wunderkind over, that's for sure. Maybe you should go talk to Wright about it. It was all about him anyways. The kid got caught in the wrong place at the wrong time."

"Was Mr. Garner angry? Did you hear anything? Threats?"

"I never met the man. But let me speak for all the trailing, adjunct, part-time this or thats of the academic world. If I came out of the boondocks like some barefoot Buckeye Lincoln, if I got a scholarship to a college which not only educated me but persuaded me that I was the American-dream-come-true, if they were proud of me and I made them prouder by winning a Rhodes and if I packed off to England for three years and worked just like I did here and then I topped things off at graduate school and applied for a job at the very school that made me what I am, thank you very much, and my whole plan was to serve where I once had been served, to take the baton from Hiram Wright's trembling liver-spotted hands, if I returned to the place that mattered most to me, if I came back home and found myself facing Martha Yeats, and if it all fell apart because of her, would I be pissed off? Hell, yeah, I'd be pissed off. But I don't know about killing her. It's been a while."

"So it has," Graves agreed. "We'll go now."

"Uh...could you give me a minute?" I asked, motioning towards the house. Linda was in there and I had to check on her before we went. Graves was annoyed, but he nodded yes. Then it came to me, I should ask Robert Rickey's permission. "Okay if I go in for a minute?"

"Hey, be my guest," he said. "It's your house." There was another line hanging in the air between us. *She's your wife.*

Linda was at the sink, splashing water over her face, her eyes.

"Don't rub. They'll turn red."

"Oh, hell, Billy," she said.

"He must have been quite a guy." Meaning: you never cried for me. I never made you feel like shit. All of which she ignored. It wasn't about me. It was this thing from years ago.

"I was the kid behind the goal post, catching the extra points," she said. "He was a quarterback, a fraternity president, valedictorian. He had it all down, that small college thing. He was the Sangy Man besides."

"The what?"

"Sandwiches. Ham and cheese, bologna and lettuce. We made them in his room and then we drove around the dorms at night. 'Sangy Man, Sangy Man,' I'd shout, running up and down the halls and the students would come out of the rooms, like prisoners coming out of a row of cells. He was Sangy Man, I was Sangy Girl. Sometimes he took me into town for chili afterward. I had a crush on him and nothing happened..."

She stopped and just sat there, not knowing how to end the sentence. I backed away, said I'd be checking on her. I guessed she heard me.

"What do you think of the G-Man?" Graves asked, on the way home.

"I don't know who did it," I said. "But I hope he didn't."

"For your ex-wife's sake?"

"Everybody's sake," I said. "But what the hell do I know?"

"You know something, Billy? You belong in the Guinness Book of Records for self deprecation. Putting yourself down."

"Well thanks a lot," I said. "I had a lot of help along the way. It was a team effort. I'd like to thank my ex-wife, my uncle, my employer and the State Police of Ohio."

Graves didn't respond to that. All he said was that he didn't need me the next day. So I dropped him off at his motel and drove away wondering how a man who didn't drive would spend his time, what he'd do in that motel room, where he'd find his meals, whether the fast food places up and down the road would be open on Labor Day. I thought about asking him to come with me, but there was no way he'd fit, where I was going.

Next morning out in Millwood, six miles from campus, I turned off the main road onto a dirt track that took me past a row of mobile homes that weren't so mobile and trailers that had come to the end of the trail and funky tar-paper-shingled cabins along a river which wasn't what it used to be, especially at the end of summer when the current's so slow, it could take years for a beer can to float down to New Orleans. Tom and Marsha's place was at the end of the road. Even before I saw the people I knew who was there by their trucks. Almost all of them college employees, one way or another. There'd be Harry Burmeister who worked on buildings and grounds and Bev Sanders who answered phones in maintenance and Woody Thomas who used to be a janitor until he retired but he still drove for the college, chauffeuring the president and visiting big shots and trustees between the college and the airport at Columbus. There was Eddie Duncan who worked for the food service, got laid off every summer and went on unemployment until they hired him again in the fall. These were the folks who watched me grow up, who'd help raise me. And this Labor Day picnic was a ceremony that went back forever.

"Look, it's the law," someone said as I came walking around the back of the shack. "I Fought the Law and the Law Won," someone else sang out. I'd been through it all, the lines and jokes. "Do Not Forsake Me, Oh My Darling" and "Go ahead, make my day." Old stuff, all of it.

I took some macaroni salad, a corn dog and a handful of potato chips, filled a plastic glass full of no-name cola out of a jumbo sized plastic bottle the size of a gasoline can. Then, like I always did, I sat at the edge of the crowd and let the talk wash over me.

Come-and-get-it-day was the topic. Come-and-get-it-day happened every May. The thing is, the students empty out the freshman dorms one weekend and the next weekend they've got families of graduating seniors staying in those same rooms, which have got to be cleaned in the meantime. Did I say cleaned? I meant scrubbed, deodorized, disinfected, damn near sandblasted. So Tom's wife, Marsha and some other local women would go walking into the valley of death with mops and buckets and toxic chemicals, working their way up the corridors room by room. And loving it. Incredible, the stuff those students left behind. Money, first. All the women carried purses for the change they found, dusty coins on bookshelves, under beds, at the back of closets, not just pennies and nickels either, all this money the students didn't bother picking up, and enough pens and papers to write a book, t-shirts and sweatshirts and socks, unwashed or washed the wrong way, bleached and shrunk and wasted. It's like a movie where a sudden plague kills off everyone, maybe a neutron bomb, and a handful of survivors, hicks who live in the woods, come into town and pick through what got left behind. Marsha's got Alzheimer's now. She's in a care center. Tom goes every day to feed her, even though she doesn't know him. "Like putting a coin in a vending machine and getting nothing back," he says. "No change, no coke."

Across all this talk about what they'd come across—shirts never worn, running shoes lightly used, a lifetime supply of tennis balls, an abandoned $300 mountain bike—I see Tom looking at me, looking hard. He points his finger at the inside of the trailer. He gets up and I follow. By the time I come through the door, he's stretched out in his Lazy Boy. I sit in a chair that's so old, I can remember picking loose change out from under the seat cushion when I was a kid.

"Look at them," Tom says, pointing through the screen door. Where we sit is dark, and out there, the picnic is in bright summer light, a little sad and smoky from the barbecue, so it's like I'm looking at my old friends from a distance, through wisps of clouds that smell like hot dogs. They're growing old, that's what I think. The picnic stays the same but folks drop off, down to Florida or the old folks places. Or they die.

"They're like house servants on some old plantation," Tom says. "We lock the doors and mow the grass. We pick up the bloody knife, the broken glass, the dirty laundry and act like Christmas when they let our women clean out the dorms."

"I guess," I say. "But they look happy to me."

"Happiness isn't everything," Tom says. He groans and gets out of the Lazy-Boy, which groans along with him. He walks over to a table with some shelves above it and turns on a lamp that's no brighter than a candle. None of what I see was here last year. It's a shrine to his son, Tony. I barely remember the guy. When I picture him I'm not sure if what I'm seeing is something I saw myself or part of a picture, like the ones in front of me now: Tony on the football field, Tony in cap and gown, Tony in uniform. He was a super kid, they say, the best pure athlete they've ever had around here. But it was Vietnam and Tony joined the Marines and you know how the story ends. The flag that draped his coffin is pinned to the wall behind the pictures. Like I say, I hardly remember him. But that doesn't stop me from wondering what all he would have amounted to, whether he would have gone from failing farm to shutting down factory to working for the college just like me. I spot a photo of Tony out on the railroad trestle next to our place, pointing a gun at the sky. Same trestle, same river, I could even recognize some of the trees, a shoal of sand and logs that's still there in the middle of the river. Everything still there but his son is gone forever. And his wife's as good as gone, too. All he's got to look at is me and himself in the mirror. And I don't think he cares much for what he sees.

"Know something?" Tom says behind me. "Time doesn't heal jack. You stop crying. You can't cry every day. But inside, you're screaming. And this..."

He gestures at the shrine he made, then sits back down. "It's bullshit! I know it. I thought I was keeping him alive. But he's always the same in the photos. And the photos get old..."

"Come on, Tom," I say. It's hard for me, putting a hand on his shoulder. Usually it's the other way around. He shrugged me right off.

"And when I'm gone somebody'll come into this place and ask who's the kid in all these pictures? And then, it'll be who *was* that kid, who's old stuff was that? And it'll go from someone knowing to sort of knowing, to not knowing and not giving a shit. Get it?"

I nod. I wonder the same thing some time, what it would take to make people remember, not someone famous, but one of us. What was a true memorial for the likes of us?

"So how's it going?" Tom asks.

"I got a question for you."

"Well...shoot."

"Why'd you take me to that meeting? The one with the cops and the big shots? They didn't need me to be there."

"Right. They didn't need you to be there. You needed to be there."

"I did?"

"For your own good. Teach you a lesson. I want you to see that college from the inside. Not keep walking around the place like a servant."

"But that's what we are."

"That's what you are," he fired back.

"Driving Sherwood Graves around is going to change that? Shutting up while I'm behind the wheel, so he can get a chance to think?"

"Maybe it'll rub off. Let's try. What do you think?"

"Of Graves?"

"Yeah. Your new boss."

"I think..." I sit there, forced to put it together, things that came to me here and there. "I think we're learning about the college and how it works and all. And we're learning about Martha Yeats. But we don't know anything about who killed her."

Tom nods. Maybe I said the right thing after all. "Anything else?"

"Yeah," I say, "I don't know what we're looking for. Or how. What Graves' game is. He gives out information on a need-to-know basis and I don't need to know nothing, it seems like. And..." This next wouldn't have come back to me if Tom hadn't pressed me, made me think. "We were out at Hiram Wright's place..."

"'The smartest man for miles around,'" he says, remembering my father's phrase.

"Yeah. And Wright made a fuss about meeting me. About Dad. And then Wright looks at Graves and says 'I know you too.' What was that about? Is Graves that famous?"

"Well," Tom says. "You learned a lot." He got quiet, the way he did when he was about to teach me something. It's like he enjoyed the fact that what came next, what I learned from him, was going to change me. "Graves is the son of Rudolph Graves. That name doesn't mean a thing these days. Rudolph was a professor here, back in the fifties. Philosophy or some such. He was kind of outspoken. A red, they said...a communist. They ran him out of here. You should ask Ave Hayes about it. He was around back then..."

"Was he guilty?"

"Shit. No revolutions around this part of Ohio. If I wanted to make a revolution, I wouldn't come here to start one and I sure as hell wouldn't start at this particular college. But if I wanted a good living talking about it, that's different. He ran his mouth like they all do."

"Where'd he go?"

"Rudolph the Red. He stayed around, believe it or not. Took an apartment in town, on the square. Drank. Became a local character. Died a few years later. Don't suppose he knew his son too well. His ex-wife was raising him someplace else, I remember. Bottom line is, his son is back. What do you think of that?"

"I'm not sure yet."

"You think *before* you're sure. That's what thinking does. It makes you sure. So think about this. He's coming back to the college where his father got destroyed. I think it's his dream come true. He doesn't look it, but the man is loving every minute. You wonder that he's taking his time? No particular target? No special rush?"

"I hope you're wrong," I say, but know it doesn't matter, what I hope. He gets up and we walk outside and before long Tom's joking about the time he took Warren Niles to the annual raccoon dinner in Danville, back in the early years, before Warren gave up on being a regular guy. When I leave, the men are playing horseshoes. I look back and maybe it's just the mood I'm in, but it feels like they're all part of a photograph that's twenty years old, Tom and his dead son Tony, me and my parents, those horseshoe-playing men, those women who warn you to leave room for pie, slipping away from me. That's what I'm thinking, something like that, and wondering what Tom was wondering, what it would take for the likes of us to be remembered. I get home and the phone's ringing inside my trailer. "Buy an answering machine," Sherwood Graves says. "Happy Labor Day," I respond. Then he tells me to come pick him up right away. He wants us to find a professor named Mark May.

III.

MARK MAY

Cards on the table: my one conversation with Martha Yeats, just as I told Sherwood Graves and Billy Hoover, when they tracked me down on Labor Day. Every couple of weeks, to encourage the idea that we're a close-knit faculty, "teaching, learning and living together" as Warren Niles puts it, the administration offers a free lunch in a basement dining room underneath the college commons. I was sitting with a guy from math and a woman from classics. They discussed the food in front of us, something called "Swedish Noodle Bake." From there we switched to weather. Touchy subject. I mentioned something I'd read about how slash and burn agriculture was fouling skies over Southeast Asia. Suddenly, there was Martha Yeats, though I didn't know her name yet. "It's *developing* world," she said. "If we can't get that much straight, we can't expect much from our students." "Okay," I said. "And," she continued, "slash and burn agriculture is a racist derogatory term that might have a place at the World Bank where people specialize in turning family farmers into assembly line slaves for Nike. Try swidden, next time." "Swidden, swidden, swidden," I repeated, watching her walk away. That was in April, May at the latest. In August she was dead. Slashed and burned. Swiddened.

That was it and that was all. If what happened on campus is a tragedy—and you'll get no argument on that from me—then I was the drunken porter in *Macbeth*. Comic relief. Even that might be going too far. Situation comedy, that's more like it. Call it *My Wife, My Provost*. When Caroline took the job here, people looked at me and said, well, that's fine, you're a poet and a poet can write poetry anywhere, that's terrific Mark, that's perfect, you're so—what's the word?—footloose and fancy free? open to experience? adventurous? No, folks, the word is portable. You don't need a laboratory, you hardly need a library, say it loud and proud, you brave bard, you're portable as in lavatory, just string that free spirit a hammock between two chemical toilets and watch those raggedy unrhymed lines come in for landings. It didn't work out that way. Until Martha Yeats' fatal final dog walk, I was the consensus choice for loser-of-the-year. I was Mark May as in Mark May-Not-Last. As in Mark May-Not-Stay-Married. And here's the double whammy: the same person who ends my career may end my marriage. My Wife, My Provost.

She likes her work, she tells me, she feels it's "challenging," but if you ask her whether she's conservative or radical, she'll ask you to define your terms. Ask My Wife, My Provost about tenure which, God knows, gets people going: either it's the last best defense of free speech or it's the last hope of gold-bricks. She'll say, yes, good question, she realizes tenure is controversial and there are deep passions on both sides, and then she'll do a history lesson, how in the not-so-distant past tenure protected professors against political pressure and although that threat has diminished it is never altogether absent. Therefore, my life's partner continues, we have to weigh the need to protect free speech absolutely and at all times against the institutional cost of providing lifetime employment to professors whose accomplishment might end when they are tenured. She pauses. She's impressive. She's impressed with her ability to impress. The real problem, she suggests, may not be tenure *per se* but the way it's administered, the way colleges recruit, mentor and review tenure track candidates. Our talk about tenure, she brightly ventures, must be enlarged. Tenure award or denial is merely the end of a six year process. If the process has integrity from day one onwards, the tenure decision will make sense. Any questions? Ah, she's something. Meanwhile, the college tenures nine out of ten, make that nineteen out of twenty people. And—this is terrific—I may be the next rare sacrifice. That would do wonders for Caroline's credibility. She shitcanned her own husband!

It's my fault, the way last year turned out, I admit it. The college made me uncomfortable from the first day. It was a country school. It was in the midwest. That didn't help. But what really tore it was the mood of the place. The college isn't wealthy but it caters to wealthy people, what with the country club looks, the humongous swimming pool, the lawns and flower beds, the high ceilings and dark wood and that snooty serve-no-wine-before-its-time atmosphere. It's like one of those noble estates in England that's obliged to rent rooms to Texans while the owner lives over the stables, counting the daily take from postcards. I hated the place. I hated myself for being here. Every day I walked to class, I felt like a costumed artisan at Colonial Williamsburg, one of those guys who dresses up in wigs and pantaloons and sits around pretending to be a blacksmith.

The first time I became the talk of the town was last fall, when the admissions department sponsored a visiting students' weekend, a round of classes, lectures, and get togethers for high school juniors and seniors and their parents. At lunch, I'm drinking lots of wine, washing down some dry, room-temperature salmon; it's not easy, flushing something like that down your pipes. I hear one of those admissions guys refer to a poll which shows that our students ranked among the—get this—"happiest" at any campus. "One of the happiest colleges in America," he proclaims. Which is when I blow it.

"That combination of country club living and easy grading gets them every time," I say. I don't shout it. I just say it.

"I beg your pardon?" the admissions guy says. I didn't fire back. But the silence is embarrassing. The guy had to say something. "That's our poet-in-residence, Mr. Mark May," he says. "Was there anything else?"

"Happy campers don't prove a thing," I say. "Free condoms at the health center, junior years abroad, passing grades for just showing up, no wonder they're happy."

"I think you've been drinking," the admissions guy says.

"So I have," I say, raising a glass of Save-Rite Chablis. "The milk from contented cows."

Maybe I should have left right then, but I wanted coffee, or what they call coffee in Ohio, a kind of brown-stained water that lets you see through to the bottom of a cup and make a wish: to be in a better place. Anyway, when I lurched out of my seat ten minutes later, a college cop was waiting.

"Professor May," he said. "I'm Billy Hoover. I got a call."

"How about that?"

"They said, maybe you shouldn't be driving home."

"They?" It was the admissions guy who called, no doubt about it. Chalk one up for the sales force. "I live two hundred yards from here. I can practically see my house."

"What say I drive you home?"

"I don't believe this."

"Yeah," he said. "Yeah, you do." That was the first time I looked at him and saw that there was someone at home in that hulking, lunky country body, someone walking around with his eyes open. One loser, it could be, who was able to recognize another. He smiled and extended his hand. "Give me your keys, professor."

That was my last public drunk. But then there were—what should I call them?—questions about my teaching. My lecture class called *Modern American Short Fiction* lumbered along alright: put modern, American and short in a course title and students will swarm it, like flies on dog shit. But my fiction seminar was terrible. "The future writers club," I called it. That didn't help. Neither did my first week's admonition that writing could not be taught, that writing courses at the college level were to writing what condoms were to sex. The course was over before it began. Doomed. Even after I weeded out submissions from I-am-sensitive-diarists, allegorists, sci-fi freaks, *Dungeons and Dragons* players, I was left with students who traded in clichés. Unknowingly. That was the saddest part. They hadn't read enough to recognize that what they were perpetrating had been done a dozen times before. A vignette from a junior year in Europe. Drift and anomie in high school. Nursing homes. Alzheimer's, especially in its early, flirting stages. One character recurred: the twenty-one year old tired-of-it-all. Soon, we were all tired. What were these students doing here with these airsickness bags of experience, disgorged and undigested? What were they doing here, when they could be studying Shakespeare? And what was I doing here, ministering to kids who didn't want so much to write as to have written and to be known as writers? Because that was what it came to, the creation—the decoration—of a persona. Well, I'll give the place this: word gets around. We swim in a broth of reciprocal evaluation, we live and breathe reputations. Students can tell good teaching from bad. They may not want to contend with it, but they can recognize it alright.

"Even the worst student is entitled to a professor's attention, Professor May. Even the worst. Especially the worst." That was My Wife, My Provost. She called me in for a conference which also included Blair McCartney, the department chair. Blair had just summarized the complaints she'd gotten about my classes. Ragged. Moody. Sarcastic. Self-centered. Blair took no obvious pleasure in this indictment. It wasn't that she cared about me particularly, just that if one professor gets it in the neck, they're all that much more vulnerable. No one had denied I was brilliant, she gamely added. I could, on occasion, be most impressive. But there were these problems that had to be addressed.

"Professor May," My Wife, My Provost said. God, she could be scary, in her straight-faced executive mode. "Surely, students are exasperating. Always. Everywhere. But no college can survive by alienating the students who select it. We grade harshly, on occasion. We say hard things, when necessary, and there are harder things that are left unsaid. But this is their alma mater, professor. And nobody makes a career out of beating up on students. Here's a letter that came in from a participant in your writing seminar. It's not the only letter I've gotten." She glanced down at her desk and this is what it came to. She had a dossier on me.

"There's quite a number," she said, gesturing towards a file which contained some posted letters, some printed out e-mails.

"I wish they'd sent them to me," I said.

"So do I," she retorted. Now she found what she was looking for. She read aloud. "Dear Provost Ives. I hesitate to write this letter which concerns a faculty member, Mr. Mark May, who is also your husband. I apologize in advance for any awkwardness this causes. You should know that whatever discomfort you feel is matched, probably exceeded, by what those of us who enrolled in Professor May's *Introduction to Fiction Writing* seminar experienced last semester. From the beginning, Professor May treated the seminar in an offhand and cynical manner. He questioned whether we should be in the course at all, whether such a course could even be taught. He demeaned our work from the start—'necessary hits,' he called his comments—but they seemed random and inconsistent. He was laughing at us and the fact that he also laughed at himself didn't make things better. Typically, he would breeze into class and ask a few of us to read our work aloud. He was hearing it for the first time. He didn't read things beforehand and he didn't mark them afterwards. Every seminar we had, he walked into empty-handed and he left empty-handed also. At first we were anxious to be called on, to have our work considered, but that didn't last long. His comments were snide and derogatory, not helpful. He didn't like how we wrote and he also criticized our subject matter so at the end, he made us feel we didn't have much to say and what we said, we said badly. He never, never gave suggestions about how to make things better. He expected us to be perfect but if we were perfect we wouldn't be taking his course. We started out with exercises and moved on to short stories but the class was always the same. Some of us left angry, feeling ripped off, and others left in tears. Sure, in the end, we all got B's. That didn't make us feel so hot. It was just another way of telling us that we didn't—and wouldn't—amount to much. Here's your B, now get out of my face. Provost Ives, I don't know if I have what it takes to be a writer. That's what I wanted to find out. I'm an honors student. I have a scholarship. Otherwise I wouldn't be here. I don't drink much, I hardly party. I work hard. I work harder than Professor May. And I can prove it. I can prove it even if it means confessing to something that I'd never do again, something I planned on keeping to myself. It's going to cost me, but I don't care. I plagiarized. I submitted a short story that was not my own. I wanted to see what Professor May would say about something that was good. I typed out, word for word, 'Daylight Savings,' by our own Harry Stribling, which appeared in *Best Stories of 1938,* after it was published in the college's quarterly magazine. It's in Stribling's *Selected Stories* and in *Hilltoppers,* the collection of stories and poems by people who have been at this college. I made it look like I'd struggled over the story. That was fun. I threw in alternative words and sentences that I crossed out, substituting what was in the original story. I turned in a faithful manuscript but it looked like I'd worked on it. The only thing that was mine was the title which I changed from *Daylight Savings* to *More Light.* By the way, I think I learned something, copying word for word the work of Harry Stribling. I went further. I slipped a copy under Professor May's door, along with a note that said I guessed this was a break-through story for me and I'd appreciate having it discussed in class. Well, that was the first time any of us saw Professor May come into seminar carrying more than a cup of coffee. I was praying he hadn't read the story someplace else, but by this time I didn't care. I was endangering my scholarship but that didn't matter either. There was something about integrity that was on the line here. Not mine. His. He ridiculed the piece, which he'd marked up and down. He had himself a field day. 'A wussy, dithering wimp narrator.' 'Ornate, self-consciously virtuoso prose.' 'Magnolia-scented writing, in love with itself.' On and on he went, about as fired up as he ever got. 'No dramatic transaction.' 'The writer chews more than he bites off.' All his favorite one-liners. His or other folks'—I'm not the only plagiarist in town. 'The longest short story I've ever read.' 'Perusing this piece is like watching an ant crawl over a face on Mount Rushmore.' We sat there watching him do his negative thing and nobody said a word. I guess we all learned something that night. It's not just that Professor May hates bad writers. He's even more uncomfortable with good ones. Well, that's all I wanted you to know. If you haul me in front of the Academic Infractions Board or lower my grade to F, I'll take the 'necessary hit.' If you take my scholarship, I'll move on. Just last week, the student paper took the number of classes we take and the number of meetings per class and divided it into the amount per year we pay which is around $25,000. It turns out that every class we take is nearly the cost of a Broadway show. This class isn't worth it. If there were an Academic Infraction Board for professors, they'd shut this guy up, or down. I still love to read and write. I'll work hard wherever I go. I came to this college because of the famous English department, the writing tradition, the literary reputation and all. I came because of people like Harry Stribling. I wanted someone like Harry Stribling. I got Mark May. I got cheated. Yours truly..."

I knew who'd written that letter. Jarrett Stark, a fragile, earnest Ohio kid, one of only two or three who'd tried stopping by during office hours, not to talk about his grade or ask whether I could get his stuff published or what was the deal with agents. He wanted to get to know me, he said, up front. He'd never met a writer before. I could see it in his eyes: he found me fascinating. He asked whether I could give him a list of "extra books," contemporary authors he might read outside of class. What I gave him was a clever reprise of Cyril Connolly's old and mostly rhetorical question, whether you could name a single living writer whose death would be a literary disaster. I ripped apart one name after another.

"John Updike?" he asked.

"Updick, Jarrett. And getting more flaccid by the minute. The old three-quarters gherkin. Goes around corners. Rabbit turning into hamster, from where I sit."

"Philip Roth?"

"*Oi, vey!* Gives self-indulgence a bad name. Read twenty pages for the sake of two. Is there an editor in the house?"

"Thomas Pynchon?"

"Strikes me like a fork off a new filling. That's not an audience, that's a cult. He and his whole law firm."

"Law firm?"

"Gass, Gaddis, Delillo, Barth and Pynchon. The great unreadables."

"Jay McInerny? Richard Ford?"

"Listen, Jarrett, there's nothing sadder than yesterday's youth movement."

"Tim O'Brien?"

"A one-trick pony. A one subject author. Vietnam. Earth to O'Brien: give peace a chance!"

"Joyce Carol Oates?"

"Save our forests."

"How about...Toni Morrison?" I sensed he was playing his strongest card. "She won the Nobel Prize."

"She deserved it." I allowed.

"She did?" Jarrett was surprised.

"Sure enough. She's as good as Pearl Buck, any day."

All the kid wanted was a list of books to read, as if I didn't have a dozen enthusiasms, famous and obscure and envied, I could have shared without being a smartass. Weren't there two or three teachers who'd intervened in my life, who'd made lists of books for me to read, who'd given me the books themselves, marked and underlined, sharing what they loved?

"Plagiarism is a serious offense," Blair McCartney remarked, but it was just-for-the-record. There were worse offenses on the table. Mine. "Here's somebody who confessed to it. I hope he's not going around bragging about it."

"Don't touch him," I said. "Don't do anything. Please. It was my fault. All of it."

"Don't touch him?" Caroline asked. "Is that for your sake? To avoid embarrassment?"

"Listen," I said. "I blew it. I apologize. I'll do better. I'll make it up to the guy who wrote the letter. An independent study or something..."

My wife studied me a minute. Shrewd, professional appraisal. Then she glanced at Blair. One woman checking in with another, not a word said, but my fate being decided. A glance, a nod. An agreement. They made it in silence. Then they shared it with me.

"This is a place where we take chances on students," My Wife, My Provost began. "We take chances on our professors, too. I've also heard that this is the sort of place where every professor has the chance to teach at least one bad course. Professor May? You've taught that bad course. You've used your chance. Do we understand each other?"

"I'll do better."

"Have I said anything you don't understand?" she pressed. Nut-cutter. Inconceivable I'd ever be naked around her again.

"I said I'd do better," I repeated. A few scraps of pride remained. "Not for your sake. Not for our sake. Not for my sake."

"Your motives..." Now she was the one who bristled.

"It's for the sake of the kid who wrote that letter," I said, inter-rupting her interruption. This was sounding maudlin. I'd regret it. In a while, I'd be rationalizing. How many kids like that were here, any-way? How many hungry, earnest kids? Surely not a majority. And once the daily drudgery resumed, it was going to be easy to forget the appalled shudder that letter had produced. So I promised I'd remem-ber. Maybe it wasn't such a bad idea, coming to a beautiful place in the middle of nowhere to profess literature, to make a life out of that. Then again, maybe it was a bad idea: complacent, elitist and, when you looked at the way the world was turning, doomed. Maybe, maybe, maybe. But I decided that this next year, I'd clean up my act and I was-n't kidding, when I told my wife it wasn't for her or me or us. That kid's righteous anger had done it. So, alright, I'd clean up my act. And then I'd decide if the act was worth playing.

I decided, as part of my second-year reform, to hold evening office hours. I was hoping to encourage thoughtful student visitors, kids who'd talk about more than grades and deadlines. It worked too, it really did. Still, some nights, nobody needed me. That was alright too. I'd sit in my office listening to music, old stuff, Jussi Bjoerling to Tex Ritter, Buddy Holly to Marvin Gaye. What they were doing, reaching out across the years, was what books were supposed to do. Mine and other people's. Anyway, Marvin was singing *Sexual Healing,* when I noticed the cops standing in my doorway, waiting for the song to end.

"I'm Sherwood Graves," the tall one told me. "And this..." He gestured at the guy who'd driven me home drunk from the admis-sions luncheon.

"Hi, Billy," I said. We'd gotten into the habit of talking, when we met. He liked talking to professors, the poor guy felt honored. I liked talking to people who weren't professors. Perfect.

"We'd like to discuss Martha Yeats," Graves said as they sat down.

"I hardly knew her," I said. I told them about the faculty lunch. That was it, I said.

"Bear with me," Graves said. "She annoyed a lot of people. As you know. But when we considered all her crusades, all we had was annoyance. Nothing more. Until we came to the fact that her killer deposited her in front of a fraternity lodge. Martha wanted fraternities out of here. Class, race, gender all came together for her in fraternities. She was death on fraternities."

"So fraternities were the death of her?"

"Not that simple. There was a related campaign. Crimes against women, sexual assault, all that. She was a speaker, a counselor. A campaigner. She represented several victims...alleged victims...in proceedings against college men. Fraternity members. Against, among others..."

"Okay," I said. "You can stop there. Now I know why you're here."

In that career suicide that was my first year here, this kid, this black kid, had sat in the back row of American Lit, just where football players are supposed to sit. He did enough to get by. He'd show up, he'd do some of the reading, scribble and doodle, and turn in a paper that didn't go an inch beyond a recap of what was said in class. He'd get a B minus or a C plus back from me. That was the deal. There was more, though. He smiled at me across the trenches, even dropped by my office to talk. He was curious about what good work amounted to, even though he had no interest in attempting it. You sensed that later on, too late, maybe, he might get serious and accomplish something and maybe—I know this sounds wishful—remember something he'd heard in class. Meanwhile, he was skating. Skating and partying. No problem. My grade—his grade, that is—no problem. He liked to bring me tales of student parties, even invited me, but they all started at midnight. I knew that student parties would be the death of me. My Wife, My Provost wouldn't stand for it. So I settled for yarns: the "caveman party," the "pimps and hos" party, the "shock your mama" party.

In spring of his senior year he told me he'd been accused of sexual assault. "Date rape bullshit," he called it. Something that happened two years before had worked its way to the surface. He'd be tried intramurally. He had a right to bring in a faculty member as a counselor. He wanted it to be me. "You're my favorite professor," he said. My degree wasn't in law, I told him, or in counseling. But I said I'd do it.

When I walked into the designated classroom, that first of several nights, Martha Yeats was there with a woman student I didn't know. There was a lot more I had to learn. Any crime victim had a right to go to the sheriff, the local district attorney, appear before local judge and jury. Or they could go to a college panel of faculty, administrator and students. In this case, the ultimate sanction was expulsion from college.

Some things were clear. Plaintiff and accused had gone to a party, sophomore year. They had gotten drunk, slow dancing, kissing, grabbing ass. They adjourned to a bathroom, locking the door behind them. They had sex a couple of times, a couple of ways. When they emerged, they hugged, kissed and parted. All that was stipulated. After that, it was up for grabs, what happened in that room, which was like no rape I'd ever heard of, also like no love affair. The woman was game, willing, wanton. Or cornered, terrified, silently screaming, breaking up inside. The guy was a coercive, abusive prick. Or a good kid who thought he'd gotten lucky. I'll never know who was harmed most, the man or the woman, or whether the harm done that night matched the harm that was done when they found my guy guilty and the president predictably blew off my e-mail, denied me a personal appointment and upheld the decision that obliged the kid to leave college eight weeks before he was supposed to walk across the stage and receive a diploma in front of his pleased-as-punch parents. I'll never know the truth of it. Not that night and not the night Graves and Billy Hoover came to talk about it.

"What about Martha Yeats?" Graves asked.

"She was there. She was sitting across from me, next to the woman. The victim."

"What was that like?"

"They were close, you could see that. I wouldn't say Martha was coaching. Not exactly. But close to it."

"Did she ever talk to you?"

"No. She smiled, kind of, the first time she saw me. It was as though it amused her...that I was the best this guy could come up with."

"Did Professor Yeats participate in the proceedings?"

"No. She whispered to the girl sometimes. Held her, hugged her during breaks. And she nodded a lot when she liked what she was hearing, rolled her eyes when she disagreed. The way the women do now on those Washington talk shows. She seemed familiar with the process, I'll say that. She'd been there before, I gathered."

"Did your student ever express any anger, any feelings at all, about Professor Yeats?"

"No," I said. "Not exactly."

"Not exactly?"

"When we walked out of the room that last time, he looked over at the two of them. The two women. 'Thanks for the memories,' he said. I thought he was talking to the girl. Maybe Martha Yeats was included."

"Maybe," Graves said.

IV.

BILLY HOOVER

Two of the three guys named in sexual assault cases that Martha Yeats had been involved in were off the hook. One of them worked for a rental car company in Phoenix, Arizona, the other was on the staff of a Washington congressman. Our calls confirmed that they'd been at work when Martha Yeats wound up in front of the Psi U lodge. That left the kid Mark May had talked to us about, the black. He was different. The other two had gotten in trouble more than once, looking for love in all the wrong places. Our man today was a first-time offender and—from what Mark May had said—a little more innocent than the others. Maybe a lot more innocent. Anyway, worth checking on. His name was Dante Gibbins.

We were off the interstate, headed into Weirton, West Virginia, before Graves opened his mouth, but only to give directions. He had one of those computer printouts, where you punch in the address where you're going and they tell you every turn you make. But they don't show what it's like, when you arrive. On both sides of the street were rows of attached brick houses, each with a porch and a tiny yard along a broke-up crazy-angled sidewalk that would give your baby whiplash, if you took her out there in a carriage.

"Stop here a minute," Graves said. We were at the end of the last street, ready to start checking numbers. I pulled over to the side. He took a folder and looked it over, close enough so that I could see a student photo. A good-looking kid with a student council smile, not that hooded, hostile look you saw on some black students.

"Remember this," Graves said. "This isn't about what he did to her or she did to him. They'll want to talk about what a raw deal it was and we'll sit through it. But his guilt or innocence in that case doesn't matter in the least. Where he was when Martha was murdered, that's all we care about. And...Billy?"

"Yes?"

"Your role in this is to nod and smile and not be threatening. Don't ask anything, even if it seems perfectly reasonable. My questions are thought-through, arranged from first to last. Okay?"

"Okay."

"Whoever we find here is a hostile witness," he said. "Do you understand that? They may glad hand us and smile, offer coffee, but it doesn't mean anything."

"Even if they're innocent?"

"No one's innocent. It's just a question of whether they're guilty of what we want them for."

So here we were at this kid's house. Were we going to pretend that we cared about the kid, that the college was worried about his kicked-out ass? Did we begin by saying we were here about some library fines or unpaid parking tickets? Or did we spring Martha Yeats right on him, maybe get him to tell us the first thing that popped into his mind when we mentioned her name?

We stepped through the screen door and onto the porch. Glancing left and right, I could sight down the porches, like looking down a row of receding mirrors, going away forever. I wondered what it was like, living here—what people missed, if they got homesick.

"Yes?" A thin, light-skinned man opened the door. He had green-ish eyes and freckles and salt and pepper hair that he didn't fuss with. He was in a bathrobe at two in the afternoon and he had a book in his hand, *The Greatest Generation* by Tom Brokaw. I studied him while Graves went into something about how we were working for the college and there was some trouble up there we needed help on. I was wondering how long it would take before the guy started shouting, rousing the neighborhood. But I was wrong.

"I know that place well," the man said. "I've been there many times."

"Well then," Graves said, as if it was time he invited us in.

"Dropping my son off at the start of the freshmen year. Before the start. Orientation, I believe they call it. Picking him up at the end. Before the end. Expulsion, I believe they call it..."

"We know there was a problem up there."

"Problem? Is that what you call it?"

"If we could step inside, just a minute," Graves said, like a salesman with his foot just barely in the door.

"On one condition, sir," the man said. "You go when I tell you to go."

"Of course..."

One side of the living room was all plants—Christmas cactus, crown of thorns, African violets, the sorts of plants you associated with old folks. That must be the woman's side I guessed, because the other wall was books, paperback and hard-cover, lots of titles about the war. After he gestured us onto a sofa and offered us some tea, the man returned to where he must've been sitting before we came, a worn-out comfortable looking easy chair with a reading lamp overhead and a hassock where he could put up his feet.

"I'm sorry," Graves said. "You're his dad?"

"That's right," he said. "I'm senior. He's junior."

"Day off from work?"

"I'm retired now. I was a teacher. Principal, at the end."

"Do you miss it?"

He sat there, like maybe he was preparing a speech about the challenge of teaching, molding young lives and all, it gets in your blood, once a teacher, always a teacher. But that's not what was coming.

"I wonder why you're pretending..."

"Pretending?"

"Pretending you care one bit about me. Why don't you just get to it? I'm really wondering what you're doing here. Or do you have another woman up there, thinking she got raped?"

"We've got a woman up there, alright. A professor who was killed."

"Oh. I see. I get it now. Makes sense. Must've been my boy who did it." He was getting angry now and Graves couldn't stop him. And it was the worst kind of anger, fueled by pain. And controlled by intelligence. I could see that, too, the way he watched us, measuring us while he talked. He was in control and somebody needed to call time out.

"Excuse me," I said. "Could I use your bathroom?"

The man was annoyed. So was Graves.

"I shotgunned some coffee on the way down," I explained.

"Well, you came a long way to take a piss. It's back through the kitchen."

I found the bathroom and, across from it, a bedroom that must be, or have been, his son's. I poked my head inside. There were shelves and plaques and trophies. The wall was covered with photos...team portraits, prom nights...and laminated newspaper clippings, plus certificates from Kiwanis Key Club and Boys State. Incredibly, our college pennant above the bed. Back in the hall, I saw something more recent, something that I studied carefully, a photo thumbtacked to a workboard, a couple of postcards around it. I pulled a few out of the board, careful not to drop the thumbtacks on the floor. I checked dates and postmarks but barely glanced at the message. It was like snooping in someone's medicine cabinet. Enough was enough.

Behind me, I heard Graves trying to get down to business. Martha's name and what a controversial person she was. Sentence fragments came to me as I stood there peeing, banking off the upper part of the bowl so there'd be no sound of splashing. And then, after I flushed, while I washed and wiped my hands on a towel, I heard silence. No more talking out there. Senior had stopped running his mouth. And Graves was quiet too, all out of careful thought-through questions.

"I wanted you to hear this, sir," the old man said when I returned. "We were waiting for you."

"Well, thanks, I'm ready now," I answered, trying to sound cheerful.

"My son messed up at college. He drank too much. He partied plenty. He chased women...and they chased him. Are you with me? Both of you?"

"Yes," I said.

"He let us down. His mother and me. She's working. You didn't ask, but I'll tell you. At the Ramada, in the office. And the reason she works...we both did...was so our son could get the chance he got...and blew. But we love him. We'll work it out. We'll get through it and move on. But what I can't let go of is what you did to my boy up there."

He leaned forward now, fire in his eyes, some for Graves—being a state employee didn't exempt him—and plenty left for me.

"Sexual assault. Deans, students, professors making like a court of law. You listen. If there's a real crime committed, get a real cop, a real lawyer, a real judge and jury. And see how far that girl gets, when she tells folks she was under-age and she was drinking and she went into a bathroom and locked a door and got laid where most folks take a shit. Try calling that a crime anywhere off campus. How in the hell did a college get into that business in the first place? Do you think you're good at it? Do you care? Do you think you owe it to the parents? The students? Yourselves? Who are you protecting?"

"I can't defend..." Graves began. But he didn't get far.

"Listen. My son—a black man accused of rape by a white woman—would've had a better chance with an all-white, all-farmer, country-boy coon-hunting jury than he had with your extra-curricular, semi-pro, student-faculty court. Since when do colleges have their own courts? Ohio law not good enough? Is that place an embassy or something? From what country? Suburban Connecticut?"

He sat back in his chair, closed his eyes, tried catching his breath. Emphysema, I bet. That or lung cancer.

"Now you come tip-toeing in, chatting up, pussy footing around, listening to me talk like I'm the most fascinating man in the world, all the time you're waiting to ask if my boy is home, which he isn't, and if I'll tell you where he is, which I won't. You're wondering if he went after that professor, which he didn't. And you want to ask if you could just have an address, a phone number, a place of employment, so you can cross him off the list, like you're doing us all a favor. But I don't want you calling his boss, his neighbors, the people he works with, a cop asking them to verify he wasn't off murdering somebody. You expelled him from college. Well, okay, consider him expelled. And now you can both go expel yourselves out of here..."

"Well, what do you think?" Graves asked, no sooner than we were in the car.

"He's been waiting forever to deliver that speech to someone. Anyone."

"Just wanted to get it off his chest? I don't think so. His son's in trouble and he knows it." Graves picked up the folder that we'd looked over. He gave the kid a hard stare, like he was turning him into a wanted poster. "That old man might get to know what it's like to have a son in front of a real judge and jury."

I let a few miles pass, wondering if this was the way it worked, rounding up the usual suspects. Graves wanted to be dropped off in Columbus, he said. Phone calls and paperwork and after that it was just a matter of time. I saw a Bob Evans restaurant coming up off an exit ramp and, without asking permission, I turned in.

"We need gas, Billy?"

"I need food," I said. "Biscuits and gravy will get me through until supper."

"Can't you wait? I've got calls to make," Now he was getting cranky. He could accept a car needing gas, not a driver getting hungry. "That warrant...I'll have to find a judge..."

"No you won't." It was odd, how power shifted between us just then, like in the movie where some average taxi driver, say, pulls a gun and turns out to be a hit-man. Graves went along quietly on into Bob Evans, and ordered a grilled cheese sandwich with milk.

"That kid isn't our man, Mr. Graves," I said, after a while. Eat first, then talk: my plate was mostly empty. "When I went to use the bathroom, there were a bunch of postcards and pictures in the hall, stuck into the corkboard. And our boy was there..."

"So..."

"In the uniform of the U.S. Marines."

"They get leave after training, Billy. They get R and R."

"They get assigned to Okinawa, Mr. Graves. APO address. I checked the dates. One of them was August. Another was September..."

He sat there a while, just sat. "I'll have to check it out," he admitted in a voice that was dead. It was just a reflex. He took a bite of the sandwich, not because he was hungry. It was something to do to buy time while he tried to cover up what he was feeling. When he put the sandwich down, he'd decided he was mad at me.

"Why'd you just sit there after you knew? You couldn't have pulled me aside? Whispered something to me? Or...was it you liked the idea of knowing something I didn't?"

"I sat there like you told me to sit, Mr. Graves. I kept my mouth shut. You told me my role was to smile, nod, and not be threatening. So you said. Well, I didn't threaten anybody, now did I?"

He thought that over while the waitress asked was everything okay and when she finished pouring coffee a miracle occurred. "Okay," he said. "Okay, Billy, I suppose I had that coming," he said. "I underestimated you..." He paused, letting his confession sink in. I can't say I wasn't enjoying myself. "I overestimated you as well. I assumed you would know enough...be enough of a professional...to share something like that with me."

"I had expectations too," I said. "Maybe we could both do better, Mr. Graves."

"Let's see if we can," he said. "We can't afford secrets from each other."

He kept on like that, all the way back north. We were partners now. Two professionals, no secrets between us. I decided to
try my luck.

"I was wondering," I began, "about Garner. The G-Man."

"Oh. Your wife's old flame."

"Could I look into him some? See what's in the records?"

"He didn't do it, Billy. Not after so long. People don't come back
like that."

"You did," I shot back and it was like I slapped him, what I said
and how I said it so fast. He sat there, sizing me up, kind of surprised.

"So you heard about me?" He sounded offended, like he'd caught
me reading his mail.

"You and your father," I said.

"Who from?"

"Well, Hiram Wright mentioned something about your background when we went out to visit. He didn't put me in the picture,
though. Neither did you."

"So...someone else..."

"Yes...someone else. Let's just leave it at that, Mr. Graves. You've
got your business, I've got mine."

"Okay, Billy," he said, but he stayed quiet for a while and I guessed
he was thinking it over. I guessed we were done talking but then he
surprised me.

"It's nice to know people still remember my father," he said.
"That's..." He didn't finish that. He got quiet for a while. Then he
stirred. "I'll tell you something. I didn't come back to kill anyone." I
nodded agreement though I could hear Tom saying, you didn't come
back to catch anyone either. "I'll tell you something else. This boy
down in Weirton? I never thought it was him. I knew it wasn't."

"Oh?"

"Any more than it's this G-Man fellow..."

"So...you know who it isn't..."

"It isn't a loner, somebody out of the past. I knew there'd be suspect individuals like that. The college graduates a few every year. The
sooner we eliminate them, the better."

"Then...what say I eliminate the G-Man?" I asked.

"You're fascinated, aren't you?" he asked.

I didn't deny it.

"Alright," he said. "Go ahead then. But Billy..."

"Yes?"

"Quietly. Discreetly."

"Sure."

"Think of it as a training exercise. Don't get carried away."

At 7:30 the next morning, a week after I found Martha Yeats sitting against a tree outside of the Psi U Lodge, I intercept Willard Thrush, the college's development vice president as he walks up the steps to his office. Ordinarily, Thrush is outgoing and informal, the kind of guy who prides himself on being able to talk to anybody, high or low, the Queen of England or a little crippled news boy. Now, things are going to change.

"Hey, Billy," he says.

"Hi, Mr. Thrush," I swallow some but before I can speak, along comes a professor, heading over to the bookstore for the morning newspaper. This guy is famous. He walks along in a daze, never says hello, not to an administrator or a cop: we're both the enemy.

"HELLO THERE!" Thrush shouts in a top-of-the-morning way. The professor shrugs and keeps walking. We watch him cross the street and stand in front of the bookstore, waiting for it to open at 7:30. "Some of us in the administration play this game," Thrush says. "You name a faculty member. Any one. And ask, if that professor wasn't a professor, if they had to earn a living some other way—a job, a marketable skill—what would they do? Factories? Farms? Can you picture them at the bank or the post office or the gas station? I don't think so. Now look at the guy in front of the bookstore. You know what we do with him, Billy? We make him into a bicycle parking rack. That's right. That's his best and highest use. Throw him on his stomach, pull down his pants and park a ten-speed right in the crack of his ass." I'm flabbergasted and then I wonder about a Schwinn, with those thick American tires and Thrush laughs back. That's the way he is, always a laugh. Until now.

"I wanted to see you, Mr. Thrush," I say. "I need to go looking through your alumni files."

"You do? What for? Who for?"

"The Yeats investigation."

"She didn't graduate from here," Thrush says. His eyes are sharper than his words.

"Yeah..."

"But maybe the killer did?" he asks himself. Again, I don't answer. We're on the same page. But it's hard for him to get used to.

"Those files are privileged. Not the people. The information. Old stuff, most of it, but you never know. The more recent stuff—the donation record—is in the computer."

"Yes, I know that," I say. "I'll be needing a look at that too."

"Well..."

"And if there's any problem, you should call Mr. Graves. Or President Niles. Or Provost Ives."

"No problem," Thrush says, but I can tell he's bothered. Here I am, the guy who writes parking tickets at two bucks a throw that get tossed onto the street or—as a joke—shoved into the president's hand at graduation, when he passes out diplomas.

"Okay." He gives in. We walk inside the office, over to the file cabinets. "What's the name?"

"No, Mr. Thrush. I can't say."

"Can't blame me for trying."

"I don't."

"Okay. I assume the person you're looking for is a living graduate. If they're dead, and we know about it, we send their files over to the archives. They're not donor prospects anymore. Not crime suspects either, I suppose."

Thrush points out an empty desk right around the corner from the last row of filing cabinets, where no one will bother me, and a Xerox machine I can make copies on. He says he'll shows me how to get into the computer files, into the giving records. He sets me up, gets me seated, pats me on the back and walks away. Then he goes into his office and closes the door behind him. I see one of the lights on his secretary's phone turn bright red. Somebody's phone is ringing, over in Stribling Hall.

If Gerald Kurt Garner is dead, the college doesn't know about it. He's still a donor prospect, his file jammed tightly among others, so tight I have to pull hard to get it out and when it comes, it carries three others with it, like bodyguards and hangers-on. The first thing is his college application. There's a photo attached, which looks like it was taken for his high school yearbook: him, in a sport coat, a white shirt a black knit tie. A face that could have been my cousin Tony Hoover, the kind of guy you picture as a newspaper delivery boy.

Father a post office employee, mother a housewife. A home address in River View, Ohio. His essay, handwritten, in ink: *I'm a team player. I work with others…If I ever become a leader, it will be because first I learned to follow. No one has gone to college before me, not in my family, not on this street, not as far as I know, in this whole little town. To me, that makes college a privilege and a responsibility…A small liberal arts college like yours seems right to me. But I should tell you that my parents aren't able to afford a place like yours. Sir or madam, I love your college already. I will do my best there and have been brought up to always do "a little bit extra." But without scholarship aid from you, I will have to try my best someplace else.*

After the application, there are clips and pictures from the college newspaper, that I don't bother copying: football games, student elections, and a spring humor issue with a cartoon that shows him on a sort of throne, the floor littered with books and beer cans, admiring professors on one hand, adoring women on the other. G-Man Rules! Then, in his senior year, there are these press releases about a Woodrow Wilson Fellowship, awarded and declined, and the mighty Rhodes, awarded and accepted. That got plenty of attention. He showed up in the college news letter and the "Alumni Bulletin." I still could see the Ohio River kid in the application snapshot, but now there was a difference. The high school kid was asking to be helped. The Rhodes scholar was waiting to be noticed.

Those first few years at Oxford and later on, at Tufts, Garner kept in touch. And the college was happy to hear from him. His doings were posted in the year-by-year class notes in the back of the alumni magazine. He traveled to Morocco and Tunisia and the college heard all about it in chatty, friendly messages, look-ma-no-hands, having fun, wish you were here. Several years out, and the college was still his audience, it was easy to see. But then, it stopped. It stopped so suddenly, I went back to check whether I'd missed a second file. The last clipping was that he'd completed and "successfully defended" his Ph.D. thesis.

I go to Thrush's office when I'm done at the copy machine, wanting him to check me out on the computer so I can get into the next chapter of Garner's life. By now, I'd be interested even if his name hadn't popped up in a murder investigation. Here's why: I couldn't think of Garner without my cousin Tony coming to mind. They were two of a kind: Great damn expectations. Well, I know what happened to Tony: a sniper laid him out on the deck of a patrol boat in the Mekong

Delta. He's dead. The G-Man is missing in action. He's a mystery. And I'm a mystery too. To myself. Mr. Withdrew Incomplete.

"Listen, Billy, you're one of us," Thrush says, inviting me to sit down. "We're on the same team here." Now here's a Kodak moment. Tom goes to the library every year and looks at the college income tax return, which includes the salary of the top five highest-paid employees. Warren Niles heads the list but Willard Thrush is in there too, nicely into six figures. So it's kind of special when he tells a guy who lives in a trailer and gets paid by the hour, we're on the same team. "I just want you to remember something. The places we compete with have two hundred, three hundred, four hundred million dollar endowments. We've got less than seventy-five. What we do have is a reputation. Word of mouth, will of the wisp, about twenty years out of date, perfume on a corpse, but there you have it. Reputation. Wright and Stribling and some others. We get the wrong publicity, that reputation is shot. We're killer campus. We're bloody ivy. Be careful..."

I agree how sensitive this all is and nobody wants to hurt the college, which sounds a little odd to both of us, once I say it. We both know better. Anyway, we let it pass and in a minute I'm at the computer. There's only one Garner. No dynasty here, no legacy. Home address the same as on his application. Still living at home? Using his folks to collect his mail? How old would they be now? College stuff, graduate school, everything that I already knew. Then it stops. No new address, no marriage, no current employer. Small contributions from graduation in 1978 until 1985, when he finished graduate school and applied to the college for a job. After that, nothing. One minute it's a television show, the next minute it's a blank screen.

I'm done, that's for sure. I push the print button and watch the pages come out, like the G-Man's sticking out his tongue at me. I count to see that they're all here, pages one, two and three. Then I notice something I missed on the screen, right at the bottom of the third and last page. It jumps out at me. It scares me. DO NOT CONTACT, it says. I head back to Thrush.

"It can mean all sorts of things," he says. "Don't phone me. We do phonathons, a room full of students dialing numbers. Some people like to hear from them, some don't. Or it could mean don't send any mail, so it's about junk mail. But there are more serious cases. Got your attention now?"

"You already had it."

"Okay. Say some graduates come back and raise hell. Get drunk, vandalize property, bother women, sell drugs. We put 'do not contact' next to their names. That's from us to them. Sometimes, it's from them to us: it's because they're pissed off about fraternities or women or compulsory chapel or gender studies or sociology. Sometimes, 'do not contact' can mean, please contact. Make me feel better. Stroke me. I got this letter, begins 'Apart from the minor inconvenience of revising my will, the college's recent policy on fraternity housing causes me no particular problem...' So I call and make it better."

"Is there any way of telling what kind of 'do not contact' it is?"

"You'd have to give me the name." He waits for me to take the bait. Then he smiles, gets out of his chair and walks me to the door.

"Not everybody loves this place," he says. Outside, the college is living up to its brochures. The road divides as it runs through the college, two lanes on either side of a gravel path, which is lined by maples that have ivy around their trunks and flowers around their roots, tulips in springtime, chrysanthemums in fall. Every hour or so, on Monday-Wednesday-Friday, every eighty minutes on Tuesdays and Thursdays, you see students marching that path, coming to and from classes, a walk they take a thousand times and the last is when they graduate. This was the path Garner walked. Where had it taken him?

"Not everybody," Thrush repeats. "Would you believe it? On a day like this, what's not to love?"

"Good morning," Professor Hiram Wright says a half hour after I leave Thrush. "This is History 63. This is not *Bitches, Snitches, Witches: Women in the Middle Ages.* This is *American History: Writing and Rewriting.* And I am not Professor Martha Yeats. My name is Hiram Wright."

A hand pops up right off, a woman in the front row, wearing a Hard Rock t-shirt and these jeans that students torture, poking holes in both knees.

"I think we should start with a moment of silence for Professor Yeats," she says.

"A moment of silence?" Wright asks. "We'll be having more than our share of those." Then he thinks it over. "Fine. A moment of silence then."

The old guy stands at the podium in Philomathesian Hall, which is one of the classiest rooms on campus, with polished wood all around and a pair of stained glass windows that catch the late morning light. Other windows, leaded glass, are wide open so you can see outside, out onto the farms east of here. It's what you think of when you picture a classroom, or a classroom used to be, before they installed audiovisual aids, television monitors and projection booths, blackboards that roll up into the ceiling, screens that roll down. And Wright is what you picture a professor used to look like. These days, they mostly dress in jeans and wrinkles, no different from the students. But Wright looks like a worn-out but still dignified diplomat from a country that just lost a war.

During the moment of silence—he's timing it on his pocket watch—late students come walking into class, the door slamming behind them. The floor is old. It creaks when they walk. Spiky hair, and baseball hats turned backwards, shirts hanging out over baggy trousers, they look around at Wright and wonder, who is this guy? Whatever. It's the first day of class and they come in tired. As soon as they sit, they slouch, like they've been in their seat for hours.

"Time's up," Wright says. "My name...again...is Hiram Wright. And the first thing it occurs to me to tell you is that, in addition to requiring faithful attendance—which I demand on the grounds that you cannot prosper in a class you do not attend..."

I see the looks going around. Who is this guy? Is this a *Twilight Zone* episode, something about time travel? Where's the usual stuff about a note from the doctor, the coach, the dean of students? What's class participation worth? What about the final exam?

"...and if you cannot prosper in a class you do not attend, it's equally true that I cannot prosper in a class which is interrupted by late-arriving students. If I can be here on time, you can be here on time. This is not New York where subways break down between stations. It's also not Paris, where you might fall in love on the way to class, whether with a person or a painting or a city. This is a residential college on an obscure hilltop in central Ohio. If you belong here at all, you belong in class on time. Any questions? Have I said anything you don't understand?"

There are no questions. They can't raise their hands. They're in shock, it looks like to me. Wright takes them back to a time when teachers could scare you. He's a regular throwback. So am I. He scares me.

"This course involves close examination of major works by

American historians and thinkers," Wright is saying. "Francis Parkman. Frederick Jackson Turner. Charles Beard. W.E.B. DuBois. Thorstein Veblen. Henry James. Vernon Parrington. W.J. Cash, to name some. These are writers whose work combines historical importance and literary merit. It is fair to say that they have stood the test of time. So far, at least. But that doesn't mean that they haven't—should not have been—tested. Here, in this class, the testing continues. And, while I speak of tests..."

Wright moves out from behind the podium, stepping in front. Every minute in class, he gets a little more pumped. In front of me, a woman draws three airplanes, three of them, each one for a Wright brother: Orville, Wilbur and Hiram.

"I will require three papers of ten pages," Wright says. "These papers should reflect your best efforts, on a topic of your own devising. I accept no late papers. I accept no revisions. I reserve the option of giving a final examination, on the chance that your papers have not sufficiently informed me of your abilities and efforts. I suspect they will have done just that."

It's clear Professor Wright's going to lecture the full fifty minutes, even on the first day of class, when students show up hoping the professor will breeze in, check registration, pass out a syllabus and leave early so everyone can enjoy what's left of summer. Now he stands in class, five minutes left on the clock. He's been working hard, setting his rules. No baseball hats, no food in class. Computer breakdowns, broken alarm clocks, power outages are no excuse. Drama club, job interview, swim meet, no excuse. Homesickness, lovesickness, attention deficit disorder, eating disorder, reading disorders, sorry. Broken spell checker, sorry.

"You may be smarter than I am. But I've been smart longer. I was your age when I read these books for the first time. I taught them for thirty years and every time I taught them, I re-read them. I have changed. The world's changed. And—in ways I look forward to sharing with you—the books have changed as well. Now I unexpectedly confront these books for what will surely be the last time. And the first for you. If all this interests you, welcome. If not...so be it. If you have any questions, I will answer them here, after class. Good morning, everyone."

"No fucking way," I hear a student whisper as he gets up. Others feel the same way, seeing how they bomb out the door. They'll go catalogue shopping for a new course. But not all of them run away, not by any means. First one, then two and three approach the podium, students who've waited until it's just me and them alone with Wright. When they're close enough, he greets them. He leans forward as they introduce themselves, gives them his hand to shake. He's cordial and old-fashioned. He makes appointments for office hours, scribbles in his date book. Then he sees me there, waiting to talk to him.

"So you decided to come," Professor Wright says. "I'm delighted."

"I'd like to try," I say and I take a syllabus. "Up to Mr. Graves, though."

"Try again, isn't it?" he says. I stand there, not knowing what to say. There's no telling how he knows I was a student here. I was hardly worth remembering. Then again, he was the smartest man for miles around.

"Professor Wright?" It's clumsy shifting from student to cop. "There's something else... there's a name came up and we'd like to know more about it." Wright shoots me a look that tells me he knows what's coming. I don't prolong things. "Gerald Kurt Garner."

He nods, picks up his papers and packs them into a leather satchel that has stickers from hotels that are probably out of business in countries that don't exist anymore. We walk across campus to the history department. Just walking is an effort for him. In class, I forgot—maybe he forgot—that he used a cane but now he needs it. It takes a while. History has its own house across campus. When the college enrollment tripled in the seventies, departments got spun off into what used to be professors' homes. All those old comfortable houses, white clapboard and slate-roofed, were cut up into rooms and offices. The porches where faculty sipped sherry in good weather are littered with cigarette butts these days.

Wright opens the door to an office where his name is thumbtacked next to Martha Yeats' name plate: MS. YEATS. Inside, it's still her office, her books and cartoons and post-its, her flowers and posters and box of Kleenex.

"I hope this isn't what I think it is," Wright says, wincing as he settles in a chair and tries getting comfortable, which means grabbing his pants leg, raising his left leg and putting it on top of a drawer he pulls out of his desk.

"We don't know what it is yet," I say.

"What it is is an ugly story with a lovely beginning and a troubled middle and...well I don't suppose we know the ending."

"No sir, that's what we're after."

"Don't make me go through it from the start, Billy. I'm sure you know some things already."

"Up to the point he applied for a position here. I get the idea you wanted him to take your place."

"Yes," Wright says. "That was the idea. So we could overlap a bit. Share the experience." The desk he sits at is at right angles to the back wall of the office. Now he rearranges himself. All I can see is the back of his head as he looks out the window.

"We don't get many students like Gerald Garner anymore," he says. "We never did, at the best of times. Those kids you saw this morning, they're second and third generation college kids. It's in their genes. Familiarity. Entitlement. Of course you go to college. It's what you do, after high school, prep school. What college? City or country? Big or little? Warm climate or changing seasons? It's not an education. It's a lifestyle choice. Garner was utterly different. Thrilled to be here. Anxious. Hungry. When I gave him a C on his first paper he came to my office, worried about flunking out of college, breaking his parents' hearts, letting down neighbors, teachers, high school coach, hometown librarian. How about that?" Wright laughs but it's a sad kind of laugh, the kind you laugh when the joke's on you.

"I've had smarter students. Tenured professors, now, six of them. They were good at the start. Excellent. The marvelous thing about Garner was that he got better in front of me, year to year. I saw it happen. I made it happen. And it happened on all fronts, all classes, everything he touched. He got the Rhodes. A crowning achievement. Then graduate school. We kept in touch. We were friends for life. Letters, phone calls, visits. He loved coming back here. It was mystical, it was almost holy, this place was to him. What he missed, I'm afraid, was how the college was changing. I wasn't the dominant figure in the history department anymore..."

"Who was?" I ask.

"Nobody in particular. Everybody..." Wright stops again. "I wish I'd persuaded him to apply to other places. But he'd be back here sooner or later, he insisted, so why not sooner? Well, he applied to this and only this place and of course he made the list of candidates invited here for campus interviews. He was the first to come. So far, things were going well, but I sensed something happening. Office doors closing more often in the history department. References to meetings, consultations, caucuses, phone calls that ended when I approached. At department mail boxes, a heavy traffic in envelopes marked 'confidential.' Then it happened—the day before Garner was scheduled to arrive, an e-mail from Martha Yeats. 'This search will have failed if it does not result in the hiring of a minority and/or female candidate.' Some of my colleagues vapored about 'the best available candidate.' Most agreed outright, from the outset, with Martha. Garner's return was doomed. He came. I wish I had told him not to. He lectured. He dined. He taught a sample class. He met the provost and the president and it was all just fine. He was a stronger candidate than even I had realized. Martha and her crew knew better than to attack him directly. She also saw that time was on her side. The first candidate to visit is at a disadvantage. He—or she—becomes a benchmark, an adequate hire, a known quantity—and simply by continuing the search you build a consensus that, well, we might do better, we can do better, we must do better. Meanwhile, impressions fade. His energy, his presence, his humor and grace, all of it, damned with faint praise. Let's see what's out there, we owe it to ourselves, to the department, the college, the profession. So they interviewed the first three candidates and brought in three more and not one was as good as Garner and they knew it..."

"So who'd they hire?"

"No one. That year. The next year they had another search. He got the message. He didn't reapply."

"You spoke about it with him?"

"Yes. But it spoke for itself. End of an era. End of the old boy network. End of me."

"Where did he wind up?"

"It was about me," Wright says, ignoring my question. "One Hiram Wright was enough. Two was too many. What happened to Garner was my fault. I knew it. So did he, I'm afraid. I wrote dozens of recommendations for him. All sorts of places. I was surprised he didn't do better. He always got interviews. But not offers, not good ones. Fill-ins, sabbatical replacements. That's what happens if you don't get a tenure track. You're a migrant worker. You kill yourself in front of classes of forty or fifty, with no benefits, no prospects. They grind you down. And meanwhile, the graduate schools keep turning out job candidates whose credentials are fresher, whose theses are more fashionable. After this went on for a while, I told Garner his preoccupation with academe—and with this particular academy—and even with me—was misplaced. Months passed. Then there came a postcard. A view of the college on the front. On the back in a handwriting I recognized: 'Fuck it.'"

"Do you think he's our man?" I ask.

"I wonder," Wright says. It sounds like a yes answer. "Why kill Martha Yeats? There are a thousand Marthas out there. But there was only one of me. And I was the most to blame."

"Where's Mr. Graves?" Hartley Fuller wanted to know. He was my next stop. A week had passed since I talked to Wright. Graves had made it clear that G-Man had low priority. No priority. In the meantime, I drove him around, to courthouses and law offices, to banks and county offices in Columbus, up in Cleveland and Mansfield. I waited for him in lobbies and parking lots, drove him where he wanted to go. He hardly ever talked about what he was doing and his only questions were about local stuff—who owned what farm, what land was selling for, things like that which he could pick up from anyone. That's the kind of partners we were.

"He had other duties," I said, not having the least idea what Graves was up to. Some days, he just stayed in his motel room.

"And you're the one to interview me?" Fuller asked. He had some industrial strength doubts. What correspondence course did I take, that entitled me to go one-on-one with the chair of the college history department?

"Yes, sir," I said. "At Mr. Graves' request."

"Well then..." he said.

"There's just one question, Professor," I said. "And it's three words long." That got his interest.

"Well, let's hear it."

"Gerald Kurt Garner."

"That's a name. Not a question."

"It's a question. It's a name with a wiggle at the end, that's a question mark. I think you can take it from there."

"Alright," he said. I'd asked about Gerald Kurt Garner. But the man Fuller started in on was Hiram Wright. "What becomes a legend most?" he asked. And answered: "Timely retirement." Stribling and Wright, the college legends. Stribling had the decency to step aside but Wright stayed forever, 'professing but not progressing, indifferent when not hostile to change.' In his last years he withdrew from departmental affairs, so that many important changes had begun without him. The problem was—and this was difficult to admit—he still characterized the department. He was the name people mentioned. "Oh, that's Hiram Wright's place." Sometimes his colleagues wondered how long it would take to shed that Hiram Wright reputation. How many years? Would time, alone, do the trick? Hiram was hostile to co-education, to team-taught courses, interdisciplinary studies, current scholarship, whole new fields of endeavor, post-colonial, gender, structuralism, post-structuralism. I could hardly keep up, taking notes on what I half-understood, nodding my head in appreciation. Once he got over talking to the likes of me, Fuller just rolled along, only pausing to let me catch up in my note-taking, because he didn't want anything he said to be lost. Even after Hiram Wright withdrew from the department, Fuller said, leaving his colleagues to "their own devices," the old man still impeded progress. He was hostile to films in class. He was hostile to junior years abroad. He had his doubts about change in the profession, about the importance of research, the role of theory. When visitors came to campus, lecturers and politicians, it was Hiram Wright they wanted to meet, was there any chance that the old man would be coming to their lecture? And in May, it was unbearable to see alumni coming in to pay their respects. They filled the hall in their springtime togs, their Docker slacks and golf shirts, waiting to hear how the college was doing, wanting to hear from Wright of all people, the person most out of touch, the least-informed, the sworn enemy of new methods and new ideas. Harry Stribling had the good grace to die on cue. Hiram stuck around, a bone in the throat of the history department, that they couldn't swallow and couldn't spit out.

"What about Garner?" I asked.

"I'm there," Fuller said. "We decided it wasn't appropriate to have Hiram Wright imposing his will...his candidate...on this department. Martha took the lead. It was her second year here. She came to me, quite bravely. We talked to some of our colleagues..."

"Garner came to campus, didn't he? For the interview and all?"

"I felt sorry for him, to tell the truth," Fuller said. "He was a well-turned out fellow. I wasn't here in his student days, as a matter of fact, none of us had been. There's a lesson there, too, by the way. When Hiram Wright was Mr. History at this college, every other department member was a bit player, a spear-carrier. A transient. Only room for one star."

"And Garner?"

"He should never have been here. If he looked bad, he failed. If he looked good, well, we knew we didn't want to hire someone Hiram Wright inspired and sponsored."

"How'd he look?"

"Good, I'd have to say. The sample class, the lecture, all the social meetings. Fine, in a Hiram Wright way. It was a little sad, how he emulated the old man. The same old-school formality—hard to do for an Ohio kid—the approach to students, the way of leaving a question hanging in the air, even the way he quoted Hiram, as if that would thrill us all."

"What I don't get is...you didn't hire anybody that year...as far as I can tell." You know that look you see in movies, when somebody says, "touché?" I'd surprised Fuller, by what I knew. Even hicks did homework. "It was in the files," I added.

"Well, it was awkward," Fuller said. He went silent on me. I could see him sorting through things, what not to tell me, how to put things. "He was the best. We looked at three other candidates. Martha was anxious that we make a hire but there she parted company with the rest of us. We were willing not to hire Garner. I've told you why. But we couldn't bring ourselves to engage anyone else...that year."

"A busted search?"

"Yes," Fuller said. "I shouldn't tell you this but I don't see how it can matter now. Garner was the best candidate in a search that was canceled. People have sued for that kind of thing and won. And I happen to know that Hiram Wright advised him to sue. Did he tell you that?"

"No."

"I'll bet he didn't."

"How do you know?"

"Well..." He faltered a little, then plowed on. "I overheard. I stopped outside an office door that hadn't quite closed and I listened to a telephone call. Hiram wanted to cause us pain. He was feeling it himself, I'm sure, after what happened to his golden boy."

"Did Garner sue?"

"No. Just hearing Hiram's end of the conversation, I could tell that Garner wasn't taking the suggestion."

"What kept him from suing? Could you tell?"

"Love of this place. Alma Mater. He couldn't bring himself to do it, even at Wright's urging. It makes it all sadder, doesn't it?"

G-Man, G-Man, G-Man, you're my man, that's what I'm thinking, driving south a few days later. Graves doesn't buy it, I know that. Someone Martha Yeats pissed off fifteen years ago? Someone who hasn't been seen or heard from since? So maybe I'm not just looking for a murder suspect. I'm on the trail of the American dream, what's left of it, wherever it's gone to, the poor kid who goes to college, wins a scholarship, waits tables, washes dishes, graduates at the top of his class...and vanishes.

Highways 661, 62, 71 go south and into the past. South is easy, it comes natural, it feels like it's downhill, all the way to Florida. I'm passing out of Mount Vernon, through a pair of white-clapboard villages, Brandon and Homer, people sitting on front porches, happy to watch traffic that slows down to forty-five. There's loads of yard ornaments, which are called yardos around here: concrete geese dressed in aprons, bright painted cut-outs of bloomer-wearing women bending into flowers, dark silhouettes of pipe-smoking men, leaning against trees. Towns like this remind me of the lives that we're supposed to live, that we fuck up. After I turn onto Route 62, closing in on Columbus, garden apartments press against the highway, golf courses surround tract homes, facing away from traffic, turning their backs to you, dropping trousers, showing their asses. Go ahead, Graves said, drive down south and poke around. But he made it sound like he was giving me the day off. Taking a joyride with my ex-wife, a pair of leaf-peepers on a late September morning, following autumn south.

"Why don't you leave him the hell alone," Linda said, when I'd asked her to come along. "He got fucked over once or twice already," she said. I told her I hoped he was living happily ever after on the banks of the Ohio River. "Well," she said, "so use a phone book. Call the sheriff down there, or the post office." "I don't want to spook him," I said. "Oh, I get it," she fired back. "You bring me along and when the police surround the house I'm the girl who says come out, we all love you, everything will be okay." "Listen," I said. "I only want to see him. Don't you?" Now he's an hour away from us, just down the road.

"Did you love him?" I ask after twenty miles of comfortable silence. We're on the other side of Columbus and she just gave up on finding anything on the radio.

"Oh, for sure. He's smart. When he's really on, really on, he carries you along. And in a room full of people, he performs. He lights up. You never know what's coming. He's remarkable."

"Hey, Linda? The G-Man, I mean. Not Robert."

"Oh..." It's as if she'd forgotten where we were going. Now, all of a sudden, the memory comes to life. A third passenger. Goosebumps. She closes her eyes and I'll bet she's picturing G-Man the way he looked back when he was a lead-pipe cinch for a Rhodes. Or maybe she's wondering what he looks like now. What time does to golden boys. "Sure I loved him. I loved him like I loved nobody else."

"Meaning?"

"I didn't fuck him."

"I guessed."

"How about that," she says. "The unconsummated love is the one that lasts."

"A lesson in there, I guess," I say. She gives me this funny, puzzled look, like she's heard something she didn't expect to hear and, we're both laughing. It feels good, being in the same car, headed the same way, deciding where to stop for lunch.

"So how's Robert?" I ask. This comes after I've finished my Italian sausage and peppers sandwich in three minutes. I don't gulp or wolf my food—I'm very neat. I'm single minded. That's what she called me. Sounds like simple-minded. One thing at a time. Like a tool. A simple tool. A vacuum cleaner at the dinner table, a jackhammer in bed. Even when I slept, I slept like I was curled up at the bottom of a deep well, out of range of dreams.

"Want the short story or the novel?" she asks.

"Short."

"Gone," she says. "Short enough? He showed me his book."

"What's it about?"

"I'm not supposed to say. It's a secret."

"Oh. You mean someone might beat him to the subject?"

"I don't think so," she says, smothering a laugh. "Johnny Appleseed."

"Oh..."

"Listen to this." There are these guys sitting around an Ohio tavern, she tells me, one of those cross-sections of people you see in phone company ads, a white, a black, an Indian—no women—going on about America and the frontier, all in the course of telling stories and drinking, how they got to the heartland and what it means and where America is headed. Appleseed mostly just listens but you know his story is coming. Rob stops before Johnny gets his turn at the mike. He asks Linda what she thinks. She blew it, she guesses. Talking to a man about the most important thing in his life, she comes up with a phrase from Oprah. "A boy's book." But she wasn't wrong, she tells me. It was a boy's book not because it was male but because it was young. It was boyish. Boyish in the things it talked about and the way it talked about them, in the way it tackled big themes, more like a history pageant or a musical, something performed on state fairgrounds, where the town chiropractor is Johnny Appleseed and the high school basketball coach is Andrew Jackson and the college Spanish professor makes an okay Tecumseh. Something you sit through once a year, out-of-doors and if it rains that night, hey, that's okay, better luck next year. So Robert goes to bed without saying goodnight. The next morning he leaves for New York to try and find an agent.

"We'll find the river at Portsmouth," I say, when she finishes with Robert. "Then it's ten miles."

"You think he's there?"

"Maybe not this minute. But it's worth a look. He didn't want the college to contact him, after he got screwed out of a job. That doesn't mean he broke contact with the whole world. Not necessarily."

"Does it make sense," she asks, "to come back and kill somebody years and years later because you didn't get a job?"

"It wasn't a job," I say. "It was a life."

So, those last miles, into Portsmouth and then, left and north, up along the Ohio, we're all about G-Man. We're in his territory, getting closer all the time. It's as if we've picked up a station on the car radio at night, when transmissions bounce across the time zones, scraps of songs that come out of the static—clearer sounding the nearer you get. I tell her about the job interview that went sour, about G-Man and Professor Wright and about the do-not-contact in his file at the alumni office. I tell her how I called other members of the G-Man's class, the senior president, his roommates all four years, the class agent.

"I've got nothing," I say. "No grounds at all. You know why I'm doing this? It's not so much about what happened to Martha Yeats. It's because I'm curious about this guy. Listen, if Graves thought we had something here, would he be letting me handle it? By myself? The likes of me?"

"What's that man doing?" Linda asked. "Six weeks, it's been."

"That long, huh?"

"Are there clues? Suspects?"

"Beats me," I said, sounding stupid. "Listen, the Sheriff did all the police work, the garden variety stuff, in the first couple of days. The crime scene, the ballistics, Martha's neighbors, friends, enemies, lovers, partners, whatever-the-hell. All that stuff. Mostly, as far as I can see, Graves is studying the college...the power, the money, the politics. Tom thinks Graves is taking his time because he enjoys seeing the College squirm. You know about his father?"

"Sure," she said. "Rudy Graves. Nice old man, I always thought. Great house to go to on Halloween. The rest of the faculty had apples and pears. He gave out as many chocolate bars as we could get our hand around..."

"So it's a homecoming, that's what Tom thinks. A dream come true. A dream case, kind of. He doesn't even care if he solves it."

"What about this little road trip? Does he know about this?"

"I mentioned it."

"And?"

"He didn't say no."

"So...is this police business?"

"I'll put in for mileage. Five cents a mile. They pay me back, it's police business."

"Pathetic," she says.

We pass through one river town after another. You wonder what people live off of, what they've got that the world needs. They live off each other, I guess—they cut hair, deliver mail, I don't know. Go to yard sales on weekends. And the river, the Ohio River, has something to do with it. Live on the ocean, you know you're hooked into the whole world. The tide goes in, the tide goes out. Here, the river just moves in one direction, which is away.

"There's one little something," I say. "I got a call from the class agent..."

"The what?"

"That's the guy in your class you send news to after you graduate, marriage and promotions and that stuff. This guy remembered someone who said he sighted G-man. So I gave this other one a call. This is a lawyer in Connecticut. And, at the start, it was dodgy, I don't mind saying."

"How's that?"

"Well, he's a lawyer for one thing and just basically a prick. He doesn't want to give, he wants to trade. Wants to know my position at the college, why I'm looking for the G-Man."

"You told him?"

"I danced around it. I said I was a student."

"A what?"

"A student of Hiram Wright's, alright? And that the President asked me to get in contact with Gerald Kurt Garner, who was a Wright student. That the college records were incomplete...see...not a lie...any of it."

She's impressed, I can tell. She thought I was too honest to lie, or not bright enough. "Did he buy it?"

"Sort of. But there's still this thing that gets into all their voices when they hear about the G-Man. Swear to God. They're horny for news. High or low. Nothing in the middle. They want extremes. It's like the whole bunch of them agreed that whatever happened, he shouldn't turn out like them."

"So?"

"This lawyer was traveling around with his daughter, shopping for colleges like they do. He wants her to go to our place but he doesn't want to push it. So they visit a lot of places, including Marietta. This is maybe five years back. He's sitting around outside while his kid is having a chat with the nice people in admissions. Anyway, there he sees someone come walking by he thinks he recognizes. The guy is bulkier than he remembers and kind of disorderly, mussed up, untogether. But he tries his luck. 'G-Man?' He half expects whoever it is to just keep walking, no harm done. Which he does, two or three steps. And stops. And turns. It's the G-Man. So, this lawyer tries to bore in a little. How are you doing, G-Man? What are you up to? Been wondering about you, all of us have, you should hear us talk about you at reunions. He sees G-Man flinch. Doing fine, he says, better all the time, got sidetracked for a while but, hey, watch out, I'm on the right track now. Watch my dust. You'll be hearing about the G-Man, sure as shooting."

"Sure as shooting? He said that?"

"It's an expression, not a confession."

"I guess..." she says, but she's not convinced and neither am I.

"He said he was in the book business. That's what he told this guy. That's all. The lawyer's impression is, he wanted to be gone. 'Will I see you at the next reunion?' he shouts it out as G–Man walks away. No answer."

"What was he doing there? Did anybody know him?"

"I called. The dean of faculty. The personnel office. They never heard of him. I called the library. Nobody knew him."

"He doesn't sound like a winner," she says.

"He doesn't sound like a murderer either."

By now we're in River View, which is a block of buildings just up from the river, where a rickety landing sank into the water and took an old ferry with it, a double drowning that looks like one of those beachheads from World War II. There used to be a movie house here, a hardware store and barber shop, gone now along with some empty places I couldn't be sure about. This is the kind of town you see in newsreels, citizens waving at TV helicopters from rooftops, after it rains a lot. Thirty-five Bank Street is part bungalow, part shack, with bare dirt in front and bug-chewed hollyhocks nesting inside white-painted tires. There are car seats on the front porch and an old man sits in one of them, watching us. He's got a piece of cloth over the front of his throat, like a curtain over a window.

"Good morning, sir," I say. He doesn't answer but there's a kind of nod. "Okay if we come up on the porch?" Another nod. The boards creak and sag beneath us. "Pardon me. Is this the Garner residence?"

"You got it," someone says. Not the old man. A woman is standing behind the screen door, as if photographed through a grainy filter. "The old man got his larynx cut on. He doesn't talk much."

Now the screen door opens and slams shut and the woman is in focus: country-western and poor, with a kind of raw-boned been-around-the-block sexiness that she's well aware of, plus she's built and she knows that too. Hungry and hurt and tough: we don't see many people like her on campus. Well-fed but fragile is more our speed.

"I'm Billy Hoover and this is Linda Thorne," I tell her. "We're from up in Knox County. That's north of Columbus. There's a little college up there that I work for."

It changes. The woman goes from curiosity to wariness. And the old man isn't just sitting there, killing time. He's alert too.

"We're looking to get in touch with a fellow, went to college up there."

"My brother," the woman says. She looks down at the old man, who has a dog-eared notebook in one hand and a stubby pencil in the other, a thick-tipped pencil like the kind that carpenters use to draw lines on boards, showing where to saw. He's commencing to write. She steps over and pats his head. "I'll take care of this," she says.

"Well, then," I say. "Looks like we found the right place." I sound cheerful and phony, but G-Man's sister doesn't look so tickled, that we found our way here.

"I guess you can sit," she says, making it sound like a real close call. I take a folding chair and Linda finds a place at the edge of the car seat, sitting next to the old man.

"The thing of it is, we're looking...that's the folks at the college...are looking for Mr. Garner. It's been a while, since they've heard from him. It's been years."

"Just what do you do at the college, Mr. Hoover?" the woman asks. "Don't bullshit me, mister."

"Alright, no bullshit, I do what they tell me to," I answer. "I'm a campus cop. I write tickets for snot-nose rich kids. I ask them nicely to please turn down their stereos and put away their open containers. I run errands, on account I'm an errand boy. This is an errand."

"What do you want my brother for?" the woman asks.

"A couple of weeks ago, somebody came onto campus and shot a history professor named Martha Yeats."

"Killed her?"

"Dead," I say. "I'm the guy who found her."

"And now you need my brother?"

"He came back a few years after he graduated. He applied for a job. Lots of people thought it was a cinch. But he didn't get it. He was sponsored by his old professor, Hiram Wright. Maybe that was the problem. Wright had enemies."

"Good old Wright," the woman says. She knows the name. She knows a lot. God, these women are something. It's like they reverse the lesson of the three monkeys, see-no-evil, speak-no-evil, hear-no-evil. They've seen, heard, said it all. And done a lot besides.

"Ring a bell? That name?"

"Sure. Heard it for years, while my brother was up there. Do the Wright thing. Making out all Wright. It was a joke in our family. Remember, Pop? Professor Wright?" The old man nods.

"The professor who got killed?" I say. "She was the one who kept your brother from getting the job."

"Oh, now I get it. And this is the part where you ask, have I seen my brother lately and I say no, I tell you to fuck off, and you wonder if I'm lying and pass over your card and ask me to call if I change my mind. And then you leave. Could we get to that part now?"

"I don't have a business card," I say. "And, lady, I'd be tickled if you told me he's having a great life in California or someplace far." Then I surprise myself. I get off my chair and approach this woman whose name I still don't know and stand right up close to her, like we're about to seriously slow dance. I'm not like this, I'm really not. I'm the kind of guy who backs away, who doesn't push things, who takes no for a final answer. "Just look me in the eyes and tell me that he's okay someplace, happy and harmless. No address, no phone number, I'll take your word for it and leave, like you want me to."

She backs away, glances down, can't look me in the eyes and lie. So she looks away, and lies.

"I got no idea," she says.

"What became of your brother, miss..."

"Lisa," she says. Then she gets her wind back up. "They made a lot of him at college, Wright and the rest of them. He wanted to go back there. He could have gone most anywhere, but he said, that's where I belong. Only he didn't. Then he started having trouble."

"Like..."

"He's better now." She's said more than she meant to say. So she puts on her shrewd look. "I don't want to talk about him anymore. And you can't make me. You're not a cop. You chalk tires."

"Yeah. And sometimes I find a dead professor when I'm out for a walk."

"Well, she sounds like a bitch to me."

"Only say good things about the dead."

"She's dead," Lisa says with a nasty smile. "That's good."

"I guess we'll go now," I say, but I'm closer to her, like when you're on a dance floor and the music stops. It takes a tapping sound to break the spell, the G-Man's father knocking his pencil against the chair, gesturing with a piece of paper he gives to me.

He never did anything I wasn't proud of, I read aloud. "Thank you, sir." I start to leave, Linda gets up to follow, changes her mind.

"Not yet," Linda says. She turns to the old man, because there's no point contending with the honky-tonk siren. "Sir, I don't work for the college. My daddy did, but he's been dead a while now. I came down here because I was a little kid on campus and I adored your son..."

She goes on, telling what she remembers, like she's flipping through a pile of old photos: G-Man on the football field, on the dance floor, G-Man and her driving around at night selling sandwiches in dorms, "Sangy-Man," and "Sangy-Girl." It was puppy love, she tells them, but it meant a lot to the puppy. The old man reaches over and pats her hand.

"Maybe you hear from him and maybe you don't," she says, "but if you do..."

"We don't," Lisa interrupts. "Okay?"

"...but if you do," she continues, "just tell him... 'Sangy-Girl' was asking…"

"Asking what?" the sister horns in. "Asking, is he a murderer?"

"Asking for him," she says. "That's all."

"Yeah, right," Lisa says. "Bye, now."

"Goodbye, sir," she tells the old man. We head out off the porch and towards the truck.

"Hey, mister," Lisa Garner calls out. From behind me, she's leaning in the doorway, beckoning me back. Linda keeps walking, opens the door and climbs in my truck.

"Yeah," I say. I'm standing in the yard. She's up on the porch.

"Hiram Wright called yesterday," she says. "Asking about the G-Man. Same as you. All those years go by and...bingo."

"Was he worried about him? That why he called?"

"Yeah, sure, call it worried."

"Well..."

"Listen," she comes down the porch one step. "Maybe we'll talk again sometime. Is that something you would like? Talking to me?"

"I'd like it."

"It's something you'd look forward to?"

"Yes, I guess."

"Guess?"

"Definitely. I'd like it." I'm ready to leave it like that. Up to her. Then I see Linda out in the truck, watching me, and I think about the way I always leave things up to her. Maybe this is when I should take things into my own hands. "Not this weekend," I say. "I'm working. But the one after that. Homecoming, they call it."

"I'll remember that," she says. She glances at her father, sitting on the porch, watching the river. "Homecoming."

"Were we wasting our time today?" Linda asks. We're headed back north.

"No."

"We'll hear from them?"

"Not necessarily."

"What does that mean?"

"Could be we'll hear from him," I say. "Maybe they're in touch with him. Or he's in touch with them. Remember when she allowed he'd had a breakdown. She said 'he's doing better now.'"

"He could have been sitting right inside, listening to everything we said," she says.

"Boo Radley? Could be. But I doubt it."

It's late afternoon and we're back on Route 23, headed north towards home, a trip the G-Man must have made dozens of times, three hours and change, but worlds apart, that college on a hill and that washed-up riverbank town. A magic mountain, it must have seemed like, top of the world.

"You could have got laid back there," Linda says. "That wasn't a kid sister. That was a heat-seeking missile."

Heat-seeking missile, I think. Hell, that might be my Homecoming date.

V.
WARREN NILES
Night Thoughts of a College President

To say Martha Yeats' violent and untimely death disturbed me is to pronounce a commonplace. I was—and am—disturbed. I worry about the college. The positioning of Martha's body outside a fraternity lodge bothered me, even as I pictured old boy alums joking that they wish she'd been dumped in front of the Women's Studies Cottage. Martha was displayed, shockingly, in a way that suggested her killer wanted to make a point. The killer was sending a message. He had other people in mind. Very likely he had me in mind. And so, as the weeks have gone by, our lovely autumn, our wisest-feeling season, my relief that nothing else has happened, my delight at our safe passage further into the semester, combines with something else. Call it panic. The kind of panic you feel at discovering an unexpected lump, death's calling card in your throat or under your armpit.

"Asshole." It's not a word I use but it's Anglo-Saxon at its sturdy best. A form of personification, more specifically, a synecdoche, using a part—the asshole, in this case—to characterize the whole, the president, that is. Now, a true night thought. As leaders, as normative figures, college presidents are a disappointing bunch. We head up processions, not causes. Civil rights, environment, Vietnam: can you name a college president who stuck his neck out, risked his career? I am part of that disappointing group. At least I can say that I have felt disappointment. And part of me has longed for a chance to do better, stand tall, play a part in a definitive movement.

Imagine...a worse confession...my disappointment as the autumn rolls along quite normally, when all our bellwether issues, our evergreen complaints reassert themselves, when what threatened to afflict the college like an Ebola virus turns out to be a passing cold. There's something oddly flattering in having caught the attention of a killer. A stranger—one hesitates to say a perfect stranger—has noticed me. Entered my house. Started a correspondence. Someone cares enough to hate me. Will I ever know who? I would feel cheated if the whole mystery dribbled away, though that would be in the best interests of the college. I confess: I picture a meeting—I walk along the path at night. A figure passes briskly by, heading in the other direction. Then I hear a voice behind me. "Asshole." It's not an insult anymore, it's a code name, a password that will take me someplace I have never been.

In the meantime, what do I do? I preside over weekly meetings of the college's senior staff. We converge in a decorous, dark-paneled room with oils of college benefactors on the walls. The metal labels have rusted: I cannot read their names. They are most noticed once a year, on the "Day Without Art," an anti-AIDS initiative, when students drape them with black cloth. A Martha Yeats initiative, as I recall. And now she is similarly shrouded, someplace. Every day. And now, in the very Fuhrerbunker of my administration, we discuss admissions. So many applications, so many acceptances, so much yield. We feel like automobile salesmen on a slow day, no customers on the lot, prices chalked on windshields, plastic flags flapping in the wind. We discuss scholarships, which are our benefaction, our investment, our potential bankruptcy. Scholarships for bright poor students, for bright students—merit scholars—who aren't particularly poor, for students black and Latino who aren't especially bright and, just lately, discounts—awards for students who want us to match a deal they've gotten someplace else. My mind wanders. I recall what it feels like when I'm traveling on college business, reconnoitering the moneyed suburbs so many of our students come from. From a descending plane, I scan horse farms, black painted fences, backyard swimming pools, gazebos. I picture perfect lawns, freshly sprinkled and dandelion-free, colonial doorways with antique brass eagle knockers. A salesman sizing up the territory, a salesman-stalker for the liberal arts, a big-ticket item if ever there were one, a vanity buy, an impulse purchase, a perfect match of leisure time and disposable income. I wonder how many of these crystal-chandeliered houses will continue to afford what we sell. I see businessmen in bathrobes, sitting at Sunday breakfast tables, balancing budgets and saying to their wives, *no more, enough's enough,* and that will be the end of us.

"Well, I've got a problem this morning," Willard Thrush announces. I bestir myself to listen. "Anybody here ever know of Duncan Kerstetter, Class of 1975?"

There are shrugs around the table. Shrugs from the Admissions, Development, Business, Provost, Library, Dean of Students. Thrush prolongs the moment.

"No one?"

Senior staffers contemplate the remnants of their dining service breakfast: eggs, unapologetically greasy bacon, par-boiled potatoes, English muffins saturated with margarine, all of which they deprecate but I notice that not many bother to eat virtuously at home beforehand.

"Well, Duncan Kerstetter passed through here quietly," Thrush says. "Pre-med. No fraternity. No activities. I called up his class agent. He says Kerstetter is a dweeb. Pocket saver, slide rule club. I bet you can guess the rest of the story."

"Let me try," I say, determined to move things along. This is something you can do, when you've been president a while. "Kerstetter has made a fortune in kitty litter and now, it's look homeward, angel. He wants respect that he didn't get the first time he was here, he wants to outshine the classmates who regarded him so lightly. He's anxious to tell us how much the college mattered to him, this or that professor. Then again, perhaps he wants us to hear how little it meant, how he prospered in spite of us. Alright, Willard. What's this about?"

"Mortuaries! Not kitty litter. A whole chain of mortuaries, hooked up to centralized processing plants."

"Didn't you say he was pre-med?"

"Yes. A respected cardiologist."

"Isn't that a conflict of interest?" asks Caroline Ives. "Mortuaries?"

"I'd call it a win-win situation," Thrush responds.

"What does he have in mind?" I ask.

"Three to five million," Thrush answers. "That's what we have in mind. That would put him among the top five donors this college ever had."

"Sounds like an honorary degree," I said.

"I'd hate to write that citation," Caroline Ives said. "To the Colonel Sanders of the corpse trade..."

"That won't do the trick," Thrush said. "Listen. Kerstetter was a biology major. Pre-med. Lived in the lab. Well, I guess he noticed these other buildings, classrooms full of kids reading paperback novels. 'I couldn't believe they were getting credit for stuff like that,' he tells me, 'figuring out whether something was ironic.' Then, too, he heard about the famous English department. So he washes the formaldehyde off and takes a course with the man himself. Harry Stribling. And it changed his life, of course."

"Of course," I say, expecting to hear how the liberal arts produced a haiku-writing rocket scientist. If only I could fast-forward all these meetings! "We change lives all the time."

"You bet," Willard said. "He hated it. He says Stribling discriminated against him, that he had a bias against science and scientists. Their approach to reasoning, their kind of knowledge, their use of language. The C he got from Stribling prevented Duncan Kerstetter from graduating as a member of Phi Beta Kappa. So he wants the grade changed."

"Now!?" Dean Carstairs asks. "This is sick."

"Certifiable," Caroline Ives agrees. "Anybody would have to say...get a life."

"He has a life," Thrush counters. "And three to five million, now. More later... maybe. Morticians die too, you know."

"The faculty would have to vote on it," Caroline Ives reminded us. "Even then..."

"You'll propose it?" Thrush pressed. "You'll endorse it?"

"I'm just trying to think it through," the provost demurred.

"Would two endowed chairs assist your thinking?" Thrush pressed.

"I wonder...I just wonder..." Caroline Ives said.

"I wish I could see a way out of this," I say. Our appetite for money is infinite. Aggressively as we try to raise it, our best efforts only keep us in step with other colleges who are also, always, raising money. Wabash got pharmaceutical money: Eli Lilly. Earlham was blessed by a stock market trader: Warren Buffet. What angel comes knocking at our door? The father of the human processing plant.

"He proposes coming back...after all these years?"

"He's been back," Thrush responds. "Right at the start of the year. He was on a kind of mid-life road trip. *Blue Highways* kind of thing. He came through here and got thoughtful. Let me just say this. Duncan Kerstetter is a huge opportunity for this college. The kind of gift that changes things. He's a big fish and he's already hooked, begging to be boated. Understand, kids? Not a trout, not a catfish. This is a yellow fin tuna, three hundred pounds of sashimi. And what's he asking for? A changed grade is all!"

"If we set a precedent..." I began. But Willard interrupted me.

"Sorry, Warren. Excuse me. Duncan Kerstetter is a huge chance for a place that doesn't get many...any...like this. I've been raising money around here for years. I know what's out there. And there's no one like him. He's huge. He's also an asshole. Okay? But my point is, we deal with assholes all the time..."

He stopped, ran his hand over his face, through his hair, the way he always did when his bottom-line corporate approach ran up against our nuanced, pettifogging academic ways. We sat in silence. Asshole. There it was again. The word was all around me, bouncing off the walls. Had some Chinese calendar turned my way? Was this the Year of the Asshole?

"No way," Martin Summers, the chair of the faculty, says. Martin's a chemist, a pleasure to work with, as a rule. Just as the years have taught me to expect better manners from the far right than from the far left—which may just be another way of saying better table manners from the well-fed than from the recently hungry—so too they've taught me that the most rabid feuding is in the soft sciences and the humanities. The hard sciences are progressive, measurable. Their proprietors are calm in possession of their knowledge, slow to anger, and...in Martin's case...boring. That made his outburst decisive.

"What Kerstetter is suggesting is obscene," Martin said. "What are we going to do? Give him a make-up exam? Because he's loaded? And if we let students come back at us, does that mean we can come back at students? Award Rutherford B. Hayes A's in all of his courses because he became a president? If a Phi Beta Kappa becomes a serial killer, do we strip him of his diploma on the way to the gas chamber? Do we start to act like one of those German universities? Hitler came to power, they revoked degrees earned by Jews."

"Well, that settles it, I suppose," I conceded. I leaned back in my chair, shut my eyes a moment, and pictured dollar bills flying overhead, south, to more congenial climes.

"I'd like to revisit this," Caroline Ives popped up. My heart leaped! Clever, clever woman!

"I think it's settled," Martin Summers objected but he'd had his turn. Will the scientist please sit down?

"There's no harm in reconsidering this," I declared. "Even if our decision remains the same—which it may well—there's no need to give an answer today."

"I'd just like to think about this a little more," said Caroline, flashing Martin a smile that was almost an apology. "Meanwhile, there's something else. People are talking about the murder."

"What are they saying?"

"They're saying this isn't like any investigation anyone's ever seen or heard about. Normally, there's a crime, there's a crime scene. They search the area, they talk to people in the neighborhood, check the victim's habits, background, record..."

"All that's been done. You know that."

"Precisely. And then they leave. Don't they?"

"Yes," I admitted. "But not here. Not yet."

"It's become a joke. 'Is Sherwood Graves up for tenure?' What is he doing? Graves and that Billy fellow?"

"Hoover," I say. "He researches college records. So Willard tells me. He's been in development, alumni affairs, human resources, the archives..."

"Maybe he's just going through the motions," Willard Thrush suggests. "A paper chase. That's alright with me. From where I sit, we've gotten all the investigation we need and just the man to man it. What do you want? Arrests? Line ups? More headlines? We've got a dweeb in charge. Sooner or later, he'll go away. Fine. We'll never know who killed Martha Yeats. That's okay with me."

"But what I don't understand..." Caroline began. She turned to me and, from the look on her face, I could tell something had occurred to her that wasn't shrewd or ingratiating. Something she almost couldn't say.

"He's waiting for something, isn't he?" she said. "What is he...what could he be waiting for?"

The next moment was strange. Intimate, almost. Caroline was a brisk, ambitious woman. So it was that much more remarkable, when I saw her shudder. She was frightened, suddenly and so was I. It happened to us at the same time, our realization. We both knew what Graves was waiting for.

Part Two: Homecoming

VI.

BILLY HOOVER

The G-Man's sister. All that next week I wondered, what was I doing? Was I such a studly catch, were my wallets so deep, my tongue so sharp, my looks so fine, that someone might drive across Ohio to visit me? Earth to Billy: call home. This is over your head. Call Sherwood Graves. Call the sheriff. Call your uncle. Yeah, right. I called no one. I was at my desk, Saturday night of Homecoming Weekend, waiting for her call, which I only half-believed would come, but it did.

"Hey, Billy," she says from her cell phone. "You've got a package at the post office."

There's a car with a downstate license plate in front of the post office, a late model Ford Wagoneer like what parents give their kids to play with at college, but this says Portsmouth Pharmacy on the side. She's come a long way. The vehicle's empty but I can see her sitting on a bench over on the path, just opposite the grocery store. We haven't lost daylight savings time yet and we're on the far side of the eastern time zone, so days are long here and, though the sun's long gone, the sky's lit up with orange and purple and I know it's her alright and I can feel the tension building, in my legs, in the palms of my hands as I walk towards her. She's dressed in a light brown suede jacket with a yellow blouse beneath and black slacks and dressy little boots.

"Hey there, Billy," she says.

"Hi," I say. I sit down beside her. I almost ask, did you find your way alright but I hold my tongue and just let us sit there, taking in the Saturday night. It's early yet. Campus parties don't crank up until past eleven o'clock but there's a lot of traffic up and down the sidewalk because it's homecoming, when the graduates of last year and fifty years ago return to take their place alongside today's students and it's as though all the generations are lined up and touching each other, from today back to the 1920s. We sit quietly, watching the kids, and it feels comfortable.

"This all takes me back," she says after a while. "Gets me thinking."

"Think out loud," I tell her. "If you like."

"My brother's four years older. He was a good brother. You saw what Daddy wrote. He made us proud, everything he ever did."

"Yeah...I believe it. I went through the records. He was something else, alright. A star. I had a cousin like that—Tony, my uncle's boy. Another wonder-kid."

"What happened?"

"Died in Vietnam."

"Well..." Now the silence isn't so comfortable. My cousin got killed. End of story. But her brother is still out there and what's he been up to? I'm not exactly asking and she isn't saying but the question's in the air. "I guess we're what's left," she says.

"You ever come up here with him?"

"Dance weekends, two or three times, he brought me up here. I was a high school kid and not college material, no sir. But...it was magic alright...all those parties...in lounges and lodges and the dance in the big hall...and the dawn milk-punch party down on the trestle...staying up all night and going into town for breakfast and falling in love with half a dozen guys who'd never touch me because I was a no-no, the G-Man's sister and so there I'd be...I shouldn't say this...standing with some of G-Man's buddies outside a door while my own brother was inside with a woman who was...you know...kind of a screamer. I'll never forget the look on his face when he came out and saw me there! Never did see him that upset...me standing in this crowd, everybody laughing and razzing...there was even a security guard there...and G-Man just grabs my hand and yanks me down the stairs onto the campus. 'I can't believe this,' he says. 'I can't believe what you did!' We walk some more. 'You can't believe what I did?' I say. 'Seems to me you were the one who did the doing.' A few steps later, he says, oh, hell, Lisa, something like that and puts his arms around me and we were close again, because we knew that whatever he did, it wouldn't come between us."

She turns away from me so I wouldn't see her face, but her voice still finds me. "He was supposed to keep on going. What happened?"

"That's what I was wondering," I say.

"I know, every year, some magazine'll do a gallery of burn-outs. Child actors and singers with one hit. But this isn't about drugs or bad marriages. G-Man didn't make mistakes like that. He did what he was supposed to do. He did it well. And you know his slogan? *Always do a little bit extra.*"

Right then, I know it's there for me, there for the taking: everything she can tell me about her brother, every downward step. And I don't go for it. Maybe she's testing me, dangling information. So when I don't bite, and after we've sat a while longer, she nods her head, like she'd decided something in my favor and we stroll onto the campus, the church on one side, the president's cottage on the other, walking side by side, then between the library and Stribling Hall, between the science building and the humanities, down to the old part of campus, where dorms are all lit up and noisy, open windows, people leaning out and shouting, different kinds of music coming out of rooms, like a jukebox playing a dozen selections at the same time.

"His room was over there," she says, gesturing to one of the dorms. "At the top, the room with the round window."

"The bull's eye."

"The G-spot, they called it."

We walk to the front of where G-Man lived and look up. I've been around enough reunion weekends to know what it's like to come back here, after years away. I've seen how big shots succumb. I talk about it with Lisa. There are a lot of places you go back to that don't hit you the way this one does, making millionaires weak and sad. I wonder why that is. Is it the river, the hill, the path, the trees, the buildings? I don't know. I don't think it's any one thing and I don't think it's all of them put together either. It's being old where you were young and had the world in front of you, I guess. The thinning in the ranks, that must get you too, the counting down to one or none, so that the freshman class of fifty years ago, newer than new, comes down to a half dozen geezers, half of them in wheelchairs. That's all part of it. But I don't think that I have the whole answer. I'm working on it, I tell her, but I'm not there yet.

"You love this place, don't you?" she says. "They treat you like a servant, pay you hamburger wages and you love it."

"I guess I do. Does that make me a chump?"

"Yeah, it does," she says. She has this way of changing character, she can do it in a wink. One minute she's tough and wised up and

sexy, the way I saw her the first time. Now she's a wide-eyed kid, innocent and easy to hurt, even when she's putting me down. "A nice
chump, though," she adds, slipping her hand around my arm and walking with me, just like we were a couple, down the college path at dusk,
walking along while the wind knocked the last leaves out of the trees.
I reached out and caught one out of the air and told her it meant good
luck was coming.

"I know that already," she says.

"Why'd you want to come back up here?" I ask.

"This place...scared me...I watched those college girls come in on
those big weekends carrying suitcases into a professor's house. I studied those college girls real close, the polite way they acted around the
professors early in the evening and later, how they drank and got
drunk, the ones who handled it cool and the ones who got lost, bird
dogged, damn near swinging from chandeliers, you'd see them walking around crying or vomiting in stairwells."

"That's not it," I said.

"What does that mean?"

"Drunken kids, loud parties. You can do better than that. That's not
what brought you back here."

"You think it was you?"

It's a challenge. We're right on the edge of an argument, if I want it.

"No," I say. "Not me. No way." I give in so quickly, she turns soft.

"He loved this place so much," she says. "He lived and breathed it.
I never saw anyone so taken over by love. I wondered what it would
be like to feel that way. About a person, about a place. And you...you
feel that way too. I can tell. And what are you?"

"What you see. A campus lawman, your friendly tour guide."

"Right. Officer, you nervous?"

"About what?"

"Me. Do I make you nervous?"

"Thirsty."

"Good answer," she says. So we go into one of the college
bars, a pizza place, and my uncle's sitting there, sitting at the end
of the bar with a couple of other security guys. They stare when
we come in. A lot of people think I'm a nice guy but basically
a loser and here I am with a woman like Lisa. We barely order
a pitcher of beer and pizza before Tom comes over. It's going to
be awkward. We don't talk much these days. Graves thinks Tom

is "a sieve." He doesn't want our business out on the street.

"I'll need to see your ID, boy," Tom says. "And yours, ma'am."

"Don't give it to him," I say. "He just wants your address. Besides, he's my uncle."

"Tom Hoover," he says, jamming his way into the booth. "What's your name, darlin'?"

"Lisa Garner," she says. Something registers right away, in Tom's face. But he's smart, he bides his time. "Well, it's nice to meet you. I about brought this guy up, such as he is."

"You did okay."

"There's a limit to what an uncle can do, though." He chugs some of the coffee he brought over with him. He likes his coffee scalding hot, emptying his cup the way college kids wallop down their beer. "My nephew can be a kind of a mope. Anything you could do, we'd all of us be grateful."

"We aim to please," Lisa answers right back to him, leaning forward to make the point, while her hand brushes the top of my leg, sort of by accident, and stays there, at home, on purpose.

"Where do you come from?" Tom asks.

"Down south of here."

"Cincinnati, you mean?"

"No. On the other side."

"You got a view of West Virginia across the water?"

"Yes, sir," Lisa says. Tom has her now. He's been working around the college for a long time. He doesn't bother asking how we met. Or why. He knows all that. He knows more than I want him to know.

"We had a Garner up here, years ago," he says. "Gerald Kurt Garner. Everybody called him the G-Man."

"My brother."

"Well, I'll be damned. He was a hell of a kid. Good at everything he did. Everything. 'Always do a little bit extra,' he said. Nowadays, it's do as little as possible. And get away with as much as you can." He gives her a long look, nothing shy about the way he stares. He doesn't bother asking how G-Man is doing these days, other than being investigated by a low-rent cop who isn't so busy, or so professional, he couldn't split a pizza with the suspect's sister. "Your brother was something. I expected he'd be president or something. Billy, this Garner guy about ran the place. He could be anything he chose." Lisa stays quiet. "Well, say hello to him. If and when..."

"Nice seeing you," Lisa says. *"Again."*

"Beg pardon?"

"I said nice seeing you again," Lisa repeats.

"We met before?"

"Outside the G-Man's room. On a dance weekend. Listening to the action from inside."

"Well then..." The thing is, Tom doesn't deny it. He blushes but he doesn't deny it. "Those were different times, weren't they?"

"I guess so," Lisa says. Tom nods and leaves. He still has us, no doubt. But Lisa had gotten on the scoreboard too. "I never forget a face," she says, watching Tom walk away. "Hey, let's go now."

I signal for the bill, and while we wait, she studies me with this smile on her face, like she knows something I don't. She knows more about me than I know about her. And now we're getting into a part of the evening that she controls. We step out into a light rain which has slicked everything down, a kind of warm rain that lovers walk through in movies. Every now and then nature plays along with you.

"Your uncle," she says.

"Yeah?"

"He got one thing right. You are a kind of mope. A nice mope, but still..."

"What makes a mope?"

"You expect the least of what's good and the most of what's worst."

"I guess," I say. We're at her car, outside the post office. Inside, a band is playing, loud. The lobby's open twenty-four hours so students use it to rehearse in front of an audience of wanted posters. "I'm doing better now," I say, looking at Lisa.

"Glad to hear it," she says. And all of a sudden we're at a moment that I guess everybody goes through in high school but in my case, I go through it still: standing across from a woman at the end of an evening, standing on a doorstep or in a parking lot or here in front of the post office, no idea what's next, nice evening, thank you or something else. I'm looking for a sign I'm scared to give and that's when she steps close to me.

"Start your car..." she says. "I'll follow you home."

I'm dumbstruck.

"Am I invited?" she adds.

"Yeah, you are," I said. "I mean...please. Yes. Thanks. All of that."

She steps into her drugstore S.U.V., I walk back to my truck and pull out in front of her. She follows me down the hill, onto the highway into town. Sure, I wonder what I'm getting into and what it will cost me. That's Billy the mope. But another Billy doesn't care. We leave the prime neighborhoods behind, the showplace houses with garages out back that used to be stables, then we pass homes with garages at the side, then these little bungalows with no garages and just cars parked out front, not all of them working, and that isn't the end of it. Where I live is the end: a trailer court where what you rode in and what you lived in were pretty much the same. I pull in front and walk over to where Lisa is parking.

"Look," I say, "could I just say something?"

"Sure."

"I'm sorry about this. I let Linda have the farm."

"Forever? To keep?"

"Till she gets her life together."

"It's your farm though. And what about your life?"

"Guess I thought that if one of us was going to end up in a place like this, it might as well be me. I'm the one who can take a hit." I check out the row of trailers. A place like this, you lived much closer together than other people do and there was no pretending anybody was better than you. We were all in the same shit. "Anyway," I say, "I'm sorry."

"Billy," she says, "I'm not here on a beautiful homes tour. Can we go inside?"

"Sure." We walk across to the fence gate and this yelping animal comes running towards me, more than happy to bite the hand that feeds it.

"Who's this?" Lisa asks.

"I guess it's a pet," I say. After thinking it over for a while, I'd retrieved Martha Yeats' dog from the pound two days after the murder. Sappho wasn't my type. I wasn't hers. But now she's running around in circles, all excited. Maybe she misses having a female around, I don't know, but this is a bigger welcome than I ever get.

"Her name's Sappho," I say, deciding not to tell her who Sappho belonged to. I go inside, grab a couple beers and pass one to Lisa, who's sitting on a bench at a picnic table, with a postcard view of the dog pound. I toss a tennis ball against the fence.

"It took me forever to teach that dog how to fetch. Specially from over there. The other side is death row. I think she knows it."

I chuck the ball again. We sit quiet but there is noise all around us, music and television from half a dozen places. No fights tonight, not yet. After a few more tosses Sappho brings the ball back and just sits down with it.

"I guess we can go in now," I say, standing up. "She's done."

"Hey mister," she says. She comes close to me, right up against me and there is no screen door between us like before. "Girls need a little encouragement."

"Sorry," I say. "I'm way out of practice." I put my hands on her waist and pull her towards me.

"Foreplay, it's called."

"Heard of that," I say. My hands come down around her ass and, grown-up as you're supposed to be, there's a point at which you half-expect to get slapped. When she doesn't do that, when she moves in closer, fitting herself right up against me, I realize that I'm not going to get slapped, and right then there are about a dozen places I want to put my hands.

"At this point," Lisa Garner says, "a kiss wouldn't hurt. Could you manage that?"

"Let's see," I say. "I was never much of a good kisser. I wind up with a mouthful of nose or an eyebrow, when I fly in the dark."

"No problem," she says. "Start from wherever you land, Billy, and just work your way to where you want your mouth to go."

She lifts up on her toes, moving upwards against me, the whole package rubbing close and I lean down and, sure as shooting, my lips land on her eyebrow and I can feel her laugh and so do I, because no map I've ever seen shows that an eyebrow is an erotic area. But I remember what she said and I find her mouth and it's waiting for me, alright, wet and open.

"That's better," she says. "Another wouldn't hurt."

Now I'm into it, into her, truly, and when we finally break away, we're both kind of shaking, trembling, and this is where, as my wife always told me, I fucked like I ate, fast and furious, finishing what was on my plate in a jiffy, and if I went for seconds, it was over just as quickly then.

"Could we go inside now?" she asks. Side by side, we walk to the back door, which I unlock. We step inside and I turn on the ceiling light. Set foot in a trailer where a guy lives alone, you expect some-thing like a student's room out at the college, dirty laundry, beer cans, pizza boxes and—added attraction—a sinkful of dirty dishes, plus a crud-colored bathroom and ten kinds of mold from toilet to towels. But I keep a neat place. The bed is made, the sink is clean, the carpet vacuumed. Where I live, things get put away.

"I'm impressed," she says, moving in for more, not wanting to break contact for long because we're on a definite roll now. "But it's too bright. Turn off that light." The way she says it, she's like a polite girl asking me to turn down a radio, roll up a car window, please. But when I look at her, she's no kid at all, she's a woman taking charge, who knows exactly how she wants things to be. And what she knows is what I'm only just discovering.

I do what she said and we're back together in the middle of the room. In the old days, by this time, Linda and me, one of us would have been in the bathroom and the other reaching for a cigarette.

"Now it's too dark. I like to see what I'm up to. Don't you? Open those windows some, Billy."

"Sure," I say.

I step over to the blinds and turn them so that more light comes in from the outside, a mix of TVs and lamps and now and then some headlights off the road.

"How's that?" I ask.

"A little more."

"Now?"

"Good," she says. "Come back here." I obey and we're together again. I like coming at her, between chores. It feels better, every time.

"What's next?"

"We're definitely getting there. You don't mind my being bossy?"

"Not so far."

"Good. What I'd like you to do now is go over to your dresser and take your clothes off."

"Everything?"

"No way around it, Billy. No getting away from it."

"What'll you be doing?"

"Watching."

"Okay." I step over to the dresser and take off my shirt and I bend down to pull off my shoes.

"Slowly," she says. "I'm enjoying myself."

Alright, I say to myself. I untie my shoes. I'm just going to bed, I tell myself, trying not to get excited. I've had a long day and now it's over. I put my shoes next to each other, take my socks and chuck them into a laundry bag, along with my shirt. I got up early, and I drove Graves up to Wooster, God knows why. She's watching me and that makes me notice the way the light crosses my body, streaks of light created by the blinds. I unbuckle my pants and slip them down over my feet. She's having it both ways, I guess. She's a spy and a peeping Tom, looking in from outside, getting off on that, before stepping into the scene. I step over to the closet and hang up my pants on a hook that's in back of the door. I slip off my boxers and toss them into the hamper. Then I turn towards her, just standing there, facing her. The light that's on me is in back of her so I can't see the look on her face, in her eyes. She's in the dark, fully dressed. I'm buck naked in the light. It feels unfair. Like a police line up. I walk towards her. She can see I'm excited. There's no hiding that: my thing feels like a divining rod in search of an underground spring.

"Fine," she says. "Just fine." I've never felt more naked in my life, more vulnerable, but no complaints from me. I'm just taking orders, anything she says. She puts her hands on me and pulls me in for another kiss. "You're a nice man, Billy."

"Well, thanks." It's good, feeling my skin against her suede jacket, her jeans, my bare foot touching the tips of her leather boots. What the hell are you doing, Billy Hoover? I ask myself.

"You've got a clock by your bed," she says. The digits turn just as I look over there. "It's 11:10. I want you to undress me."

"Yes...you bet..." I reach for the buttons on her suede jacket, buttons that are snap buttons, that would pop open in no time at all. She grabs my hands.

"I want you to take your time," she says. "That's the whole thing. I want you to finish at 11:15. I want you to take five minutes and not a second less."

"Anything you want me to do? In particular?"

"Anything you want," she says. "But slowly."

Slowly. One thing at a time. One piece, one patch, one layer. The suede jacket is first to go, which draws me to the curve of her neck, the tips of her fingers, the backs of her ears. I take my time. I've been wrong all my life. It's all a turn on, every curve, every inch, every opening. Even eyebrows. Then her boots, her socks come off. I discover her feet, the curve of her soles. She watches me take my time. A naked man, undressing her, slowly. It pleases her. What next? Her slacks, I decide. Slowly. Hung in the closet door, right next to mine. Before now, I thought I'd seen her. I could have given a description: brown hair, edging into reddish, pulled back into a bun, and an oval face. I've been around police identi-kits. Green eyes that drill right into you. But now I discover her legs, which are muscular legs, like you see on dancers. Time, I take my time. I take a minute on her legs. She watched me undress and now, the tables are turned but not so, because she was watching me undress her, discover her. Her shirt and bra are next. She's built and that was no surprise, that was what she led with down behind the screen door, and I have no trouble loitering around there and then, all of a sudden she steps back and out of her underwear.

"You did that real well," she says.

Lisa Garner made it all new. Her strategy, at the start, was to pro-long everything, insisting, begging, commanding that I make the most of every step along the way before I moved on and then, when I was inside her, she fended me off again, she pleaded with me not to come, not to, not to, not to, like she wanted to take every second off the clock, hit the basket right at the buzzer and then, all of a sudden, it changed, a new command, the last and most important, Lisa to Billy, yes, yes, yes. Then, before I could reach for a cigarette and light hers, like they do in the movies, when they talk about the war, she had me up again and she was on me, all over me and this was a spring, not a marathon, it was a dash, all out, all the way. Then, not a word more, she was ready to sleep. She fell asleep right off, no tossing and turning, no tarrying at all.

Now, I always have trouble sleeping in a strange place and to tell the truth, I have trouble sleeping with strangers. I even had trouble sleeping with my wife. And I'm wondering about the G-Man's sister, how she got so good at what she did, how she stayed in practice, and what it meant to her, and what I meant to her, all those questions that the woman usually asks but now they came to me. It's amazing how thoughtful you can get after it's too late to make a difference. I stepped over to the window and checked outside. Sappho had started barking, up at the fence, barking at a truck, a truck with an unmistakable ping-ing valve that was moving slowly by. I should have known. It was Tom's truck. He could tell I was home and I wasn't alone. Lisa's S.U.V. was right next to my truck. So he knew what I'd been doing. That was the bad news. The good news was, now I wouldn't have to answer any questions. I looked down at Lisa Garner, naked and defenseless, breath-

ing evenly and sleeping deep, here in a trailer with a guy who was
twenty-four hours and two sex acts away from being a total stranger.
Next thing, hours later it must have been, I sensed her stirring, sitting
up at the edge of the bed. It was early yet, just getting light outside.
When she started to get up, I reached out and held her.

"Don't go," I said.

"I've got to go," she said.

"What about breakfast?"

"Time's up," she answered. "I've got to get a move on. It's eight
o'clock."

"Seven," I said. You wake up often enough at the same place you
can tell what time it is by looking at the strength and angle of the
light. Eight it was. But this was the night that time changed. "Spring
forward, fall back," I said. "You've got an hour. A whole hour."

"Oh hell, Billy," she said, mussing my hair like a mother trying to
make a hurt kid feel better. "Tell you what. I'll split the difference. Half
an hour?"

"Okay," I said.

"To do as you like," she said. Kittenish. "We can have breakfast, just
like you said. We can sit in your backyard and throw the ball to your
dog. That would be nice." She gave me this sly smile, this challenge.

"I want you again," I said. And that was that. I honestly tried to
have it both ways, to talk with her while we were closing in on each
other. "I want to keep seeing you." She stands over me, naked, pulls off
the sheets, all business. She sits, runs her hands down my belly, likes
what she finds. "I want to know you. Where you work and who your
friends are and all..." She likes this new game we're playing. Talk...not
dirty talk, anything but...and sex. "Nice morning," she says. "I guess it'll
warm up later."

Getting right on me, she leans forward, her breasts roving across
my chest, her elbows at my sides, her eyes locked into mine. She's like
a kid reading a book, ready to discuss what she's been reading, only
this kid moves up and down and around on me, hovering, gliding, up
and down, like she might break loose at any minute. And she talks. "So
what's on your mind, Billy Hoover?" Moving slow—rolling, rolling on
the river. "Go on, Billy. Ask me anything. What's on your mind, Billy?"
She knows where my mind is. She looks down at me like a wrestler
pinning an opponent, like a fisherman who hooks a worm, wriggling
away. "I want more of you," I say. "Not just this." Moving. "But this,"

she says, "is what you chose. We could have walked to the public library but oh no..." Just then, she tosses me a little move that about tears the top of my head off. "Yeah, I know but..." Hang on, Billy, I tell myself. I close my eyes, because if I look at her, I'll be a goner, but I can still feel her, and a goner is what I am going to be. It won't be long now: inside I'm screaming. "This isn't about fucking," I say. "Could have fooled me," she says. "I don't want to pry, honest," I say. "I can feel you prying," she counters. She leans forward. "Time's up," she said. She kisses me, stops my mouth with her tongue, so she's in me like I'm in her and down south she turns a few spirals and circles, she's a gyroscope, she loops the loop and now the whole thing gets out of control, out of her control too, we both make it happen or, put it another way, it happens to both of us. She's been directing me, riding me, landing and taking off at will, teasing me trying to talk, but at the end she's as lost as I am and, after the explosion, only for a moment, she rests upon me, like she belongs to me. And, of all the things I could ask, personal and professional, I just put my arms around her, I hug her, which she likes and say "I've got a farm here I'd like to show you some time." And I hear a little gasp of surprise.

"You're a sweet man," she says.

"I'm trying."

"Shitty cop, though."

"Off duty..."

"What are you, Billy? I'm wondering..."

"What am I?"

"You have a farm, that you don't live on. Or plow. You have a wife you're not with anymore. You're sort of a cop, but not really. And a little bit of a student, when you find the time."

"Student..." I think about it. It's something that hadn't occurred to me. "Yeah, maybe that. I'm learning all the time."

Like that the moment's over, the evening, the morning after, the whole thing. As she slips out of bed and away from me, I wonder if we'd ever get this close again.

Another kiss, a quick touch of mouths and she's out the door without looking back. I watch her back out and drive away. I toss Sappho the ball, walk her to the back of the trailer and thank God for the end of daylight savings.

VII.

MARK MAY

It might have been the best day of the year, maples flaming red and yellow, oaks a stubborn brown, the lawns about finished growing but holding onto their darkest green. The college uses these magic times. This was Homecoming Weekend, graduates and current customers and prospectives gathering on this hill and Caroline and I out on the porch at the back of the house, setting up our Sunday breakfast, which is an eastern custom we'd continued in Ohio, even if the bagels were frozen and the paper's the Columbus Dispatch. For the record, our Sunday breakfast followed our Sunday morning love-making, which was a habit we'd resumed. Caroline and I had been doing better lately, I thought. I'd bet even money we'd make it. Then, all of a sudden, the church bells were ringing, going on and on.

"What's that about?" Caroline asked, coming out with a tray of orange juice and coffee.

"I don't know," I said. There was alarm in the bells; they were more like sirens or air-raid warnings. "I guess we'll find out."

It was a joke, how quickly news traveled in this town. You could start a rumor—a professor on the job market, devil-worshiping on a nearby farm, somebody's house for sale—you could start it by pledging one person to secrecy and just wait for it to boomerang back to you. Just then, Caroline went into her office to take a phone call. She had a whole network of women friends who talked to each other about their careers. These calls never lasted less than an hour. I decided to try grading papers for my writing class:

"They're coming this way", Jessica said defensively, running a finger through her long blonde hair. "Yeah". Megan sighed. Her conscious bothered her. After that night at the lodge. It had started the summer before with Josh.

Punctuation around quotes. Stop coaxing dialogue. Impose a moratorium on the use of flashbacks, until after graduation. I arranged the papers the way army medics sorted battlefield casualties. Triage. The lightly wounded, the serious but treatable, the lost causes ("sucking chest wounds,") whom you sedated and set aside. This, from a paper entitled "The Last Kiss:" *A golden, gibbous moon gilded her body, a wet lunar tongue licking into every curve and crevice, a last loving caress, so beautiful, so much more beautiful, she being dead and all.*

It was like teaching song-writing to people who had never heard music. Sometimes, I cut through these papers like a hot knife through butter, sharp, perceptive, even helpful. Sometime I got impaled by the first paragraph. This was one of those. Words, words, words. We read them, we react to them, we spit them out into the air, we excrete them onto paper. But not this morning. Not with the bells still ringing. Maybe Caroline couldn't hear them, busy on the phone, but they rang for me alright. I pushed the papers aside, stepped out the door and walked towards the village. Crossing in front of the dormitories and proceeding into town, past the bank, I could see the entrance to the main campus surrounded by yellow tape, a crime scene, a sheriff's duty standing guard and—I saw as I came closer—a television reporter in front of the deputy, glancing over her notes while a cameraman scooted in front. One minute she was a harassed woman, checking what might have been a shopping list. When the camera was on, so was she, brightly lit performer.

"Traditional. Beautiful. Conservative. Selective. Expensive. These are words that commonly describe this liberal arts college. But today, new words apply. Murdered. Shocked. Frightened. The violent deaths of two students at the gates of the college..."

She gestured behind her and the camera followed along, through the gates, along the path, towards the bench and the grass beyond.

"Entering classes march—'process'—down this mile-long path when college begins. Four years later, they take that walk again, at graduation. A lovely ritual at a proud school. But this year, Amy Plimpton and Jarrett Stark will not be among them..."

Plimpton and Stark! I stood there, dumbstruck, while the woman went on, tying these murders to the death of Professor Martha Yeats last August. Suddenly, the deaths were something that happened to me, in my life, in my neighborhood. I stood there, shuddering, on the edge of tears. I was a walk-on, a part-timer, a spousal hire, but I'd gone two-for-two on dead students. Both mine. I stood there, picturing people I would never see again. Kids. College students. Kids who couldn't be counted on to deliver and...this was something I'd only just learned...also didn't always disappoint. Just when you wrote them off, one at a time or a whole generation, they came through for you. And now, two of them were murdered. Both of them were mine. Mine. I claimed them now, now more than ever, and they claimed me. I remembered the way Amy Plimpton curled her finger in her hair, while I was lecturing, like she was turning a fork in a plate of spaghetti, I told her. An English major, a New Yorker with a patina of Manhattan sophistication, an air of grown-up familiarity and no particular aptitude for literary study, Amy acted as though college was something to get through as agreeably as possible. She appreciated good work when she saw it and—unlike some English majors—actually liked to read. It would be nice, she thought, to get A's, if only it weren't such work. Still, she dropped by my office regularly, not conniving for a paper extension or "kissing butt for a B." It was because she thought of herself as an adult; she liked being around grown-ups.

"Hey, Professor May," she'd say, leaning in my door, reluctant to put out a cigarette before coming inside. "How's it?"

"Come on in, kiddo," I'd say. It was a relief dealing with someone who didn't want to go to graduate school or get published.

"You busy?"

"Molding young lives."

"I bet you could use a break," she'd say. She'd sit down and—have I made this clear yet?—on a campus where an unusual number of women were prematurely matronly, Amy was food for my paper-grading eyes. She was lean and willowy, a sports car on a parking lot filled with trucks and utility vehicles.

"So what's it like being married to a provost?" she'd ask, with a directness that made me laugh. "Is it like Margaret Thatcher and...uh...Dennis?"

"Nope."

"You show her your poetry?" She reached into her bag and pulled out a copy of my book. "I'd ask you to sign it but it feels like brown-nosing. Maybe after graduation."

"The rarer copies are the ones that are not signed," I rejoindered.

"You put yourself down," she said.

"Just beating the world to the punch," I countered. "Have you read any of that stuff?"

"I've looked at them," she said, leaving it at that. Amy Plimpton was one of those students who believed that it wasn't necessary to read the poems, if you just could get to know the poet. English professors offer literature as a criticism of life. To Amy it was a poor substitute for it; literature was ribbons and wrapping paper around a present. "So answer me, Professor. You show your wife your poems?"

"I'm not sure the marriage could take it."

"Oh..."

"You pictured me reading to her in bed?"

"You never tried it?"

"I didn't say that," I tried. I couldn't resist adding a line. "I said, I never tried it with her."

"Oh..." Every now and then it dawns upon our students: professors have lives. Have pasts. What we are now, we have not always been. How startled they are, when they see us at an airport—he travels! he flies! he leaves Ohio!

"So how's class going?" I asked. "From where you sit?"

Amy always positioned herself in the front row. She played with me. Sometimes she gazed out the window dreamily, at other times she stared at me, stared hard, undressing me with her eyes, whether to torture or caress, I couldn't tell. She had long, tanned legs, toes equally long and graceful, that I couldn't resist studying: she turned sandals into peek-a-boo wear. I pictured her toes in my mouth. Single toes, pairs of toes, whole clusters. I wasn't surprised to learn that Amy had spent her last night in a student's room at the south end of campus. She'd mentioned her love life, using "love" ironically, wriggling her fingers to make imaginary quotation marks. She disparaged college men: "macho, hormonal youths." She spoke of adventures in Manhattan, limos and hotel rooms, an affair with a married man. She wanted me to know this. She was testing me, tempting me, in a good-natured sporting way. As if it were an abstract subject—black holes, tectonic plates—we discussed sex between professors and students. I had told her it was a bad idea. This was a small place and faculty had power over students. Any sex would be an exercise of power. "What if she's not a student of yours?" Amy asked. And then she gamely added a line that won my heart forever. "I could always drop your class." "No difference," I said. Besides, I wanted her to stay. Amy nodded, smiled. "Never say never, Professor.

Never say always." I wondered where she got that. Students often surprise you with what they don't know...and sometimes with what they do. "Never...here," I said. I didn't go further. I didn't tell her that if I'd been a single professor—a wretched prospect in this sexual cul de sac—I'd have been waiting for Amy at the edge of the graduation stage, suitcase packed, tickets in my pocket. "Well, bummer, professor," she'd said when I'd made my position clear.

"Class is going good," she reported. "Some of the women hate Updike. That Rabbit guy's a heel..." Her voice trailed off. These were English majors, mostly. They were, I warned them, students of literature, not consumers of books. But half were kids whose critical pendulum swung from *I-liked-the-book-it-was-well-written-and-I-cared-about-the-characters* to *it-sucked-I-couldn't-relate-to-it*. As for the distinction between an author and the characters—the idea that they weren't the same—that was so much professorial nitpicking. "They dig the class, though," Amy added. "The way you talk and get excited about the books. A lot of people I know are doing the reading. Say, is it true you're kind of on probation this year?"

"Where'd you hear that?" It still surprised me, how word got around. Amy shrugged. She'd heard it. It was in the water, in the air.

"Well," I said. "That was last year. I've reformed. Hadn't you noticed?"

"You're doing terrific now," Amy assured me. A student consumer enjoying a meal well served, entertained by my jokes, my anecdotes and factoids, my enthusiasm and occasional anger. I was on my way to becoming a popular professor, a colorful character. I was grateful to Amy. She wondered about teaching English in Japan and I'd have perjured myself into hell to help her. "In the novel *To Kill a Mockingbird*, by the author Harper Lee many important questions are discussed." That's how her last paper began. Bummer.

In my writing seminar, I resolved to be generous and funny and un-ironic, a brand new me. They were kids after all, they wanted to know about writing, they were taking a chance on something that involved more than memorizing facts and lectures and putting them in an exam book. In going through writing samples, I looked for funny moments, the spots that came to life, the well-turned phrases, here and there. We'd have our good and bad days, we'd be in it together, I'd share my work with them, they'd show theirs to me. This was where I got to know Jarrett Stark, last year's plagiarist-complainant. Caroline had decided to give him a WP—withdrew passing—for the course. He agreed to give me another chance. A fire-eater on paper, in person he was a shy, skittish kid, a total loner. After our first seminar, he trailed me to my office. He said he sensed the other students were laughing at him, he wasn't sure he belonged in the same room with them, he wasn't certain about college either. As a rule, I think you shouldn't be in college unless you want to be. But why are the best students the ones with doubts, while the slugs never dream of leaving?

"I'll be paying off my student loans until I'm thirty," Stark told me. "For what? Up and down the hall from me there are kids who wait until the night before a paper's due to start working. Then they crank out some junk, some total bullshit, and they get a B and some of the kids who've been killing themselves, writing and revising get maybe a B plus..." Then he caught himself. "Not that I care about grades."

"Okay," I said. "What do you care about?"

"You know," he answered, so intensely I wondered if he were making a pass at me. "I want some of what you have..."

"Some of..."

"I want," he corrected himself, "more of it than you have. Understand? What you have and more."

"Which is..."

Without hesitation, he pointed to that spot on the bookshelves, that sacred half inch which accommodated *Mistakes, Corrected,* my book of poems.

"I want some magic," Jarrett said.

"Magic?"

"That's all. All the other stuff I can get cheaper, at other places. On my own, even."

"And...I'm the chosen magician."

"I guess."

"Well then," I said. "Let's give it a try." Next, Jarrett Stark did something that almost never happens between professors and students. He offered me his hand. I paused a second. Then I shook it, sealed the deal. He nodded, his eyes radar-locked on me. It was all a matter of time, only time, that separated Jarrett Stark from me, from T.S. Eliot, from you name it. Only time. He had lots of time, he thought. He dressed in black, he stayed up all night. He wasn't sure if he was writing poetry or prose "or something new." My first assignment was a sense of place essay. The others brought in vignettes set in bars and dormitories. Stark came in with a piece set in genocidal Rwanda,

Hutus slaughtering Tutsi, told from the point of view of a mountain gorilla. He always came in with something different. And I worked with him, worked through the manuscripts he slipped under my office door in the wee hours of the morning, a random scene set on a winter night at a roadhouse outside a military base, during Vietnam. Told—God, Jarrett!—from the point of view of the jukebox. It was easy to make fun of work from a kid, desperate to be different, whose spelling could always be counted upon for a laugh: a sailor coming in from the cold is worried about *penal* frostbite, then spots a bunch of *semen* sitting in the corner. Still, there was something nice going on, a resonance between the songs and the sentiments on the jukebox and the people at the bar, out on the dance floor. The music commented, consoled, prophesied: it did what art did, for people. Now he was dead, killed the same night he dropped the paper off. So there it was: two lives over, two fewer papers to read. A little news, a lot of bad. In the sadness I felt just then, I think, was my discovery that I had a vocation for teaching.

Amy, it turned out, had been making what they call the "walk of shame," which is what happens when a girl spends the night with a hook-up in a dorm at the south end of campus, where the fraternities are housed, gets out of bed early and heads home along Middle Path, cross-eyed and messy-haired and wearing the same things she was wearing the night before. Amy had hooked up with Jordan Matthiessen from Darien, Connecticut. Their last night together was also their first: they didn't know each other all that well but a spooked and shaken Jordan—"I never slept with a dead person before this"— explained that some kids started their senior years with lists they want to get through before they graduate, and we're talking bodies, not books. It's like the game seniors play in spring before they graduate, when they draw names and chase each other all over campus with water pistols, water rifles, eliminating each other one by one, ambushing each other outside of classrooms and dorms, in bathrooms and from behind bushes. *Killer,* it's called. This year a real killer was playing with bullets. One of them found Amy in the back of the head. She was sitting on a bench, waiting for sunrise maybe. When shot, she tumbled forward, onto the gravel path, but the killer must have lifted her back on the bench, displaying Amy the way he'd displayed Martha Yeats. Later I heard people wondering whether he had wanted to dump her right on Warren Niles' doorstep, a hundred feet across the lawn. But he heard someone coming, another student. Maybe the student saw something, maybe he heard something, so he came rushing to help and took a bullet in his chest that stopped him and spun him around and landed him on the wet grass ten feet behind Amy Plimpton. That was Jarrett Stark.

At seven a.m. an early morning jogger, a student's mother, runs down Middle Path from north to south, from the old divinity school to the old fraternity dorm, down an alley of maples and chrysanthemums. She enters campus through the gates, sees the bodies, the shock of one and then the other and she finds out for herself that no, this is not a prank or a protest, not an art or drama project. She screams and screams again and no one seems to hear her. She's wrong. Tom is smoking outside the security building. The minute he hears, he's on his way but meanwhile the woman rushes to the president's house. Warren Niles, an on-and-off sleeper in recent years, comes out in his bathrobe to confront the sobbing jogger. Still in his bathrobe and slippers, the college president crosses the lawn in front of his house, arrives at the bench where two dead students and Tom Hoover are waiting for him. In the distance, sirens home in on the little village, ambulances and state police arriving from all directions and a small cluster of onlookers quickly growing as early birds, the ones who pick up their coffee and their New York Times at the college bookstore, find their way over. Every minute brings more people, more vehicles: cops put barriers in the road, divert traffic and now the word is out, it gets into the dormitories, it runs up and down the halls, room to room, bed to bed, shower to shower and stall to stall and the dorms empty, sleepy-eyed, hungover and bleary kids—the good, the bad and the ugly—as soon as they get close to the gates of the college, they're stunned, they're sobbing, because this is a place where you know, or sort of know, lots of people, two murders touch everyone, and the morning looks different from the morning that was supposed to be, it's blurrier and more shadowed, that kind of hazy change, and now some students have gotten into the steeple of the church, less than fifty yards from where the bodies are being slipped into zip-up bags and the Dean of Students is going into his office to make a pair of phone calls and the cops are telling everyone to go home, it's all over here, and the Dean of Students' phone calls are just two of hundreds that come in and out of town all morning, and add to this those students up at the church, where a student club plays regularly, the chapel chimesters, not just for Sunday services but on Commencement, joyfully ringing, ringing, ringing, and Friday afternoon, clunking away at hard-to-recognize standards like *Hooked on a Feeling* and *Three Times a Lady* and *Alone Again, Naturally*, but now they're just up there pounding away without rhyme or reason, the bells are screaming, and it won't be long now before the jogger woman, showered and dressed, has her station wagon backed up to the door of her daughter's dormitory, moving out her clothes, her books, her mini-refrigerator and stereo and now, an Amish buggy comes up the hill, negotiates its way around the vehicles, this mess of lights and sirens, and a couple of dark-dressed heavy-bodied women start unpacking pies and quilts for sale, not knowing how the world has changed.

That night, the college's main meeting hall was jammed and Caroline needed to identify herself as provost or we'd have been diverted to the fieldhouse, where what proceeded here would be projected. The balcony and main floor were full, students sat in aisles, and no one worried about fire laws. I'd seen full houses before—Jane Smiley, Naomi Wolf—but nothing like this. Those others were celebrations of celebrity, high-priced whistlestops. This was a funeral. All day long, the campus had been a Woodstock of grieving, students standing in circles, silent, students hugging each other, sobbing. Youth was privileged, college kids more privileged than most, so they fell apart when death crashed the party.

Caroline and I got seats in front—vacated, grudgingly, by students—but then Warren Niles spotted her. I saw him first, motioning her towards the stage, already bathed in hot camera light. Caroline didn't notice, she was looking around the auditorium, as if she were counting the house, which was standing room only.

"The president wants you," I said.

"Oh, shit," she said. My wife left, her seat immediately occupied by a short, bald, heavy-set man, the kind who can turn an airplane flight into a torture exercise.

"Hi," he said. "You a professor?"

"Yes," I said, unencouragingly.

"Well, what do you profess?"

"American literature. Fiction writing."

"Hey! You're the man. We should talk…"

"They're starting up there," I said. Someone was moving towards the podium. Dean of Students Herb Sullivan.

"There will be other occasions," he said, "a memorial service. But I think we should begin with a minute of silence." There's something about a crowded hall going silent that's like a suspension of life because life is noise and now all we had was some coughing and sobbing. I studied Caroline. She dressed up the stage, even though she didn't want to be there. She reverently lowered her gaze but, as the silence lengthened, she looked around, right into the camera, tears in her eyes.

"Moment of silence," my neighbor whispered. "He should have said moment. He said minute. A minute is sixty seconds."

I turned away from him. People were noticing. His whisper carried. Did Warren Niles peek my way? I was on plenty of shit lists already. I didn't need this.

"Thank you," Dean Sullivan said.

"Forty-five seconds," my neighbor remarked. "It felt like forever."

"Do you mind?" I said, louder than I should have. People heard me. To make it worse, the guy looked at me and shrugged as if, go figure, I was the source of all the noise.

"Some of you may not know me. I'm Herb Sullivan, Dean of Students. Behind me are our President, Warren Niles..."

Normally, Warren shone at public occasions. He had a trademark smile, congenial and conspiratorial, he combined gravity and mockery, he wore his authority nonchalantly, like an out-of-style sports coat that was too comfortable to discard. But not tonight.

"...and Provost Caroline Ives. And Special Agent Sherwood Graves of the Bureau of Criminal Investigation and Identification."

Graves was an odd one, no doubt about it. A bean pole of a man, you'd think his name was Ichabod, all bones and angles, looking dead pan at the audience of scared kids, worried parents, up-in-arms faculty. He was all business. The college didn't expect much of him. I knew that from Caroline. The Martha Yeats case hadn't gone anywhere and the College hoped Graves would leave before they had to complain. But now the question was moot. The spooky geek from Columbus was going to be with us a while longer.

"This is a sad day," Dean Sullivan continued. "This morning two students were murdered at the gates of the college. Amy Plimpton and Jarrett Stark. Funeral arrangements are incomplete. As details become known, I'll circulate them. Tonight's meeting is to inform you about what has happened, what is planned and how the college will protect itself in days ahead. Mr. Graves will speak first. To be followed by me and by President Niles. Then, we'll answer questions. But please remember, there are limits to what any of us can say, at this early point. Mr. Graves?"

Sherwood Graves leaned down into the microphone, not bothering to adjust it. It was as if he didn't expect to be speaking much.

"Evening," he said. Give him that much. He knew better than to say good. He reviewed what had happened, the death of Martha Yeats, still under investigation, and the death of two students that morning, also being investigated. After that, it was all boilerplate: how the full strength of state, county, village and college would be brought to bear until these crimes were solved and the college could return to what he called "normalcy." "Underwhelming," my neighbor said. I couldn't disagree. Did Graves go out of his way to be this dull or did it happen naturally?

Dean Sullivan returned with a list of measures the college was taking—cops patrolling, hot-line for suspicious activity, call any time, operators on duty, students marching in groups at night, escorted walks from library to the dormitory and a virtual ban on activities off the hill. No walks down to the river, no jogging on country roads, no hitchhiking, no fraternity initiations, no midnight runs for food in town. It amounted to a stage of siege, a declaration of martial law, the college contracting, folding in on itself. The question hung in the air, though Dean Sullivan didn't touch it, whether a college that operated like that should operate at all. Then it was Warren Niles' turn.

"This day," he said, "has been a nightmare." He reminded me of an ex-head-of-state, overthrown and brought before a peoples' court, disoriented, bedraggled. Shrunken. "Martha Yeats' death was appalling. But this—the death of a student—of two students—goes beyond that, beyond everything that we have experienced, beyond our worst fears. Our community, our college has been violated. What now? What is to be done?"

The old Warren would have shifted gears then. He'd have a way of saying, yes, there's a problem but we're on our way to solve it. Trust us. Trust me. You might disagree with this or that individual decision but we're doing something. Now he stood there as if he were searching for answers.

"I can't tell you what to do," he admitted. He sounded plaintive. "I don't have that power over you. I don't want it. But I can tell you what I wish. What I hope for. We are being tested, very cruelly. If some of you choose not to take that test, to absent yourself, I would understand. I would accept that. I would hate it. I wouldn't hate you but I would hate it. As I would hate to see a college broken and humbled...everything suspended...our very integrity..."

He faltered then, turning away from the audience, away from the cameras, brushing away tears I guessed. Anyway, it gave me goosebumps.

"He's good. I heard he was a hambone." My next-seat neighbor again.

"Listen," I said. I leaned over. "Shut...the...fuck...up. Have I said anything you don't understand?"

"Jeez, Professor May," he said. "You're touchy." It startled me, that he knew my name but before I could follow up, Warren was back speaking.

"Integrity..." Warren said. "Integrity... integrity... integrity." Chanted like a mantra. Was he losing it in front of us? Would someone lead him offstage? "Integer...to see an integer become a cipher...zero, nothing...is more than I can bear. I suggest we proceed. All of us together. Faculty, students, administration, community. That we endure. Not endure. Prevail..."

"Isn't that from Faulkner?" my neighbor conjectured. "Nobel Prize speech?"

"...that we accommodate the severe but necessary rules that Dean Sullivan has just outlined. That, just as we have gathered to learn together, we gather together for protection. And that we continue as a college. That's my suggestion. That we go about our business, not in spite of what has happened but because of it. That is my wish. The other choice is death, for this college. I choose life. Thank you..."

What next? The star of the show had spoken but the audience was still restless. I saw Dean Sullivan lean over to consult with Niles. If he answered at all, it must have been no more than a word. All I could see was a shrug. He checked on Sherwood Graves who shook his head, no, and so it happened that the only person who hadn't spoken was propelled towards the microphone.

"We'll take questions now," Caroline said. "And we'll be as helpful as we can. Questions?"

If you attend lectures and readings at a small liberal arts college, you're familiar with what usually happens after lectures, a mixed and delicate silence in which the audience's desire to show polite interest contends with a collective urge to hit the streets. Only now, things were reversed. The speakers were the ones who wanted closure, the crowd wanted more.

"Any questions?" Caroline repeated, scanning the hall, hoping it was over already. She was like an auctioneer: going, going, gone. Then the hands started going up and she was dead meat.

"Yes?" Caroline said, pointing to a woman I knew from the library, Miranda Simmons. A poet and a sort of friend. We'd agreed that we'd never attend each others' campus readings. As a result, we got along nicely.

"This is for Mr...is it...Grave?"

"Graves," he said. "Plural."

"Well, that's my question. We've had three deaths. So tell me, are we talking about one murderer? Or two? Or three?"

Graves shook his head, as if this were a question he knew was coming. He thought it over for a little while. A little too long for Miranda.

"Sir," she resumed. "It's not like I'm asking you to answer if you don't know. But if you do..."

Graves nodded. "I understand your question. And your concern..."

"Then answer it!" someone shouted from the back and now it was clear that everything that happened so far hadn't worked, Warren's speech included.

"Here's your answer," Graves said. "Ballistic tests on the bullets we recovered today...and we recovered them both...are preliminary. I have to be cautious. I'll just say that unless things change...and I doubt they will..." He paused. Now he'd committed himself. He glanced out at the audience, sensing he was one second away from changing the way people looked at themselves and this place forever. "...there's nothing inconsistent with the conclusion that the bullets were fired from the same weapon." He stopped and let it sink in: I could picture car doors being locked all over town, houses bolted, people looking over their shoulders. "The same weapon," he repeated.

"Are you saying...are you saying what I think you're saying?" Miranda pressed.

"Yes."

"Then why don't you say it?"

"A serial killer. Alright? The same shooter...for Martha Yeats as well as the two students we lost today."

You could feel the shock pass across the room. Serial. Serial killer. Serial code. Movie serial: *Perils of Pauline*. Daytime serial: *Days of Our Lives*. Serial killer: Boston Strangler. Ted Bundy. Here.

"I'm Hartley Fuller," the history chair announced. "I've been teaching here for fifteen years. I appreciate President Niles' concern that the college go about its business as usual. But isn't there a point at which caring for an institution has to be matched by consideration for individual lives? You can hire more security officers and install phones and patrol the streets. But how long can a college go on that way?"

"I'll second that," someone shouted, not waiting to be recognized. "My name's Howard Parrish. I've got two daughters at this college. I'm paying $50,000 a year to send them here and, let me be clear, so far I've been well satisfied. So much so I serve on the Parents' Advisory Council. I've sponsored college get-togethers back in Lake Bluff. You know me, President Niles."

Warren waved from his chair, nodding regards. Or forgiveness.

"You know I love this place," Parrish said. "And I know you've got a problem. But so do I. I can't gamble my kids' lives, keeping them here while you catch the maniac responsible. I'm sorry if I'm letting you down. But I came here to pick them up and bring them home. Alive."

"Is there a question? Caroline asked. She was trying to control the meeting. But she miscalculated.

"All sorts of questions," Parrish fired back. He'd been forbearing with Warren, tiptoeing around someone in obvious pain. But My Wife, My Provost elicited no such sympathies. "And yes, Mrs. Provost, I know there are things you can't talk about. I hope there are. But here's an easy one. Do you have kids?"

"No," Caroline responded, flushing lightly, and I'll bet she contemplated saying that the students were her children.

"So make it a hypothetical question. If you had kids in college here...would you let them stay?"

"I'd have to think about it," Caroline said.

"Well, thanks, but I've thought about it," Parrish responded and sat back down. Now there was real applause. It had hung in the balance for a while but the verdict was coming in. I could feel the college just draining away.

"Thank you," Caroline said. She pointed to another hand which belonged to a student I didn't know. I could see she was a mess.

"My name is Kim Hetherington and I'm Amy Plimpton's room-mate," she said. "I spent this afternoon packing her clothing and her CDs and stuff in boxes. Just sort of stripping her half of the room down to like bare bed and bare walls. Hopefully, you'll catch some-body. But what I'm wondering is...does anybody know...why us? Why here? Why now? I mean, I know this stuff happens but it's in big places isn't it, like at state universities or in cities? Not here..." She'd held on so far but now she was crying. On stage, no one wanted to speak. It was break down, vapor lock, their sitting in silence while Amy's room-mate stood there. All I could hear, all around the room, was crying.

"If I may," someone said from down in front.

"Yes," Caroline said. "Professor Wright."

"Thank you," the old man said as he moved—with the aid of a cane—to the edge of the stage, turning away from the college administration, facing the audience. I'd seen Wright around, without knowing who he was, but now that the legend had been identified, I took him in: the ancient pinstripe suit, the suspenders, the unex-pected checked flannel shirt open at the collar to expose one of those old-fashioned undershirts, with buttons at the neck. They'd brought him out of retirement—it looked like hibernation—to fill in for Martha Yeats.

"Some of you know me, some of you don't," he began. "I am Hiram Wright. Say it quickly and the name becomes a slogan. Hire-em-right. Known to my enemies as Hire-em-wrong. I've listened carefully and I appreciate that the worthy people on stage are having a difficult time." He had the excuse of his cane for not turning towards the administration, but there was something extra nonchalant in the way he gestured their way over his shoulder, acknowledgment and dis-missal combining in one move. So much for them.

"And if I appreciate their dilemma, I also—more deeply—appre-hend what the people in front of me are going through. These deaths are obscene. They are also—I suspect—gratuitous. Those two students were not killed because of who they were or anything they'd done. Nor—I suspect—was Martha Yeats singled out because of her posi-tions or her politics. I may be wrong. I'm ready to be corrected. Are there any hands behind me? Any stirrings on stage..."

Wright asked his question without turning to check. "No, no," the audience told him. "They're clueless!"

"Well, then, I suspect these people did nothing to earn their deaths. Except for one thing which connects me and you and them. That is...this college, this place. To which we make our way to teach and learn for four years or...in my case...forty...forty years."

He had the audience now. The lights were hot, so he pulled a motley-colored handkerchief out of his pocket to mop his brow and no one stirred.

"Who gets to play him in the movie?" my neighbor asked. I didn't answer but I couldn't help casting the part, thinking about smart, strong fat men, bodies like monuments, tongues like snakes, eyes like hawks. Burl Ives, Jackie Gleason, Orson Welles. All dead. We don't grow them like that anymore. Belushi, Candy, Chris Farley—we lose our fat men early. And we don't teach rhetoric anymore either, those cadences and rhythms, shifting modulations, careful, balanced sentences.

"These three deaths are frightening and tragic. The death of a college is worse. And, when this is over—and it will end, and soon—I predict that we'll find someone hated...all of us. Someone wants to shut the college down. Someone who hates us. Or who loves us. Do you follow me, Miss Hetherington?"

The tear-stained roommate glanced at the professor with the kind of urgent regard you hope students will give you in class. You rarely see looks like that, outside of admissions videos.

"Do you follow me?" Wright asked again.

"I'm trying."

"A college like ours generates strong feelings. Like a parent. Love and hate, you think of them as extremes. Opposites. Way apart. But they're connected, they truly are. They need each other, I sometimes think. They're both a kind of caring. Someone wants to hurt this college. I can't say who or why, whether it will turn out to be something we did that was right or wrong, whether it was by design or accident. I ask myself, could it have been something I did—or failed to do—that inspired this madness? A bad grade I gave someone? Or—just as likely, just as pernicious—a grade too generous? Did I make too much of someone? Or too little?" He took a deep breath. He kept the audience waiting. "But I will not abandon this place. I will remain. I will teach classes on schedule, day and night, for nothing, if need be, to an audience of one. I will keep office hours. Daily, I will proceed from my home on River Road to campus. If the killer wants me, I will be at work or home, on my porch. An easy enough target. Meanwhile, I see some of my students here tonight. I remind those in American History that they have papers due tomorrow. Thank you."

What a gambit, I thought, watching Wright take his time—maybe a little more than usual—to get back to his seat. The applause started slowly, a clap here and there, then it caught and swelled and people were on their feet, a standing ovation for the living legend. The administrators looked at each other. Do what now? Say what? Huh? Then they rose as well, sensing a chance to close the meeting, all of them but Sherwood Graves, who left the stage immediately.

"Thank you for coming," Caroline said, before the audience could sit back down and ask more questions. I didn't want to chat with the guy at my side, so I exited down the aisle away from him, not looking back, and I rushed out through the rear of the building, where a backstage door opened out onto the old college cemetery. There I decided to kill a few minutes on a bench, waiting for the crowd to thin.

Old Wright had his moment, I thought: the grand old man meeting a crisis head on. Good footage. Wright as an I'll-take-my-stand professor, a rare talent, a curmudgeonly breed, a hybrid of local character and national reputation. His kind was rare these days, when a lot of faculty divided between stayers-on who were pumped-up prep school teachers and passers-through who were waiting for that call from Duke.

In evening light, the cemetery looked like the cover illustration of a copy of *Spoon River Anthology* I owned. Row on row of graves, high and low, some mossy and hard-to-read, some newly cut. Settling in a college like this put you in a collective frame of mind. Like it or not, you became part of something, something larger than you were and yet, small enough to know. You thought of *Our Town,* of *Winesburg, Ohio,* of people anchored in—and consumed by—obscure places. I bet Hiram Wright had his place reserved at this cemetery. It was only a question of time, and not much of that. You had to wonder what it felt like, to come to a place and say, this is it, here's where I'll have my career, this is my home forever, there are other places out there, maybe better, but this one is mine. Was it wisdom or cowardice? Copped-out complacency or serene contentment? No more resumé-publishing, no more networking. I was a mover, at least I had been until now, and Caroline was definitely upward and outward bound. So there was always this false suspense—which we called adventure—about where next, and when. Not for Hiram Wright. He'd be here, in among these tombs and markers and one lonely mausoleum, these trees and shadows, with the sun going down across the river.

I thought the pizza place would be empty, students disinclined to double cheese and pitchers of beer on such a night. But they were there, with parents who'd raced to campus. They sat in quiet groups, out of practice in family dynamics. Visiting parents made college students younger: it tamed them for a while. I chose the bar, a lair of locals, working guys I usually avoided because, when they found out you were a professor, they struck up a conversation, testing whether you were a snob or a regular guy. I took a stool at the end of the bar, ordered a beer, and feigned interest in the telecast of a high school football game between Zanesville and Danville, stubby, scrubby kids on a half-lit field. I had the set to myself, until the news-at-ten.

"An Ohio college adds murder to its list of electives," the announcer said. "Coming up next."

"Hi, Professor May." It was the guy I'd sat next to at the meeting.

"Have we met before?" I asked.

"Duncan Kerstetter," he said, offering his hand and sitting down beside me. "I guess we'll be getting to know each other. One on one."

"Is that so?"

"That's still the style here, isn't it? Get to know your professors in and out of class? Rake leaves, take walks, maybe get invited to supper?"

"What?"

"Well, sherry and cheese at least."

"Are you a student?"

"Your student. Didn't they tell you?"

"Who the hell is Duncan Kerstetter?" I asked as soon as I came into the house and before I noticed that Caroline was on the phone. She gave me what amounted to a busy signal: a raised hand that said, back off.

"Shit!" I said, loud enough for whoever was on the other end to hear it. I stalked to the refrigerator for a beer I didn't want, I scraped some skin off my finger before remembering Sam Adams didn't use twist-off caps. I rattled noisily around in a drawer before finding a bottle opener, enough to get a *do-you-mind?* from my wife. I stepped outside, using one hand to pour beer into my mouth and another to unzip and pull out and piss on the lawn. I knew what was going on inside. I'd seen it before, back east, when this college and Caroline were courting. There were phone calls she couldn't take at the office, messages on our answering machine to call "her friend in Ohio."

"Are you drunk?" she asked, when she was done.

"Not drunk," I said. "Pissed. As in pissed off."

"Listen. I'm sorry I forgot to tell you about Duncan Kerstetter." Then she briefed me on this crazy mortician millionaire who had a score to settle with Harry Stribling. He wanted a grade changed. Caroline's bright idea had been to offer Kerstetter an independent study. Stribling's grade wouldn't change but now Kerstetter would finally have a chance to get an A in English. From me. A grateful student would remember the college and a grateful administration would remember me.

"You promised him an A up front? Just for showing up?"

"Of course not. I suggest you start him off with a C plus. Then you can bring him up to an A. A-minus anyway. Happy ending all around."

"Thanks a lot," I said. I thought I'd learned to live with a wife who had more power and money than I did. But this ratcheted things up a notch. Turn your poet trick, Mark. Easier if it had been a B. B's are nothing. But damn it, maybe because all other grades are basically gas-station give-aways, we're kind of fussy with our A's. We might be prostitutes but, when it came to A's, we were prostitutes with principles: you can do what you want down below, honey, but just don't kiss me on the lips.

"Why didn't you offer him an independent study with Hiram Wright? He and Stribling were Butch and Sundance, right?"

"Hiram wouldn't do it."

"Did you ask him?"

"He wouldn't do it. We didn't have to ask."

"And I would. You didn't have to ask."

"It's up to you," she said, in a way that suggested it didn't matter what I thought, the deal was done. "Was there anything else you wanted?"

VIII.
BILLY HOOVER

"Okay," Sherwood Graves said, looking around the Security Office, the afternoon of the double murders. "Who'd want to kill a college?"

The Security Office was jammed, like the first day of a popular class, people sizing each other up, sizing up the teacher too, all these cops and sheriffs, uniforms and suits, wondering what they could get away with, how weird it was going to get. From where I sat, near the back, next to a window, it was plenty weird already. Half an hour after watching Lisa Garner drive out of the trailer court, I drove up the hill and into the middle of craziness. Sunday of homecoming weekend and the highway was blocked, right at the gates of the college. I saw ambulances and sheriff cars and state cruisers and a mobile crime lab and I knew right away there'd been another murder. While Lisa Garner had been visiting me, a killer visited the campus. And now, Sherwood Graves was the man of the hour.

"Who'd want to kill a college?" Graves repeated. Sure, he admitted, it sounded like an odd question. Colleges weren't people, they were institutions, like a church. They went on forever, they were bigger than the people who ran or attended them, they were where past, present, future came together. No one would want to kill a college. So I thought. Then I saw what Graves had been doing, while I was mooning about the G-Man. He'd been preparing for this day. His list of suspects was endless. Check that. The lists. He had lists of every employee who'd been let go or left under a cloud, a secretary messing with petty cash, a maintenance man asleep on a leaf mulcher, a business manager who tangled up accounts. A few years before, there'd been an effort to unionize some of the guys in maintenance. The skilled trades. There'd been pickets out and a lot of e-mail. He had a faculty list.

People who'd been let go. That didn't mean fired. That almost never happened. But there was still a chain of hurt alright, visiting professors who had been denied tenure and tenured professors who vapor-locked at associate professor level and never made full professor.

Then, the students: students who were suspended or asked to withdraw, who had major disciplinary problems or court appearances, who were convicted of felonies after graduation, who asked the college not to contact them. He had a list called "Town and Gown." This was all the beefs that had arisen between college kids and locals, country boys who crashed fraternity parties, college kids who'd acted up in bars or shoplifted the local supermarket, messed up at the all-night diner. There was a local businessman who'd wanted to build a shopping center right outside town and another who'd broken ground for a trailer court at the bottom of the college hill.

The next list was a shocker. Other colleges. That's when I saw it, this look that passed between Sheriff Lingenfelter and one of the suits, the way the sheriff rolled his eyes and another guy kind of shrugged. So this was what he was up to, all this time! Graves was all over the place, advancing on all fronts, looking into everything in general and nothing in particular. It was like you walk into the doctor's office with a knife sticking in your gut and he decides he wants x-rays, MRI, blood, urine and stool samples. Just then I sensed someone looking at me and when I turned I saw Tom, grinning at me, nodding towards Graves and rolling his eyes, then winking at me as if we both know better. Hint, hint, nudge, nudge. We shared a secret. We both knew I was pitching the high hard one to G-Man's sister last night. But that was between us, our little secret. Meanwhile, we'd let Graves make a fool out of himself.

"This college is a business and businesses compete," he was saying. "These expensive liberal arts places most of all. Their market's shrinking. Don't take my word for it. Talk to people in admissions. Not what they say about themselves. Listen to them when they talk about that other college up the road. Here. Look at this."

He read from a printed-out e-mail that had been sent to Dean of Admissions Carstairs and forwarded by him to Graves. It was about a phone call an admissions officer at another college had made to California, to parents of a girl who was considering our college and his. Had the parents heard what was happening at our college? Terrible news and everyone hoped the culprit would be caught, but in the meantime, how safe could any parent feel, sending their kid to our place? Especially with a place waiting at a school that was, by golly, just as good.

"I rest my case," Graves said.

When the meeting was over, a few people stayed behind, talking to Graves and most of the others just filed out, some shaking their head, a lot like after that first class of Hiram Wright's. This was Professor Graves' seminar, that he'd been wanting to teach forever. And I was enrolled. Our texts were these lists, text and syllabus all in one. Extra credit if you caught the killer.

"Hey, Billy," Tom called out to me. He'd been in the Graves meeting, so he must have been the first out the door. Now he was sitting on a bench at the side of the building, the smokers' bench, taking in some autumn sun. "Sit down with me," he said.

I walked over and plopped down next to him.

"So," he said. "Are we having fun yet?"

I shrugged, I wondered if he was ragging me about being with Lisa last night. Turned out I was wrong.

"Why am I not surprised?" he said. "That was his whole idea...sit around and wait till another one happened..."

I couldn't argue with that. Martha Yeats was just the start. And who knew where the end was?

"They'll get someone, Billy. They'll need to get someone. They won't be fussy."

"Any idea who?"

"Anybody. Push comes to shove, they won't be particular. They'll just want it over."

Just then, Sherwood Graves stepped out of the building, surrounded by a half dozen lawmen, some in uniform, some suits. He gestured for me to come over.

"Nothing like autumn sun," Tom said. "The way it warms you up on a cold day." He closed his eyes, just sat there soaking it up. "Go get 'em, Billy."

That same afternoon, Graves took over the whole back room of the Security Headquarters, evicting Tom who was moved out front, next to the switchboard operator. I had a desk in the inner sanctum, next to a guy named Wesley Coward, a three hundred pound, junk-food addicted computer guy Graves brought up from Columbus. It turned out Wesley was a hacker, a snoop, a wizard. If you gave him your driver's license, he could come back with your whole life, the medicine in your cabinet, the magazine underneath your bed. Wesley worked mostly with Graves, all of it hush-hush. I was in charge of faculty suspects. That left the list of former students. We needed help with that. By Wednesday morning, my ex-wife was sitting there looking over the list.

"How's it, Billy?" she asked.

"He hired you?"

"You bet. That okay? You don't mind do you?"

"No problem," I said. Linda looked happy to be in an office. Her jeans had a crease, her blue denim shirt looked good, I liked her turquoise necklace too. On the farm, it was old clothes. She'd dressed and, like they say around here, she 'cleaned up good.'

"How's Robert?" I asked.

"There's some good news and some bad news," she answered. "He came back from New York. He packed and left."

"What about that book of his? The Johnny Appleseed thing?"

"Don't hold your breath," she said. We sat there for a minute, me and the woman I was still married to. Ever since she'd left me, ever since I knew her, she could have me with a wiggle of her finger. Until now. When I thought of women now, it was Lisa Garner I pictured, Lisa who drew me on and scared me. I'd thought of her all day long, while I worked for Graves, making phone calls, talking to people about a murderer. And all the time wondering if the murderer and his sister—maybe his partner—weren't a phone call away. That was the call I didn't make.

"Did Graves say how long he'd be needing you?" I asked.

"For the duration," Linda said, wiggling her fingers to show she was quoting someone. A phrase from war movies. "He said he was looking for someone who knew the college and could handle people. What's your specialty around here?"

"Me? I'm a phone guy. Dial 1-800-UNHAPPY. Press #1 for tenure denial, #2 for no promotion, #3 for tenured and promoted but unappreciated. And if you got this kind of non-specific infection, just stay on the line and an operator will get to you."

"Where'd you learn all that?" she asked.

"Graves ran through it," I said. "Some of it I knew already. Mostly, you've got to be willing to lie a little."

"That must come hard for you."

"It's getting easier. Graves trained me. Just yesterday, took a solid hour of his own time. He said I should just get people talking about the college and let him know if they say anything funny."

It wasn't funny. It was a damn good thing we closed the office door, once we started working on the lists, because in no time at all the room got filled with a whole world of hurt. Close the door, this room was where the poison flowed, this was bad news central, this was where the chickens came home to roost, a graveyard, a Bermuda Triangle, a black damn hole. You saw the bad side of everything. Here's me on the phone, Bill, not Billy, Hoover. I was a researcher employed by the college or, if it helped, someone "assigned" by the state to investigate the college. We were interested in the way colleges hired, oriented, promoted, tenured faculty members. Or didn't. "Use the word mentor," Graves suggested. "That's the open sesame these days. Everybody needs a mentor."

Marshall Thackeray was one of the college's first black hires. In the music department. Tenure track. So far as I could tell, he'd had it made, our Jackie Robinson. But after a while, he'd withdrawn, stayed at home, "recused himself." After a year, he resigned. That, roughly, is what I knew, from the provost's file. But it felt strange, calling someone up, offering a kind of reunion they weren't looking for. These were smart, troubled people and the hardest part of it was pretending that the college remembered them, the college cared, the college wanted to hear their thoughts, share their pain. It wasn't an obscene phone call but it was in the neighborhood.

There was a long silence out in California, after I said where I was calling from, but I could hear a kid rattling around in the background. More silence after I explained how I was looking into mentoring. When Marshall Thackeray spoke, he was cautious, he was choosing his words carefully.

"Did you get a fair shake? Looking back?"

"You mean did I leave feeling angry? Rejected? Hurt?"

"Well...yes."

"Enough to come back and kill someone?"

So much for my researcher impersonation. Now it was my turn to be silent. And ashamed.

"We get newspapers out here, Mr. Hoover. And television. Are you a cop?"

"Not really."

"Well, where were you before you started calling up people like me?"

"Campus Security, actually."

"Campus Security! Campus cop?" He laughed. "They've got you doing this?"

"Yeah, it's a hoot alright," I granted. "But you wouldn't laugh if you were here, Mr. Thackeray. Or if you were me. I found one of the bodies. It wasn't so funny."

"Okay. Sorry." After a while. "Am I a suspect?"

"Not really. We're just going through a list of people who left...who came here and changed their mind about the college. Or the college changed its mind about them."

"God, you must be desperate."

"We want to end it."

"Okay. Cross me off your list. I teach at a community college. I'll give you the name and number. I've been teaching three courses all semester. I haven't left the state. I haven't left town. I don't have time to commit a crime."

"Fair enough."

"They wanted me, they wanted a black on the faculty back there, okay? They treated me well, went out of their way. Good people. An A minus faculty, B student body. Better than the other way around, I guess. A good place, a little too high on itself, but good. But I wasn't about to spend my life teaching rich white kids."

"Okay," I said, ready to sign off. "I hoped it worked out for you."

"It did and it didn't. Community college, you get all kinds—the little old ladies, ex-cons, welfare mothers, street kids, undocumented. Three classes, forty in a class, one semester after another. Their skills aren't close to what your kids have. But they're hungry. That's what I missed out there. Difference between something you just do and something you need. Was there anything else you wanted, Mr. Hoover?"

I crossed him off my list. One down. Or was it one up? Marshall Thackeray was a nice guy, over the phone and a call to his dean's office confirmed he was in California all along. At that, it wasn't much of an investigation. He could have gotten someone else to lie for him, could have skipped a class and flown to Ohio. But I had to move on. I talked to a visiting professor who'd been bypassed for a tenure-track position that got filled by another professor's spouse. He was still pissed. "National search, my ass," he said. "It's bullshit. It's like one of those Hollywood talent hunts that eyeball a jillion candidates to play Dorothy in the remake of *The Wizard of Oz* and when it's all over, envelope please, the winner is...by golly, she was here all along...the winner is Tori Spelling!" Another tenure tracker was brusque, when I asked why'd he'd left. "Food and sex," he replied. "Okay? I rest my case." "I lied," said a third. "I said how I loved the small college environment, I loved teaching, I was sure my research would be enriched if it were anchored in classroom teaching, et cetera, et cetera. Well, after three years in the hatchery, I flew the coop. I brought my graduate school professor in for a talk. I saw the place through his eyes. I saw myself. I was gone." Next, a political scientist, denied tenure. "I hadn't thought about the place for years, until the first murder," she said. "It's odd, Mr. Hoover. When you're there, you think it's the center of the world, the universe even. After you leave, hey, it's just a little college in Ohio. It's a place that fools you and deceives itself. It sounds like the place is under attack now. That's crazy." Why crazy, I asked. "Someone's got it wrong," she said. "It's an institution. Institutions don't have feelings. They don't say thank you or I'm sorry, or you were right and I was wrong..." I let her go: she was off to lecture on a cruise ship. But she wasn't done yet. "Institutions don't go around phoning disgruntled employees, asking what it all meant to them and could it have been better. Do they?" "No, ma'am," I told her. "They don't." I don't suppose I fooled more than half the people I called. I'll bet Mr. Graves knew that most of them would see right through me. It didn't matter one bit, what I did, because there was no way he'd let me close to anything he thought was important. That's why he let me chase after G-Man. That and all the rest of it, the phone calls, the records, it was homework. As for Graves, God knows what mattered to him. All I could see was he seemed happier. Sometimes he smiled, sometimes he even hummed a song I couldn't recognize.

"Hey, Billy," Linda said, coming over to where I was sitting. "You working late?"

"Yeah, I've got calls out," I said. "And a call to make."

"So let's eat."

"What if a call comes in?"

"There's answering machines," she said. "And how long did it ever take you to clean a plate?"

"Okay," I said, not sure I was ready for her now.

"You really sweep a girl off her feet," she said, kind of teasing me, but just barely. As a matter of fact, she was looking grim. As soon as we get done ordering food, she reached out for my hand, squeezed hard, like something is wrong.

"He called me," she said. "The G-Man called me."

"When?"

"Friday night." Friday night. The weekend of the killings. The night his sister had me every which way. Homecoming Weekend.

"I pick up the phone," Linda said. "'Is this Linda Thorne?' 'Yes,' I say. 'This is someone out of your past. Guess who.' I say I don't know, then he gets me. 'Sangy Girl,' he says. I go, 'G-Man?' 'I hear you've been asking about me.' I say yes and how I have nice memories of him and I'm half expecting him to say, yeah, well, do you always walk down memory lane with a campus cop at your side? But no, he keeps calling me 'Sangy Girl' and says maybe it's time we had a reunion and I ask when and he says 'next time I'm in the neighborhood...'"

"Next time?"

"Right. Does he get up here much, I ask and he says 'when I'm in striking distance.' On business or pleasure, I ask and he says 'it's all the same to me.' He'll try to let me know but maybe he'll just pop in and surprise me...'"

"Was there any...could you tell if it was a local call?"

"Can't say. It didn't sound long distance to me..." Then she got what I was after. "Oh my God, you think he was here that night the kids got killed...you think..."

"Did you tell Graves?"

"No," she said.

"Why not?"

"Because I'm still rooting for the guy. I don't want it to be him. And I would like to see him again. Even though I'm scared to death. I'm scared, understand? It never bothered me, living in the country, living alone in a farm house, until he called."

I looked at her, I got the cue. This was where I was supposed to say, well, maybe I should move back in, at least until this blows over. But I didn't say it, didn't say anything. I just looked at her because I knew we'd come to the moment that would change things forever.

"Okay, Billy," she said. "You want me to say it? You know you've changed. You're livelier, more thoughtful than you used to be. You read people better. You're more interested. And...more interesting."

"Well, nothing like some time in a trailer court to shape a guy up. That and a ton of rented movies."

"See? That's what I mean. You're faster. You make wisecracks. You went from movies to books to Hiram Wright's class."

"And from parking violations to triple murders. Yeah...All trends are up. And maybe, maybe I'm worth your time now Linda. But I really want the farm back."

"Billy, you can have it back. Of course you can."

"Okay. Good."

"And...me." Soon as I heard it, I knew she'd never forgive me for making her say it.

"I'll just take the farm, thanks."

"What?"

"The farm. That'll do just fine."

"Just the farm?" She couldn't believe me.

"That's all I want," I said. I thought I was being low-key and gentle but this see-saw we were on, if I were down on the ground, that only meant she was up in the air and angry.

"You've found someone else." It didn't sound like a question, so I didn't answer. Silence meant yes. "That..oh, Billy...that girl behind the screen door...that junkyard bitch from Dogpatch...is it her?" Silence again from me. At least I wouldn't say anything I'd regret. "Have you fucked her?" she asked. And answered. "Of course you have. What does courtship amount to for someone like that? Sharing a six pack in the back of a pick-up truck?"

"Don't," I said, raising my hand. "Don't do this."

"She is so..." She stopped and began to lose it. "She is so...unworthy of you."

"Sooner or later, we get what we deserve," I said, reaching for the bill.

"Is that so?" she asked, in an oh-really tone. She had her edge back now.

"You want to make an honest woman of her, right?" Then she snorted. "That'll be the day."

"Okay," I said. "Stop it."

"She'll eat you alive, she'll chew you up and spit you out," she said. "How do you think I got that call in the middle of the night? She told him I was down there. You're making a terrible mistake, Billy."

"Well," I said, "it won't be my first."

She got up and walked out, headed to the office. I stayed behind a while, giving her time to pull herself together. Rejection isn't easy to handle. Well, I knew that. I'd learned it from her.

When I stepped into the office, Linda was gone. I reached for the phone and made the call I'd been avoiding. Knowing for sure, I decided, was better than not knowing. So I got an answering machine which gave me another number. "River Lanes," she said, but it was her, working at a bowling alley.

"It's me," I said. "Trailer court trash."

"Could you narrow it down a little?" she asked.

"It's Billy."

"Hey, Billy. I was wondering how long it would be, before you called me."

"Sorry," I said. "It's been crazy up here. I guess you know why." I didn't know how else to put it. What was I supposed to say? I missed you something awful and by the way could it be your screwed-up-brother is killing folks up here? "I was going to call you..."

"Listen," she said. "I'll be in Columbus tomorrow night."

"What for?"

"State Pharmaceutical Convention. Not the whole shebang, just the planning committee. Back to back meetings all day...So..." She sounded different, normal, perky. None of that heavy, sexy, hit-me-with-your-best-shot challenge I'd heard before. "Tomorrow night is free."

I meet her on the sidewalk, outside a little bungalow in a nice Columbus neighborhood that's called German Village. It's kind of a movie set. Where I come from there are old farm houses with lots of small rooms and there are new houses, ranch houses, that plan for a visit from every living relative on the same day. Here, the houses are no bigger than the shacks on River Road, but there the resemblance ends because these are houses that people worked on. Some are old but kept up, some new and made to look old but it comes out the same and it looks good, I have to admit, everybody all close and sociable, restaurants and bars mixed in with houses. As we walk, we look in windows, peek over fences into backyard gardens, try out a few back alleys. We come to a park with people in it, dog walkers and kids playing and a bench just waiting for us.

"Whose house are you staying at?" I ask. Friend of a friend she says, travels a lot, leaves the key under the doormat. She can have the place whenever she wants it, she says. How often is that? I ask. Whenever she wants to be alone. She likes being in a neighborhood where no one knows her.

"How have you been, Billy?" she asks.

"You told me you heard the news. We lost two students."

"Yes."

"It was the same night you visited," I say. I hate it, but there's no point in dancing around it. She nods, like oh yeah, now I remember fucking your brains out, at least that's what I think she thinks because women like to go into that vague number, like your world-beating night is ho-hum to them.

"I've got an alibi alright," she says. "Question is, do I need one?"

"No," I say. "But your brother might."

She tenses immediately, pulls away, sits forward. Now we aren't such park bench buddies anymore, all comfortable and easy. I've screwed it up and now it feels like one of those end-of-the-affair scenes, conducted in autumn, in fading light, out in the open, in a public place, two people about to walk away forever, closing credits coming up while leaves blow across the sidewalk.

"I told you he didn't do anything," she says. "I guess you didn't believe me."

"Just listen," I say. "The professor who got killed was the professor who wrecked his chances at the college."

"You told me already."

"Those students who got killed that night? The night we were together..." I didn't add, *that night before the morning you were in such a rush to leave.* "Chances are, it was the same weapon that killed the professor."

"It doesn't matter. He's innocent. Period. You've got nothing. Leave it alone, Billy Hoover." She is trembling when she turns to me. "You can believe me or not. It's up to you."

"Ten minutes of his time, talking to me, and he's off the hook. He can move on and God bless him."

"Yeah, right," she says. "It's amazing what you can do to a person in ten minutes." She didn't have to specify: kill them, screw them, make a baby, end a life. "If that's all you came down here for, you can turn right around."

"That's not all I came down here for," I say. "I guess you know that."

She nods and we sit together, saying nothing, letting the minutes pass. It's tense alright. But then, while we're sitting quietly, things change. It feels like something good is taking over. Time out. She smiles at me after a while, takes my hand in hers and rests the two of them on my leg and those things don't just happen by accident.

"So what else is new, up your way?" she asks.

"I'm taking back the farm," I say. "She's moving out."

"Sounds good."

"She works in the same office I do. Hired by the cops."

"Doing what?"

"She's got a list of names. All our less-than-happy-graduates..." Then I stopped myself. "All but one, I mean. I'll take care of him, Lisa. I really will."

"Maybe you will," she says, and it's in a low, quiet non-arguing voice. And right then, right in Schiller Park, is I guess where I fell for her. Don't get me wrong. She's still the hot number behind a screen door, wearing a *fuck-me-I-dare-you* look on her face, so sexy she scares me. At the same time, though, she's like a kid on that park bench. When I lean over to her—she sees me coming, eyes wide open—and tuck a closed fist under her chin, the softest possible uppercut, kissing her, tasting lips and mouth and the littlest bit of tongue, I prolong the kiss the way you do, just daring the world—or the other person—to laugh at you. I close my eyes—a double dare—and after a while I open my eyes, she's staring at me, surprised, amazed, even, as though this woman who's sure as hell done everything has never tried this before.

"You always keep your eyes open?" I ask.

"So I can see what's happening. Seeing is a turn on."

"Well, try closing your eyes. That's a turn-on, too."

"Billy!"

"Come on," I say. I feel like I'm in the back seat of a car, trying to get a girl to lose her bra. "Try it," I say. Amazingly, she does what I tell her. We kiss again and when she opens her eyes, she finds me looking at her.

"You cheated."

At the restaurant, Lisa attracts attention, especially with her coat off, wearing black slacks that might have come off a man's silk suit and a white blouse that isn't too frilly so it's the kind of basic outfit that's

the sexiest thing in the world on the right woman, like a nurse's uniform, which is why nurses show up in lots of porn movies, I figure. As
a hostess leads us across the dining room, I see folks are checking her
out, guys shooting sneaky glances her way and women noticing
because women always notice stuff like that so they act puzzled: you
mean you actually think she's something special?! They question the
guy's taste, act disappointed in him, only it's a no-win situation,
because the no-taste guy who stares at Lisa is the no-taste guy who's
out with her. You can't blame a guy for looking, even if it's rude, like
looking at food that showed up on somebody's plate and wondering,
are you gonna eat at all? Okay if I have a bite?

"So tell me about your farm," she asks, after she orders for us. I'm
not sure whether she's humoring me, like people do, when they know
you're from the country and they wonder about watching corn grow
and riding into town on Saturdays to watch haircuts, but there's such
a thing as having a home and when the home is a farm the stakes get
larger, it's double or nothing in your heart, and when the farm goes
back a hundred years, the stakes get doubled again, all that land and all
that time.

If she'd only just walk around the place with me, I say, maybe she'd
get it. I don't want to build it up too much but there's four hundred
acres, almost half in woods and half of those woods were never cut,
oaks and ash and sycamore and walnut, not just maples, and a stream,
actually two streams that we call runs that meet and go down to the
Kokosing River where there's a quarter mile of frontage and sure,
nobody gets rich farming, but if you own the place to start and have
a day job to give you some kind of salary and medical, you can make
a little money in corn and soya plus there were possibilities I'd
explored, sitting in my trailer, Christmas trees and u-pick raspberries,
and a couple fishing cabins I could put along the river and rent or
maybe loan to friends, not just friends but strangers who might like to
come. Take it all together, I have to admit, it could never match what
I'd make selling to Averill Hayes, who was always telling me what this
or that Florida-bound neighbor had sold out for, $2,000 to $6,000 per
acre. Hayes had always had an eye for land. "Just let me be the first one
you talk to, whenever you're ready," he said.

"And there's the college, too," I say. "That's extra. I'm sitting in on
Hiram Wright now and then and he says he'll tutor me all I want, long
as I like and set me up with other courses, maybe scholarship aid too."

"You're going to be a college guy?"

"Not like most," I say, thinking of the college kids I dealt with, before the murders. "I'm too old. Too poor. But there's a place for people like me who come out of nowhere and don't count for much...There's a place."

"God, Billy," she says, shuddering. "You sound like my brother."

I just nod. Her brother's off-limits, those are the rules.

"They built him up," she says. She's like one of those people you see on television, in a documentary, reflecting on someone famous they used to know, famous and dead, James Dean or somebody. "And they brought him down. I can't forget that."

"Can he?"

"Could you?"

We step outside into a chilly autumn weather, good sleeping weather, people say, but I doubt I'll be getting much sleep tonight and I'm up for it, not only because I want it but because I'm curious, whether I'd get a replay of her first night, fine by me, or something different, a tad kinky. The deep end of the pool, she called it. We walk home slow and quiet, a respectable couple on an old fashioned street, lights shining on cobblestone, wind kicking up leaves, arm in arm, all the way to the little toy house she's staying in.

"This is where we say goodnight," she announces.

"I can't come in?"

"No, Billy, not tonight," she says, her lips on my ears, like she was whispering some sweet nothing, not bye-bye.

"Okay," I say. "Okay, then." A sad step at a time, I walk away from her, back away actually, seeing her in her raincoat, reaching under the doormat for her keys. Not much of a hiding place.

"Hey, Billy." When I turn she's standing in front of the door, which she'd unlocked and just barely opened. "Come on back a sec."

About face. A replay of our first meeting, down on the Ohio River, standing behind that ripped screen door, tempting as could be. Now she was a demure lady in a raincoat. But it was the same pattern: hook the guy, reel him back in. Catch and release. For now.

"I think it's time for you to meet my brother. If that's what you want. Do you want it?"

"Yes, I sure do," I say. But it comes out sounding queer, like I was on a stage, playing to an audience I couldn't see. And, I swear to God, I wondered if the whole night, the walk, the dinner and all hasn't been leading to this minute.

"Alright, then. Maybe you should get to know him. You'll get a call. You won't tell anyone. And you'll come alone. That's the deal, Billy."

"I'll be there," I said.

We worked on Sundays because it was supposed to be an emergency; no telling when the killer would strike again, but Wesley Coward would have worked anyway. The computer spy had nothing else to do, not here, not anywhere, it was all the same to him, no roots in the community, as the parole officers say. He could sit in his chair with a Bob Evans biscuit-and-gravy special congealing on the floor, a Domino's pizza, a Long John Silver fish and chips, but he'd be sailing into a courthouse somewhere, or motor vehicles, into your bank account, your will, your insurance records.

"Yo, Billy," he said when I came in, friendly enough but all attention on his screen.

"Wesley, I got a question. Maybe you can answer it, maybe you can't."

"You want somebody?"

"How'd you know?"

"People always ask me. They see one of those ads on TV, these places that say they'll find somebody, run a search. Army buddy, schoolyard buddy, lost love, where are they now? Just wondering, they say, don't get me wrong, nothing kinky, this isn't *Fatal Attraction*. I'm just...you know...keeping in touch. So who is it?"

"It's a house, actually. A small one, more like a bungalow. Down in Columbus. If I give you the address can you find out who lives in it now? And...if you can...who owns it? Is that sort of thing possible?"

He sat there, shaking his head as if to say, now I know I'm really in the country.

"Billy," he said. "You're taking me back to *Ding Dong School.*"

"Here's the address," I said, handing him the place that Lisa Garner was staying.

"Old girlfriend?"

"New girlfriend."

"Piece of cake," he said. And he got to it. Sometimes, just showing off, he hit the keys of the computer like he was playing a piano, Van Cliburn or somebody. He'd raise his hands up high, he'd look out the windows. I watched over his shoulder, watched him find the neighborhood, sail through property tax records, utility bills. I got more than I expected. The place belonged to Hiram Wright, since the 1960's. The current occupant? Gerald Kurt Garner. When Lisa and I were outside there, saying goodnight, he could have been standing there, just inside the door, listening to me say that when she called me, I would come.

The college was dead, not the way a bar is dead on a slow night, stools empty and the bartender by himself, watching TV and polishing glasses. More like dead dead: the bar is closed, the bottles are gone, the chairs are up on the table, and there's a UPS notice tucked in the door, that nobody cares about. But the lights were on down along the river. No students around Wright's place this late but he wasn't alone. There were always river people around, hanging around the porch, in the kitchen. Down there, what with odd jobs, odd shifts, you could count on one thing. Anytime, day or night, someone would be sleeping and someone would be awake.

"You missed class this morning," Wright said, first thing. Sitting on the porch, a blanket wrapped around him, to protect against the cold.

"Sorry. I can't always be there..."

"That's not what you came about," he said.

"No sir. There's a little house you own in Columbus."

"So I do, Billy."

"Well, I have an idea who lives there. Not that he's there much, lately. I don't know where he is. Not there."

"No, I don't suppose he's much at home these days," Wright said. "You want to know about the house? I've owned it for thirty years. I haven't set foot in the place for fifteen. But there were times before..."

"Kind of a getaway?"

"You could say that, yes. I don't need it much anymore. I'm beyond getting away. And, to answer your question, Garner was in distress some years ago, after Martha Yeats spiked his candidacy here. He needed a place to stay. I let him have the cottage."

"Did he ask you for it?"

"No, not in so many words."

"Did he thank you for it?"

"No."

"Has he visited you here?" Another no. "Have you visited him there?" No again. "Why'd you give him the house?"

"I gave him the house out of friendship. Respect. Guilt. Disappointment. Because I helped create him and I stood by while others destroyed him. Because I missed him. Because I never wanted to see him again."

"Are you afraid of him?"

"Yes and no."

"Give me a break, Professor Wright."

"Sorry." He fell silent. I could have nudged him along but he was still my professor and my father's old friend and when he looked up at me again, he nodded as if to thank me for holding my tongue. "There hasn't been a day in the last dozen years, I haven't wondered about him coming back here. I used to worry more but only because I was younger. Now, at my age, it doesn't matter much. It hardly matters at all. What am I protecting? A matter of months?"

"What you're saying...you're saying you're worried he would come back and kill someone?"

"Yes."

"Who?"

"Why me, of course," Wright said, a little annoyed. "Who else? You don't think I was losing sleep on Martha Yeats' behalf?"

After that, it was time to go. He hooked his hand into my arm and walked me towards the door. "There's something you should know."

Down on the river bank, one of his neighbors slouched in a seat that somebody had taken out of a truck. He was listening to country music on the radio, Hank Williams or someone just like him, singing "Hey, Good Lookin'!"

"I'm not asking for it," Wright said. "But if G-Man comes, I'm ready. I still can't believe the rest of my life will pass, without our meeting one more time."

IX.

WARREN NILES
Night Thoughts of a College President

I didn't know either dead student, so the prospect of attending their funerals made me feel like a hired mourner. In the end, I called both families and asked if there were any particular professors whose names had turned up in phone calls and letters home. And so it came to pass, as they say, that I attended funerals at the Ethical Culture Society on Manhattan's Central Park West and the Founders Methodist in Sherman Courthouse, Ohio, in the company of Mark May. Well, odd things happen on a small campus and even the most obnoxious professor develops a cultish following. Try denying tenure and you'll see. There he was, neatly dressed and apparently sober, in the college car that took us to the airport, then beside me in the plane. I'd expected him to wallop down Bloody Marys on the flight to Newark. He abstained. Polite, reticent, speaking when spoken to. And when necessary. At the funeral service, there was an awkward moment when struck-by-lightning mourners were invited to stand up and remember Amy Plimpton aloud. I looked at him, he looked at me. I nodded and crossed my fingers.

"My name is Mark May," he began. "and this is Warren Niles. Dr. Niles is the president and I am a professor at the college where Amy lived...and died." Pause, rest. "Okay, she wasn't a great student. C plus, B minus tops." Heads turned. What goes on here? Isn't it enough, she got shot on your picture-pretty country club campus? On your watch, Mr. Asshole President, on your own damned lawn? I was about to intervene. This was madness.

"I'll go further," Mark said. "It's as though the mistakes she made were what brought us together, something we shared, so she kept making them. A lot became one word: alot. Conscious and conscience were interchangeable. And as for punctuation, well, let's just say that in Amy's world, apostrophes were unidentified flying objects. You never knew where they came from or where they'd land. I'm almost done and if I linger, it's because these are fond memories. I can't count the times I showed her why hopefully was almost always misplaced at the start of a sentence. I diagrammed sentences in front of her, again and again. Still, Amy said hopefully the way Hawaiians say aloha, meaning, hello, meaning goodbye..." Now he stopped and faltered. He choked up. Had he planned it that way? Was he that good? Make them laugh, make them cry? He was doing both at once. Doing it to himself, besides.

"She was the sort of student who made me question whether it was worth my time, being a college professor," he continued. "Whether the things that mattered to me—books, ideas, ironies, paradoxes, the rest of it—would matter to her. Not a great student. I read her last paper last night. I had to laugh. I hope for Amy's sake there are spellcheckers in heaven. But a great, great kid. Whom I am going to miss forever. I don't know if I changed her life. For sure, I didn't save it. But she changed—and maybe she saved mine. I'm a writer and most of the stuff I write is poetry, which means I have to do something else to earn a living. So I teach. This isn't only me, this is every poet in America who isn't born to or married to money. It's inevitable, but that doesn't stop you from hating it. And yourself. When Amy showed up in my class, I was coming off a bad year, wondering whether a teacher had any business being a poet or a poet being a teacher. And Amy saved my life..."

He wasn't so much delivering a eulogy as telling a story. And the story was working. He was around forty, still fit, a head full of curly black hair, a handsome face in which you could just discern the old man he was going to be, the long nose and bushy eyebrows and dimpled jaw that would make him an easy target for caricaturists, if he ever became famous.

"She liked my class," he said. "She read my poems. Well, so she said. She dropped by to talk. She told me something 'grabbed me' or 'passed me by.' She winked and smiled and high-fived me on my good days. She rolled her eyes and made faces on my bad ones. She liked me, more than I liked myself. She thought I was worth knowing. She thought, before I did, that a teacher-poet, a poet-teacher, was a good thing to be. So she saved my life. And…somehow…lost her own. That's the worst that can happen, to her, to you…to me. We can kid about our children, compare them to what we were, once. We can joke about our students, the funny mistakes they make—penmanship, grammar, spelling—going, going, gone—the whole world going to hell. But we cannot…I cannot bear…the loss of her…of…let me just say the name aloud…of Amy Plimpton."

Another rest. Gathering himself for the finale, I supposed. No need for me to speak. I was grateful for that. Also resentful.

"And her life is over," Mark said. "Abruptly. Brutally. That, as Amy herself would say, is 'something I have a hard time wrapping my brain around.' I'd like you to know that, in the end, Amy would have been just fine. She had spirit and humor. She was sly and, in some bottom line way that never shows up in transcripts, she was wise. I wasn't worried about Amy, not one bit. I wish it had been me sitting on a bench that night. Me or…" Now—what nerve!—he gestured my way—"…or him. All I can say is that she was one of those students I expected I'd be hearing from in years ahead. I will miss her. And I won't forget her. Thank you."

Later that day, on the short plane ride back to Columbus, I complimented Mark on the performance he'd given in Manhattan. And I couldn't resist asking him, as one professional speaker to another, whether what he'd said was true. Or, if he had not exactly lied, had he 'pumped it up a little.'

"Christ, Warren, she died with a book of my poetry in her bag," he said. "That's a first, as far as I know." He shook his head and glanced out the window, down at the hazy farmland checkerboard. Natural haze, we tell ourselves, wondering meanwhile if the world isn't wrapping itself in a shroud as it spins through space.

"One of the things I like about a college our size is faculty can get to know students, outside of class," I said. He didn't reply. "Did you get to know her well, outside of class?"

"Sure," he said. "She dropped by all the time."

"How well…how close were you?" Now my intent was clear, even to me. These things happen. At worst, they involve sex and grades, quid pro quo. Sometimes they end a marriage, sometimes they end in marriage. One rule doesn't fit all cases. But if it lands on my desk, I deal harshly, with a predisposition against the faculty member, the presumed adult. Inviting Mark May to confide in me—two gents chatting between funerals—I was angling for a confession that would enable me to reassert myself over him. When you discover quality in another person, it's helpful to acquire an offsetting sense of what is bad; for every positive, a negative—a double entry bookkeeping that keeps accounts in balance.

"Mr. President, are you asking me if I fucked that poor girl whose funeral we just attended?" He took my embarrassed silence for assent. "If so, shame on you. And no."

"Oh," I said, taken aback. "Sorry."

"It was there for me if I wanted it," he continued. "We talked about it, even after she knew it was a no go. She's sitting in my office one afternoon. It was right after school started. Summer weather, still. Humid, hot. I say, 'I've got to go home now and take a nap.' 'You take naps?' she asks. 'Every day,' I say. 'It's why I became a professor, because there aren't too many other jobs in the English-speaking world, allow you to take a nap every afternoon.' 'I love naps too!' she exclaims. 'They're the best! I love my naps. That makes two of us.' I arrange piles of papers on my desk, check e-mail while she waits for me at the door, stretching, yawning luxuriantly. 'Hey, Professor May,' she says. 'In connection with your naps do you ever…get after it?' 'Not lately,' I say. 'Bummer,' she responds as we walk across campus, cutting in back of your so-called cottage. Right then it seemed like the nicest thing in the world and no harm done, if she and I curled up together. I don't know what you think, Warren, if you've got a presidential opinion on this…"

"Chances are, you'd have regretted it later."

"Yeah," he said. "Well, there are a lot of things I've done I regret. Some you know about. There are memories, make me wince. I wake up at night and say, what an asshole…" That word again: the killer's name for me, in my hair like a horsefly buzzing around.

"But at the end of the day," he repeated, "it's the things I didn't do I regret most."

"Amy?"

"Top of the list." We're now on our slow descent to Columbus. "Mr. President? Warren? Do you have a list too? The things you didn't do?"

The second funeral was altogether different, a ceremony in a charmless, metal-roofed rectangle of a church set in an unlandscaped field five miles from the farm where Jarrett Stark lived, until his parents consigned him to our care. At the Ethical Culture Society, Amy Plimpton's mourners were familiar with ceremonies. Jarrett Stark's death stunned a congregation of farmers and small-town shopkeepers. There was shock and anger in the air. They had doubts about colleges like ours and now those doubts were confirmed. To them, the liberal arts were a course in manners, not necessarily good manners. When May and I stepped into the church, heads turned. We were not invited to say anything and, between the lines of other people's remarks, their pointed references to Jarrett's death away from home, I heard accusation. They sent us a student and we returned to them a corpse.

"Tell me about this one," I said after the interment, as I pointed our rental car towards a reception to which Jarrett's grim-faced father had summoned us.

"Jarrett? I'll bet he was the town freak before he left. Long hair. A ring through his eyebrow. Dressed in black from head to toe. Not your 4-H club type."

"A poet?"

"Poetic, anyway," Mark replied. "A good kid, underneath it all. He liked to read and he liked to write. You know something? That... just that... made him special..."

With that, he put his face in his hands. Genuine emotion startles me. I have a hard time with it. "I'm sorry," I said.

"Me too," he said. "I'll miss him. He dropped by my office all the time...to talk about books...get recommendations from me...opinions...and he'd come back wild-eyed after reading what I told him to read—discovering things for the first time, lighting up. Everything he wrote was influenced by the latest book he'd read...but that's okay. He was coming along. He was a work in progress..."

"Was he...talented? Jarrett?"

"It's not the talent, Warren. There's always talent around. The thing is, he wanted it so badly. To be a writer, to be known as a writer." He took a deep breath, stared out the window, stayed quiet for a while. "But, yeah, he could write. He had talent. And...speaking of talent..."

"Yes?"

"And considering the sudden rapport between us..."

I nodded, even as I could feel myself contracting, like a fresh oyster squirted with lemon juice.

"Do you think my wife will ever be a college president?"

I can't say. Three magic words. I could feel them coming. But, having seen Mark May take chances at the Plimpton funeral, I decided to return the favor.

"Not at our place," I said. "It's not about gender. Not about ability, really. It's about the lack of a certain...gravitas."

He nodded, as if that were what he'd expected, possibly hoped, to hear. If he'd pressed me, I'd have expanded on gravitas. Local gravitas. What you missed in Caroline Ives—what college missed—was commitment. Ours was a place that required a commitment that went beyond shrewdness. And Caroline was, at the end of the day, a mercenary.

"Will she be a president anywhere, then?"

"Oh, I suppose. Someplace will want her."

"Shit."

"Which answer did you not like? That she would not be president at our place? Or that she would be president someplace else?"

"Both."

The Stark farm was surrounded by cars and trucks, shining in the afternoon sun. Picnic tablecloths stirred in the breeze and, as we parked, I glimpsed farm wives carrying covered dishes out of the house. We waited at the edge of the party, glancing around for someone to acknowledge us. Eventually, a boy came across the lawn, on someone's orders.

"The other college fellow is over there," he said, pointing to where some men were sitting in folding chairs on the shady side of the house.

"Was anybody else supposed to come?" Mark asked.

"Not that I know of," I said. We wove around picnic tables, past a rock-bordered fish pond, to the men who were gathered at the edge of a horseshoe pit. They weren't playing, but you could tell they wanted to.

"Hey, Mr. President," someone said. It was Billy Hoover, the security officer we'd given Graves to use for errands. "Hi, Billy," I responded. I started to introduce Professor May, but it turned out they'd met. We stood, silent and awkward, around the horseshoe pit. Jarrett's father was there, red-eyed. I felt I was supposed to speak.

"I'd like you all to know," I said, "that Jarrett was a special young man. We thought the world of him. Mark May here was just telling me about his talent. As a poet." I signaled to Mark but he hesitated and missed the opening. Now, as the silence lengthened, I realized that my little elegy hadn't worked at all. A total misfire. They weren't out to produce poets.

"He marched to his own drummer, that's for sure," Billy Hoover said, breaking the silence. "I worked nights a lot and we used to shoot the shit at three in the morning, pardon my expression. Hey, Professor May, what's the name of that character, always went to bed at dawn?"

"Dracula," someone volunteered before Mark could speak. I admit, that was my guess too.

"No, not him. Played music."

"Orpheus," Mark said.

"That's the guy. That was Jarrett. I went into town at three in the morning, he came along. The night watch, we called ourselves. Talked about everything under the sun. And the moon, too."

"He died bravely," I said. "He heard a shot. He saw a fellow student on a bench. He rushed to her aid..."

"I guess," Billy Hoover agreed but I saw a flicker of doubt cross his face, and Mark's as well. I had sounded a little too sure of myself. The official with the official story. What a relief when we were summoned to eat, to feed: corn on the cob, slabs of ham and chicken, macaroni and cheese casseroles, jello rings, salad that involved marshmallows and—it has the force of law in Ohio—leave room for pie. I foresaw correctly that I would be asked to take the first plate: that way everybody could see what I took and how much.

"At least it was over fast," someone said as we neared the tables.

"I guess he never knew what hit him," his father agreed.

"That's the problem," I heard Billy say to Mark. "Neither do we."

Twenty students withdrew from campus—a damaging but not mortal loss—and some of these might return. Since tuition and fees are paid a semester ahead, October withdrawals entail no immediate loss of cash. We worry more that students may not return from Christmas vacation, but time, we tell ourselves, is on our side. It's over, it isn't over. It's over. A maniac landed and killed and moved on. A terrible but transient event at one college, one autumn, a certain time and place. But what a difference a month makes! Except for oaks, the leaves are gone, the fields are vacant, the hills across the river stand out in sharp gray lines. You see further over the land, into the land. Maybe

what happened here was one of those freak conjunctions of geogra-
phy and climate, the sort of timing that churns up El Niño or brings
locusts out of the ground...but it is over now, over because the weather's changed. The place doesn't look the same. Passionate crimes need
heat, don't you see? A killer likes cover. It's over.

Over. Amazingly, college routines assert themselves, job searches
in half a dozen departments. People still want to work here. A tenure
denial going to court. People still want to stay. There's a review of the
college's curriculum, an agony marathon we go through every now
and then, replete with meetings, forums, consultations and this year,
posters which show a group of students, one oriental, one black, two
male, two female, above the headline: WHAT DO WE NEED TO
KNOW? I sympathize with the uncaught student who scrawled WE
NEED TO KNOW WHO KILLED THEM. But doesn't our tenacious
silliness and self-interest suggest that the college is returning to normal patterns? It's over, I tell myself, it's over. All day long, I say it to
myself. But at night, it changes and the worst fears come to me. I
fidget, I pace. Things occur to me. And, one unbearable night, I called
on Averill Hayes.

"Warren," Ave said, as soon as I stepped out of my car. "Welcome."
He was holding a drink. Never drunk but almost always sipping.
"Come on in." I followed him onto the porch, into his gazebo. Not
many nights left for him to sit out here: it was nippy, flannel shirt
weather. I glanced across the lawn, where a deer trail skirted the
woods. Beyond, on the hill, I could see the lights of the college
through the trees.

"Fog rolls in," Ave said, handing me a gin and tonic, "and up there
looks like a ship. You half expect to hear foghorns."

"Listen, Ave," I said, skipping preliminaries. "I had an idea tonight
that I can't let go of. So I need to run it past you."

"Okay."

"Our Mr. Graves says these murders aren't individual crimes. They
are part of an attack on the college. Which of course gives him a
license to review twenty years of God knows what. It's like an autop-
sy on a patient who's still alive."

"He does get into it, I hear."

"He loves it. He's having the time of his life. Ask me who has ben-
efited from these crimes, he tops the list..."

"You don't mean to imply..."

There came an odd silence and all sorts of thoughts were in the air between us. Or perhaps just one thought. Could it be that Sherwood Graves was the killer, returning to avenge himself on the college that destroyed his father? Ave suggested it. Or said it was what I'd suggested. Anyway it was there, hanging in the air, untouchable.

"No," I said. The idea was more than I could deal with. "It's just that he's made a mistake. He jumped from considering individual crimes to considering a crime against the college. He jumped that way...because that's the way he wanted to jump. But he missed something in between. Another individual, another victim."

"That would be you..." Ave surmised. "It sounds...you'll forgive me...egotistical."

"Please," I said. I waited before saying more. I was about to tell him what I hadn't shared with anyone and my confessor was a classic C student, whose undergraduate memories were of copied papers, slept-through classes, doodled blue books. "Let me ask you something, and answer me immediately. No editing, no politeness. Alright?"

He took a drink, walked over to the bar and poured a refill. He gestured to me.

"No, I'm driving."

"Fair's fair, Warren," he says, handing me another gin and tonic. "I guess you can make it home."

"Ready?" I asked.

"As I'll ever be," he said, raising his glass to his lips in a kind of salute.

"Am I..." I leaned forward in my chair to study him closely, watching for a wince, a flush, anything to betray him. "Am I...an ASSHOLE?"

"Jeez—" He bolted in his chair, choked on his drink, which had gone down his windpipe, ice and all, up his nose and out his mouth in a mix of gin and tonic and chopped ice which covered my face like a new aftershave. I pulled a lime wedge out of my pocket and held it towards him. He was laughing now, so was I.

"Asshole? Warren? No, hell no. Listen, we have our bad days. And our off days. But no...So tell me. What is this all about?"

Now I told him. It was easy. Martha Yeats' library card in my bathroom and that first note. *Act of faith,* in lipstick, on my bathroom mirror. And, I pointed out, *act of faith* was no boilerplate phrase that I served up every year. It was part of my departure from prepared text. Someone—how could it not be the murderer?—had heard my speech, then written that hateful note on my bathroom mirror.

"So...you're the man," Ave said when I had finished.

"So I resign. What's another year or two at this point, anyway? You can't say people aren't wondering about me. Is he what he was? Has he already made his contribution? Are his best years behind him? You can't tell me there hasn't been talk. Informed, tentative, off-the-record, et cetera, et cetera. Among the trustees. Not all of them. But some. Including..."

"Me?"

"Yes," I said. Our trustees were...trusting. They liked getting respect in a respectable place. Mostly, they heeded what we told them, their assigned chores, their particular committees. In spite of that, I always knew that, at the end of the day, one of them would come to me. And it would be Averill Hayes.

"Well, hell, Warren. What do you expect?"

"You think I'm past it?"

"It's not fair, I admit. You forget something when you're young, it's because you're distracted. Same thing happens in middle age, you're overworked. Forget something at your age, you're senile. But there's something you've got to remember, Warren."

"What?"

"Till now, you've been very well treated."

I couldn't disagree with that. The worst turmoil of the sixties and early seventies was over when I arrived, and what's more, by the time they got to Ohio, to our campus, they were road-weary and stale—the demonstrations, sit-ins, teach-ins and all. Times had been mostly good, the college had prospered. I'd made a difference in this place, I supposed. So they'd tell me on my way out. But it was no different from the difference a thousand other men might have made.

"Anyway, you can't resign," Ave said. "Not now."

"Of course I can resign. I can resign anytime."

Ave took a deep breath and studied the lights of the college as though he couldn't believe that command of such a ship had been entrusted to the likes of me. When he turned to face me, Hayes had a look I'd seen him aim at others—faculty members at their whiniest—but not at me.

"These murders are the best thing that ever happened to you," he said. "You want to stay a while longer—and you do, Warren, you do—these bodies are your tonic. Elixir. Fountain of Youth. Is there talk about retiring you? There was. Consultation? A certain concern? Yes. An inclination—no, an obligation—to picture this place without you? You bet. You've been here a long time. People take your strengths for granted. Your weaknesses stand out more. The mistakes you've made."

"What mistakes?" Again, I bristled. He held up his hand, like a school crossing guard holding up a pedestrian. Stop it, Warren. Don't do something. Just stand there.

"But you can't go now. The college would be defeated. Cowardly. Unconvinced of the importance of its mission. You'd be joining the twenty students who left. Not the hundreds and hundreds who've stayed."

"Yes, but if I left, they might be safer. If it's about me, if I'm the asshole."

"You're an asshole if you go. 'College president offers self as a sacrificial figure. Message to murderer: kill me not my students! I'll be waiting for you down at Hilton Head. Just aim for the little alligator on my golf shirt!' Please.... Everybody is somebody's asshole. But you're the captain of this ship. Listen, Warren. This college has been here a long time and will be here even longer. It will outlive everyone who is here now, yourself included. It has more resources than you realize, more strength..."

Ave paused a moment and studied me. More resources, he said, and now he waited, watching to see if I understood.

"Oh, hell," he resumed. "I shouldn't have to tell you this. It's not about you. Much as you might wish it were."

It felt like a reprimand. Suddenly Ave Hayes outranked me, Ave Hayes was stronger. Had he just grown or had I diminished? We stood facing each other as if we were both measuring something. Each other, I suppose.

"We have business in front of us, Warren," he said. "Decisions to make." Then he walked me out to the car, clapped me on the shoulder. I nodded gratefully. I turned the key, switched on the headlights and heard the scrunching sound a rich man's driveway makes, raked and even, no pings and pongs, every pebble in place. Behind me, he stood on the porch, watching me drive away. I admired his decisiveness. I'd been like that in my first years. But in recent years, I'd learned that in academe, nothing is ever decided. Every yes and no is provisional, a temporary adjustment, shifting weight on a see-saw.

Driving home, I saw where the river lay just across some floodplain cornfields, hidden in a line of trees. Harry Stribling had written stories about hobos camping out on the doorsteps of the college during the Depression, about a Kristallnacht-traumatized professor arriving by train in the middle of the night, wandering up the hill towards the shining lights, about a country girl—this was in something called "The Mixer"—invited to a fraternity party, plied with drink, attacked from behind while leaning out a window, vomiting. Stribling had his dark side. Dead fifteen years but still around, no doubt about it. He cast a shadow, still, a shadow over the land.

I should have felt better, because of what Ave told me. He'd confirmed that trustees were watching me. But he'd also convinced me that, in this crisis, I was the necessary—or inevitable—president. Captain of the ship. But then, I wondered, was I the captain destined to pilot the college vessel through stormy seas or was I the captain tradition-bound to go down with the ship? "Oh captain, my captain, the fearful trip is done." Whitman's elegy for a dead president.

I turned home at last, speeding up the hill and then my blood froze. I saw some flashing lights and heard a siren—all this a quarter mile from home, so close to being back in the castle that I debated slowly driving home so that the officer would know who I was and behave appropriately. But I pulled to the side. Some local deputies had an attitude towards the college and would cheerfully write me up for resisting arrest, along with speeding and, God forbid, driving under the influence. There might even be a photo: the president walking a chalked line. Further proof that it was all falling apart. I waited behind the wheel while someone stepped out and walked towards me. It was late and I might be lucky, no one coming up the hill at this hour. Everyone in town knew my car. The law walked toward me slowly, while red and blue lights lashed across my face. He paused in back, walked around, shone a flashlight inside. As soon as the beam hit my face, it snapped off.

"Mr. President? You okay? It's Tom Hoover."

"Tom!" I said. "Thank God it's you."

"I thought someone was joyriding in your car. I never figured it was you. Something wrong?"

"No," I said. "I mean, yes. It's—you know how it's been around here. The pressure. I had to get out tonight. So I just took off and drove like a teenager."

"I see you hit the back roads," Tom said, running a finger over the door, covered with dust. "Blowing the carbon off the pistons, huh?"

"Exactly."

"I can't say I blame you. It's a rough patch. We get three times the normal number of calls. Anybody steps on campus is a suspicious character. I hope it's over soon."

"I hope it's over already," I said, leaning forward to turn the key and make my escape, before someone drove by. But Tom Hoover was shrewd. He was doing me a favor, no doubt about it, but I owed him. I hadn't been excused. He leaned down, resting his elbows against the roof, so that his stomach and face filled the space where I'd rolled down the window.

"This Graves guy coming up with anything? My Billy won't even tell me. Ever since Graves turned him into a junior crimestopper, he treats me like a stranger. Not a word about what they're up to."

"I don't know. They're into all sorts of things. We're cooperating but...I don't know."

"What did we do to deserve a guy like Graves?"

"That's a fair question, I'd have to say. Just between us."

"Man takes his time, don't he?"

"He takes *our* time. It's our time I'm worried about."

What had we done to deserve this? What had we done to deserve the murders? Publically, I maintained that what had happened to us might have happened anywhere. That was what I wrote to graduates, what I said to reporters, every day. Much as we praised our uniqueness there were a dozen, a hundred colleges not so different from ours, equally virtuous, equally vulnerable. Yet at night, I wondered whether this was a fate reserved for us, something I should have seen coming. What did we do to deserve the likes of Sherwood Graves? "A guy like that." Tom Hoover's phrase recurred when Graves sat across from me this morning. I'd decided to call him in, invite an update or what I wishfully termed a "progress report."

"Mr. Graves," I began. "This is a crime scene to you. That's what it is, that's all it is. To me, it's a college. And I don't want any more deaths here. This place has been profoundly wounded. Are you here to end its agony? Or study it? I don't want any more deaths here. Should we cancel what's left of this year? What, sir, is your professional opinion? Shall we empty the college?"

"You want a clear conscience, Mr. President," Graves replied, "go ahead and shut her down. Nobody to kill in a ghost town. Shut it down, though, you'll have to shut it down for years. That's like shutting it down forever. Is that what you have in mind?"

"Is that what you're hoping for?" I retorted. "I know you hate this place—and I know why." Anger is a luxury I rarely allow myself. I've permitted myself to seem angry, sometimes, but those are displays, carefully calculated.

"You want us to catch someone, Mr. President," Graves said, "you stay open."

"And risk more funerals?"

"We're working on this every day."

"Is there anything I can do? Anything at all? Anything you can tell me?"

He studied me, as if deciding whether he'd heard anything more than routine politeness. He decided he had.

"Come take a walk, Mr. President," he said. A moment later, we were sitting out on Middle Path. The trees were past peak by now and the leaves that covered the gravel, wet from a shower the night before, were smelling like mulch.

"You're not going to like this," he warned me. "I've been looking into all sorts of things. Maybe you think I take pleasure in this." Now he turned to face me. "Maybe I do. Private pleasure. But my pleasure doesn't come into it, Mr. President. Or your displeasure. Shall I go on?"

"Yes."

"Then talk to me about Averill Hayes."

"Averill Hayes?" It took me a while to recover. There was only one reason Sherwood Graves would ask about Hayes. "Some of this you must know. Mediocre student. Distinguished graduate. Generous donor."

"Friend?"

"Of the college? Of course."

"Of yours?"

"I suppose so," I said, hating myself for my lukewarm response.

"Fine," Graves said. "A generous donor. How generous?"

"I don't have those figures memorized."

"There were large donations in the sixties. About a million, altogether. Real dollars."

"In a time of real need."

"Probably his wife's money. Still..."

"At one point we needed a loan to meet our next payroll. Ave was there for us. He co-signed the note."

"Fine. But in recent years, things have tapered off. Lately, it's been two hundred dollars a year."

"Well, he's retired. Living off assets and pension, I assume."

"What assets? What pension?"

"How would I know? The point is...there's more than money involved here." Beat by beat, Graves was undercutting a man who was at the heart of our college and our community. His agenda was becoming more clear. Red Rudolph's son, the scourge of the college, pointing a finger at a president's—a U.S. president's—descendant. And the maddening part of it was that whatever he found—insider trading, unreported income, unexpected debts—would have nothing to do with three homicides. It was something for Sherwood Graves to do, while the college perished. It was a puzzle he worked on while he sat, dry-eyed, at our deathbed.

"Mr. Graves, I'm going to take a chance on you that you wouldn't take on me. I'm going to confide in you. I'll let you in on a secret. That place of Ave's...and it's quite a place...is ours when he dies. In fact, it's already ours."

"So he takes the tax benefits when he's alive."

"You could look at it that way, I suppose, if you're determined to take the lowest possible view of human motives. I don't."

"Okay, Mr. President," Graves said. "Calm down, just calm down," Graves repeated, sounding like a hypnotist.

"And answer this," Graves said. "Averill Hayes is interested in land around here..."

"If you say so..."

"If you say so. Please, Mr. President. He's been sniffing around for years. More talk than action. He hasn't got the money. He has some options to buy, that's all, options that are running out on him. But he's a dabbler. He doesn't have the money. Or the land. He wants the Stribling Tract. He wants the college to develop the land. Am I right?"

"In a sense..."

"You're measuring your words, Mr. President. Senior Years, Mr. President, the magic word is Senior Years. Want to elaborate?"

So that was it! Senior Years. He'd found out about it and now I had no choice but to describe it. A few years ago, I told him, Ave Hayes took me for a drive. So far as the roads allowed, we drove in circles around the college, a one-mile circle, a five-mile circle, a ten. Ave did most of the talking. The college founder, he said, had purchased eight thousand acres, some to develop, some to sell. These days, we owned fewer than 1,000. But there was a lesson in what the founder had done. And in what Stribling had added. Look around, Ave said, and you saw farms abandoned, brambly untilled fields, falling-down barns, rusted plows, not a mile of road without a for-sale sign. That was the past. And the future? Look again. Trailers and mobile homes, tract subdivisions, horse farms, mini-ranchettes, golf courses. We could be on the side of the losers—those forlorn farms—or the winners. Why leave development to outside investors, why let them take advantage of our presence—"quaint college town, lively cultural life"—while contributing nothing to our survival? Thus: Senior Years. Use the Stribling Tract to build a housing development aimed at the kind of people who loved association with colleges like ours—all the games, concerts, lectures, all our traditions and ceremonies. And the best of it was that these people would be retired. "The Elderhostel Crowd." We could count on them to live graciously, die gratefully and be replaced by more of the same. Senior Years could be a gift that kept on giving, if we could get it past the Trustees.

"Does Mr. Hayes have a financial interest in Senior Years?"

"You mean, has he invested anything?"

"Yes."

"Only hundreds of hours of unpaid labor."

"I see. That's your way of saying he hasn't put any money into the project?"

"One dollar."

"What did a dollar buy him?"

"A participation," I said. "You'll have to ask Willard Thrush. He's on top of the fine points." Just then, I sensed that Graves had already been to Thrush, already knew that Ave's cut would be one-third, which seemed high to Willard and fair to me.

"It doesn't matter," I continued. "Don't you see? Everything that Ave has is ours. It's in his will. The college receives the residue of his estate. In a way, he's not selling Senior Years. He's donating it."

"A proxy for the college. A cut-out," Graves said. "Or is the college a cut-out for him?"

"As you like," I said, shrugging. "We thought it would be better if

he approached landowners. Farmers and such. If word got out the college was aggressively buying land, the market might go up."

"So Ave buys some land. And opens up the Stribling Tract too.
Piggybacks what he's bought and optioned and folds it into the
Stribling Tract."

"That's the idea."

"In the interests of the College."

"Yes."

"Have the trustees approved all this?"

"Not as yet," I said.

"Have they voted on it? Up or down?"

"Not as yet." I hated the way he made me sound, like a corrupt
official on a witness stand. I decided to take control, if I could. "It's sensitive," I said. "The land wasn't given to be developed. Harry Stribling
loved this place—the woods, the fields, the rickety barns. The dirt
roads, those especially, that he sped down on dark nights, driving out
in the country in a state that was—what to call it—like a diver going
deeper, rapture of the deep...the land drew him into it. Whatever else
came and went, he wanted the land to stay. So, until now, there would
have been resistance to any scheme that involved development. And
lots of legal questions. But now that the college is in desperate shape—
I endorse it."

"Okay, then, Mr. President," Graves said, getting off the bench.
"That's all I want." We walked together across the street, towards the
post office. He put a hand on my shoulder as we stepped on the sidewalk. It felt companionable. For a moment I felt reconciled to his presence. I wanted him to appreciate life's complexities.

"I went to two funerals this week," I said in my lonely-at-the-top
tone of voice.

"Oh, my," he said, sounding sympathetic. "Don't think of
them as funerals."

"No?"

"Think of them as groundbreakings."

X.
MARK MAY

After Jarrett Stark's funeral, Billy Hoover got into the habit of dropping by my office, just to "shoot the shit." We both missed Jarrett. I'm safe in saying no one missed him more. We were his late night buddies. Now I was the one who went with Billy for chili. At first he was tongue-tied, talking to a professor. But after a while, he got comfortable. He talked about his father, whom he'd lost in an accident he thought might have been a suicide. The man drove his truck into a river. He talked about his farm, which he wanted back, and his ex-wife, whom he didn't. He talked about Hiram Wright, a living legend, the smartest man for miles around. And he wondered about a famous student, the G-Man, whom he worried might have something to do with the murders, though Graves wasn't buying it. Finally, he mentioned Graves. It took time for him to get around to it, though. He was tense, awkward, shifting in his chair, like a student begging to get into a closed class. Or out.

"This is between us," he finally said. "Okay?"

"Sure."

"You're the only one I'm telling. So if it..."

"Okay," I said.

"You're the only one I can tell," he added. Still, it took a moment before he could bring himself to speak. "Averill Hayes. That's who Graves wants."

"He's the killer?"

"Not the killer," Billy said. "The killer's employer."

"Why?"

"Because that's who Graves wants it to be."

He said until lately he was out of the loop with Graves, kept busy with "window dressing and make work." Graves had promised the press he was "looking everywhere, leaving nothing to chance." Billy was there to make it look that way. But Hayes was who they wanted. It was hard to know what they had on him, Graves and Wesley, the way they whispered. Maybe if they said it out loud, if they shouted it, he still wouldn't understand it. "The likes of me." Income tax records, court proceedings, deeds of ownership, wills and trusts, they were going all through Hayes' affairs. And they'd discovered his wealth was smoke and mirrors. He was leveraged to the hilt. He owed money.

"So what?" I said. "He's like half the rich people in America."

"Right," Billy nodded. "But there are some bank withdrawals he made, right last August. Twenty thousand dollars in cash. Who was he paying?"

"You think he's guilty?"

"Guilty as hell. Of being a president's relative. Of having gone to this college that dumped Graves' dad. Of being a trustee of that college. Of being the kind of guy Graves hates."

"Still," I persisted. "You think he's the wrong man."

"Hey—I'm not the boss."

"But you have some ideas of your own?"

"That no one listens to. That I don't want to listen to myself. That scare me shitless..."

Billy sat there, wanting to say more and worrying that he'd said too much. I could see him decide he didn't want to stay. He got up, opened the office door, stood there a moment.

"I have my guy," he said. "Graves has his. Who isn't a suspect? Is there any end to it?"

"Hang in there," I said, watching him walk down the steps, out across the frozen lawn. I would keep his secret. That, in itself, was a sad change. This used to be a town that gossiped. Secrets were told. Now we carried them around and kept our mouths shut. Everyone had someone they wondered about. Once the unthinkable had happened, we looked at each other in a new way. We knew that there was something we'd missed, in our colleagues and ourselves. Disappointment, anger, rage were suddenly in easy reach. No one was immune, me least of all. I had my own candidate for killer.

"I've got a short shit list," Duncan Kerstetter told me in our first conference. "My father. My first wife. A lawyer or two, naturally. A short list, really. But once you're on it, you're on it forever. And Harry Stribling leads the parade."

Our agreement was that he attend class—and he did so faithfully—and then drop by to chat with me, in a tutorial mode. I kept office hours twice a week, in three-hour segments, and Kerstetter never failed to show. He waited until near the end, so that other students wouldn't have to sit out our conferences. The man loved to talk and, clearly, he wanted his money's worth out of me.

"Anybody would have to ask," he said one night, "considering what we've been reading, do you guys ever come up with a book that shows people winning? That has a happy ending? It's not just your course, professor. I read this so-called canon that people complain about—dead white males, establishment authors, you name it—and I've got to laugh. Poe?! Melville, Thoreau, Crane, Twain, Whitman, throw in dickless Dickinson and I ask you, is there one, just one of those characters that could qualify for a mortgage at any prudent bank? That you'd trust to house-sit your summer place? Hemingway, Faulkner, Baldwin, Wright, that whole crew of drunks and exiles and closet cases? Sinclair Lewis for Christ's sake! And yeah, I can hear it coming, I can hear old Stribling now—*trust the art and not the artist.* Well, he's half right. I don't trust the artist because they're not trustworthy, they build their own short, shitty lives on not being trustworthy, okay?" He stopped to catch his breath. How different from the students who scanned the course syllabus with a yeah-well, whatever. "And this is what they're paying to study, a hundred K and more for four years. You're not even teaching them to write, let's face it. I've seen the papers you put out in the hall after you've graded them. You circle this and underline that, you sprinkle words like *awkward* and *vague* like so much pepperoni on a pizza. You comment on their writing but you don't really teach them how to write..."

"Sometimes, they improve," I demurred, but only mildly because these things happened unpredictably, and, though you took credit, it was hard to know whether it was our doing or would have happened anyway. If the grimmest felon comes out of prison an exemplary human being, is it because prison was an enlightened correctional institution that put him on the right path? Or an appalling hell-hole he never wanted to see again?

"Now, about your course," Kerstetter continued. "You're lively, you're smart, you know a lot about a lot of different things. Trust me, if I were in the same town, I'd look you up once a week, dinner on me, so we could talk about books. But this course. One wrist slicer after another. Willie Stark to Bob Dubois to Gatsby, Bigger to Babbit to Rabbit. Can you mention one happy marriage in all we've read? One trip that isn't a disaster, one business or investment that doesn't bottom up? One trial that's fair, can you give me that, one jury that brings in the right verdict for the right reason? One politician who isn't a whore? Tell me, does anybody have a night of wing-ding sex that does not lead to heartbreak and betrayal? And money, is it ever not ill-gotten, not pissed away? Does it ever fail to corrupt? Anybody ever buy anything that's worth having, at a fair price, huh? Does a business ever just start and struggle and grow and not wind up in feuds and bankruptcy? It happens in life, now and then. But not in books. And another thing. This country I live in is full of monuments and parks and streets named after people who died for—and believed in—their country. Do they ever make it into your serious literature? Has there been just one war that was ever worth fighting, one sacrifice that wasn't for nothing? God, Professor May..."

"Okay, it's a puzzle," I said. "So let me ask you this, Mr. Kerstetter. You read. You read a lot. That's clear."

"So?"

"Why?"

"Why do I read?" He repeated the question, the oldest trick in the book. When they repeat the question before answering, it means you have them. They're stalling, but time won't save them. There are no exceptions to this rule. "Well, there's the language thing," he said.

"The language thing?" I returned. "Kerstetter, please, we're grown ups here."

"Alright, already. I like the way they use words, when they really cook. I like the English they put on the ball, okay? The words, the rhythms, you know, because a new way of saying something is a new way of seeing something..."

"That's it?" I asked.

"No, that's not it, you know it's not. There's places they take you, you can't drive through without thinking of them. Every time I come in from Kennedy Airport, headed through the Bronx, well shit, it's *Bonfire of the Vanities.* And I go down to Key West, it's that sorry-assed Bob DuBois that guy Banks wrote about—you know, the New Hampshire furnace repairman who moves to Florida, talk about a shrewd career move, he could have stayed home and planted orange trees, it would have turned out the same. *Continental Drift,* right? They're all sad. But yeah, what you read, it becomes part of your luggage, when you travel. Takes you places you'll never get to, wouldn't even want to go, takes you to other times too. *Studs Lonigan, Absalom, Absalom, U.S.A.*—Jesus, does that guy cover ground! The characters you forget but the writing...did that guy play a mighty Wurlitzer!"

Kerstetter's enthusiasm embarrassed him but he didn't take it back. If Harry Stribling were still alive, he wouldn't remember Duncan Kerstetter and—if memory were jogged—he'd summon up a game, sincere, inept kid, lost among the acolyte belletrists, the whole thing an awkward episode that should never have happened, like a foreign student drifting into a fraternity party. He'd be wrong though. A lifetime reader was born in that seminar. Lively, excited conversations, passionate debates. Two people caring about books, he was a dream student. And a nightmare. Because he always came back to Stribling. That's when he frightened me.

"Know something?" he asked me. This was out of the blue. We'd been talking about *A Fan's Notes.* More literature-about-losers, I warned. He ignored me. "When the old fart croaked, I felt worse than when my own mother died." Then he fell silent, waiting for something to come. "You know what? I've never told anyone this."

"What?"

"I wished he'd come into one of our shops in the end."

"Your shops?"

"One of our plants. You know? Stribling. For processing." He'd gotten carried away and he knew it. He pictured Harry Stribling on a table, the storyteller of the South, magnolia scented, transfused with embalming fluid, his brains on a scale, the unexercised body, the ironic pouting mouth. Now the college was on the mortuary table. Could you blame me for wondering if he'd put it there? He'd been on campus when Martha Yeats died, when my two students were killed. Was that a coincidence? That moment—that brief, almost accidental confession—was the beginning of my suspicion. If a crime contemplated is a crime committed, he was a killer.

Often, after we finished talking, we'd head out across the campus together, the murder-shadowed campus, with its looming buildings and empty paths and here and there, the blue-lit phones that connected the caller to the security office, glowing now like prayer candles in an empty church. I never declined these walks with Kerstetter, but that didn't stop me from wondering if I weren't strolling with a killer. On one such walk—it might have been our last—I tried to test him.

"I've been wondering," I said, "whether the same impulse that draws you to books, 'loser lit' as you call it, is what drew you back to this college."

"Oh boy," he responded. "This better be good."

"No, listen. After so many years, after lots of success in other places, marriage and kids..."

"Marriages—plural—and kids, professor."

"After all that, you come back here, where you say you were hurt. You deny that nostalgia had anything to do with it. It's the ghost of Harry Stribling. But I think it's the opposite. Know what, Kerstetter? You're a lover."

"Well, shit—"

"Hold the applause. Just think about it."

He did just that, at least for a minute, until we reached the spot where Plimpton and Stark had died.

"Love makes the world go 'round, that it?" he asked. "Love keeps colleges going. You really believe that?"

"I was talking about you."

"You think love's enough? I don't. Could be a coral polyp loves a reef. Could be a dog loves its master, though I've got my doubts. Not people."

He glanced at Amy's bench, at wilted flowers and melted down candles.

"You knew them both, I heard," he said.

"Yeah. She was in our class. You must have noticed her."

"Can't say I did."

"You like it? Like watching the college squirm?"

"It's funny," Kerstetter said. "I looked back on it, the whole place seemed unreal—a liberal arts college, for Christ's sake—hard to believe it was still around. Hey, do they still have spelling bees? Fuller brush men? County fairs?"

"When you decided to come back, when you approached the college to set this up..."

"They didn't play so hard to get, I'll tell you that much. That Thrush guy had been in touch for years. My new best friend."

"But did you know that the place was in trouble? I just want to get the timing straight. Did you contact the college before Professor Yeats was killed? Or after?"

"What are you? A detective?"

"Never mind," I said.

"Before. The murders were an extra." He gave me an odd parting look, as though something had come to mind, an idea he didn't want to share. "Thanks for your time, Professor."

Part Three:
Fall Break

XI.
WARREN NILES
Night Thoughts of a College President

"There was a time when I thought I might move on to another presidency," I confided to Caroline Ives. "There were conversations, after I'd been here a while, conversations with Brown and Princeton. Did you know?"

I must have sounded like an old man owning up to a youthful affair—poet laureate Wordsworth recalling a long-ago love child in France. How like me, Caroline must have thought, to refer to a job application, a failed job application that everybody in town knew about, as a "conversation." A conversation was what we were supposed to be having now, the kind of "periodic mentoring" I'd promised her from the beginning, though it felt odd, under the current circumstances. And yet one look told me that she'd learned all she was going to learn from me. At least she thought she had. She sat in front of me with a blank yellow legal pad in one hand, a motionless pencil in the other, like a student in a gone-dead lecture.

"And I'll tell you," I continued, "even then, with my eye on larger places, I thought, well, it wouldn't be the worst thing in the world to remain here."

"Maybe not," she granted.

"You run a capital funds campaign every ten years," I droned on, "and it's brutal. You're doing it to stay in step with all the other colleges, to stay with the pack. You appeal, promise, placate, wheedle money. And you get it, eventually. Then it's time to leave. That's when you feel the tug. Move on, move up. But then you wonder—at least I wondered—wouldn't I be running another campaign, asking for more money from bigger donors? Is that a promotion? I'd still be pumping gas, more of it, into a bigger tank. But wouldn't it be nice to drive the tanked-up car for a while? Make those shaping decisions that..."

"Oh my God!" The shout came from the outer office, through the door. In burst my secretary, Cindy. "They found another one!"

"What?"

"Right in the village. In the alley, right by Security."

"Dead?" I asked.

Cindy nodded yes. "I park right near there," she sobbed.

I leaned forward in my chair, head down just above my knees, hands on my ears, roughly the position stewardesses tell you to assume in a crash landing. I stayed that way for a while. I heard the secretary crying, I sensed Caroline watching me.

"Faculty or student?" I asked. I wondered if I had a preference.

"A prospective student."

"It couldn't be worse," I said. There was no doubt about it. Martha Yeats' murder was a shocker. The loss of two students was appalling. But a prospective student, a high school kid touring the college! A dead prospective! This was a torpedo below the water line.

"I'm going home," Cindy announced. "In the daylight."

"It's 8:30 in the morning," I reminded her. "You just arrived."

"I've got to go," she said, shaking her head. "It's not safe here." She grabbed her purse and ran out the door, leaving us sitting there. I pictured offices emptying out all over campus and, as it turned out, I wasn't wrong.

"I didn't think we were getting many prospectives this year," Caroline said. "Harry Carstairs said they were few and far between."

Fewer and farther now. This was it. The college had its handful of celebrated graduates. A few professors had national reputations. But famous names weren't what made the college work. Appearance was what counted—the hill, the paths, the one-block village. Make no mistake, this place was admired for its looks, not its brains—its looks and the promise of a good time. Make that a good, safe time. Once we lost that, we lost everything.

I'd never have said what came next, had that prospective student not been murdered. His death, and the likely death of the college, made me weary of the charade I'd been playing with Caroline Ives. It was the worst possible moment to test her. And the best.

"I've been meaning to ask you about your ambitions," I said. "Whether they are here or elsewhere. I wonder if you know."

She nodded, swallowed. It was something she'd thought about but that didn't mean she was ready to answer. So she flushed and floundered, which was out of character for her. And I pressed, which was out of character for me.

"Whether you're the sort of person who aims for the top of the field. Whether you want—or need—to associate yourself with recognized excellence. The Ivy League. A small well-endowed New England college. Or whether you might settle in a place like this. A good place. Sometimes, very good indeed. That was my question. Perhaps it's inappropriate. Shall I withdraw it?"

"If you don't mind."

"Besides, I think I know the answer." I added.

"I think you do," she said, glancing downward, feeling (or feigning) shame.

"I can't blame you," I said. Of course I blamed her. And we both knew it.

"I want you to know," she said, "that I have nothing but the highest regard for you, Warren. And for this place. I'll never regret..."

"That'll do," I said with unexpected decisiveness. Never bullshit a bullshitter, they say.

"Jeremy Alan Gould was college material," Dan Rather said. "An A student from suburban Chicago, student council president, swim team captain. He was courted by state universities with hefty scholarship offers. But Jeremy insisted on visiting this small, liberal arts college in Ohio. His parents had their doubts. But this was his first choice." Rather was standing on Middle Path, at the gates of the college. "And it cost him his life." He strolled down the path, towards the bench just inside the gates. "He was not the first to die here lately."

"These days, debate about the future of higher education—its cost, its purpose—is commonplace," Peter Jennings began. Jennings stayed in New York. "And often, the debate focuses on small liberal arts colleges, proud, private places like..." And now a clip from the college's promotional film, a heart-stopping overhead of the hill in autumn, accommodated by a student chorus singing one of the college's wistful anthems. "Places like this are routinely described as endangered. But tonight there is a college more endangered than most. And more dangerous." Then it was Martha Yeats, then the students. Amy and Jarrett. Next came that prospective student, a body under a rubber blanket, tucked into an ambulance. Then Graves and Niles and Peter Jennings again, how the University of Texas was stunned when Charles Whitman started shooting from that tower. But Whitman was dead at the end of the day, the mourning and healing had already begun. We were smaller, poorer, more isolated. And so, tonight, this picture book campus slept in fear.

I missed Tom Brokaw but later I heard he positioned himself in front of the college's oldest dormitory, which had burned in 1949 with nine students losing their lives. A tragedy this feisty little college had survived, he said. But tonight, with dorms emptying, parents arriving to pull their offspring out of college, the trustees arriving tomorrow for an emergency meeting, it was anybody's guess whether the college would pull through. Brokaw was the only one who noted the college's tuition dependency, that eighty percent of this year's budget derived from this year's tuition.

At first, I wanted to meet the trustees off campus, at one of the places we use for annual retreats. There's an inn in Amish country, just north of here. But Willard Thrush talked me out of it. The word retreat sent the wrong message, he said, and I suppose he was right. There's a room in Ascension Hall, wood-beamed and dark paneled that they say once accommodated the entire faculty, thirty years ago. There, the Trustees awaited me, accompanied by Deans Sullivan and Carstairs, Provost Ives, Vice President Thrush. Photographers snapped our photo as we walked from Stribling to Ascension. The network TV reporters were gone, but local affiliates filled in and there were a dozen newspaper reporters too. Groups of students stood behind them, red-eyed and dumbstruck, some of them with parents, protective and concerned. It was sad, seeing this drizzly November ceremony, right where our colorful rituals took place, this parade across the grass to the room where capitulation awaited.

Dean Sullivan reported that, as of that morning, at least 300 students had already left the college. They drove off in their cars. That was only the first wave though, the ones who fled in a panic, leaving dorm rooms full of books, clothing, stereo equipment, mini-refrigerators. They just took off. This was when Willard Thrush leaned towards me, his lips close to my ear. "Well," he whispered, "I guess we finally solved the student parking problem." An unknown number of parents were arriving to pull their kids out of school, Sullivan continued. We didn't know how many, we wouldn't know until they actually were gone. All we could do, he said, was count the empty rooms, the unserved meals, and make an estimate. The Dean of Students swallowed hard. He was the only one of us who had much contact with students. Each May, he was the heavy favorite to win the trophy seniors awarded to the staff or faculty person who had meant the most to them. "The real honor," Willard Thrush once said, "would be if a Dean of Students got through a career around here without receiving that award." The dean had about finished his report. But, he said, one question wouldn't go away: refunds. We were well past the date when the college was obligated to make even a partial refund on the semester's tuition payments. Someone would have to decide whether the college would adhere to its written policy. Or not. After Sullivan finished, it was Caroline Ives' turn. And she was ready.

"One-third," she said. "I walked the campus yesterday. I walked through most of the buildings in which instruction takes place. I did this at period three, 10:10 to 11 a.m., one of the busiest slots. I'd say that one-third of the classrooms were occupied, sometimes by a handful of students without a professor, sometimes a professor without a student. My guess is that the earlier sessions had fewer than one-third. As for evening seminars..." Her voice trailed off for a moment, while she let her message sink in: no one was showing up for a class at night.

"One more thing," she said. "The question Dean Sullivan raised about tuition payments also arises in regard to faculty contracts. I don't mean to be heartless, but we'll need a decision about continuing payment to faculty who have absented themselves from classrooms and, in some cases, from campus. Granted, of course, these are unusual circumstances. There's no provision I can find for acts of..." She almost said it, she came close enough so that we could fill in the missing word: acts of God. "For acts like this," she said.

Already somber, the mood in the room got darker, heavier. Its very weight pushed me into my chair, determined never to rise and stand again, in this place. Still, there was something else. I noticed it in Willard Thrush's face and in some of the trustees, the business types who regarded tenure, sabbaticals, release time, leave and other faculty perks with skepticism, even contempt. In the midst of all the bad news, a possibility glimmered. End an arrangement of lifetime employment, an arrangement unmatched anywhere, now that Japan had discovered pink slips. Get rid of them all, a total housecleaning, and bring back the ones worth keeping. Bring them back on contracts—one year,

three years, five or seven—and wouldn't that strike a blow for everything we said we esteemed, for teaching, scholarship, community service, for plain civility? Was there a college administration anywhere that
wouldn't take advantage of that opportunity, if they thought they
could get away with it?

"Next year's freshman class?" Dean of Admissions Harry Carstairs
began. "Forget about it." He stood there for a moment, letting the brutal news sink in. "I'm not going to tell you that admitted students are
changing their minds, but that's only because our acceptances don't go
out until March. I can feel it happening, though. In a routine year our
yield is thirty percent. Thirty percent of those we admit end up coming to campus. With this...well...I'd be surprised, as a matter of fact I'd
be suspicious, if anybody came. We're a costly, private liberal arts college. The chance of a student, especially a full-fare student, choosing
to enter..." He waved it away. This was hard to bear. Our Mr. Outside,
our recruiter, was telling us that the game was over.

"I'll say this," Carstairs said. "If the killer is caught tomorrow, if we
can convince ourselves and our clientele that what happened here is
definitely over, then there's a chance we'll survive. As a matter of fact,
flourish. I don't mean to sound cynical but, if you look past these murders, we've had huge publicity these last few days. Our promotion film
on network news, television and newspaper correspondents all over
campus, discovering this college and—make no mistake—liking what
they see. If we can get through this, soon—I mean not in weeks, but
in days—there's hope."

There it was again, that stirring of interest, like a shaft of sunlight
breaking through a skyful of thunderclouds. A brand new faculty,
stripped of attitude and entitlements. And, for Carstairs, the chance
of an all new student body drawn by the publicity the college's
tribulations had generated. How many other colleges made the
evening news?

"About money," Willard Thrush began. "I'll tell you what I
know and then I'll speculate a little. Without this year's tuition, the
college can struggle through in a reduced way, assuming anyone
wants to go to college here. We'll take a hit but we can do it, for
one year. Maybe longer, if we're willing to sell off some assets,
some non-essential assets..."

He held up for a moment, waiting to be interrupted, challenged
even, waiting for someone to say what, pray tell, was or was not essen-

tial. Waiting for someone to ask about our secret treasure, our castle keep, the Stribling Tract. That, of course, would lead to prolonged debate, the soul of the college at stake. What was the land without the college? What was the college without the land? Amazingly, no one asked. Did I see Thrush's eyes meet those of Averill Hayes, in a moment of detente, a sense of ripeness?

"There are people discovering this college every day, wondering about it, pulling for us," Thrush said. "Wealthy players, foundations that like our style, a lot of new friends. Then again, there's someone who hates us. If we get him...or her...soon you might be surprised how strong we come back. If we don't—soon—we're dead. You can't have a college that no one attends. Period." Wealthy players, new friends. I heard it for the third time. Yes, we might hate ourselves in the morning and yes, it wasn't appropriate but there you had it: we contemplated the college's near-death experience with excitement. On the edge of extinction, we glimpsed magical possibilities. We looked around, too polite to say what we were thinking, yet the looks on our faces told the story: do you see what I see? Like a lost Atlantis, no sooner glimpsed than it disappeared. Because then it was my turn to speak.

"I'll open discussion in a moment," I said. "But let me anticipate some questions. I spoke with Mr. Sherwood Graves, the lead investigator, just before coming here. Point one: These killings are serial. Probably the same weapon, almost certainly the same killer. Point two: with the possible exception of the first death, these victims were targets of opportunity, randomly chosen and probably unknown to the killer, certainly unknown to each other. Point three. The killer's target, it becomes more and more clear, is this college."

I felt a stirring in the room, surprise, perplexity, anger. Murders were familiar. Crimes of passion for the most part. Maniacs shooting up elementary schools. But to learn that a school—our school—was itself the target was startling. Not one of them raised a hand to question the logic, or the absurdity, of murdering a college.

"Point four—last," I resumed. "Mr. Graves' investigation continues. But for reasons of—and I quote—'logic and law'—he declines to be more specific or to indicate when we can hope for peace. Alright then, I have a recommendation I must offer. And not just to promote discussion. Let me be clear. I want you to pass it. I am recommending that we close this college..."

I heard a groan through the room. But they'd have groaned if I said, *keep it open.* A groan from the same people, I'd bet. For a moment I just stood there, though not as long as I'd planned to. I thought it was a moment to take note of, a moment that would change things forever. When the moment rolled around, though, I just wanted it to be done, and quickly. Like an execution.

"I am recommending that this semester's tuition be partially refunded," I said, "that our faculty be furloughed at half pay, that other staffers be similarly furloughed, that caretaker and maintenance functions be consolidated into one or two locations, off campus if necessary, and that appropriate security personnel be hired to police and protect the vacant campus. I'm recommending these actions be effective immediately and continue until circumstances permit our reopening."

I said all of that as if it were one long sentence, a recitation, rushing through it, and when it was done I heard people crying. Then hands started going up around the room, voices were raised. "If you think that..." "There was a time when..." "There's a lot more at stake than..." And then: "How's it feel to be this college's last president?"

I was startled. It was a question for a tabloid journalist, a low blow that landed and knocked the breath out of me.

"This is a time when the college needs your wisdom and your courage," I said. "I'm not sure, however, they're the same thing."

"What's that supposed to mean?" someone fired back.

"It means that I wish they'd come together," I answered. "But if it's to be one or the other, coming from you to me, let it be wisdom, please."

"Why not courage?" Another voice. "That's what's in short supply around here. This place is in the hands of the undertaker!"

"Stop it!" Ave Hayes shouted. "Before these deliberations go any further, I think we should excuse those of us who are not trustees."

So we took a ten minute break. I watched my team depart—the Provost, the Deans, and Willard Thrush marching out into a nasty November morning, windy and spitting rain. The leaves were gone and that made the campus seem skeletal.

Ave chaired the meeting, when it resumed. He fielded the howls of pain, declarations of love, professions of faith. And the questions. How did this happen? Why hadn't we seen it coming? Why hadn't someone—anyone—been arrested? What about an appeal for federal aid, a call to the National Guard? After that, they got to specifics, asserting themselves in small ways. They decided against refunding tuition, which would set a dangerous precedent: any malcontent student could fire a few shots, stop worrying about his grades, and live off his tuition refund in Portugal. The faculty wouldn't get half-pay either. Another bad precedent. So, without asking or even saying much, the trustees revised my soft-hearted recommendations. But when it came to the main point, closing the college, there was little they could do. They formed a committee, headed by Ave, to decide if and when we would reopen. They decided, at Ave's suggestion, on a decent interval, an evening of reflection. They would meet the next day to cast a final vote. Nonetheless, some trustees wanted to pull the plug right then. Why spend another night on a campus that wasn't safe?

That was yesterday. Last night, I stayed at home, alone. I called Maine, where my wife urged me to leave, and soon, to join her in our new home. There's no escaping it: she never liked it here. If I were to linger here, I would do so alone. I sat in my study, picturing the years ahead. We would travel, I supposed. There were trustees with places in California and the Caribbean, in New England. And, Averill Hayes had made clear, if the college reopened, there would be a place for me. He did not specify what that place would be. He did not say President. Meanwhile, if Phillip Nolan were "the man without a country," sailing back and forth forever, I could be the president without a college, attending a board meeting here, teaching a course there, writing the occasional op-ed piece on violence in schools or crisis in the liberal arts. This wasn't a tragedy, I told myself, except for the four who died their unlucky deaths. Some people had done pretty well. Before the murders, trustees were contemplating my retirement. Now, as it turned out, I would outlive the college. Wasn't that a kind of victory? Add Caroline Ives to the list of winners, a college president-designate, somewhere in California, so I'd just heard. And Mark May, his drunken writer days long behind him, a serious teacher now. He'd be a hit with students someplace. And Hiram Wright, plucked from exile, suddenly America's favorite grumpy professor. And, as for the college itself, had we ever been better known, more highly regarded than at the hour of our closing?

I turned on the television, to see what the newsmen had made of us. In the absence of hard news—a vote to close the college—they dusted off Hiram Wright, down on the river, where the venerable one treated them to a reprise of what he'd said after the second and third murders.

"Trustees are not the college," Wright told them, sitting on his porch, the image of a cracker-barrel philosopher. "Administrators are not the college. Presidents come and go. Provosts come and go more quickly." Ouch! Someone had tipped him off about Caroline. "Professors and students are the college. And as long as I am here, I will teach whoever comes to me. One or a hundred. I'm a professor. I profess literature and history. The flame that has burned in this far corner of Ohio will flicker. But it will not go out."

At closing, the camera found the network reporter, sitting across from Wright, adoring him. He wrapped it up. "On this night of decision for a small beleaguered college, Hiram Wright summons up Geoffrey Chaucer's famous description of an Oxford clerke. 'And gladly wolde he lerne, and gladly teche.' Wright will be here. About the rest of them—about the college itself—we'll see tomorrow."

So, the last president steps outside his cottage and proceeds down a path lined by photographers, students, faculty members, farmers, janitors. "Sorry, Warren." "Don't do it, Mr. President." "Did you get my e-mail?" Am I Lee at Appomattox? Wainwright at Corregidor? Surely not. Death and imprisonment don't await me, just more invitations than I can open, an infinity of symposia and summer homes, sympathy and condescension all the rest of my days. I try looking around me, taking it all in, its last moments of life, this ancient gravel path—again and again, we fought off those who wanted to pave it—those rows of trees that 19th century presidents planned and planted, they reproach me, those classroom buildings and laboratories, that ugly Greek Revival auditorium, that dining hall with stained glass windows, each celebrating a great work of literature, that got controversial when we became co-educational and people complained that Cristina Rossetti was the only female writer. Those venerable spirits watch me walk these last steps, and, oh, those grassy, carefree lawns, those empty classroom windows, they watch me, from distant dorm windows, open, curtains flapping in the breeze like flags of surrender, windows where students had strung blown up photos of the first three victims from window to window, like fans mark strikeouts at a baseball game, they reproach me. "Give 'em hell, Warren." "Hey, Mr. President, it's not your fault." "About my sabbatical..." They all reproach me, the presidents who were passionate builders, shrewd administrators, zealots, time servers, and the faculty, their anger and talent and pretensions come to rest in a small place, they reproach me, and the students most of all, the ones looking out of ancient yearbooks, rows of young men, all dead, long dead, yet they took comfort in knowing that this place would live on, that other lives would pass through here, they reproach me, for closing this college tips them into oblivion, as much as they remembered this place they equally believed that the place would remember them and this morning is the end of that, the end of all remembering, so they reproach me along with students who'd left yesterday and the day before, the ones who other colleges had courted, sweeping down like vultures, cooing like trauma counselors, sorry about our misfortune and so anxious to accommodate its victims, these students whom murder had turned into refugees, would they talk about this place forever, would they have reunions and if so where, and would they invite me, and would I accept? I look up as I neared Ascension Hall, which had been covered, make that buried, in ivy when I arrived and I had permitted that ivy to be cut away, because the arguments were irrefutable and yet, I remember and miss that tall, brown and green building, that marriage of plant and stone that would be our tomb today. I should never have let them take the ivy.

It was over quickly. No speeches. The time for that was past. No agonizing. We put together a committee—Ave Hayes and three others, with me ex-officio—to monitor the situation and make further recommendations. Then we voted and the only odd thing was that someone requested a secret ballot. A strange idea, I thought, but when we counted the votes, there were twelve votes not to close the college. Then I understood. Later, anyone could claim that they had cast one of those negatives, the same way any member of a firing squad could walk away from the scene of the execution, telling himself that his weapon held a blank. Still, there was something dead on the ground, a person or a college. Close to two centuries of college history had ended and the trustees were in no mood to linger. Some left with hugs—"let me know what you decide...if there's anything I can do." Others departed with no more than a nod. Being a trustee was supposed to be an honor.

Quickly, the college emptied. The dormitories first, of course, those were vacated in three days which were the longest and worst of my life, because the village filled with a false flush of business, cars and campers crowding into parking lots, parking on the grass, just as they did in May and August. This was different—sullen, shoddy. And final. The dining halls closed too, all the cafeteria ladies, dishwashers, cooks gone, the kitchen sealed and fumigated. One by one, our systems shut down, the student health service, the college bookstore. The athletic facilities, the swimming pool and weight room, showers and saunas, locked down. All of this was over in a matter of days. The town would die a slower death, more disorganized. Some people left right away, no one knew whether temporarily or forever. They probably didn't know themselves. Certainly, they didn't tell me. About half the faculty remained in town for various reasons but even the stayers-on were outward bound, except for Hiram Wright. He stayed down on River Road, holding class for a handful of renegade students. The place was as I had never seen it before, this winter emptiness that began in late November and continued past New Years' was terrifying. I felt it most in mid-January, when the campus had always filled up with students returning from vacation. Coming to central Ohio in January, then plodding to class on February's muddy paths, hawking and coughing through classes, inhabiting dormitories where overheated air flushed out the smell of stale food and unwashed clothing, enduring a succession of sunlight deprived days, that surely was the act of faith I'd mentioned in my latest—and last—college address. But now the migration was interrupted, the tide didn't roll in, the river stopped flowing and I faced the reality of our death.

"Closing a college turns out to be a tricky business," Willard Thrush said. Thank God, there was some work to do during the day, reason enough to go to the office. And, like him or not, Thrush was lively as ever.

"Your business is bankrupt," he said, "there's Chapter Seven, Chapter Eleven, depending on how bad it is. There's a bankruptcy judge, bankruptcy law. It happens all the time. But this—as I hardly need to tell you—is a non–profit institution. The State of Ohio is very interested in what we do, how we liquidate, how assets are distributed. You can't hold a yard sale. What we're going to do, Warren, is set up a foundation. That's what Monticello College did, when it died. And Alliance College too."

"I never heard of those places," I said. Not only had I not known that they died, I was unaware they'd ever lived. But I wondered what became of their presidents, whether they told themselves that time changes all things, that nothing lasts forever. Did they inventory all their decisions, asking themselves if anything they did or didn't do might have made a difference? I had. Did they worry. Blame themselves? I had. Did they have correspondence from a killer who labeled them an asshole?

"Those other places were way down the food chain from us," Willard continued. "Still, the precedent is there. They took what they had and formed foundations. They make grants. So that's what we'll do. We need to be able to accept money that's coming in, even though most of what we'll get is contingent on reopening. Which I hope we will. But if we have to sell the college..."

"Sell the college?"

"Well, yes," Willard said. "It never occurred to you?"

"Has it ever happened?"

"That's what I'm saying. There's the places I mentioned. Plus, the Unification Church took over a place in Connecticut. Some Maharishi snapped up Parsons out in Iowa. No such luck for us. The obvious purchaser would be Ohio State, opening a branch here. But that's not in the cards. They're set up in Lima, Mansfield, Newark and Wooster already. And besides, we're not their style."

"So..." I couldn't resist asking what came next. It was like sending in that card to Social Security, that tells you how much you get, if you survive to collect and they're around to pay. "How much are we worth?"

"There's no market, no demand...not for a whole college. Sorry."

"Oh," I said. Sometimes it was amazing that there'd ever been a college here. Maybe that was the way to look at it, improbable from the beginning, lucky to have lasted this long.

"As for the component parts," he resumed. "About a dozen dormitories ranging from 1901 to a few years ago. Miscellaneous bungalows and cottages, your place included. We've got millions of dollars of science labs, those were the big ticket items..."

We'd invested heavily in science in recent years, $30 million just lately. The humanities people weren't pleased, our carving Los Alamos into local woods, while poets and writers holed up in rickety houses, routinely warned to please ease up on using the copy machines.

"We've got faculty and administration offices, we've got athletic buildings, baseball and football fields, maintenance facilities, what else? Oh, the library. I forgot the library. Think anybody needs a library around here?"

"How much?" I pressed.

"And two theaters. Plus tons of beds and dressers, chairs, computers, dining tables, weight room equipment. Trucks and vans and tractors and stuff, a whole fleet."

"How much?" I persisted.

"Prepare yourself…" Willard said.

"I'm ready."

"…for a disappointment. Five million, that seems safe. Ten million, if we're lucky."

"That's incredible. It's…"

"A dime to a dollar? Fifteen cents? I know. But listen, Warren, you've got to wrap your brain around this. If this college isn't sold as a college, and it won't be, its constituent parts depreciate. Because no one's looking for a chemistry lab right here, right now. And the fattest cat in Cleveland or Columbus doesn't want an indoor Olympic-sized swimming pool that has two locker rooms and a basketball court attached."

"Is that all?" I asked. I meant to ask whether he was done now, whether he would soon leave. But Thrush misunderstood me.

"Not quite," he said. "There's the land. A thousand acres under our direct control…that's the hill, the lawns, the athletic fields…"

"Yes…"

"And the Stribling Tract…wherever…whatever it consists of…"

"I always enjoyed not knowing," I said. "Guessing. Hoping, even."

"Well, enjoying, guessing, hoping are out of style right now, Warren. Call the lawyer. The Stribling Tract lawyer. Or have him call me."

"Alright," I said. I could feel him writing me down, marking me off. I was fading. But I had to speak. "Sorry for being so…It's just that…this college we had. I liked the place just fine. I really did. Just lately I've been hearing about all the things that were wrong with it, with us, all the ways we'd gotten weak and soft. Giving faculty what they wanted. Giving in to students. To parents. Weakness and compromise and drift. But Willard, tell me. Wasn't this a good place? At the end of the day?"

"End of the day is where we are, Warren," he cruelly rejoindered.

"But didn't people love it?" I persisted.

"Sure, Warren," he said. "Lots of people loved it." He arose, I stayed in my chair. I saw pity in his face, looking down at me. "I'll see myself out," he said.

These days, the college has become a kind of weekend drive des-
tination, even a tourist attraction. Cars cruise through town, drivers
rolling down their windows to ask where, exactly, the bodies had been
found and what am I doing here, was I around when the shit hit the
fan? There are inquiries about staging a solve-the-mystery weekend
here and some movie producers were interested in location shooting.
I confine myself to home and office during the day, but at night, I
wander. It's not recommended, but I walk, sharing February darkness
with whatever might come out of it and half inviting it to come. I
walk the mothballed campus, the rows of faculty houses, half of them
dark, realtor signs out front, others announcing "for sale by owner," a
circumstance which describes the whole college. Cars sometimes stop
if the driver recognizes me. "Are you alright, Warren?" "Just out walking, Mr. President?" "You sure you're alright?" Every house I pass has
a history. I've been president long enough to have seen them change
hands, sometimes more than once. I remember old professors, the ones
who regarded me with skepticism when I arrived, dead a long time,
most of them. But here, more than most places, the ones who'd pass
on linger in memory for a while, not the books they wrote or didn't
write, but their styles, their quirks, their presences. Now we've come
to the end of that, the end of remembering. Can I be blamed if I felt
old feelings returning? Old regrets? Can I be blamed if at last I drive
down to River Road, to pay my respects to Hiram Wright?

"What's he doing here?" I hear someone ask as soon as I step up
on the porch.

"That'll do for tonight," Wright says, glancing my way. The seminar he's been leading disperses. Reluctantly. A dozen students have
been sitting around a fireplace, books in their hands. This is education
for people who want it, education for free—no charge, no credit,
virtue its own reward. It's like seeing an old dream, a college in the
wilderness. That was how we began.

"Bummer," one student says. He glances at me as he departs. I see
accusation in his eyes. *What did we ever do to deserve that guy?*

"Get yourself what you need, Mr. President," Wright says. I proceed to the back, where a bottle of Calvados awaits me. My bottle, my
glass. When I let him go, I avoided him. It was as though I'd pulled the
trigger on the last of an endangered species, a nationally known scholar content to make his life at a small college, to let the world find its
way to him, not he to it. Then, one day at the post office, he invited

me to visit. Now, at the end of everything, I turn to him.

"How's your little college?" I ask, once I've filled my glass.

"Marvelous," he replies. "We're back to basics, back to beginnings...unenriched, undistracted by..." He gestures in the direction of the hill. "All the other things that grow up around it." That's my life's accomplishment, he dismisses with a nonchalant wave. "They're here because they want to be," he says. "Not because their parents sent them. Not because of the parties or the swimming pool or the easy B's."

"Where do they stay?" I ask.

"Since you locked them out, you mean?"

"Hiram, I had no choice."

"I know that," he replies. "Well, they live down here. With me. With my neighbors. In shacks and huts and trailers. Sleeping in cars, some of them. Others in tents. See what I mean? It's a college in the sticks, in the middle of nowhere. Heartbreaking autumns, killer winters, spring just in the nick of time. Nothing to do but read and write and think. And drink..." With that he nods to the kitchen. I refill his brandy glass. I might defend myself against his criticism but why bother? My college is dead. And, besides, I agree—not in my mind but in my heart—with some of what he is saying. I was a builder president. I built dormitories and labs, an athletic center which Hiram claimed never to have noticed. But even as changes occurred—good changes in some cases, inevitable in others—I liked hearing about that college in the wilderness, a pure small place, without the summer camp counselors and the country club trappings. So I listen, nodding, letting the scorn and nostalgia wash over me, until Hiram notices something wrong.

"What is it, Warren?" he asks, studying me. "You're more hangdog than usual. As a matter of fact, you look awful."

"My wife. She keeps telling me it's time to go. Go to Maine. Where there's a home waiting for me. And the rest of my life. Carefree golden years. This is over she says, this is our past. And everything she says makes sense. And yet...I can't bear it."

"Stay," Hiram says. "I'll keep you company. Really. Stay. Better you than someone else. I enjoy your company. This is a small place but it amazes me, how years pass and you never get to know some of the people you see every day. Beyond a certain point. We assume smallness guarantees intimacy. Yes and no. It also enforces distance. Until just lately, anyway. Lately barriers come down. We're getting to know our-selves better. So, once again: stay. If I can stay, you can stay. See this out."

"Alright," I say. He's told me what I wanted to hear. And then it comes to me, my boldest stroke ever. "But I have a proposition for you."

"What might that be?"

"Don't react right away. Just listen to me."

"I'm listening."

I meant much less than has been imputed to me, naming Hiram Wright our provost. I don't deserve the blame that has been piled upon me, or the credit. I wanted to correct an old wrong, repair a slight to our college's legend. A small courtesy, that's all, the last college president looking for a little company in Stribling Hall. To my surprise, he accepted my offer. A few days later, anoth-er surprise awaited me.

I'm not sure I had ever seen the two of them together, Hiram Wright and Averill Hayes. Granted, there must have been occasions, receptions of some kind, where they shared a crowded space with many others. But they did not consort until now, when they entered unannounced, sat down unasked.

"Have we interrupted anything?" Hiram asked.

"No," I said. "Nothing." What they'd interrupted was my study of a winter sunset, one of those gaudy orange and purple productions that looks like the world is ending, just west of here.

"Well then..." Hiram continued. And stopped, just stopped, which was odd for someone who traded in complete sentences and well-turned paragraphs. It was Ave who continued.

"Look at us," he said. "I guess this is what they mean when they talk about 'the old boys club.' A handful of duffers sitting down."

"Old we certainly are," Hiram agreed. "And boys too."

"Till recently, it would feel like an illegal meeting," Ave said. "The old boys have been pretty well shredded, but...funny thing...the ones who hate the old boys, they're not around right now."

"No," I said. Caroline Ives was gone. And Martha Yeats. And the younger faculty, most of them had melted away. In the end it came, it came back to us. An odd trio, any day. The daunting professor, Wright. Ave, the epitome of the gentleman's C. And me.

"We've talked," Ave said. "And we decided that, if this college stands any chance at all, we have to do something. Act, not react. We can't just..." He gestured at me, or out the window at the sunset, "...sit."

"We want you to call in Sherwood Graves," Hiram said.

"I see," I said. "What shall I tell him, when I call him?"

"Oh, Warren," Ave said. "Just make the damn call. You're the president."

XII.
BILLY HOOVER

Nasty weather. Slushy ground and cement colored skies. But I was sitting out in front of the post office with Sherwood Graves when the end came. He was talking to me about Ave Hayes and where did I think a man like Hayes would go, if he wanted to hire a killer, and I was dumbfounded, wondering what to say to a man who was getting weirder by the minute, when Wesley Coward came over and said the President called and Graves was wanted in Stribling Hall, right now. My guess is that Graves knew what was coming. He stayed quiet a while, nodding to himself. Then he asked me to go with him, for no reason I could see. Maybe he just wanted company.

Looking back, I suppose everybody was surprised when we entered Niles' office. Graves expected Niles but what were Wright and Hayes doing there: president, provost, trustee? And those three were surprised to see me trailing behind. Just a mild surprise. All of them wanting to be thought of as regular guys, they let me stay. I wasn't worth bothering about.

"Sit, Mr. Graves," Ave said, as if bringing a dog to heel. "We decided it was high time we had a talk. Six months after Martha, five or so after the two students, two weeks after that poor high school kid. Time to talk. This is unofficial, confidential, off the record, all of those words. Would you mind talking to us that way, sir?"

"I'm not sure," Graves said, a cautious response which Ave was ready for.

"Not sure. Well, don't talk then. Try listening. Hiram?"

"'Looking everywhere,'" Wright quoted. "'Leaving nothing to chance.' Those are your words—virtually your only words to the press. Fine principles, Mr. Graves. They could guide a scientist to the Nobel

Prize. But you are not a scholar. You are a law official investigating crimes. Can you tell us, sir, about results?"

"I don't report to you," Graves said. "You know that."

"Let me report to you then. It comes to this. Four people are dead and buried, the college closed and still you are here, in residence..."

"Doing what?" Ave added. "On what kind of schedule? Reporting to whom? Waiting for what?"

"World-historical books, pioneering theses have been written in less time," Wright complained. They sounded like a tag team. It was Ave's turn.

"I supposed that, the longer Mr. Graves stayed, the more information he would have," Ave said. "Perhaps I was wrong."

"Not all my students are mendicant scholars," Wright said. "Some are men of affairs, down in Columbus. I've been chatting with them. I shared our concern about the progress—no, excuse me—the status of this investigation."

"I made some phone calls too," Ave said, "and no scholars on my list, that's for sure. But the governor, he's a left-handed relation of my wife's, I don't know if you knew that. I knew that kid before he had a pot to pee in. Anyway, he's concerned. Believe it or not, Graves, he doesn't like the idea of the state's crown jewel of a college going out of business. He seems to think maybe we need a whole new team on this job. Nothing personal..."

Hayes and Wright worked well together. As for Warren, he was about as useful as a referee in a pro wrestling match.

"Now, it's up to you, what you say or don't say," Ave said. "But before we go further, let me ask—it's only fair—is there anything you want to tell us? Anything you've got. Or think you've got?"

"I've got you, Mr. Hayes," Graves said. I guess he couldn't help himself, blurting out like that. It wasn't a professional speaking. It was the dead professor's son. We all just sat there a minute and it was real unpleasant. Warren had his head in his hands. Wright studied Graves, pleasantly, like you smile when your opponent in a card game makes a dumb move. And Ave just nodded, almost like he agreed with what Graves had said.

"You've got me? Care to elaborate?"

"Not now," Graves said. But it was too late for that.

"Now," Ave said. "Right now. I'll tell you what you've got. Connections, relationships, contingencies, privacies. I confess. Want me to say the damning magic words? Here goes. Senior Years."

Graves flinched when Ave mentioned the name. He was supposed to be the one to bring it up, when the time was right.

"That's right," Ave said. "Senior Years. Say it loud, say it proud. My idea and I'm not ashamed to mention it. It's not a criminal enterprise. I have an interest in seeing that the college controls and develops land around the campus. In conjunction with those initiatives, I've been looking into buying land myself. The college would profit. So would I. But...in our moment of greatest need...I think we should consider the Stribling Tract. Does this incriminate me?"

"Your brilliant idea—you never even put it up for a vote," Graves said. "You knew you'd lose. Trustees weren't as keen as you were about condos in the cornfields."

"There was opposition," Niles said. "But there was also some feeling that the project might be revisited at another time."

"And now, it's time," Graves said. "I wonder how that happened?"

"Ah, I see," said Hayes. "So that's my master plan. Murder people to move my project along. Did I tiptoe around the campus executing people myself?"

"I didn't say that," Graves said. "I never dreamed you'd do the dirty work. You'd pay someone. In cash. I've looked at your bank withdrawals."

"Now I get it. Smoking gun evidence. Mysterious cash withdrawals. God, Graves, you must hate me."

Graves sat there. Waiting. He didn't deny the hating. "Twenty thousand dollars," he said. "In cash."

"It hurts to let you down," Ave answered. "I mean it. This means so much to you. And it's so mundane, in the end. Listen, Graves. We have these people around here who shun electricity. They wear black hats and plain shoes and pants with no zippers. They drive horses. They hire out as carpenters. They build fences, repair barns. They work for cash. Names and dates available. I hope you don't scare them to death. They're plain folk, Amish."

"Let me add a point," Warren said. "There are people around here, more than we like to admit, who resent the college. We're snooty, we're spoiled. In contemplating Senior Years, in considering adding to what might be in the Stribling Tract, we needed someone who was not a college official. Someone we could approach as a partner and friend. And what better friend that someone who has left us his estate...Really, Mr. Graves...we're his heirs!"

"After he pays his debts? After he revises his will?" Graves kept fir-ing but he sounded desperate, like he was rushing to finish a lecture to a class that was already leaving the room.

"You've got nothing," Ave pronounced. "Am I right? Warren?"

Warren nodded.

"Hiram?"

"Agreed."

"Billy?"

That startled me. I never expected to be included and now they were all watching me.

"Think out loud, Billy," Hiram Wright said. It took a while but they were patient. Interested, even, not knowing what I would say. I didn't know either.

"I'm sorry," I said, turning to Graves. He was a goner already. "But it never felt like..."

"No need to apologize, Billy," Wright said.

"Definitely not," Hayes said. "Because we haven't gotten to the point, have we Graves? Do you want to tell them? Or should I?"

Graves didn't answer. But, with the slightest nod of his head, he signaled Ave to go on.

"I did a stupid thing once," he said. "Oh, I've done a lot of stupid things. But one in particular. I was a student, of sorts, when Rudolph Graves taught here. I belonged to a political club, more or less Republican, that was called the Edwin Burke Society."

"Actually, Ave," Wright said. "It was Edmund...Edmund Burke."

"There you go!" Ave said. "I thought maybe something was wrong there. Well, this Burke crew mostly drank beer and talked about what was in the papers. Kind of dull. I took it up a notch. We marched in a few parades, protesting a professor they called 'Red Rudolph.'"

"They called..." Graves protested.

"I guess I made 'Red Rudolph' up. You know how it is with nicknames. Sometimes they just stick. Well, Mr. Graves, I'm sorry about your dad. If he were here, I'd say as much to him. Now I'm saying it to you. It was just a campus flap that escalated. It wasn't the end of the world."

"That's exactly what it was," Graves fired back, glaring at Hayes. I suspect he felt cheated. A nonchalant and slapdash apology like that. Something he'd been waiting for, that didn't satisfy him.

"Regrets aside, Mr. Graves, I still wonder what on earth you're up to here. I'd be tempted to call your investigation purposeless but that wouldn't be fair. There is a purpose. The purpose was revenge..."

I waited for Graves to counter, to come back with a declaration, an accusation, anything: suspects identified, arrests imminent. But he stayed silent as a punished schoolboy. He had nothing to say. And just then I was certain we would never know what happened to us. At least, we'd never learn it from Sherwood Graves.

"What strikes me," Hiram Wright offered, "is how much your techniques resemble the ones that brought your father down. Your father was still alive when I came here. Not teaching, but in the neighborhood. I met him more than once. He'd been badly treated, no doubt, but to the end, there was a courtly, gentle nature about him, something almost...sweet. I don't believe he'd have wanted you to revenge him in this way."

"The hell with it," Hayes said. "I'll tell you what bothers me. Every minute Mr. Graves diverts himself with me—my offshore this, my silent that, my undisclosed this and that—is a moment the murderer breathes free. The case Mr. Graves makes against me is false. The case I—and this college—have against him is true. Malfeasance, misfeasance, the whole drill. Of course I hope it doesn't come to that. But it's there alright. It's only a phone call away."

There was no doubt about it. Now I felt sorry for Sherwood Graves. What son wouldn't want to return to a place where his father had been ruined? *There, there,* I wanted to tell him. *It's alright.* But now wasn't the time. It wasn't my meeting.

"Now, Mr. Graves," Hiram said. "Let's talk about your investigation. I know you have been looking into wounded, grieving faculty. No question, we have some of those. But...do you have a bona fide suspect?"

"No," Graves said.

"And what about unhappy students and graduates? Every kennel has sick puppies. But rabies?"

"Not that we found."

"And the fabled friction between town and gown. Lots of fights over the years. Even a shooting death, I've heard."

"That was years ago," Graves said. "There's nothing I could take to the D.A. A lot of things looked promising for a while..."

"Not as promising as me," Averill Hayes couldn't resist interjecting.

"That'll do, Ave," Niles said, but Graves overrode him.

"No, sir," he conceded. "No one looked the way you looked to me."

"Oh...well, you looked wrong," said Hayes.

"I'm not done looking. Fair warning."

"Look away," Hayes said. Something seemed funny to him. Then he started to sing, echoing "Dixie"— "Look away, look away..."

"That'll do," the President repeated, a little more firmly. "Is there anything else that we should..."

"Alright," Graves interrupted. "I've listened to you and now it's your turn to listen to me. Okay?"

"Please," the President said.

"A killer moves quickly, moves randomly...it's the hardest thing in the world to solve. Also...happily...the rarest. Most murders solve themselves. Not this. There were no connections, no trails to follow. It was all about the college. It was where I wanted to look, look into everything, anything..."

"And nothing!" Ave burst out. "Six months of snooping and this is all we get?"

"That'll do, Ave," Niles repeated, taking control now that it was over. Wright and Hayes sat there, satisfied with themselves, looking to have a jolly post mortem, replaying the punches they'd thrown and how they landed. Graves might have had more to say but he decided not to bother. He got up out of his chair, nodding goodbye, and I followed him towards the door.

"Actually," Warren said, "I'd like a moment with Mr. Graves."

"Okay," Graves said. "And Billy."

"Fine," Niles said. "And Billy."

Hayes and Wright left, not saying a word, not so much as a nod to Graves.

"Sit down, both of you," Warren said. "Sit here." He gestured to the chairs where the provost and trustee had sat, right next to his desk.

"I'm a glib man, everybody says," Warren told Graves, who was sitting like a kid called into a principal's office, a basically good kid who'd messed up. "But I'm not sure how to say what I have in mind. Would you give me a minute?"

Warren clasped his hands in front of his head, thinking, or looking like it. This meeting, which had begun in the late afternoon, had continued into early evening. A few strokes of deep purple were all that lingered in the west. The office was dark; no lights turned on. Night claimed the abandoned campus, the president's office.

"You came to us highly recommended. The people we called in Columbus believed—still believe—that there was no one better to help us out of our predicament. And I don't doubt them. And...if you went off the track here...it's for reasons that I understand. That I honor. One of the discoveries I make as I grow older is that I think more and more of my father. The older I get, the more he's with me. It doesn't make sense. He's been dead so long. And every day that passes adds another day to all that time that's come between us. I had thought of him as a figure on a horizon, moving away from me. Now something is bringing us together, closer and closer. A paradox, I guess. I'm older now than he was when he died and yet he's in my thoughts. I don't understand why this should be. And I don't know how many other people feel this way. But I wanted you to know that I understand what brought you here...loyalty and love and righteous anger..."

Another pause for thought. I noticed the deep, grainy polished wood in the president's desk, the carpet under my feet that had the college seal woven into it. I liked what Niles said about the connection between fathers and sons, how it doesn't wear away with time, it stays, it even gets stronger. I was impressed by him, just then.

"You had an apology of sorts from Averill Hayes. I don't know what it meant to him. To you, it cannot have been other than disappointing. But what happened to your father here was wrong. And I wouldn't want you to leave this office without hearing from me, the president, these words: I apologize. I am sorry."

He came out from behind the desk, reached his hand out to Graves. "I'm sorry," he repeated.

"Thank you," Graves said. They shook hands. "I'm sorry too."

Tom was waiting for us outside the Security office. He knew what had happened, it was written all over him. Glancing through the door, I saw that Graves' world had been dismantled, the computers, maps and files all gone. Wesley Coward was a memory, some fast food cartons and silver foil envelopes of mustard and soya sauce were all that was left of him. Linda was gone too.

"Wild goose season is over," Tom said. He gestured across the alley, at a college vehicle, then glanced at Graves, who was standing next to me. "Take him back where he came from," Tom said. "And come straight back. You're on the night shift."

So, after a stop at the Motel 8, we rode through the village, turned right onto the road that goes down the college hill, into the river valley, past fields of corn and soy, brown and stubbled now with half frozen puddles between last year's rows. On River Road, we passed Hiram Wright's place. Hiram was keeping his personal college in session; our latest class was filmed by a TV crew, some cable series called "People Who Make a Difference." There were TV trucks still in the driveway, cars along the road. A few miles later when we found the road that runs south to Columbus, Graves finally spoke.

"Relax, Billy," he said. "I'm not mad at you."

"Yeah, but I'm still sorry it wound up this way."

"My fault. I made a mistake here. I wasn't working for the people who got killed, the way I usually do. Those are the ones who employ me, dead strangers, at least that's how I think of it. But when I came to this place, I was working for my father. And that means I was working for myself. I took on the whole college. You were there. I was convinced that what was going on there was deep and complicated. It's what I believed and what I wanted to believe. Well, I turned up stuff, all kinds of stuff. But I didn't have a killer. At the end, I was just waiting to catch a break, waiting to get lucky. Waiting for the killer to kill again. That's sad. But the saddest thing of all is, I wasn't wrong. If this is ever solved, it'll turn out to be complicated and deep. And, I guarantee, it'll involve more than one person."

"A hired killer?"

"No," he said, shaking his head. "This isn't hit-man-comes-to-campus. A hit man wouldn't last five minutes, nervous as this place is. No, it's not that. It's a coincidence of interests, a manipulation. An alliance. Call it that. Possibly a very unlikely one. I didn't find it. But I guarantee you one thing. The killer is local. Has to be, to move around campus. The killer is local and so is his boss. You'll know them both, if they're ever caught."

"What are the chances, now you're going?"

"They might get lucky," Graves said. "But I wouldn't bet on it. They'll do what the college wants and the college wants it to be over. Even if it isn't, they'll act like it is. Get rid of me and the problem goes away, they hope..."

I kept driving and waited for the next installment. It came at Sunbury, at one of those interstate plazas—motels, gas, fast food—that makes you feel like the whole purpose is to keep 'em moving. We were sitting at the last traffic light, watching huge rigs head out for Columbus, Indianapolis, Wheeling.

"It's not as if I didn't learn something," Graves reflected, more like he was talking to himself than having a conversation with me. "I came in to settle a score. And you know what? I actually liked the place, never mind all the dirt I was digging. Every day I walked around, I liked it, I liked it in spite of myself, this little college, full of shit and charm. I saw why my dad came here, why he stayed, stayed in the neighborhood even after his career was destroyed. Walking where he walked, those lawn and paths, those lines of old trees, those classrooms he taught in..."

He fell silent once again. He was telling me what he wanted to say, which was all about himself and nothing about me. I was always the last thing on his mind, the bottom of the list. He was saying goodbye to a place he'd fallen in love with, which was nice, but I was going back up this road and there was no love waiting for me at the end of it.

"The G-Man," he finally said. We were in the parking lot of a state office building. "The magic word. At last you hear it. You've been patient."

"Thanks..."

"I could tell that your interest in him was exceptional. From the minute you heard his name, out of your ex-wife's mouth, you were hooked. You'd come across a life you wanted to know about, a lot like yours in its background, and a lot different in its accomplishments. As for its outcome...horribly worse, it could be. You'll notice I said could be."

"I know you never thought it was him," I said. "You were doing me a favor. Indulging me."

"I was, Billy. And it was unprofessional. But I liked you and felt sorry for you...and wanted you to have something that you wanted."

"You make me sound like a chump."

"You're not. Bear with me. It seemed impossible that an honors student would come back after many years to kill a professor, more impossible that he would kill two students and a high school kid. It was inconsistent with my sense of...human likelihood. And inconsistent with what I've told you about these crimes, which I continue to believe are the result of an alliance that is deep, complicated and...local. So I gave him to you, Billy, the same way I let you sit in on Hiram Wright. For your benefit..."

"I see," I said. Looked at in a certain way, I'd done alright out of these murders. I got a new girlfriend, a college course for nothing, and a free dog. But it didn't feel like I'd come out ahead.

"Well," he said, figuring out how to say goodbye, I guessed. Wrong. "I don't suppose you've learned much from me. I wanted Averill Hayes, more than anything. That's unprofessional. So is this. This last thing. This is between us." He reached into his coat pocket and pulled out a plastic envelope, zip-locked.

"It was on the body of the fourth victim, the prospective, tucked into his pocket. That's why there's blood."

I opened the envelope and found a piece of paper inside, cheap paper that had sponged up the kid's blood, turning from red to rust. Careful block letters that were between the lines. Stay between the lines. The lines are your friend. ALWAYS DO A LITTLE BIT EXTRA. The G-Man's slogan.

"With that, you can get the sheriff to put out an all points this afternoon," he said. "I thought you might want to try something else."

"Does this mean he did it?"

"He did it," Graves said. "Or someone wants him to look like he did. Anyway, you weren't wrong. G-Man's involved."

"'Always do a little bit extra,'" I quoted. "If it's not him, it's someone who knows him."

"And knows you, Billy. I guarantee it."

"It's not over?"

"Of course not," Graves said. He reached out and put his hand on my shoulder, left it there a second. "Good luck, Billy."

I get back from Columbus in time to pull the night shift and around midnight I'm parked out by the tennis courts, smoking a cigarette and listening to oldies but goodies on the radio, "You Don't Send Me Flowers Anymore," wondering what to do about that bloody note Graves gave me, when all of a sudden there are sirens screaming up the highway, like coon hounds on a hunt. They pass the entrance to the college—we're spared—but I call in to Dottie, who tells me there'd been a report of shots fired at a house in the country. My house.

When I drive up, the place is a crime scene, two police cars, a fire

truck, an ambulance parked out front and Tom's truck too. He's standing on the lawn next to Sheriff Lingenfelter. The house is all lit up.

"What happened?" I asked.

"You don't know?" Tom says.

"I did, I wouldn't ask."

"Okay. About an hour ago someone came down the driveway—
on foot, seems like—and stood about over there..." He nods toward
where my Dad's truck's been parked for twenty years. "...and shot out
every damn window in the front of your house."

"Linda?"

"She's okay. Hit the floor, crawled over to the phone."

"Where is she?"

"Coming."

I see Linda step out onto the porch, accompanied—steadied—by
a deputy who's carrying an overnight bag. They walk towards us. She
looks shaky, red-eyed and trembling. When she sees I'm there she gives
me a look that says it's my fault, what happened.

"Well, Billy," she says, "I guess you got your farm back."

After a long hard stare, she walks away from me.

"What's that about?" the sheriff asks.

"It's nothing," Tom says. "She just needs a man around the house,
is all." Tom asks can he help me clean up the mess and I say no, it's my
mess, but I appreciate the offer. "Okay, son," he says and he drives off
in that pinging truck of his. I head towards the house, spend the next
hour sweeping up glass. When I go out to the barn looking for ply-
wood, everyone is gone. I nail the wood over the windows. That
would keep the weather out. Not people. Whatever keys we had were
lost years ago. Anybody could walk right in.

I sit on the porch, just tasting what it would be like to live here
again. Sappho a country dog? That's the first thing I think about.
Going up against groundhogs? Hard to picture. Still, she's got a nasty
streak. My father's truck sits out across the lawn. You can hardly tell it
was a truck anymore, thistles and weeds. Nature as destroyer and con-
soler. That's something Wright talks about. He loves stuff like that.
Paradoxes. I sit there thinking and then I stop thinking and just sit.
That's okay, too. It's nasty—temperature in the thirties, damp and
mean—but I don't want to leave yet. I wonder who came down the
driveway that night. G-Man after Sangy Girl? Maybe not. What was
the phrase Graves had used? "Human likelihood." Besides, Robert

Rickey had been out of the house a while and it could be Linda picked up some guy, jumped his bones and told him to go. Some guys wouldn't put up with that.

Back on shift, I do a few more circuits and drive home at dawn. The farm is mine again, things are looking up for me, even though the killings haven't been solved. Could it be possible, I wonder, for life to be good, with things rattling around in the past, four people dead and a killer unpunished, no justice done? Could the world work that way? Or had it been working that way all along? A big question, the kind of headscratcher that might come up in Wright's class or afterwards, when we stayed around to talk with the old man, the way we always did, because among the students at that makeshift one-man college, there's a sense that he won't be around much longer. Since I've known him, especially since they made him provost, he's been going down steady. "One long retreat from the gates of Moscow," he says. "The weather gets colder, the snow is deeper." Then he pulls himself together. "But not tonight," he says. "Not tonight." Another thing that doesn't help, he isn't sleeping much. He says he's terrified of dying in his sleep, he wants to see his death coming.

Next morning, someone was hammering on my door. No doorbells in trailers, no sound of knuckles on wood, just a kind of metal rapping that would worry you, if you heard it from your car. While I stumbled out of bed and put my legs in my pants, I glanced out and saw the sheriff's car. I opened the door, Lingenfelter was standing there.

"Hi, Billy," he said. "Did I wake you up?"

"I work nights," I said. "Sleep days."

"Sorry. Guess I knew that. Can I come in?"

"You really want to?"

He looked behind me and didn't see much. "Not really. But we got to talk."

"Can I have a minute? Brush my teeth? Throw some water in my face?"

"Sure thing. No rush."

While I was in the bathroom, I asked myself what brought him. Old Donny Lingenfelter had been sheriff forever. Unopposed. Look at him and you'd think of Jackie Gleason in all those movies where he was running after Burt Reynolds. That was his trick, getting you to think he's some dumb, fat goober.

"Well then," I said when I sat down next to him. He was trying to play with Sappho and having no luck.

"Billy, you want to chat a while or should I just cut to the chase?"

"The chase," I said.

"We're just talking here. I knew your dad real well and I watched you grow up..."

"This the chase, sheriff?"

"Getting there. I know you married that college woman. I know you had trouble. When I heard you let her stay in the house after you split—hell, after she moved another man in—I said that's Earl's boy alright, that's Earl all over again..." He stopped and shook his head, like he couldn't resist lingering among memories of my dad. When he spoke again, he made it sound like a reluctant return to business.

"So there I am last night, standing outside your shot-up house. Out comes your wife, ex-wife..."

"Ex-wife, to be..."

"And she snarls at you and says, 'Well, Billy, guess you got your farm back.' Son, look at it from my side. Can you blame me for wondering if you maybe gave her a little nudge? Hold it..."

I'd been ready to answer but he didn't want to hear it yet.

"This is chickenshit, Billy. Four broken windows on your own property. Hell, I wouldn't know what to call it, not sure it's even a crime. What I'm saying is we can handle this, we can end it right here, just the two of us."

"We sure can," I said. "I didn't do it."

"Uh-huh. That's your answer?"

"I didn't do it."

He sat there waiting for more. When it didn't come, he sighed deep, like he was blaming me for wasting his time.

"Okay then, that's the way you want it."

"That's not the way I want it. It's the way it is."

"Okay. No need to get touchy."

"I'm not touchy. I'm innocent. And the flip side of that is—someone else is guilty."

"That'll do son," he said. Now he was being patient with me. "That'll do for now." He hoisted himself off the bench and Sappho started barking.

"Is that a dog?" he asked. "Or something you knitted?"

After Lingenfelter left I went straight back to sleep, no trouble, no guilty conscience here. The trouble was staying asleep. I closed my eyes and the phone rang.

"Billy? It's Linda."

"How you doing?"

"I'm leaving," she said. "I wanted you to know. I'm going to stay in Columbus with my aunt. Take it from there. From here I mean..."

"Huh?"

"I mean Columbus is where I'm calling from. I'm not just going. I'm gone."

"Oh..."

"This return to Ohio thing didn't work out. I guess we both know that. I just wanted to say I'm sorry."

"That goes for me."

"Well...I said it first."

"Okay."

"There's something else, Billy, that I'm sorry for. It's what I said to you last night, with Tom and the sheriff standing right here. I was scared and angry. I wasn't accusing you of anything. But I think that's what they thought."

"It's alright," I said. "Sheriff came sniffing around this morning. Woke me up. I told him I didn't shoot those windows out. No big thing."

"Oh, Billy, but it is..."

"What?"

"That's what I wanted to tell you. I went to the office this morning, first thing, cleaning up. Sheriff was there and Tom and they've got a match..."

"A what?"

"The bullets from your house? They match the other bullets from those kids. Same gun."

I couldn't speak. Broken windows? Chickenshit? Watched you grow up, knew your daddy, just us talking? Bullshit. The bullets matched. Matched each other. Matched the Smith and Wesson .38 the killer used, that we'd been keeping quiet about. No doubt about it. Lingenfelter had come to my house to collect a murderer. He wanted me.

Things hadn't been right between Tom and me since Graves came to town. But Graves was history now and Tom still kept his distance, communicating through notes, acting pissed off. I wasn't sure why. Was it because I hadn't shared every step of Graves' fouled-up investigation? Or because I'd slept with Lisa Garner while conducting a screwed up investigation of my own? Did he prefer me alone and mopey? Was it that I was hanging out with Hiram Wright? Did my uncle prefer me stupid? It was something I'd done, no doubt about it, but I wished he'd narrow things down a little, pick one off of a long list of things he wanted me to apologize for, so we could get back to how we used to be. Meanwhile, tonight's work order: "Stay sharp. There's a basketball game in Danville. They might come down here drunk, joyriding, tearing up the grass." So I parked outside the upper-class dorm, walked out onto the grass, found an Adirondack chair and sat, just near enough to hear the basketball game on the radio, Danville versus Mount Vernon, farm kids see-sawing back and forth on a court I could picture, parents and girlfriends screaming in bleachers, the whole place damn near levitating. Some of those kids, tonight might be the best night of their lives. Count on it. There's a peak that you don't even know you're on, until you're back down.

"Billy Hoover. You there?"

Dottie was calling me from the Security Office, her voice rising above the background of the basketball game. Somebody had a flat tire in the parking lot above the football field. I told her I'd be right there. Football was over, so was college, but sometimes folks with campers and RVs parked down there, where the ground was flat.

It wasn't a camper, though, it was a van with Franklin County plates. That's Columbus. I got out, grabbed a flashlight and walked over. No one was sitting inside, waiting for me. And the tires looked just fine.

"Hey, Billy Hoover." It was Lisa, leaning against the stadium fence.

"Hey, yourself," I said. "I've been thinking about you." Now I was facing her, wondering about a hug. It didn't feel right. Something was up. I didn't believe in happy coincidences any more, lucky meetings, star crossed lovers, casual drop ins. Neither did she.

"Got a question for you," she said. "Are you armed?"

"No."

"And the radio that connects you to the office? You left it in the car? You're not carrying a beeper?"

"Nope. In the car. What is this, anyway?"

"You wanted to meet my brother, right?"

"He's here?" I looked around. No one else in view, no traffic. A shrewdly chosen place and time, I realized.

"I'm asking. You still want to meet him?"

"Yes," I said. And—I don't know why—I did what I'd done when we met, down on the river, came right up to her, an inch away. To see if it was still there, the feeling.

"Okay, Billy," she said, moving in towards me, like we were just about to slow dance. There was feeling, alright. Most of it was fear. "He's down on the field. Fifty yard line."

"He knows I'm coming?"

"Sure does. He's looking forward to it."

The light from the parking lot died at the top row of seats. After that, I stepped into a dark bowl, down the aisle towards the field. I saw Lisa standing at the top, watching me go. I went slowly, asking myself if she was testing my faith in her—which was possible—or waiting to hear a shot—which would be the end of me and my amateur detective career, my late education, all my half-assed wondering. I could picture Lingenfelter standing over my body tomorrow morning. "I knew his daddy..." And Tom recalling a lifetime of lessons he'd wasted on me. "In a restaurant, never order anything stuffed." "Any beer that's worth drinking is worth drinking out of a glass." All his winks and jokes and his warnings, wasted. Linda wondering if I hadn't taken a bullet that was meant for her. Wondering what to do and doing nothing. Hiram Wright, ripe in years, remembering all the students whose lives he'd changed and a few—just a few—who hadn't worked out.

At the bottom of the stands, I stepped out onto a macadam running track that goes around the football field. I couldn't see anything out there in the middle. If I couldn't see him, did that mean he couldn't see me? Maybe not.

"Yo," I called out. And then, after hesitating. "G-Man!"

A moment of silence and winter wind came next and me just standing there, wondering what was being prepared for me.

"Over here," someone said. A voice that came from mid-field. I stepped out onto the grass, not seeing where I was headed. So I sensed him before I saw him and all I saw was a dark, bulky something ahead of me.

"That you?"

"Yes." In front of me, I sensed a hand rising, pointing. A flashlight, shining right in my eyes. I was a deer in the headlights, Tom would say, dead meat. I put my hand over my eyes, then dropped it and looked away to the side to avoid the glare. It was like that night, with Lisa, when she inspected me as I undressed. A kind of family thing, that led to sex, in her case. Where G-Man was headed, I wasn't sure.

"Sorry about that," he said. "It's rude. But you're a sort of cop and Lisa says you've been looking for me."

"That's for damn sure."

"You want to see what you've found?" he asked. "Here." He tossed the flashlight my way. I caught it and turned it back on him. I found the top of his head, light brown hair, then a face that hadn't changed much from what I'd seen in the college yearbook. Or, if it had changed, like his classmate had told me, now it had changed back to what it was when he left there. Bright, trustworthy. Smiling at me in a Will Rogers kind of way. He was sitting in a wheelchair, I saw now. It was impolite, like staring at a scar, but I ran a flashlight down his chest, his stomach, over his legs.

"I got hit by a drunk near Newport, Kentucky. Uninsured. I've been learning how to walk. Takes time."

"I'm sorry."

"I've got motel receipts. I've got medical records. Where I've been."

"Forget about it," I said. "You're off the hook." He could forget, alright. I couldn't. Somebody had tried to hook him. That blood-soaked note: ALWAYS DO A LITTLE BIT EXTRA. We were both in trouble. But he had an alibi. I didn't.

"G-Man?"

"Yeah."

"Could I just shake your hand?" I held the flashlight at my side and walked towards him. "Billy Hoover," I said. Then I started pushing his wheelchair out the far end of the field, up towards the parking lot.

"You don't hate this place?" I asked. We were sitting at the only restaurant in town that was still open, eating pretty good chili and drinking watery coffee.

"Hate it?" G-Man asked. "I loved it! They took a kid from...you know where. And they made me something special. You might say, well, it might have happened anywhere. I'm not so sure..."

"But after you didn't get that job."

"That was tough, finding out what you always thought was meant to be...wasn't in the cards. There were years, I thought I'd never come back up here. Then I started sneaking back, like some guy who drives past his old girlfriend's house. I guess you didn't know that..."

After he got shot down by Martha Yeats, he took lots of fill-in teaching jobs where they expect you to be bad, feel threatened when you're good. Then he knocked around for a few years as a book jobber, one of those guys who goes around faculty offices, buying text books that publishers send out to professors, free samples, working out of a van, moving from college to college. That was his job in "publishing." He'd been back to this college lots of times, he said, walking the same campus where he'd been a star, poking his head into faculty offices. It was like he'd never been a student here. No one knew him. Then his luck got worse: a highway accident, broken leg, shattered kneecap. He was getting better but he'd never play football again. He wouldn't go around buying books either. He'd written one. While he was recovering, he started writing a collection of stuff, just for the fun of it. He wrote it for himself, killing time in therapy. He couldn't imagine anyone would pay money to read it but it turned out a publisher was willing to bet on a book of sketches that reminded them of *Blue Highways* and *Travels with Charley*, only smarter.

"Why didn't you call us, when you heard we were looking for you? 'I've been in a car accident...'"

"She told me not to," G-Man said, indicating Lisa.

"Not so fast," Lisa said. She nodded at her brother. "Tell him the rest."

"I said some unkind things to Hiram Wright, way back," G-Man said. "After the job fell through. I hit bottom after that. And worked my way further down. Then he heard about me. Set me up in this cottage he owns. On one condition. We wouldn't communicate directly. A third party, if I had problems."

"Who was that?"

"The guy who gave me the keys. Tom Hoover," he answered. "Kin of yours, I guess."

"Yes," I said. "Kin."

"I wasn't supposed to get in touch until I'd done something we'd both be proud of. That seemed fair."

"Billy," Lisa said. "He wants to see Hiram Wright."

"Sure," I said.

"Now..."

"Let's do it."

In a minute we were driving out to River Road, the headlights poking into empty cornfields as we took a curve. It's amazing, how all that winter mud and stubble comes up green and tall each year. Then we pulled into Wright's driveway and I got out, opening the door for G-Man.

"You know something?" G-Man asked. "I'm nervous. He always scared me. Lisa says you're in his class. Is he still scary?"

"He's still scary, alright."

"It's as if he knows you better than you know yourself. Sees into you. Not just what you are but what you ought to be. The whole rest of your life, you feel him watching you. It's spooky."

There was a light inside the house, the professor's reading lamp and, on the porch, that night's sentry stood up and watched us come, one of the River Road neighbors keeping watch. Scraps of sad-assed country music marked our path, growing louder the nearer we got. Inside, I could see Wright hoist himself out of his chair and lumber towards the door. I headed towards the house. Behind me, Lisa handed her brother a pair of crutches.

"Hello, Billy Hoover," Wright said. Then he saw G-Man coming along behind me but he couldn't recognize him.

"I brought you some company, Professor," I said. Then I just watched. I watched G-Man slowly make his way across the lawn, a man who was learning to walk again approaching a man who was less able to walk each day. Two damaged generations; it wasn't like passing a baton in a relay race, it was a lot shakier than that. G-Man got to the steps, which were going to be a problem. I offered him a hand. He shook me off. He lifted his right leg onto the first step, pulled it up, working hard, then the left leg. It was an effort, his head was down, watching what he was doing, careful not to lose it. It wasn't until he reached the top that he looked up at Wright and Wright knew who was standing in front of him.

"Hello, Professor," G-Man said. And then, well, I shouldn't have been there but I'm glad I was, seeing something I'd never seen before and would never forget. First a look of panic and shock, almost fear. And then—more of a surprise—the old man's eyes watering, hands trembling, like you would if you came across somebody you never expected to see again, the kind of feeling I had when I saw my father in my dreams and tried to talk to him but the words caught in my throat and by the time they came out they were sobs, not words. Then Wright moved forward to where G-Man was standing and hugged him, the kind of hug that moves past the look in someone's eyes or the expression on their face and it's all about contact, pure touch, two people holding on. After a long moment, Wright recovered a little. Still holding onto G-Man, he saw me and nodded as if he were saying it was alright, my being there, seeing this and hearing his first words to G-Man, to both of us maybe.

"Forgive me," he said.

We sat out on Wright's porch, listening to him and G-Man talk. You know how it is, some people can sit down after years apart and pick up right where they'd left off. Books and ideas, stuff that was always there for them. They'd go until dawn, I supposed, knowing how Wright felt about going to sleep. After a while, we just excused ourselves. They wouldn't miss us.

"Hey, Billy Hoover, you there?" It was Dottie, back at the switchboard.

"I'm here," I said.

"Doing what? Tom was just asking. He phoned in."

"That flat tire got complicated. I'm running people around all over. It'll take a while yet. Got to take the driver home." Lisa put her hand on my leg when she heard that and gave me this look that said, good answer, Billy.

"Okay," Dottie said. "I'll let him know you're tied up. Sounds beyond the call of duty."

"We aim to please," I said and cleared the channel. Then I turned to Lisa. "Let's go."

The trailer camp was crazy, like it gets some nights, cars and trucks jammed up against trailers, no room to park except way down at the end. As we walked back, we couldn't avoid looking into a world where every meal was macaroni and cheese, all clothing got washed in laundromats and television sets got turned on the day they were bought and played until they died. "We won't be here much longer," I said when we came to my place. "Who's we?" she asked. But I guessed she knew what I meant. So now we were sitting in back of the trailer, bundled up against the cold. We could see our breath in the air. The stars were bright. We sat close together, letting Sappho bring the ball back from the Animal Shelter fence.

"I've got to ask," I said, "why you made it so hard on me. Why you couldn't just have...you know...confided."

"My fault," she said. "It's how I am. The more I like a guy, the harder I make it for him..."

"Well...in that case..."

"I liked you plenty. There. See? I'm confiding." She took the ball that Sappho brought her—the two were right—and tossed it against the fence. "You're just what I want in a man. You're quiet and decent and loyal. And smarter than you let folks know. And I been looking forward to tonight an awful lot, I'm warning you."

"That another test? I thought you tested me last time."

"That?" She got up off the bench, turned and sat on me, her legs over mine, her body against my chest, her breasts against my face, her lips in my ear. "That was a pop quiz. True and false. Tonight's harder. Multiple choice."

Right then Sappho started barking. Out of jealousy, I thought. But it had a different sound, watch-doggy. And then I heard what set Sappho off, the kind of pinging that came from Tom's truck. And a door closing. And the creak of the gate in my metal fence, opening and closing quietly.

"He's got keys," I said. "He's going inside."

"Who is it?"

"Tom." I had to see him. To know, not guess—to find, not lose. "You stay here."

"No," she said. "I'll come."

We walked to the back door. I turned the knob and like that I was in the trailer which, except for the bathroom, is one big room. I saw him standing with his back to me, fussing at my dresser.

"Hi, Tom," I said, switching on the lights. He didn't spin around the way people do when you surprise them. He turned around, real leisurely.

"Well, well, well," he said, nodding hello at Lisa. "On duty, my ass."

"That's my dresser there," I said. "T-shirts in the bottom, socks in the middle, underwear at the top. Boxers, just like you wear."

He smiled at that, at least he gestured in the direction of a memory: jockey shorts, he told me, were for kids in gym glass. Men wore boxers. "I taught you to keep a neat house," he said.

"Right. Looking for a change of underwear?"

"Nope."

"What's that in your hand?" I asked. He didn't even try to conceal it, a plastic bag with a drawstring that the college bookstore uses, with a college seal on the outside.

"I think you know," Tom said.

"Smith and Wesson .38?"

"Bingo," said Tom. "You guessed right. And there's a silencer that I made myself, with a beer can, some steel wool and a few inches of plastic pipe. Hell, murder's one thing. Disturbing the peace...that's something else again."

"So..." My voice was breaking. "It's you."

"Me," he said, smiling, studying me, the way an eye-doctor watches a nearsighted customer read a chart.

"Why?"

"Hell, son. You wouldn't understand."

"Try me."

"Little bit at a time then. Begins with, you get old, you look back on account there's more behind you than you can see in front. I looked back and—hell, we even talked about it—I wanted to make a mark. Settle accounts. For what happened to Tony, dying while they partied and protested. What they did to me and your old man..."

"What about him?" I asked.

"You don't even know. Hell, you don't even realize what they're doing to *you*. What they've done. Maybe old Hiram can turn on the lights for you. I sure can't..."

"Tom..." The feeling surged up in my throat, choking. "A professor. Two students. Good, good kids. And that poor high school kid, setting foot here for the first time."

"Hey," he said glancing over at Lisa. "'Always do a little bit extra.'"

"Why'd you bring my brother into it?" she said. "What did he ever do to you?"

"That was a side deal," he said, waving her off. "'Always do a little bit extra.'"

"And why shoot out my windows?" I asked.

"Like the man said...*a little bit extra*," Tom answered. "Anyway, I wanted that wife of yours off your farm. Never liked her."

"So now," I said, "you drop the gun off so that it'll be resting in my underwear when Lingenfelter shows up with a search warrant. Tomorrow, is it?"

He laughed at that a little, shook his head some, like he used to do, whenever he taught me something. "Thing about you, Billy, is you always try your honest best and you always get it wrong. I wasn't dropping the gun off. It's been dropped off, sitting there all along. I was picking it up..."

"Picking it up?" I asked. "Because...you're not done?"

"Not quite, son," he said. "Listen, it'll be over in a jiffy. The next one won't hurt anybody...no loss at all. Painless, practically."

"Why'd you leave that thing in here in the first place? You want to get me for this? Frame me?" My voice cracked like a kid's. I couldn't believe he wanted to hurt me that bad.

"No," he said. "I wanted you to find it someday...and have it. From me to you...Someday you'd come across it and...you'd know...something in common. Because we're connected."

He stood there, waiting for an answer that wasn't in me. He was right. We were connected.

"I wonder how long it would of took," he said, scratching his head like he was puzzled, "for you to work your way to the bottom of the underwear."

"I wash all the time," I said. "Same three pairs off the top of the pile. Never get to the bottom of it."

"I figured that," Tom said. "Well, damn, this is all fascinating, but I'm going now."

"Leave the gun, Tom. Please..."

"I got more use for it. Thing is, you do something you want people to know you did it. You want credit. Anonymous donor don't make it. No point in hiding your light under a bushel."

He was talking fast, like a performer at the end of his act, working towards a big closing, heading off stage.

"You gonna stop me, Billy? This is the part where you tackle me, you and your girlfriend? We struggle, all in a pile, a shot goes off and the audience doesn't know..."

"I won't fire it," I said. "Not at you."

"You sure?" he said. He held the bag out to me, offered it, dared me. "You want it?"

"I got no use for it," I said. "Oh hell, Tom."

He walked past me and I let him go. He paused, though, right in the doorway, and looked back at me. "You know where I'm going."

"No," I said.

"Yeah," he said. "You do."

I stood there, watching him cut across the yard, Sappho barking, him shaking his head.

"Aren't you ever going to train that dog?" he called back. Then he climbed in his truck, drove down among the trailers, turned and passed by on the way out and my throat was tight, watching him.

"Billy," Lisa came up behind me, "you let him go."

"It's alright."

"With a gun. He could kill somebody!"

"It's alright," I said.

"Where's he going?"

"Wait," I said. "I'll show you."

We drove slowly through Mount Vernon, headed east, talking along the way. How Tom wanted credit for what he'd done, wanted to make a name for himself and leave a mark behind and not be forgotten. A monument. And it was going to happen. He'd be a name that people whispered, that kids scared each other with. He wasn't going to go to prison. He'd gone off to kill himself. No need to leave a note. Whoever found him would find the Smith and Wesson, which would be as good as a confession, once they ran a ballistic test.

"So where are we going?" she asked.

"Where his brother died," I said. "My father. That's my guess."

"He said the college did something to your father. What was that about?"

"I don't know. Not yet."

So we came to Millwood, where the river runs deep. Not as deep as it used to, but deep enough. I parked near the trestle, looked around for Tom's truck, stepped out onto the bridge. No one was there. No Tom, no truck. There was a rope tied to the trestle, swinging back and forth, just above the water. That's when I knew I was wrong. That's when I remembered another place. Home. And another death.

Tom's truck was parked in the driveway, next to what was left of my father's truck. Two brothers who worked for the college, loyal, lifelong employees. "You don't have to come with me," I told Lisa.

"You telling me to stay?" she asked.

"No..."

"Then I'll come."

"This is my farm, by the way," I said. "It's not the way I wanted you to see it, the first time."

"It's okay, Billy."

"I pictured us walking hand in hand," I said. "Another time, I guess."

"Take my hand now."

We left the edge of the lawn and took the path that cut through the fields, curved towards the river, passed the trestle and cut in towards the ruined barn. The same barn where I'd found the hanged student and where Tom had found me. Where he was waiting for me now. He hadn't hanged himself. I thanked him for that. He was sitting against an old stall, the gun in his hand, shot through the heart, not the head. In the end, he made it easy for me.

"I'm sorry about this," I said, on my knees in front of him, taking the gun out of his hand.

"You shouldn't touch that," Lisa said behind me. "The sheriff..."

"The sheriff doesn't come into this," I said. "Besides. It's my gun now."

I carried him to the edge of the field, right where the woods began, went back to the house for a shovel. It was dark and we were out of sight of the road. No one comes onto our property, after hunting season. So there was time to dig.

"I don't feel so good right now," I said before I started. "He loved me, he raised me..."

"He killed four people."

"No," I said, forcing the shovel into the ground. "Five."

"Okay," Lisa said.

"No one's gonna know about this. They'll blame him anyway, after they notice he's missing. The blame, the credit, whatever. But they won't get him. They'll never know for sure."

It takes time to dig a decent grave but I got as far into it as I could. "Turn your body into a machine," Tom used to say. A grave digging machine. Dig, dig, dig, don't think. Don't feel. Put him into the hole, don't think, toss that first handful of soil, aiming away from his face, pick up the shovel cover him with dirt, cover the dirt with leaves and branches. Then stand back and study what you made, wait for winter, wait for snow and rain and time to swallow a corpse and build a legend, right up there with Harry Stribling and Hiram Wright and

Johnny Appleseed.

"This is how it's gonna be," I said. I had Tom's Smith and Wesson inside the bookstore bag with the college seal. "He's out there, damn it. Out in the world. He got away, you understand? Took right off. Could be in these woods or Las Vegas or Key West or up in Alaska, maybe, running a fishing camp and taking folks on trips and teaching kids how to cast and shoot and pitch a tent and..." I was crying, not the way you cry when it's a sad occasion and tears are expected so you talk yourself into it and squeeze out some tears, like an actor on camera, crying on cue. Really crying. "Most of my memories of this man," I said to Lisa, "are going to be good."

Me in Tom's truck, Lisa in mine, we drove to Sunbury, the exit on the interstate between Cleveland and Columbus, and parked his pickup at a truck stop. Then we drove home, went to bed, I lay there with my eyes wide open, just trying to sort it all out. Sometimes you know too much, sometimes you know too little, you never get it exactly right. Sometimes you know more than you think you do. But that came later.

Part Four:
Second Semester

XII.

MARK MAY

Warren Niles' appointment of Hiram Wright as provost was a public relations gesture. That's what they said, the faculty gang that gossiped at the post office. The old duffer was our new poster-boy, gallant defender of the liberal arts. He showed up on news shows during the murders, was interviewed on *Nightline* when the college closed, had *Good Morning America* down to his cabin, where students sat on his porch while river people guarded the property. Hiram's Bullet-Proof Symposium they called it, and the nation cheered. Just lately, he'd made the cover of *Modern Maturity* magazine. There was some grousing from the Hartley Fuller types that there hadn't been a national search but, come on, what kind of job posting would you put in *The Chronicle of Higher Education*? "Respected college, now closed as a result of unsolved serial murders, seeks provost to preside over empty campus, shredded faculty, uncertain future." Who'd apply for a job like that? G. Gordon Liddy? So Hiram Wright wasn't a real provost, he wasn't even a caretaker. He was there to turn out the lights or, considering his age, blow out the candle.

Then he started doing things that were hard to believe. E-mails started showing up, e-mails from a man who never learned to use an electric typewriter. Long, crafty messages which described a reorganization of the faculty, the curriculum, the entire college. The faculty was scattered, half of them someplace else and the others selling houses and setting up job interviews. The most they could manage was a committee to bargain for furloughs and, when it came time, severance. The college might not have students, they contended, but it had an endowment, it had assets and it owed its professors support—we're talking pay, plane tickets, travel expenses. This was supposed to be a closing, not a lockout! So at first, Wright's position papers didn't draw much of a response. People were busy doing other stuff and anyway, his plans would never be implemented, not here, not anywhere. "What's sadder," Hartley Fuller was heard to wonder, "than an old man's wet dream?"

That was the trick, though. The fact that the college was moribund gave Wright his chance. He got away with—I'm just saying what other people said, when they cottoned to what was going on—he got away with murder. The faculty ignored him at first, derided him later. But other people noticed—some of the journalists who'd been to campus, network parachutists and feature writers and eventually, education editors. Soon, Wright's messages were showing up on op-ed pages, getting quoted on talk shows, inserted into the *Congressional Record.*

Wright's Modest Proposals, as they came to be known, are soon to be published as a book. I only summarize. He raised faculty salaries by half, across the board. And all but eliminated tenure. There'd be one or two tenured professors in each department, one of whom would serve as chair, an appointment without limit. Other professors would be on contract, one or two years to start, up to seven years later on. Who decided about that? The administration, basically the president, the provost, the department chair. This, Wright admitted, was a command structure and so be it. Faculty committees were dismantled. A professor's job was to profess. And professors—the nature of their work, the course of their careers—were his next subject. Or target.

Before the murders, the college consisted of big departments that offered a smorgasbord of courses—"richly articulated" was their self description—and little departments, service departments that lived off introductory courses and struggled to attract majors for advanced courses. Also, there were interdepartmental programs, concentrations, mix-and-match synoptic majors. Wright attacked the small departments first. Some he enlarged and others he folded into larger departments. "I oppose the Balkanization of the curriculum and of the faculty," he said. "We must contend with each other. Let the wearers of dashikis confront tweed coats and rep ties, let sandals and Birkenstocks, Hush Puppies and wingtips walk together. Let there be an end to territoriality, separation, an end to distance and diffidence masquerading as diversity." At first sight, the big departments looked like winners. But keep reading. All departments were obliged to offer agreed upon and relatively uniform introductory and survey courses, those grueling and, if you taught them year in and year out, repetitive basics. No one was exempt from this, not the senior professor with an endowed chair, not the heavily recruited grad school whiz kid who pined to teach the latest scholarly dance steps to students who hadn't learned to walk yet.

It got interesting, at least to me. Wright was touching things that smart people had talked about forever, addressing questions that were thought to be insoluble or, at least, insoluble by us. Grade inflation. Lots of people regretted it. But who was going to be the first to beat up on the kids in his or her classroom? These likeable kids, why should they be the first victims of reform? Why should this college be the first to put its ass on the line when everybody knew—hint, hint, nudge, nudge—that the problem was just as bad, maybe worse, at places more highly regarded, more deeply endowed? But Wright didn't buy that. "Let us confront this problem where it occurs, our own small patch. Looking ahead or behind, gesturing left and right, implying that all vices originate elsewhere, all virtues are local, is self-serving sophistry. Let us deal with the campus we see every day. Let us contend with what we see in the mirror."

His broadside on scholarship and teaching, a constant tension in a college like ours, drew the most notice. To its credit, the college always insisted on superior teaching as a *sine qua non:* if you couldn't deliver in the classroom, you couldn't stay. Some professors would have been happy to leave it at that. But there was a countervailing force, especially among younger faculty, who wanted to make a name in their field, who traded in articles, conferences, papers, panels, encyclopedia entries. Teaching enriches research, research enriches teaching, that was the mantra that accompanied requests for reduced teaching loads, release time, pre-tenure sabbaticals. That was what they were up to: the name they made in "the profession" mattered more than the professing they did at college. Or, as My Provost, My Wife put it, "it's the wine, not the winery." Along came Wright. "A commitment to teaching and research can be admirable," he wrote. "But either one can be the refuge of a failure. Forced to choose between teaching and research, I choose the former. The students' interests demand no less. We are a college, not a research university—more a conservatory than a laboratory. Happily, for us, we aren't obliged to choose between teaching and research. We shall have both. We have had both in the past and will again. I offer current and future faculty the same terms of employment Harry Stribling enjoyed. I invite great teachers to come here. We will know them when we see them and if they are great, truly great, they shall stay. Greatness in scholarship, research, creative work we shall also have. We will recognize it as well, when we see it. I said greatness. Greatness of the kind that resonates beyond this hill, that resides in publications, public recognition, that comes to rest between hard covers. Scholarly articles, conference papers, letters to the editor may be a prelude to greatness, one hopes, but greatness does not reside in them."

That got Wright on *Nightline*. Hiram sat on River Road, Ted Koppel was at his desk in New York, and a frighteningly smart English professor, Michael Pike, was in his office at Duke. Pike took the offensive. He accused Wright of mounting "a romantic, reactionary putsch." He was more than ready for Wright. "Far from rescuing a college, Wright is embalming it, dismantling governance, disenfranchising faculty, disregarding research, disregarding developments in academe and the requirements of the marketplace. He proposes returning curricular structure to hidebound, straight-line patterns more appropriate to a military academy than a liberal arts college. He ought to be ashamed of himself."

"Pike's Pique," *Time* magazine called it. But that was the subheadline. "Hiram's Right" was at the top of the page. You should have seen him respond to Pike's accusation that he was "a Gauleiter of the Great Books," that he was returning the college to dead white males, that he was reprising Matthew Arnold's moldy definition of literature as "the very best that has been thought or said," dusting off a list of texts that Matthew Arnold himself would surely recognize because you could count on Wright's not including anything that had been written since Arnold's death more than a century ago.

"Please, sir," Wright said, erupting in laughter, just chuckling to beat the band and everybody had to wait for him to collect himself. "Alright. Very good! Let me say a few words. Won't take a moment. All of this comes down to books, doesn't it? The books one requires, recommends, neglects. It comes down to hard choices. But has anyone heard me prescribe what books should or should not be taught? Have I banned a single book? Or required one? I think not. All I require is focus, perspective, order. Mr. Pike teaches the latest things first, what happens now, his own personal Cuisinart, described as cutting edge. I teach first things first and move on from there. As to specific titles, I'd be happy to teach a course, co-teach a course, with Mr. Pike someday, a course in literature or history. I ask to be permitted to choose half, no more than half, the texts and I accord him the same right. And I am content to let our students decide about what they got and what they needed."

"Everyone knows that student evaluations..."

"Let me finish. The century which Mr. Pike accuses me of neglecting comes at the end of twenty other centuries. I do not neglect our times but I insist they be studied in connection with the past. Mr. Pike speaks for now. I speak for then and now. He trades in waves. I consider the ocean. I dive, possibly I drown, I sail in the ocean of time. He...surfs."

That probably was the height of the media attention. Lots of professors at other places screamed in pain. They saw a threat. The joke was that, if this place needed to be finished off a second time, and Hiram Wright along with it, they could recruit volunteers at the December meeting of the Modern Language Association, just put a sign-up sheet on a table in the lobby. But outside of academe, Wright sailed. At the moment of its death, *The New York Times* said, our college's last offering was a road map to the future. The only question, sadly undecided, was whether bigger places with lesser men would have the fortitude to follow Hiram Wright.

What turned out to be Wright's last epistle didn't resonate the way the others did. It wasn't meant to. Wright was first and last a local hero, at least that's how I think he saw himself. If he'd stayed at Rutgers, then gone on to Stanford or Berkeley, he might have turned out like Michael Pike. But he'd come here and it changed him, like it was changing me. So he saved his finale for the community. Even as the place was emptying out, and the place became known for the classiest yard sales in Ohio, even then he came up with an essay called "The College Community."

"There's no way of knowing what might have become of me, if I hadn't come here," he began. During the early years he chafed, like people still do, missing all the things that weren't here. We all had our lists. But then he realized that he wanted to stay, stay in a good place he could make better, a good place—as he had come to see recently—that he could save from getting worse. Place? What did that mean? A location? A dot on the map? Here, not there? No. A college community, where people lived and taught and learned together. Not a university, a college; not a city, a village. Getting to this place had been an accomplishment, staying was a challenge. Before long, he believed that no matter where in the world he went and was honored, this was what mattered. So it had distressed him to see his place changing, apologizing for its limitations, departing from its mission. He aimed to restore the college and the community to its rightful function. The essence of the community was that people lived there. To that end he was reimposing the long dead residence rule that obliged college employees to live within a certain distance of the campus, a distance that was measured from the flagpole in front of the village post office. Once, the prescribed distance was three miles, then seven, then ten. Wright chose twelve: "We draw a larger circle," he said, "and let that circle be unbroken." Surprisingly, he endorsed Averill Hayes' controversial Senior Years development, provided that faculty housing be included as part of the project, some of which would be located in the Stribling Tract.

What about the students? If faculty presence was required, surely student attendance wasn't too much to ask for. Or require. Attendance at classes was henceforth to be enforced throughout the college: three unexcused absences permitted, the fourth resulting in expulsion. Student attendance would be further encouraged by his decision to end all study abroad programs and close the off-campus studies office. No more junior year vacations. Furthermore, Wright restored Saturday classes, a casualty of the sixties. It would be a miracle if he pulled that one off, I thought. That's when lots of people were sure he was mad.

"Fantasyland," I heard. Another conversation at the post office. It was the only place people met each other anymore. It was crazy, Hartley Fuller said, preaching community values in a ghost town, extending classes on an empty campus. It was delusional. Raising salaries he'd never have to pay. Still, it was all hypothetical, so much singing in the shower, poignant, if you liked what you were hearing, pathetic if you didn't. So that was that. But then the faculty started getting phone calls. Would you believe it? One by one he was calling them into his office. Some, of course, had left. Others blew him off. "Fuhrerbunker fantasy," Fuller said. "Phantom armies. Secret weapons. Madness." Still, when Wright called, I came.

"Sit down, Mr. May," he said. "Thank you for coming. Give me a moment." There he sat, where My Wife, My Provost used to sit, same desk, same office, though Caroline's furnishings were on their way to California. Still, she'd left my dossier behind and Wright took his time reviewing it.

"Stark and Plimpton," he remarked. "You had them both I see."

"Great kids," I said. "I guess they're part of the reason I'm here."

"I see," he said, in a way that didn't invite me to proceed. He kept reading. Then he threw the dossier back on the desk, looked at me hard and all of a sudden laughed.

"'Pandering to sickos,'" he cried. "'the milk from contented cows!' 'That combination of country club living and easy grading gets them every time.' Are those accurate quotes? You really said those things? In a meeting of prospective students?"

"That was my first year, Mr. Wright. I was a bad boy."

"A very bad boy. A very boyish boy. Have you grown up at all since then?"

"Yes."

"I had wondered..." He glanced back at the file. "...what it was like being married to a provost."

"That's over," I said.

"How's that, sir?"

"Well, Caroline's not provost here anymore, as you know. She's also not my wife. I don't know if you knew that."

"I'd heard," he said. I should have known. In a town like this, which I proposed to love, a secret was something you told one person at a time. The thing, though, was I hadn't told anyone. The culture of gossip was so fertile here, you didn't need a seed to grow a rumor.

"Tell me more," Wright said.

"She said it was over here. She'd had it with Warren. Then she came home and said there wasn't going to be a college here anymore. She said this place was going to be a trivia question, a crossword puzzle clue: name of a dead college, six letters, begins with a K."

"Half the world would fill in Kansas," Wright said. "Where is she now?"

"Crane College, outside of San Diego."

"Provost?"

"President."

"Were you included in her plans?"

"Initially. Part of the package. A tenure track in the English

Department, sight unseen. They were excited about meeting me, she said. What's more, they're a pioneer in study abroad—operations in Edinburgh, London, Copenhagen, Vienna, Florence."

"Daunting challenges, all of them."

"It gets better. We were invited to tour them. Before Caroline's inauguration."

"And you said no?"

"She couldn't understand why. There were some students I knew who died here, I said. Wrong answer. She warned me. Even if this place has a future—which she doubted—I'd be a writer-in-residence. Out of place in the English Department, out of place in the college, out of place in Ohio. And the teaching! Three courses a semester. When would I write? What would I write? One haiku per weekend? A short story per summer? The place would destroy me, she said. Maybe it already had."

"Your wife," Wright said, "has things in your dossier that should have resulted in your dismissal. I could accommodate you now. Accommodate your wife as well."

"I hope you don't," I said. "I'd like to stay. If there's going to be a college here, I'd like to be part of it. And if it's like the place you're talking about...well...I'd like a shot."

"What kind of life do you picture yourself living here if you stay?" he asked. Again, I felt the oddness of it, talking about employment at a shut-down college.

"Teaching," I said. "And writing, of course."

"Which comes first?" he asked. "And please, spare me the dosey-do about how they go together like a horse and carriage. Horse and miscarriage is just as probable."

"What comes first," I said, "is whatever I'm doing at the time." He smiled at that. I'd dodged another bullet.

"Well, if you're here, you'll be teaching most of the time. And most of the teaching you will do will be introductory and survey courses. Not more than one seminar. God knows what you'll write. Or when."

"Summers," I said. "Vacations. Sabbaticals. If it's important to me, I'll do it. You said as much yourself."

"I did? Where?"

"Harry Stribling's conditions of employment. Just give me the same deal he had. I won't complain."

"Well," he huffed. "I'm not so sure we can do that, right off."

"I was joking," I said.

"Oh. I see."

"But this part's not a joke. The writing that I do here, I won't be doing in order to leave. I'll be doing it in order to stay. I want you to know that."

"Well then," he said. He picked up that dossier he'd been studying, My Wife, My Provost's collection of my abominations. He held it over the wastepaper basket. "Do you want your biographers to find this?" I shook my head. He dropped it into the wastepaper basket. "You can stay."

"That's it?"

"Yes. Why? Is there a question?" There were a lot of questions. How many courses, how many years, visiting appointment or tenure track, full time or part time, what about medical and retirement coverage, when would I have to move out of the provost's house? But those were for another college or another time. For this place there was just one question, for now.

"Have we been playing a charade here, Mr. Wright?"

"A charade? That's what they're saying?"

"Will this place ever be a college again?"

"I don't know," he said, which was disappointing. "It depends..." I'd expected something more ringing and well rounded. "We'll see..."

"Mark May!" Willard Thrush exclaimed. "The man, the legend."

I didn't know why he'd called me in, a few days after I'd spoken to Hiram Wright. He wasn't popular with the faculty, I knew that from Caroline. "What's the difference between a dog and a faculty member? A dog stops whining when it gets what it wants." Jokes like that were his style. He cast himself as a man of affairs, someone who dealt with real budgets and hard money. A lot of people thought he'd be out of here lickety split, once the college closed. But my wife won that race.

"So..." he said. "What are you doing around here?"

"Writing. Waiting to see what happens."

"California?"

"Not in my plans," I said. "Why are you staying?"

"I like it here," he said. "You spend twenty years learning about a place, honking people off, you can't just walk away." He stopped and studied me and for just a moment we connected. We were both here and I wondered if, years from now, those of us who stayed around, this skeleton crew, might not amount to a freemasonry. When we met, we'd know each other. It would be in our nods, in our conversation and in our silences, what we'd shared.

"I was wondering, how did Duncan Kerstetter do in that course your wife cooked up?"

"He did alright," I said.

"A pain in the ass, right?"

"I got used to him."

"So the question...envelope, please...is, did you give him an A to make up for all the pain and suffering Harry Stribling inflicted on him?"

"A student's grade is confidential. I sent it to the registrar."

"Give me a break. There's no one in the registrar's office. I could walk over, unlock the door, and look it up myself."

"Okay. B plus."

"It was supposed to be an A."

"B plus. Lots of energy. Lots of attitude. He wrote pretty well and what he said was interesting."

"Sounds like an A to me," Thrush said. "These days."

"But there was a tone of impatience in everything he did. An indifference to craft. An over-eagerness to get to the bottom line. Not 'what does it mean,' but 'what does it mean to me.' It all came down, way too quickly, to whether or not he liked something. So...B plus. I could show you his final paper. A comparison of Toni Morrison's *Beloved* and William Peter Blatty's *The Exorcist*. Blatty holds his own, it turns out. But...in the end...B plus."

"Well," Thrush said, tilting back in his chair, pulling out a lower desk drawer and stretching his legs across it. "The joke's on us. Duncan Kerstetter calls the other day. 'How much does it cost to endow a chair?' he asks. 'Three million,' I say. Silence on the phone. Then, 'Bullshit. A million and a half.' 'Duncan,' I say, 'that's not a chair, it's a stool. You want your new best friend sitting on a stool?' That's you he was talking about."

"Damn," I said. "I should have given him the A. I'd be getting a chair."

"It's alright. He came up with the three."

There was one condition, of course. The college would have to reopen. If that happened, there was a place for me here, a tenure track that led right to an endowed chair. No national search on this baby, this was home-cooking at its finest. Oh, they might have to go through the motions—applications and interviews and inviting two chanceless candidates for campus interviews. I'd worry about that, because you always worry about something, about Seamus Heaney walking into the room. But it was all there, all waiting for me. Which made me that much more certain that the college would never come back. And that maybe Duncan Kerstetter wasn't being generous. Maybe he was being incredibly...even criminally...cruel. Maybe this endowed chair was a killer's parting joke.

XIV.
WARREN NILES
Night Thoughts of a College President

"Don't thank me," Sheriff Lingenfelter said. "Tom didn't disappear because we were looking into him, Mr. President. We started looking into him after he disappeared. And what we found was interesting."

How surprising, how banal, it all turned out to be, that the crimes against our college were committed by Tom Hoover, a local man, a low-level employee. And that the account of his disappearance should be rendered to me by a county sheriff whose voice and cadence and grammar made it sound like a garden-variety domestic quarrel or tavern punch-up and not an assault against a respected and beloved college. The stupidity of it all, the meanness of it contaminated us. It stank of anti-climax. But an anti-climax was better than no climax at all.

Tom owned and was licensed to carry a Smith and Wesson handgun. That weapon had not been found but it matched the make and model employed in the killings. And, it turned out, Tom was bitter. The college had rejected his son's application and the boy, his only child, had died in Vietnam. This was from Hiram Wright, confirmed by Billy Hoover, who added that Tom had made puzzling references to moving on but not before leaving something behind that would make him remembered.

"He was on duty the night that Martha Yeats died," the sheriff said. "Hell, he was right there for the next two. Those students, the girl and the guy..."

"Oh no," I said. "Wait." I held up my hand, pleading for a time-out. I remembered the awkward funeral. Jarrett Stark's. How I'd lauded a brave boy who'd heard a shot and rushed forward to be of help, only to be slain himself. Everyone seemed puzzled by the picture I'd given. No wonder. It was wrong. The boy had run towards a uniformed College Security officer, his executioner.

"Alright," I said to the sheriff. "Sorry. I just remembered something."

"Sure. Anyhow, that high school kid? Right outside the Security Office. Like Tom's getting tired of walking. Another thing. We found his truck out at a restaurant on the interstate. That was this morning..."

"You think you'll find him?"

"We'll look. But Tom's no fool."

"No," I said. I remember our last conversation, when he stopped me speeding up the hill. Our talk about the college. I always liked it, when lower-salaried employees fretted on our behalf. It was good, they felt they were part of the college.

"Do you think," I asked, "that Tom was working with someone?"

"With? You mean for? Well, we couldn't find any money. Then, Tom only used banks for checking. Hundred dollar balance. I told you he was smart. Wherever he is, he's probably kicking himself about that $100 he left behind."

"Still..."

"He was smart enough to work alone, sir. He didn't need supervision. That's what I think. You want to look for a conspiracy, bring back Sherwood Graves."

Night Thoughts of a College President. For now, the bad times are over. The college has reopened, one third smaller than before. Our applications are higher than usual, despite the fact that our competitors made the most of our weakness. It's hard to know, but the publicity that came to us in our distress may, in the end, outweigh the damage done by the murders. Next year's freshman class may be among the best ever admitted. Really. Our time in hell was a little more than a semester, but it was bad enough and long enough to answer my years-long musing, whether time—longevity—is itself enough of a monument for a man like me, and a college like this. The answer is mostly yes and a little bit, no. Bear with me. On that gray morning when I walked across the campus to Ascension Hall, I felt a huge sense of impending loss. To think of this college's dying was more than I could bear. It was an imperfect place, but mostly good. So, when our rescue finally came, when I summoned the Board of Trustees to our reopening, relief surged through me; not relief, but joy, sheer jumping joy. One more year seemed like a huge gift, just then.

There was something else, though. I could sense it in the trustees, after the cheers and the heartfelt embraces—an unmistakable sense of let-down, knowing that our brief moment of national fame had passed and we were back to being a pretty good liberal arts college. Large issues of life and death receded and we were returned to a world of budgets and staffing, what to do about fraternities, minorities, student parking. Later, Willard Thrush confided that he regretted that the solution hadn't come a few weeks later. "There's no telling what might have become of us," Thrush said.

That sense of disappointment, of a sudden return to earth, is something I share. There was something not quite first rate in the way I accepted Tom Hoover's guilt. I hate to admit it, I may be wrong reopening the college. We may have missed something. A larger truth. Maybe Tom was someone's instrument. Someone might still be out there, brooding, plotting, planning to come back at us again. Could it be? Is there a more substantial antagonist than poor Tom? Someone who desires our death or designs our transfiguration? Classes meet, professors profess, our college lives again, yet sometimes I find myself wondering whether it is truly over. These intimations come to me at the oddest moments, not when I am worried but rather, when I am mostly relaxed, hosting a reception for parents, putting in an appearance at a poetry reading, sitting in the stands at a swim meet and it comes to me like that, while I am watching, the sense of someone watching me. "Asshole." Could that have been Tom's judgment, his alone? Could there have been a confederate, an associate, a boss? Was there so much hate in Tom, that produced so much harm? Unlikely, I tell myself. But not impossible. I must never underestimate the abilities of a common working man, I tell myself, hoping I'm not sounding like an asshole.

Coming to the end of my night thoughts, seeing that this manuscript has not amounted to what I had hoped it would be, I remember a conversation with Harry Stribling. The first years of my presidency were the last years of his life. Even had his health been good, we would never have been close. He was a shy man, a tired man, and if he confided in anyone it would not have been me. Hiram Wright, perhaps, but not me. Yet I remember meeting him one summer day, when the absence of students encouraged us to chat. I had read a novel that fell apart after a promising start, ending in unbelievable contrivances.

"Closure," Stribling said, "is hard." He was talking about literature. Or life. His own was ending, that was clear. He'd gained unhealthy weight and his skin had a yellow cast. "You want endings," he continued, "happy endings preferably, meanings made clear, questions answered. But when you get them, you resist them. It's a problem." He glanced up at me, as if only just realizing he was talking to an unworthy audience in an unguarded moment. He started to leave, to shuffle forward down the path and, at the last moment, he said something over his shoulder that returns to me, as I prepare to shuffle off as well. "Things don't end the way they should, Mr. President, and neither do we. Still, we end." And so we do.

XV.

BILLY HOOVER

Spooked and dodgy, like deer at the end of hunting season, the students returned to campus. They came back jittery, those that came back, to a school year that would end in August. They flinched, kind of, when they walked through the college gates. They still put candles and notes where Amy Plimpton died. Not so much where Jarrett Stark had fallen: that was lawn which needed liming and cutting, once spring rolled in. If anybody showed up on campus that the students didn't know, they called Security. They called about a BancOne interviewer smoking a cigarette outside the dining hall, a visiting speaker—a poet—who didn't look like "our type."

You couldn't blame them. Tom Hoover was still out there. He could be anywhere. Some cocky kids put his picture on a t-shirt they had made, a picture of Tom at a fraternity party, standing at a keg, guys around him on his left and right, raising beers in the direction of the camera and Tom pretending to be shocked. That was the Tom that everybody used to know, the sunny-dispositioned, easy-going good old boy. He's a legend now, a bogey-man, and the t-shirts are just the start. There'll be Tom clubs and parties, Sons of Tom, down the road. Our Freddy Krueger. You never know, he might be back. I like the feel of that. The feel of his gun, when I take it out of hiding sometimes, when I hold it, my fingerprints on his.

They picture Tom in Manila or Mexico or Guam, when they talk about him, someplace where lots of people speak English, nobody asks questions and money talks. He's gone far from here by now, they say. Or, he's right in the neighborhood, that's the other theory, hunkered down and hiding out in some shack along the river, in somebody's trailer, on an abandoned farm. There's lots of places to hide around here, don't kid yourself, and Tom had lots of friends. So people spot him at Kroger's supermarket or down on River Road or—this had to happen—driving an Amish wagon with a hat and a long beard. Tom lives.

At the start we were like someone who'd been real sick, cancer or something, but we kept going for tests, which were all negative, everything free and clear, no bumps or spots of any kind, but old fears continued. The whole place reminded me of one of those ex-patients who says, *I'm just taking my life one day at a time.* Which isn't a bad way to live, because nothing is for sure. If I've learned anything this last year, that's it. I learned it from Tom and from G-Man and even from old Sherwood Graves, from all the phone calls we made, the stories we got told. It's no more than what the college teaches and says it believes, about the importance of the past. There's this line that Hiram Wright kept quoting, said it was from a William Faulkner novel, that the past isn't dead, it's not even past. Everything that happened seemed to show that, one way or another, but the real clincher was when Mark May took me out for breakfast. We'd gotten to be friends. He was living in the provost's house until the end of the year—Hiram Wright wasn't going to bother moving in—and sometimes Mark cooked a meal for me. I returned the favor, which was breakfast out in some little town with a farmers café: trucks in the parking lot, these heavy lumbering guys making a cup of coffee last an hour. We always wondered where their wives were. Did these guys run away from them? Or were they run off? Then we talked just like they did about sports and real estate. But not this morning.

"I told you about Kerstetter," Mark said.

"The mortician."

"When he left he said he'd send me some things Harry Stribling wrote. Unpublished. Odds and ends." Mark reached into his pocket and pulled out an envelope. "This is for you. We can talk about it...there's a reference to a novel by a French writer. Benjamin Constant. Otherwise...it speaks for itself."

"Okay."

"It's about Hiram Wright," he said. "Turns out...I'm pretty sure...it's about your father. And your mother."

Hiram Wright was waiting for me, sitting just inside the door of Stribling Hall.

"How are you, sir?" I asked. He was always happy to see me, like I made his day. Underneath, though, he seemed depressed.

"I can't walk," he said. "That's today's news." He pointed towards a wheelchair next to the door. "G-Man looks after me at home. Security carries me up the steps when I come to work. Quite a spectacle."

"I'm sorry," I said. "Anything they can do?"

"Issue me wings," he snapped back. "Listen, Billy, could you wheel me out onto Middle Path?"

"Sure." It took me and Harry Carstairs to maneuver him down the steps. But it was good being outside. Spring in Ohio.

"That's better," he said. We were right on Middle Path, under the maples. "Back when I was in my prime, there came a year when I got fed up with student papers. It happens to all of us. This was my year. Maybe I realized that student writing skills were headed south, that the papers I was getting were all shake-and-bake."

"Shake and bake?"

"Students waiting until the night before, sitting down in front of a word processor with their lecture notes on one side and their books, all peed upon with yellow marker, on the other and you know...a little of this, a little of that..."

"I see."

"Maybe it was them. Maybe it was me. Or the weather. You know what it was like? Just like today." He waved a hand in front of him, sweeping from left to right, like Thomas Mitchell in *Gone With the Wind,* standing in front of Tara, telling Scarlett about the love of the land, if you're Irish it's in you. I took in what he was taking in. Everyone was saying they couldn't remember a May as fine as this one. There were violets and daffodils around the church, so woven into the lawn you'd think the grass was blossoming. And those rows of maples, gradually turning the path into a shaded tunnel which the seniors would pass through at a graduation we never thought would come. Around town, there were flowers in all the trees, flowering pears and plums and cherries and crab apples, whole trees that were nothing but flowers right now, each one as sweet-smelling as an orchard.

"Anyway, I decided to give a new kind of final exam," Wright said. "Instead of having them fill blue books, which I would have to mark, students were invited to take a little walk with me, a walk around campus to chat with me about the books we'd read. Walking the plank, they called it. It didn't catch on, needless to say."

"Is this my final exam?" I asked.

"I think not. More likely, mine." He studied me, waiting for me to take his cue. "How's your new job?"

"Fine," I said. "I guess you had something to do with that."

"Just a little," he said. They'd made me the new head of security, replacing Tom. So parents would relax, the college had contracted a private security firm, mostly retired or off-duty troopers and cops. Men with weapons were chalking tires, stamping palms at parties, counting beer kegs. By all accounts they got—and took—much less shit than we did in the old days. For the time being, I was what they called liaison.

"It's not what you'd call the busiest job in the world," I allowed.

"More time to read," he said. "And write."

"And think," I said. "Would you like to know what I've been thinking, Professor?"

"Of course I would."

"It's just a hunch. And it's nothing that'll change anything. Still interested?"

"Please."

"My hunch is that Sherwood Graves was half right. Tom wasn't alone. He was working with someone else. Or for someone else. And it wasn't Averill Hayes. Professor Wright, it was you, sir."

He didn't flinch one bit. He nodded, like this was something he'd been waiting for. "I might have to change your grade, Billy," he said. "Keep talking."

"All year, in and out of class, you kept saying how love and hate are tied together. 'Symbiotic and inseparable,' those were your words. Reminded me of an old movie, *Night of the Hunter,* where Robert Mitchum has L-O-V-E written on the knuckles of one hand and H-A-T-E on the other and he showed the two of them struggling against each other but always in touch, like a pair of wrestlers. He was this corrupt preacher, a killer preacher..."

"Is that what you think I am? A corrupt preacher? A killer?"

"Not corrupt, I'd never say that. But something else. That's what I'm trying to work out here. Graves thought the murders were done because someone got greedy, like Ave Hayes. Or maybe someone hated the college and, God knows, we found lots of haters. Including Graves himself. But then it came to me, an idea I can't shake which is that it wasn't hate or greed. It was love. And that brought me straight to you, sir."

"I see," he said. "Well...I do love this place."

"What's more...I think you wanted me to come to you. You were leading me to you, all along, leading everybody, maybe. That night you spoke to the students, the parents, the TV cameras, asking yourself was it something you did, something too harsh or maybe too kind. Damn straight it was. You were dropping clues left and right, you were confessing right then and there to everybody who listened. But you were talking to me. Inviting me into your class. You figured we'd be sitting here like this someday. So I guess this is a final exam. How'd I do?"

"Interesting. But, anyone would have to say, weak on proof. As a matter of fact, unprovable. At the least you need a confession from Tom. Do you think Tom will be confessing, Billy?"

You should have seen how he looked into me, when he asked me. Turned the tables, without warning, without half trying. I wasn't able to hold things in like he was. I'm sure he saw something on my face.

"I don't think they'll be getting a confession from Tom," I admitted.

"Too bad," Wright said. "He was a man who loved to talk."

"He talked plenty alright, professor. He told me you could turn the lights on for me. What I'm wondering is if he talked to you, before all this started."

He sat there, thinking it over. I watched his eyes as they glanced from one place to another, back to me and off again, across the grass, over the tops of the trees, into the classroom buildings, into the woods that sloped down to the river and back to me. Almost like a caress. He didn't want to kill the college. He wanted to save it.

"I'll give you an A-minus," he said. "What now, Billy? Do I get that one phone call before you cart me off?"

"I just want you to tell me what happened," I said. What I knew was more important than what I did. I wanted to know. I was still his student.

"Alright then," he said. "But what I tell you is for your sake. Not mine. I want you to know that. Tom wasn't working for me. If anything, it was the other way around."

The past wasn't dead alright, not when Hiram Wright could close his eyes and shut out Warren Niles' cheerful, healthy college—the new labs and dorms and swimming pool—and return in memory to the smaller, poorer place he'd loved. If a person could love a place the way you love a person, this was a place that you could love that way, almost hold it in your arms. Five hundred students, forty faculty, up on a hill in the sticks, heart of Ohio, where the nights were dark and the stars were bright and the cornfields rolled away forever.

People were closer in the old days, all sorts of unlikely friendships, between a professor and say, two brothers who were college employees, who shared nothing with him in terms of books or jokes or politics. It wasn't because the professor was being sporting and democratic. Chances were, they'd never vote the same in an election—a professor, a campus cop and a college maintenance man. Or sit around a table and share a meal, he couldn't even picture what would be on their plates or in their glasses, they were so different. But what brought them together was those autumn mornings that came back to him, those crisp, focused dawns, that old love. What else to call it? Oh, those miles he'd walked along ridgelines, across fields, along runs that fed into the river, ceremonies of pure joy that drew and held them so that, all the rest of the year, the dreary inward winters, the now-you-see-it-now-you-don't springtimes, the heavy, nearly tropical summers, none could compare with those October hunting days they shared with each other and the land.

"I loved your father, Billy, he never knew how much, we never talked about it, it wouldn't have worked to put it into words, because words were my business and to say something would be like giving a gift that he couldn't return. I think he loved being around me, just for that, the way I spoke. Thrilled to be in the presence of a professor. Honored. But not as much as I was honored by him. His instincts, his grace. When we went out, his sense of direction, his feelings for the land, the weather, the wind even..."

"How'd Tom fit in?" I asked.

"Tom!" He laughed at the memory. "Tom just included himself. No saying no. Jabbering, joking, no shutting him up. The looks your father gave him. The looks he gave me, *sorry about this, professor, sorry about my loudmouth brother.* To Tom, silence was time wasted, unless you filled it with words. A terrible hunter. An early-warning system for wildlife. A wretched shot. I guess his marksmanship improved, just lately..."

There it was again, hanging in the air, another silence, waiting for me to fill it with words.

"Happy times," Wright resumed when I didn't oblige him. "Went on for years. I thought we'd go on forever. At least until we couldn't walk, like I can't walk now."

"What happened?"

"I destroyed it. Do you want to hear about it?"

"Yes. I want to hear it from you. But I should tell you—it only seems fair—I already know." I took out an envelope and showed it to him. "I got this from Mark May, who figured I'd be interested. He got it from Duncan Kerstetter, who got it out of his collection of Harry Stribling's unpublished papers. Here you go. A note from your old pal."

"Old Harry," Wright said. "A voice from the grave."

"Those are the ones you said we should listen for," I said. "In class. 'Listen to the voices of the dead. Hear them. Heed them.'"

"So I did," he nodded. He read it, a paragraph that I'd memorized.

" '*Droit de Seigneur...*'" he read aloud. "'Hiram's downfall. The devil drives. Cunt hunting. He quotes Benjamin Constant. 'It hurts them so little and it gives us such pleasure.' Now, his friend drives a truck into the river. Story here?'"

"*Droit de Seigneur,*" I said. "Mark May told me what it means. Right of the master. Nobility gets first shot at a peasant girl. Kind of an entitlement, in the old days."

"Alright." He sat a minute, shaking his head back and forth, reliving it the way he always relived the past when he thought about it, the past that wasn't past. "It was the worst mistake I've ever made. Nothing compares with it. I had an affair...no...that's not the word...oh damn, Billy..."

"Final exam," I coached him. "Not the farmer's daughter, was it? The farmer's wife." He still didn't respond. "I used to hear you got around a little. A free-range chicken, they used to say. How did it happen?"

"Does it really matter?"

"I want to hear it," I said. "You and my mother."

"I had a house in Columbus that I know you know about. A hideaway. Not all my trips to town were to use the O.S.U. library."

"A love nest, you mean?"

"In its time."

"You took her there?"

"Listen, Billy. She deserves better..."

"You got that right."

"Better from you, I mean. She was a decent woman. This was her only mistake."

"Not your only mistake."

"No. But my worst. May I proceed?"

I nodded. I hated him, just then. But I still respected him. I didn't think hate and respect could go together. In his case, they did.

"We left to drive back here, after our little time together. Feeling wretched, soon as we were in the car. And then we saw Earl pull out behind us in that truck. He knew. He'd known. He could have stopped it, could have prevented her coming, could have burst in on us, could have done and gotten away with anything at all..."

He sat there, shaking his head, thinking of that hour's drive home when anything might have happened and nothing did.

"He stayed behind us a safe distance. He kept his headlights on low. Signaled left and right turns. Obeyed the rules. Till, when we turned towards this place, fully expecting him to follow...he kept on going. Perhaps we should have followed him...When I reached the farm, your mother walked inside without a word. I never saw her again, not even by accident. Or your father. His ride ended in the river. I've always wondered if I could have met with him, talked to him..."

"You being so good with words..."

"It wouldn't have worked. He'd have listened to me, I'm convinced. He'd have nodded. He'd shake my hand. Hug me. Forgive me. And then he'd have driven into the river. The best man I ever knew..."

"With friends like you..."

"Quiet, Billy."

"You're telling me to be quiet? You ripped a hole in my life!"

"Be quiet so you can listen. You haven't heard the whole story. Your father left a note. A note I never saw. At least Tom said there was a note. Take care of my boy, that sort of thing...and more. I doubt the note. Not the knowledge."

"Tom knew."

"From the start. But he waited. That was Tom's style. To scratch and chuckle and bide his time. He waited for years, all the time I thought it was over."

"I thought you knew better. The past is..."

"...not over. Of course not. But private. For me to engage with on my own terms, at moments of my own choosing, which was often. No one needed to remind me to hate myself. Then, one night, he came into my office. He wanted his son to go to this college, on a scholarship. Essentially, he was applying on Tony's behalf. He wanted me to make sure it happened. And, to underscore the importance, he told me what he knew..."

Another rest. You always had to wait with him. He walked through the past, but slowly. Maybe for the last time. The past might not be over. But he would be. Soon. The past would claim him. Tom the college bogey-man, Hiram its savior. Local history in the making. Local heros.

"I told Tom I would not deny it. I would never lie. Two people were dead. I hadn't killed them but they were dead because of me. That was the burden I would have to carry. I had thought of moving on, believe me. But I couldn't bear the thought of leaving this place."

"Tell me about Tony."

"It was hopeless. He was a lovely boy, a natural, but his test scores were wretched. He might as well not have shown up. In some cases, he didn't. He didn't want to go to college, not here, not anywhere. He was a happy, loyal, lively youth who wanted to go to Bangkok in the worst way."

"Hope to hell he got to Bangkok before he died."

"He didn't," Wright said. "He didn't get to Vietnam either. He died in Texas, Fort Hood. An automobile accident, off base. The closest thing Tony Hoover saw to a sniper was a Texas Ranger with a speed gun."

"Shit," I said. "That cheapens his death some, doesn't it?"

"No, Billy. Not at all. It only makes it sadder."

"It is sad," I granted. "Could I ask you something? I'm just wondering."

"Of course," he said. "Anything. No secrets between us."

"So Tony wasn't college material. You've made that clear. But could he have gotten through here, some way? I guess I'm asking, are all the kids we get here college material? I've been around. I've sat in your class. Aren't there others like him?"

"Yes," he said, closing his eyes. "By the dozens."

"Well then," I said. "That's what really makes it sad, then."

He didn't answer me. Not with words. He only nodded.

"So what about Tom?" I asked.

"Tom remained as deferential and funny as ever, when we met in public. 'How you doin' professor?' 'Lookin' good today, sir' 'What's new in history?' That sort of thing. I couldn't look at him without being reminded of your parents. If I'd left, I'd have been rid of him. I didn't believe he'd follow me. Tom's not the kind to leave here. Is he?"

"No," I said.

"A local boy, born and bred. Not the kind to run off." He kept signaling, he had my number. I just sat. It was his turn to confess, not mine. "Last summer, a few weeks before the first students came back to campus, the football players and the rest, he visited me, down on the river. We talked about this and that. Everyone knew what happened to me, how Martha Yeats had engineered, how Warren had colluded. He asked if I was bitter and I did not deny it. Then he talked about himself and I realized how the issue of Tony had mutated, how the college had sent him to his death, the college had shrugged off the war, the college had offered a haven to rich kids, a sanctuary for goof-offs, for folks who acted 'like their shit don't stink.' I saw in Tom a bitterness that matched, that outmatched my own. Then he said something. It was all he said and he said it on his way out the door. Understand that, Billy, he wasn't consulting, he wasn't asking permission, he wasn't specific. He wasn't asking, he was telling. 'Professor,' he said, 'I believe it's hunting season.'"

"Did you know he was the killer?"

"I wasn't sure. There was all that talk about the G-Man. Evidence, too, I gathered. I thought it might be him. Or Tom. In either case, I couldn't say. Understand? I could not say. Even if I knew, if I were sure, I could not say." Then he recovered some. He faced me. "Billy? I wonder where Tom's gone to. Can you say?"

"I can't say. Let's just mark Tom missing. I like it better that way."

"Well, then," he said. Another look, like we were partners. "So do I." And it felt like the end of a session, some straight talk, some hints and nudges, an agreement to leave things be and to keep in touch. No meeting with me and Wright could end differently. But it was a little too soon.

"Professor Wright," I said. "I'm going to wheel you back to Stribling Hall and leave you there. And then I'll drive home wondering about what you told me, running through it, studying. Close, careful reading like you require in class."

"That's fine," he said. "I'd expect no less."

"And I'll be asking myself how much you lied to me right now and wondering if I'll ever know. Here, we've got Tom. Tom was bitter, Tom killed, and there was nothing you could do but sit, and suspect but not be sure, and anyway you were honor-bound or some such. And I'll ask myself if there wasn't more. I'll wonder if Tom and you didn't talk a lot more than you let on. You'd worked together before, setting up G-Man in that Columbus place, all quiet. I wonder if you didn't take that anger of his and launch it. Could be you primed him, Professor. Could be you primed him like a pump."

He sat there and something came down over his face. Maybe he was angry at me. Maybe he was disappointed.

"He wasn't always bitter, Professor. He was a cheerful, joking kind of guy. He liked people, people liked him. Not just locals. Students, professors. All of a sudden he turns bitter. Goes on a killing spree. So I'm wondering...let me just wonder, aloud..."

"Yes..."

"...whether the bitterness wasn't a lesson that you taught him...that's what I keep asking myself. He wasn't always the way he was the last time I saw him."

"The last time you saw him..." Wright said. "That's a meeting I wonder about. The when and where and why of it."

"He was so bitter about Tony," I said, brushing off the confession that he was waiting for me to make. "He built a shrine at his river house—the flag they wrapped around his coffin. Photographs—and then..." It came to me all of a sudden, one of those times something occurs to you while you're talking, not later. "Professor, you just said Tony wasn't college material."

"Yes."

"And I asked whether we didn't have other kids here who were no better than him—who weren't college material. And you said yes. You answered fast, you didn't have to think one bit. And I said, well, that made it so much sadder...and we left it at that. Sad and sadder. But now I'm thinking that's the kind of thing you were telling Tom. Educating my uncle. Priming him. Poisoning..."

"Oh, Billy," he said. "You think he needed to learn bitterness from me? That he couldn't discover it on his own? Without my coaching? Do you think so little of him? Or yourself?"

That stopped me. I wondered, was this what all his teaching came to, all that talk of standards and discipline and tradition and listening to the voices of the dead, about words carrying us across time zones and through time itself? Did he make Tom a murderer? Or was it all Tom?

"I don't know, Professor. I don't know."

"You don't have to decide today, you know. Or tomorrow. But when you wonder, as you say you will, ask yourself what you would want that answer to be. That Tom was his own man? Or mine?"

"They'll blame Tom," I continued. "Blame him for everything. Blame him forever. But I'll be wondering about you."

"You have a lot on your mind," he said. Which wasn't an answer. I waited for more. But he was done with me. "Take me back now."

"One other thing, Professor, and then I'm done. That kid who got killed in the alley near Security had a note in his pocket. I wonder if you know what it said."

He didn't answer.

"'Always do a little bit extra.' The G-Man's famous slogan."

"Tom..." he said. "It must have been. He knew I feared the G-Man."

"Oh, Tom again..."

"You shouldn't discount him."

"It couldn't be, you told him to tuck that note in?"

"Never," he said. "Not that. Don't think that. Please."

"I've got no control what I think about."

"Take me back now," he repeated and this time I got behind the wheelchair and started pushing him down the path.

"I'm sorry," I said. "What you did, whatever you did, you did it for love, I guess. Still, four people dead. A professor and two students and some poor high school kid who never got as far as freshmen orientation. Four people dead. That is something I can't get past. I can't get past. That's huge."

"Four?" he said. "Why not six, counting your parents? And why not seven?" There it was again. Tom. He knew. He didn't have to say it. Tom was the seventh. "I've killed no one," Wright said. As if he were thinking aloud, trying out a speech in front of a camera. "I've ordered no one killed, the courts would find me an arresting figure, tragically flawed but hardly culpable. An elderly professor, rallying to the defense of his college, even though coerced and threatened by the instrument of its undoing. If I were looking for Tom, I'd check your property, Billy. If I were looking for the murder weapon..."

His voice trailed off, as if he were tired of talking about it. He thought I'd killed Tom, I saw that now. I was ready to correct him, to protest my innocence. But then I decided to leave it between us, let it stand. I hadn't killed Tom. But I had the body, I had the weapon. That was close enough.

"Never mind, Billy," he said. "Our guilts are private. We carry them inside us, we contend with them each day. We're our own prosecutors and our own judges, if it comes to that, our own executioners. But consider this. Consider the return of the G-Man, an instructor in the history department next year. Building a house on your property. And there's you, out of the trailer, back onto your farm, living with the G-Man's sister. Promoted a notch, enrolled half-time in the fall. And what about the College? That's what matters most. Think of it, Billy. A chance to build a great college. Here. Now. A faculty of great teachers, original thinkers. A curriculum that gives students what they need, not what they feel like taking and professors feel like teaching. Promotions that are based on merit, not habit. Scholarships that are based on ability and need. Grades that are honest, transcripts that aren't funny money, diplomas that the world respects. It's up to you son, whether or not that happens." That seemed like a stretch, I said. "You have the same power over me that Tom had. If you ask me, or ask anyone else to ask me, I will tell them what I told you and what happens, happens. It's up to you."

So there I sat, in the Security Office, staring at the telephone. One call to Lingenfelter and it would all start over. One call to Sherwood Graves and we'd be famous once again. I couldn't picture it. I was in an odd spot, no doubt about it. I had scary knowledge in me and terrible power. I had dead people living in me and a murderer's weapon in my dresser, under my boxer shorts, and if I said the word, I could crack this college wide open. Wright knew it and I knew it. I could tell whenever our eyes met, his wheelchair speeches, that great voice of his echoing off the buildings, an audience of students and parents all before him, all confident this is a place that's not like any other and though I was on the sidelines, keeping order, waiting to be of assistance if anybody fainted from heat, I believed the same thing. Our eyes met. *Anytime,* he said to me, *anytime you choose.* And I looked back at him—a security guy answering a provost. *Not today* was my response. *Not yet.* I wasn't sure how much to believe his story about Tom, Tom just going off on a killing spree and him, sitting home, not able to do anything. I wondered whether, over all the years, he hadn't been preparing Tom for this, coaching, hinting. Teaching, even. Who was the organ grinder, who was the monkey? I'll never know for sure. They're both gone now, anyway. A few days after that late August graduation, they took Hiram Wright to the hospital. A coma. At the end, death cheated him, sneaking in by the back door, knocking him over the head, hanging him out in limbo for a week. When he died, we were in the papers all over again. Willard Thrush was busy raising money, Harry Carstairs was snowed under applications, Warren Niles conducted a memorial service that got televised. Then, there comes a morning, I walk to classes, text and notebook in my hands, I enter Ascension Hall, go up those creaking steps, into those rooms that smell of wood and stone in late summer heat and I sit back, in the middle of kids who wonder what I'm doing there. That's alright. And I have no doubts about belonging here. I know where the bodies are buried and where the gun is hidden. The people around here need me, more than they know.

About the Author

Novelist, journalist and teacher, P.F. Kluge is Writer in Residence at Kenyon College. His six previous novels include *Eddie And The Cruisers* and *Biggest Elvis*. His non-fiction books include *The Edge of Paradise: America in Micronesia* and *Alma Mater*, an account of a year in the life of Kenyon College. Two films, *Dog Day Afternoon* and *Eddie And The Cruisers*, have been based on his work. His journalism appears in *National Geographic Traveler*, where he is a contributing editor, and elsewhere. A native of Berkeley Heights, New Jersey, Kluge lives in Gambier, Ohio with his wife, Pamela Hollie.

Praise for P.F. Kluge

The Day That I Die (novel), Bobbs-Merrill, Indianapolis, 1976

"If you like suspense, this one's perfect. The plot is full of twists, the characters are well drawn...I read *The Day That I Die* in one sitting."
  — Ronn Ronck, The Pacific Daily News

"Comparable in suspense to LeCarre's *The Spy who Came in from the Cold* and as elastically modern as *Rosemary's Baby.*"
  — Joe Murphy, Micronesian Independent

Eddie And The Cruisers (novel), Viking, New York, 1980

"Sparkling dialogue, wonderful characterizations and a plot which dazzles."
  — Leo McConnell, Enterprise Sun

"An excellently crafted book. The dialogue is sharp, the book is packed with exquisite description and a surprise ending."
  — Bart Becker, Sunday Journal and Star

Season for War (novel), Freundlich Books, New York, 1984

"Kluge has the ability to evoke scenes that give the readers a sense of participating in the events portrayed. He brings life to his protagonist and to the members of the 25th Cavalry, and he raises many questions about the morality of war..."
  — Lynn Eckman, Roanoke Times and World News

"*Season for War* is a startling, magnificent novel that demands you try to read it in one sitting...It's a first-class story."
  — Terry Pluto, The Plain Dealer

McArthur's Ghost (novel), Arbor House, New York, 1987

"Fascinating, timely and rich. Kluge does more to explain the Philippines and the Filipinos than a year's subscription to Time, while telling a fine and intricate adventure tale."
  — Kirkus Reviews

"...an evocative, riveting saga of war and its aftermath in the Philippines, reminiscent of Michener's early South Pacific tales."
  — Publisher's Weekly

The Edge of Paradise: America in Micronesia (non-fiction), Random House, New York, 1991

"Both instructive and pleasurable, *The Edge of Paradise* recalled for me many exciting days in those islands and told me things I had not known. It's a top-quality travel book."
  — James A. Michener, author